Praise for

FLOWER FROM CASTILE: BOOK ONE
THE ALHAMBRA DECREE

"GAFNI'S UNDERSTANDING OF THE TIME period seems paramount, and her plot is solid. Isabella's movement between different cultures allows readers to explore what it was like to be a Catholic, Jew, or Moor during one of history's darkest periods." ~ Kirkus Reviews

"*FLOWER FROM CASTILE TRILOGY: BOOK ONE – THE ALHAMBRA DECREE* is an accessible novel that inspires interest in, and relays the complexities of, a fascinating period in history." ~ ForeWord Clarion Reviews

"GAFNI USES HISTORICAL FICTION TO retrace the steps of displaced Jews during the Inquisition. She writes with passion—her experiences a springboard." ~ The Desert Sun/My Desert

"THIS BOOK IS A MONUMENT to the Marranos that suffered and lost their lives." ~ Manuel Luciano da Silva and Silvia Jorge da Silva, authors of *CHRISTOPHER COLUMBUS WAS PORTUGUESE!*

"A MASTER STORYTELLER, GAFNI WILL reveal to you a world that will open your eyes and show you a piece of important history while keeping you riveted wondering what will happen next. A must-read!" ~ C. S. Lakin, author of *SOMEONE TO BLAME* and *INTENDED FOR HARM.*

"BOTH MY HUSBAND (who has very different literary tastes than me) AND I loved this book and enjoy discussing it. Gafni is a superb author!" ~ Ann White, Rabbi and Chaplain, Radio Host, Transformational Author and Speaker, and author of *LIVING WITH SPIRIT ENERGY: BRING BALANCE AND HARMONY INTO YOUR LIFE AND WORLD, THE SACRED ART OF DOG WALKING MAKING THE ORDINARY EXTRAORDINARY,* and *PEBBLES IN THE POND TRANSFORMING THE WORLD ONE PERSON AT A TIME*

Flower from Castile Trilogy

BOOK TWO: THE NEW WORLD

Lilian Gafni

First printing
Published by Lifeline Publishing Books
Book and cover design by Ellie Searl, Publishista®

All characters and events in this book are a work of fiction as well as those based on true historical accounts. Any resemblance to actual events or living persons is purely coincidental.

ISBN-13: 978-0970273529
ISBN-10: 0970273525
LCCN: 2013935721

Printed in the United States of America

10 9 8 7 6 5 4 3 2 1

LIFELINE PUBLISHING
BOOKS
La Quinta, CA

Also by Lilian Gafni

FLOWER FROM CASTILE: BOOK ONE
THE ALHAMBRA DECREE

HELLO EXILE

LIVING A BLISSFUL MARRIAGE: 24 STEPS TO HAPPINESS

Praise for

FLOWER FROM CASTILE: BOOK TWO
THE NEW WORLD

"History has never been so exciting. The author marries historical events and fictional characters to create a page-turner. I awaited the release of this book with high expectations after reading the first of this trilogy, The Alhambra Decree, and I was not disappointed. I enjoyed every page of this novel; I like the short chapters and could easily keep up with what was going on in the new world with Columbus and his crew and in the old world with the spirited Isabella. I am looking forward to the final book; I'm sure I won't be able to put it down."

~ Patty MacFarlane, founder of *IMMIGRANT SHIPS TRANSCRIBERS GUILD*

"Although it would be best to read the first book in the trilogy, The New World stands alone beautifully. However, it is wonderful to pick up with the characters from the first book and watch the tense and heartbreaking adventures they go on in this installment. The first book showed Spain during the time of the Inquisition and the Alhambra Decree, which forced hundreds of thousands to flee Spain and seek a safe place to practice their religion. This second book follows the characters as they try to find safe havens, and it features Columbus on his journey across the Atlantic to the New World. Gafni has done a tremendous amount of great research, which shows so keenly in her novels through the detail and care she takes to convey the era and locales. These novels are filled with pain, hope, romance, history, danger, and excitement. You don't want to miss either of these two novels, and I'm excitedly waiting for the final book that will resolve all the riveting story lines!"

~ C. S. Lakin, author of *SOMEONE TO BLAME and INTENDED FOR HARM*

"The sequel does a fine job of balancing the plot for both the first time readers, (where readers are engaged and will not be at loss,) and also for the followers of the first book, (where readers are engaged with the progression of the story.) As I had mentioned in my first review, I had observed how there is a connection to the Holy Trinity with the first three Isabella's. I see another connection of threes- the three stories that focus on Isabella and her husband, the infamous Columbus, and Queen Isabella. This continues to hold an important theme, which could either lead to success or tragedy, much like the enterprise of maintaining any business of running a country. There are other themes that permeate in the squeal: risk taking, faith, and endurance. Despite the social positions of the main characters, the challenges they face hold a common ground- which I find intriguing. Not only is it just great story telling, but also it leaves one to ponder the validity of history and humanity. That is equally as important, to me, as good drama. Like its first predecessor, The New World is tightly enticing, and it flows with the rapid movement of true adventure without depleting the weight of history. Again, it is worth 5 stars."

~ K.P. Kollenborn, author of *EYES BEHIND BELLIGERENCE*

Dedication

I DEDICATE THIS BOOK TO the 200,000 men, women, and children exiled from Spain in 1492 . . .

. . . and to Dr. Manuel Luciano da Silva who was an author, great physician, historian, archaeologist, and epigrapher. Dr. da Silva and his wife Sílvia da Silva, co-authors of the book *Christopher Columbus is Portuguese!*, discovered the secret monogram that Christopher Columbus affixed on his letters that proves the discoverer had a hidden origin.

Acknowledgments

M Y GRATITUDE GOES TO SUSANNE LAKIN for her wonderful patience and impeccable editing skill and to Ellie Searl, Publishista®, for the great cover and design content.

I also want to thank my husband Joel for reading the first draft, and his unlimited patience in willing to help while I disappeared for hours on end to write this story.

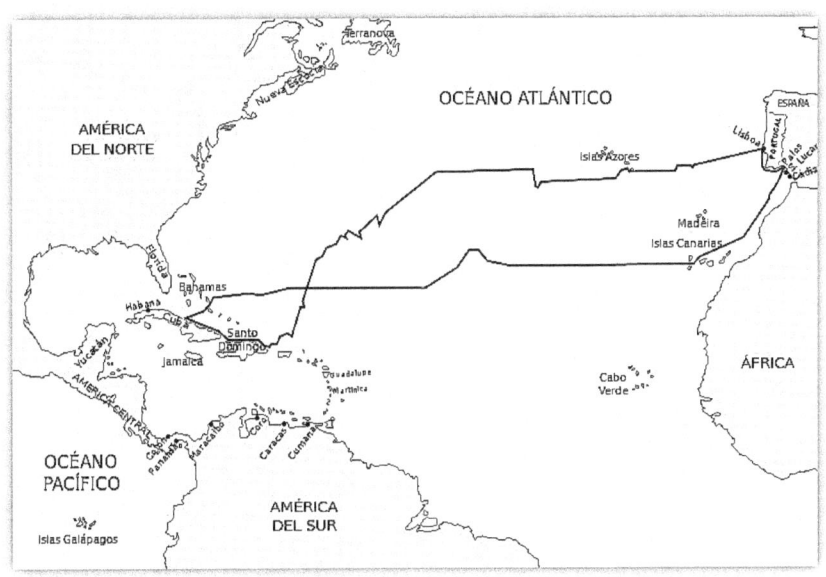

Courtesy of Wikimedia Commons

The Route of the First Voyage of Columbus

Ruta seguida por Colon en su primer viaje

Author: viajes_de_colon.svg Phirosiberia

A character list is found at the end of the book.

1

Passage to Tangier

A BARNACLE-STUDDED BOW PARTED dark waters, and a gentle breeze propelled the square-sail caravel toward Morocco. The ship had sailed peacefully on the Atlantic Sea and once in Tangier, Miguel knew that his life with Isabella would begin. He sat on the crowded main deck and reveled at his young wife asleep in his arms, her chest rising with each breath. Studying her peaceful features, he delighted in how dear she was to him. They were both free from Inspector Guerida's reach now, and from Grand Inquisitor Torquemada's tentacles. Since they had left Seville's port, and plied along the meandering river, the Guadalquivir, the last two days had gone by smoothly with good weather into the Atlantic Sea. The small vessel, El Mouro, had glided along the shores of the Guadalquiver River in the heart of Spain, while refugees sat grieving for their lost homeland. In a few days the sights of Africa's northern coast would be in view. For now the sea moved along with the ship, helping transport them to a new life.

Isabella stirred, opened her eyes, and smiled at Miguel.

He grabbed her hand and pressed it against his face. "My precious and beautiful wife. Did you rest?" he asked anxiously.

"I had a dream of a little house overlooking the sea. You were standing on the beach, chopping logs, and I was calling you." Her eyes held a vision.

"Did I come running to you?" he asked playfully.

Her face suddenly lost its color. Her emerald eyes dimmed and looked at him with fear. "Yes, you were running toward me, and men were chasing you." She came close to him for protection, held him tightly while her hands slightly trembled.

"Shh, shh," he reassured her. "It's only a dream."

She buried her head into his chest, but her breath remained shallow and fast.

Miguel helped her to her feet, grabbed her hand, and fought his way through the throng of people and bundles lying on the upper deck. Weary women and some suckling newborn infants looked haggard from lack of sleep, and old men with a vacant gaze in their eyes tugged at their white beards, smoothing them to unravel tangled, matted hair. Both Miguel and Isabella advanced to the ship's bow and held on to the rigging tied around the conifer foremast. The Levant wind, now increasing a few knots, came at them more forcefully than at first as it blew their long hair around and into their faces and eyes, and they swayed under its power.

"Hold on!" Miguel shouted at Isabella. He came close and wrapped her with both arms, trying to protect her from the sudden wind now lashing at them mixed with sea spray.

Captain Juan de Luna, standing on the upper deck shouted orders to his seamen. "Raise them! Furl the sails!" he bellowed to the lower deck while his men furiously scrambled to pull on the coiled ropes. Like a curtain rising before an oceanic audience, all the canvas sails were clewed up and furled tightly to the beams above their heads. From their vantage point, Miguel and Isabella watched the scene unravel while the water sprayed on the decks and washed over the travelers. Miguel felt glad they had found the small quarters below in the hold. Below the decks, the Beneluz family was huddled in the hold and sleeping close to each other.

He recalled that his uncle, Isaac Beneluz, had compensated the captain with a handful of gold coins for the coveted space below. His aunt, Rivka Beneluz, had taken it upon herself to make the small space into livable quarters. She wrapped two blankets from the rafters to enclose the space into a cubicle where all of them, including their four sons Avram, León, Guerson, and Mica, would feel some privacy.

As the winds increased, visibility decreased exponentially while the waves washed the deck continuously. Their faces and clothes now soaked, Miguel and Isabella marched toward the hold and descended the rope ladder. Their eyes adjusting to the dark and cavernous space below deck, they made their way to the opposite side of the vessel and to his uncle's small cubicle. Miguel parted the blanket hung from a rope and found them still asleep. He went to his uncle and shook him gently by the arm.

Beneluz uttered with eyes still heavy with sleep, "What is it?"

"We're hitting rough seas," Miguel told him. "We may also get more refugees from the upper deck down in the hold."

"If we do, we'll make room for them." Isaac Beneluz quickly woke the rest of his family and urged them, "Move closer."

Still the rabbi helping everyone! No sooner had this thought crossed Miguel's mind than the huddled masses from the washed-out deck began to descend the rope ladder in their wet and dripping clothes. Their soaked bundles were thrown from above to land on the families camped below. "Watch out!" Fists were raised by indignant passengers.

Miguel whispered in Isabella's ear, "They must've parted with some of their gold.*"*

Their small space began to shrink as the ones already there moved to accommodate the new additions.

Meanwhile, his Aunt Rivka had prepared a cold meal of bread, dried meat, cheese, scallions, and cakes.

His Uncle Isaac reached into their bundles and retrieved more provisions. His Aunt Rivka raised her eyes at him, and before Isaac could stand up from his bent position, she reached for his full hands.

"No!" She raised her voice. "You won't!"

"We must! It's pitiful how hungry those children are."

Rivka looked down at the provisions in his hands. She grabbed half then handed him the rest. "All right. But that's all we can give. We'll starve ourselves." She then reached across to feel the foreheads of her two youngest, Guerson and Mica. "They're burning with fever," she moaned to Isaac.

"Give them more water to drink. I'll see if I can find the ship's doctor."

On his way up, Isaac went to give the extra bread and cheese to the hungry children. The parents thanked him by nodding silently and watched as the youngest children devoured the bread.

"Aunt Rivka." Miguel addressed her. "We should be coming to port within a couple of days."

"That is if we have good weather," Rivka replied.

Isabella, who had been quiet until now, went to sit by Rivka and grabbed her arm affectionately. "We will, Aunt Rivka. You'll see." She tried to reassure her.

"May I have some more bread, Mother?" Mica said in a weak voice.

"There's no more for now!"

Rivka's hard voice startled Mica. Avram, the oldest Beneluz son, moved sluggishly on his mattress and offered Mica his own bread. The young lad took it gratefully and ate it slowly.

Rivka broke out crying bitterly.

Isabella comforted her. "It won't be much longer now, you'll see. One more day and we'll be there. By then their fever will be gone."

Rivka wiped her tears as she saw Isaac returning to their small space.

"Did you find the ship's doctor?" Rivka said to Isaac.

"He said many are sick on the ship, and he ran out of medicine."

Rivka took her linen cloth from her pocket to dry new tears. "What are we going to do?"

Isaac shook his head and lowered it.

"We have another long night ahead of us. Let us rest," she then said.

Everyone around them bedded for the night in their blankets. Soon the only sounds heard were a few passengers chatting quietly and the sounds of quiet breathing around them.

Miguel hugged Isabella as they huddled on her blanket and, covering their faces with a corner of his blanket, stole a kiss from her lips. She kissed him back and said, "One more day."

2

The Canaria Islands

August 6, 1492

THE DAWN LIFTED GRADUALLY ON the *Santa Maria* headed for the Canaria Islands. Once there, water and provisions would be loaded onto the ship for the long voyage. Trailing behind the *Santa Maria*, the *Pinta* and the *Niña* followed each other at two nautical miles behind her. Christopher Columbus leaned on the top deck, his hand grasping the handrails while balancing his body, swaying to and fro, and riding the waves with the ship. He filled his lungs with the salty air and savored every breath slowly, conscious that this air was leading him to his goal. *That's what I've been waiting for all these years. To enjoy this crisp air—the mother of life.* Since the three ships had left Palos, the sea had cooperated. He deeply believed that the waters were unusually calm because of the Savior's guidance for all three of his ships.

"Admiral!" The voice belonging to Sancho Ruiz, his pilot, sounded overjoyed. "We're closing in on the Canaria Islands."

"Inform me as soon as you see Gran Canaria Island."

Columbus fell back into his reverie and his outlook on the voyage. He felt a warm feeling at the thought of what awaited him in the weeks ahead.

His discovery of the Indies by sailing west, and using the power of the trade winds to push them forward west; to reach Asia and the treasures he expected to find, according to Marco Polo's notations in the margins of his book, and the new souls he would bring for España intoxicated his brain. His head spun from anticipated joy at the rewards that would come his way. Not the vain rewards for himself but for his two sons, Fernando and Diego. Their future would be assured with titles and monetary rewards. That's what he desired most from this voyage. He must succeed. No other outcome could be acceptable.

Except for the *Niña* yawing badly so far, the voyage had been smooth sailing from Palos as the ships made their way south into the Atlantic, then sailing past the coast of Africa. The Canaria Islands would be a godsend, allowing them to restock their provisions, tools, and water and begin their Atlantic voyage into the unknown. Everything must be just right to prevent any future problem during this voyage.

He then decided that to help the *Niña* from yawing and pitching, she must be rerigged from its lateen sail to a square rig, a *vela redonda*, at Gran Canaria. Otherwise she might not be able to undergo the great voyage and, under great winds, might be lost with her men aboard. His heart tightened at this last thought. What if he didn't come back, or lost the men in his charge?

He turned around abruptly and left the quarterdeck for the hold. On the main deck, the sailors worked hard at washing and polishing the wooden planks with seawater splashed from wooden pails. In a corner, by the forecastle, Diego Sanchez, his cook, was busy by the sandbox, where a fire burned underneath a cauldron stewing a meal for the crew. Columbus then descended into the hold below deck to inspect provisions.

The crates were stacked along the walls of the hold, along with additional empty water barrels. Upon leaving La Gomera, one of the last islands in the Canaries, water will be supplied along with the food provisions loaded in Gran Canaria. These must suffice for the voyage. With careful monitoring and wise distribution, they would stretch until they reached the Indies. Deep down, however, he felt a tinge of anxiety rising to the surface. *What if the voyage takes longer? Will the men die of starvation, or lack of water?* He wiped his forehead as if to obliterate the morbid thought.

Everything will work out fine, he assured himself. Wasn't it the Lord who had put him on the path of this holy mission, the passage to the Indies by sailing west and the sacred calling to convert the heathens to Christianity? Yes, it was.

He turned to the task at hand and began to count the tuns of wine. The hogsheads were stacked along the halls of the hull, and he made sure all were accounted for. The rest of the food supplies to last them until Gran Canaria seemed plenty. He noted down how much food and water to divide among the crew and sailors.

"Admiral Columbus?"

The voice behind his back made him jump. He turned around and raised his lantern to face the same sailor whose eyes had left a disturbing impression upon leaving Palos.

"And who wants me?" he asked the sailor.

"João Treves. Forgive me, Admiral. I believe I've known you before. A long time ago."

Columbus looked him straight in the eyes. "Why should I know you?" Columbus stood a full head above the sailor, looking down at him, his jaws clenched.

The sailor hesitated for a moment. "I'm not sure, but I believe you knew my sister Sarita."

Columbus startled momentarily but remained calm. "You must be mistaken. I never knew anyone by that name."

"Her name was Sarita Treves. She lived near Sintra, Portugal."

Columbus continued to remain calm. "I have no recollection of what you're talking about. Now get back to your post."

The sailor stood still with burning eyes remained fixed on him.

Columbus lowered the lantern, then turned his back on João. Fleeing the suffocating air below, he climbed back up the swaying rope ladder to the deck above. When he emerged from the hold, he took a long breath of sea air.

"Almirante! Almirante!" a voice from above in the crow's nest called out.

He looked up to see the sailor pointing in the direction of the *Pinta*, and falling behind the *Niña*. A distress signal was posted by a black flag on the mainmast, and several smoke signals were sent in succession.

"Reef in the sails and slow down the ship!" Columbus yelled at his men and Sancho Ruiz, his pilot at the stern. The sailors rushed and clambered to furl the sails with yards half hoisted.

With a grinding sound and vibrations felt throughout the *Santa Maria*, the ship slowed down to allow the *Pinta* to approach. Their only boat was released into the water, and Columbus went down in it and made his way toward the *Pinta*.

Martin Pinzón was at the top of the rope ladder. "Admiral, we have a broken rudder."

Columbus approached the steerage deck and saw that the big outboard rudder had jumped its gudgeons. The tiller's long and heavy wooden handle had broken in half. He thought hard for a solution. He then turned to Pinzón. "You're a man of wit and resources. I know you can repair the damage. We will slow down the *Santa Maria* for you to follow us at your own pace. Pray that no great winds come our way."

Pinzón's face showed surprise at Columbus's praise. "All right, my admiral. Slow down the *Santa Maria* until the repairs are done."

Columbus nodded, then returned to his ship. *This was poor workmanship by none other than the caravel's owner, Pinzón himself*, he grumbled. It was a troubling circumstance for his voyage.

Throughout the two three days, all three ships crawled toward the Islas Canarias. Early at dawn, with no breeze helping the three ships, Columbus stood on the starboard deck and scrutinized the horizon.

"Look!"

Columbus raised his head to the crow's nest to see his sailor pointing to the nearest island coming into view. "El Tenerife!" the voice shouted again. All eyes turned to the island spewing flames and fire from its highest peak. Black smoke filled the atmosphere in a plume reaching over the vast ocean. Columbus saw the men fall to their knees and cross themselves, warding off a bad portent.

"It's a natural phenomena!" he yelled at the men. "A natural phenomena." He repeated. "A volcano gets rid of pressure in the earth by throwing excess fire and rocks." He swallowed, then continued. "Remember Mons Vesuvius and Mons Etna?"

The men looked up to him peevishly after his explanation, but still crossed themselves again.

An hour later another large island loomed ahead.

Standing below him on the main deck, Juan de la Cosa, the master and owner of the *Santa Maria*, cupped his hands and called out to him, "Admiral. We're approaching Gran Canaria Island!"

"Very well. Have the men ready to go ashore!" He looked straight ahead and saw the island rising before him. The tall mountain of Gran Canaria with its ash slopes seemed like a giant lost in a long sleep.

Columbus called down to Juan. "We will do the repairs on the Pinta, and I will give orders to the ship builders in the harbor to equip the *Niña* as a square-rigged sail! See to it!"

De la Cosa nodded.

3

The Obrigon's Home

ARTURO OBRIGON KNEW FOR CERTAIN he was getting on in years. At the age of fifty he felt old. Life had taken a toll by depriving him of his wife, Estrella. The years past with Estrella had been filled with her ebullient personality and her sudden burst of ideas on where to visit or vacation in the country. No wonder Isabella had had the same characteristics. When Isabella was young, she had infected the household with her laughter and playing her buffooneries on the servants in the kitchens or wherever they were working. Isabella would hide the brooms or sheets that were being changed, leaving the maids puzzled.

"Little señorita, where are you hiding?" the maid would call out. A giggle reaching her ears would clue her where Isabella had been hiding. "I have you!" the maid would cry, then fall upon her. Isabella would scream in delight, then erupt in a series of chuckles and laughter.

Where have these days gone?

A child's laughter reached his ears. Arturo perked up in his chair, listening with delight. *Is it Isabella?*

The door to his study opened up, and in ran José with a smile on his lips. An out-of-breath servant ran after him to catch him.

"My apologies." Carmelita bowed to Don Obrigon. "José was chasing me all over the house." Carmelita looked down at the red tile floor trying to hide a smile.

"But I didn't, I didn't!" José protested while trying to withhold a smile of his own. He then burst into laughter.

Don Obrigon stood from his chair and walked slowly over to hug José. "It's all right. Only make sure you don't waste the servants' time. They have chores waiting for them." He smiled affectionately.

José bowed his head in obedience.

"Now go and play outside, my child." Don Obrigon gave José a pat on his rear end.

When the door closed on his study, Arturo found himself alone again. José had somehow adjusted to not having his older brother, Miguel, around him. The two brothers were close in their affection, and especially after hearing of their mother's death in prison. From what was explained to both brothers, their mother, Téresa Costa, had died a martyr, but Arturo knew what "martyr" meant. It meant she had been tortured until the poor woman's heart stopped.

Since that fateful day Isabella left with Miguel, never to return home, Arturo pined for the young couple. He still remembered the crucial moment when his love for his daughter had to be quashed for her to be safely out of reach from Constable Guerida's tentacles. He knew that the Beneluz family had hidden Isabella and Miguel from the inspector and soldiers that came on the ship to arrest them. His unbounded gratitude to the Beneluz family was sacred. Now he cared for José as his own son.

His whole Obrigon family had felt the blow of the Inquisition and the church. "Damn them!" He made his right hand into a fist. "I will get my revenge someday!" he screamed out loud. Outside, José's giggles and laughter came to his ears.

He turned his attention to his books and continued to jot down numbers, adding columns of debits and credits of his latest patients' payments. The columns of numbers didn't jibe. There was more owed to him than what was paid for his services. That was curious. Never before was such a large sum of money owed by his patients, nor were they so late paying their debts. He got up from his chair and went to look at José playing in the front yard. José was kicking a leather pigskin ball back and forth to the Obrigons' longtime faithful servant Emilio Gomez.

Arturo turned away from this peaceful scene and went back to his desk. No sooner had he sat than he heard screams. *José must be back to his antics and chasing Emilio this time.* When José's screams were joined by Emilio's screams for help, Arturo ran back to the window.

There, before his eyes, José was fighting to be freed from the arms of a soldier preventing his escape. Guerida was standing with his arms on his hips, and with a satisfied smile on his lips. He saw Guerida's lips form words, but Arturo didn't wait any longer. He ran as fast as he could out of his study to the hallway leading to the front entrance. The door flew open, and he lunged for José. His hands reached for the boy, but another soldier stopped him with one blow to the head with the butt of his sword. Arturo swayed under the pain. Emilio ran to him before Arturo landed on the ground.

Arturo cried in pain and shock. "What's the meaning of this?"

"I came to undo what you did to me last time," Guerida said mockingly.

Arturo put a hand to his head and felt blood on his fingers. "And what did I do to you? Tell me!" His voice came out terrible.

"You stole this boy and his brother from under my nose. Remember— the day you brought the fake tax collector Don Senior!" Guerida barked back at him.

"You better not say any derogatory remark about Don Coronel. That's what he's called now after the queen saw to his baptism. And King Ferdinand was there too! You will be punished for smearing Don Coronel's name!"

A hint of pallor spread across Inspector Guerida's face. "I didn't mean to imply anything. Don Coronel has my respect." Guerida bowed with those last words. "Now. We will take the boy away—"

Arturo grabbed the boy's arm, but the soldier held him in a tight grip. José squirmed to be let free.

"You can visit the boy at the nearest military barracks in the outskirts of Seville. We won't harm him, I promise." Guerida put his hand on his heart.

Arturo felt tears rolling down his face. This was a nightmare he hadn't predicted. He turned to José. "I will get you out of this. I promise!" he told him.

The boy was now in tears, and Arturo's heart was about to break. He turned to Guerida. "At least let me hug him?" he begged.

Guerida nodded to the soldier, who let the boy free. José ran into Arturo's arms. Arturo held him tightly and whispered in his ear. "I promise I'll get you out. You'll see." To which José cried now in earnest. His cries rose in the front garden as the servants ran outdoors to witness the arrest unfolding. The servants' cries joined his, and dada Hannah, Isabella's past nanny, ran to hug José.

"*Mi povre niño, mi povre Josélito. No tengas miedo.* Don't be afraid, my boy." She pressed him to her bosom.

"But why? What do you want from a ten-year-old boy! He's innocent of any wrongdoing!" Arturo's voice rose with harshness.

Guerida gave the order to the two soldiers standing alongside, and they grabbed José and tied him to the horse standing outside the yard. The boy screamed in fear and reached with both his arms to Arturo, whose heart felt crushed. Dada Hannah fell to her knees crying with hands in prayer. The other servants stood with contrite faces under the shock of the scene before their eyes. Don Obrigon, too, fell to his knees and tried to comfort dada Hannah.

Within minutes Guerida, the soldiers, and José were gone.

Arturo gotArturo got up with difficulty and shuffled back into the house, his shoulders low.

4

High Seas Pirates

THE SEA ON THIS GLORIOUS morning was as flat and calm as a mirror's surface. The children on the ship were playing at who could be first to find fish swimming below the surface. The water was clear, and shouts of delight burst from their mouths as they saw schools of flying fish swimming alongside the ship.

"I see hundreds of fish!" a boy of twelve years shouted in delight.

"Where, where?" Another girl his age rushed to look. She held on to the railing and bent over to see well. "I can't see anything." She sighed. "Besides, you can't count them!"

"Step aside!" shouted a sailor at the youth. "If you fall in, the fish will eat you!"

The children yelled in disgust and fear, then fled, each to their respective family. The parents sat gloomily, grabbing their children with cross faces.

"We ought to get back down below," Miguel whispered to Isabella. "Let's see how my cousins are faring."

"Please, let's stay a while longer. It's so stuffy down in the hold, and so many people are sick."

Miguel tried to look serious, but Isabella knew how to win him over whenever she wanted something out of him.

"All right," he then said to her, raising his arms in a relinquishing gesture.

"Look! Look! Right there!" a passenger yelled, pointing to the horizon, where another ship sailed.

Isabella and Miguel scurried to the railing. Isabella squinted, watching a vessel approaching them.

"It is getting closer," Miguel said.

Isabella turned to Miguel and said calmly, "I'm afraid for us."

"You have nothing to fear. I'll protect you."

No sooner had Miguel reassured Isabella than a cry rose from the passengers. "Pirates! A pirate ship!"

All eyes turned to the caravel now advancing slowly toward them. They clearly saw the skull-and-crossbones flag attached to the flagpole and pirates balancing on the rails, their swords unsheathed.

"Come! Hurry!" Miguel pulled Isabella away and ran to the hold down the open hatch. Tripping and sliding, they both reached the bottom and ran to their quarters, where the Beneluzes were huddled.

"We're in for trouble!' Miguel said out of breath to Isaac.

Isaac blanched and went to speak to Rivka. She turned white too, and began to hit her head with both fists. "My poor children, we're doomed!"

Isaac looked cross with her. "Control yourself, woman!"

Those words worked like magic on Rivka. She stopped her panic and turned to her two younger sons lying helpless in the throes of fever. They were weak with burning foreheads and feeble from hunger.

"You, Isabella, come here!" Isaac said. He pushed her to the wall and grabbed their bundles, then stacked them high, covering her completely. Isabella had complied without questions. Now, however, a moan came from her.

"Miguel, Miguel. I don't want to be separated from you." Her muffled cry came through.

"Hush," Miguel replied loud enough for Isabella to hear him. "We will be rid of them in no time at all. Stay silent."

A loud thump shook the sides of the ship, shaking their every fiber. The bales concealing Isabella tumbled down, revealing her hideout. Isaac ran to her and piled them up against her. Isabella grasped Isaac's arm to stop him, but he continued until she was hidden again. He then turned to his sons, who were sitting frightened. "We're going to face these evil men together."

They all nodded.

A sea of cries rose from the ship like a wave that came down to their ears. "Save us! Save us!" The words came tumbling down the open hatch. Next a series of footsteps sounded from sailors running above them on deck. The voice of the captain rose. "We don't have gold or silver! These are poor refugees that left España without money!" Next a muffled cry came, then a deep silence crept in.

All eyes in the hold turned to the top of the landing, where cutthroat pirates with swords attached at their belts trickled down the ladder through the open hatch. A fearful hush spread among the passengers huddled with their belongings. Miguel thought that if the pirates could be overcome, the rest should be easy. After all, there were more passengers than those pirates going through the passengers' belongings. Isaac met his eyes and he saw in them a muted message of caution. *How many more pirates were above them on deck?*

The pirates' search proceeded through the passengers' bundles, ripping them apart and digging for valuables. Next, they yanked each passenger and began searching their bodies for gold. As the search kept on, Isaac made a gesture to Rivka, who was eyeing him. Miguel tried to understand the message that passed between his aunt and uncle, and his aunt's eyes held fear in them.

Their turn came to be searched. The bales were torn from the wall, and as they came tumbling down, Miguel was astounded to discover that Isabella had vanished! Where was she?

A disheveled and bearded pirate stinking of sweat with liquor on his breath searched Isaac. A cry of victory rose from his bearded mouth. "I found gold!" He brandished Isaac's robe, and the pockets were torn to reveal gold coins.

"Do you have any more?" the bandit yelled in his ear. Isaac, repelled by the pirate's noxious breath, stood back and shook his head.

"Well, we'll see about that." He scattered all their belongings looking for more coins. He then fell upon Rivka and searched her unashamedly.

"Get your filthy hands off of me!"

The pirate slapped her several times in the face. She swayed and fell back on the floor. He then lifted her skirts and searched her undergarments. Rivka yelled at the top of her lungs. "Don't touch me! ¡*Ladron!*"

Isaac put his arms out to hush her. "No! Don't!"

Rivka spit in the pirate's bearded face. To their amazement, the pirate stood laughing at her.

"You old hag. Stop your screaming." He then turned his back to her and moved toward Guerson, and Mica lying down on the floor.

Rivka yelled, "Don't touch my sons! They're sick with fever!"

The pirate hesitated for a moment then turned away to his next victims.

Isaac ran to Rivka and tried to comfort her, but she wouldn't stop crying.

Miguel, who had watched the whole scene, and had been prevented from interfering by his uncle's glance, stood helplessly, his thoughts jumbled up as to Isabella's disappearance. The pirates had now completed their search, and dragging along a few resisting young men in their grasp, they left one by one up the rope ladder and through the hatch to the upper deck.

"Quickly, let's find Isabella," Miguel cried.

"No! Wait until the pirates leave the ship," his uncle said. "If they find her, she'll be sold to the highest bidder!"

Defeated, Miguel dropped his arms alongside his body. "Where is she?"

"Be still," Isaac said. He then went back to Rivka to comfort her.

They all sat in the hold in complete silence. A faint moan rose now and then from some of the passengers, but it quickly died down. They were still frozen with fear; some were injured from beatings, while others sat stunned having lost all their fortune. On the deck above, the scurrying feet stopped running. Miguel sensed they were those of the pirates scrambling to finish the rampage and gather as much gold as possible.

Within minutes all was silent above them when a shout went out, "They're gone! The pirates are gone!"

A sigh of relief went out from the passengers as they sat still.

Miguel sat tight, gripped by anxiety. Had Isabella vanished from her hideout? Unless. . .

He grasped on to his thoughts, got off the floor of the hold, and walked toward the wall near their gathering place. Isaac, who eyed him, looked puzzled.

Miguel tapped the side planking making up the wall and received a hollow sound to his ears. He kept tapping, when his eyes picked up a discrepancy among the boards. With his fingers, he pulled on the board, and it flipped open sideways. Grasping the next board, he pulled again, and a cavity opened before him. Isabella stood shaking there in front of him. She fell trembling into his arms. Miguel held her tightly in his arms.

"I thought I'd lost you," he whispered in her ear.

She hugged him back silently.

Isaac, who had witnessed the entire scene, came close and put his arms around them. "Elohim is looking out for us and protecting us," he said.

"You can also add a little ingenuity on the part of Isabella," Miguel added. "What I don't understand is why the pirates didn't take me hostage like some of the others?"

Rivka, who had recovered from the vicious search by the pirate, said, "Perhaps the boys' fever scared them away."

Despite the precarious situation they were in, they all laughed with relief.

5

At the Palace in Madrid

IN THE DIM LIGHT IN the chapel, Queen Isabella prayed at the altar, her crowned head bent down to her chest, her lips moving slightly in prayer.

Carmela, watching her in an alcove, also prayed distractedly while she observed her mistress. *The queen is worried more than usual. I wonder what's troubling her.* Carmela knew Queen Isabella to be extremely and deeply lost in her morning prayers. After all, the Pope had dubbed her the *Reina Catolica.* Somehow this morning the queen lingered with her prayers. Carmela finished her prayer, crossed herself, then waited for the queen to finish hers. She approached the queen and remained at a respectful distance, and heard her voice murmuring softly.

"*Santo Dio y Santa Madre,* free me from my doubts. Have I been too harsh? Was I a punishing queen to my subjects? Please show me a sign. Did I condemn these poor wretches to their death?"

Was the queen speaking of her ousted subjects, the Jews who had been forced to leave Spain? Carmela loved the queen with all her heart, but felt disturbed, nonetheless, by this revelation. *It's now too late to atone,* Carmela murmured to herself.

The queen suddenly rose from the pew and walked down the church aisle. Out of a side door, her lady-in-waiting, Beatriz de Bobadilla, rushed to aid the queen with her train.

"My queen, there are two delegates from the Pope waiting for you in the Ambassador Hall," Beatriz said a few paces behind her, while balancing the queen's heavy train.

"I don't recall any scheduled appointments from the Pope. My Fridays are dedicated to my subjects only."

"They only indicated to request an audience with you," Beatriz replied.

"Any news from your sister Leonor in the Islas Canarias?" Queen Isabella quickened her pace despite her long and voluminous damask skirts slowing her down.

"No, my queen. No word yet. Your advisors are monitoring the flotilla under Admiral Columbus, and no letters have arrived."

The queen's face didn't show her concern from the lack of news from Columbus's voyage. She now walked faster, followed by Beatriz, with Carmela walking at a distance in case the queen had need of her. They arrived at the hall, where the envoys waited patiently for her. Queen Isabella smiled at them as she sat on her throne, then nodded in their direction to commence.

"Dear Queen Isabella de Trastámara," one delegate said, "we're sorry for the absence of your husband King Ferdinand in Naples; we came with haste from the Pope to deliver his words."

"We're still mourning the passing of Pope Innocent. May his memory be blessed." Queen Isabella crossed her chest, followed by the envoy copying her gesture. "And how is Pope Alexander? I'm sure he's been getting to know his new flock since his election on August eleventh."

"He's well and thriving. That's why we've been sent on this mission," the envoy said. "Pope Alexander is wishing both you and your husband well." He quickly continued, seeing that Isabella was about to interrupt him. "Pope Alexander is conveying his wishes for a speedy voyage for Admiral Columbus and with much success. The Pope is also reminding everyone connected to this voyage to follow the treaty between Spain and Portugal concluded at Alcáçovas on September 4, 1479."

Isabella rudely interrupted the envoy. "I need not be reminded of the treaty. We've abided by this treaty and have not interfered in any way with Portugal's sovereignty."

"The Pope is well aware of the cooperation on the part of Spain and Portugal. Now, however, with this new voyage undertaken by the admiral, under your benefaction, the Pope wants to make sure that all parties agree to the terms of the treaty."

Queen Isabella nodded, resigned to listen to him.

"In the treaty," continued the envoy, "it's stipulated that Spain will abide to limit her explorations to north of the Canaria Islands, and not cross the line south toward Guinea and its gold mines, or trade in any of Portugal's held islands, coasts, or lands, or beyond the sea in Africa."

Queen Isabella concurred with the envoy by nodding again. "The admiral is well aware of those details. As a matter of fact, this was his decision for the voyage to sail the course past the Canaria Islands, then follow in a straight course west for the Indies." Her voice rose volumes.

The envoy seemed to understand the conveyed assurance by the queen. "In that case we will report to the Pope that all parties are agreeable to the treaty and are abiding by it." He bowed to Isabella, and followed by his aide, left the audience room.

Queen Isabella turned to her advisors. "Make sure to draft a letter to Columbus of said audience and its content, then convey it as soon as possible to La Palma in the Canaria Islands." She then turned to Carmela and said, "I'm very fatigued; please help me to my chambers."

6

La Gomera

August 15, 1492

THE SAILS WERE BLOWING AGAIN in the winds coming at them safely but also persistently. *At this rate we're bound to reach La Gomera in a few hours*, thought Columbus with joy in his heart. He stood tall on the quarterdeck observing his sailors toiling with washing the decks and checking the ropes and the rigging. The men were from strong stock, tanned by the sun and with bulging muscles taut by their labor.

He observed one sailor in particular. This same man had accosted him before in the hold. The encounter had reopened the memory of Sarita, his first and only love. He had been very young then, full of hope for the future and with dreams still forming in his soul. He recalled confiding to Sarita that his travels and those of others were showing him the way to more explorations. Marco Polo, Henry the Navigator, and Abraham Zacuto were the navigators who had most influenced him. He kept Zacuto's map at his fingertips and checked it periodically for navigational instructions. His most fervent belief in his aspirations to discover a passage to the Indies relied on biblical prophecies. The book of Isaiah showed him the way: "*The isles shall wait for me, and the ships of Tarshish first, to bring thy sons from far, their silver and their gold with them. I create new heavens and a new earth."* He felt compelled by these words pointing the way for him. *And the gold will usher in reconquering Jerusalem by the Crusaders.*

He suddenly felt eyes resting on him, and those were none other than those of João's face fixed on him. Columbus became irritated. João was stalking him and preventing him from gathering his thoughts. He motioned with his head for him to climb to the upper deck. João dropped the ropes in his hands and climbed the three stairs to the quarterdeck.

"Your name is João Treves, isn't it?"

"Yes, Admiral. I'm honored that you remembered."

"How can I not remember? You've been watching me since we left Palos," Columbus said with a harsh voice. "What do you want?"

João turned somber at being rudely addressed. "Admiral, this is regarding my question to you about my sister, Sarita—did you know her?"

"Why must you know?" Columbus spoke lower this time while glancing at the sailors working on the lower deck.

"It's important that I know."

Columbus scrutinized João for a long moment. "All right. I knew a Sarita long ago. Are you satisfied?"

João flushed a smile. "You see, Admiral, I recognized you from the start. You came on many occasions to see my sister around the spring of 1475."

Columbus thought for a moment about those long-ago visits. He now recalled João present there as chaperon for his sister, but Sarita had found a way to meet him in a secluded and abandoned farm. They were so much in love, he remembered. Sarita and he had made a pact that they would be faithful to each other till death broke the bond. Then his dreams of exploration began to torment him. He had told her about his plans to sail west and reach islands east, where gold waited for him. He had also, foolishly, told her secrets about himself that he now feared may be damaging to his quest.

"Admiral?"

João's voice pulled him out of his reverie. He turned to him and said, "I must get back to my ship. We'll talk later."

João opened his mouth to say something, then stopped, nodded, and returned to the lower deck.

Columbus followed him with his eyes while his hands gripped the handrail in front of him.

"La Gomera!" yelled the watchman.

Columbus turned his face upward to the caller in the crow's nest pointing west. He clearly discerned the low-lying beaches and tall mountains in the background. Clouds and mist shrouded the tall mountains that were frequently visited by the trade winds. As the *Santa Maria* approached the harbor of San Sebastian, flags on the mainland with the cross were hoisted on the flagpole. The native population of Gomeras ran to the beaches and swam toward the ships. His master-at-arms, Diego de Arana, made a call to all hands on deck.

Deafening sounds of grinding metal chains against the floorboards of the deck were heard as they were pulled. The anchor was dropped, and Columbus was followed by Juan de la Cosa, owner and master of the *Santa Maria*; Maestre Alonso, his physician; his master-at-arms, Diego de Arana, a cousin of Beatriz Enriquez de Arana and the mother of his son Fernandez; and Rodrigo de Escobedo, his secretary.

Columbus turned to his boatswain and said, "The crew can go ashore for two hours only. I don't want them drunk on their first day on this voyage."

Bartholomé Garcia replied, "With all due respect, Admiral, I will monitor each man, but you know how much they drink."

"Yes, I do. But this isn't a wedding or a holy day. I want them sober by dawn." With that last word, Columbus descended the rope ladder to the rowboat moored by the ship. From the last rung he slipped into the boat, followed by his men. The oars pushed against the side of the ship, and the rowboat set off toward shore. The Gomerans, native islanders, swam around the boat and when they stopped, communicated with a whistling speech. The islanders latched on to their boat and pushed it forward with sheer strength, while Columbus noticed their muscled arms, smooth black hair, and gentle features. These Gomerans resembled their Guanches neighbors to the east and the natives of Tenerife Island.

A thud was felt as the rowboat landed on the beach. Columbus stepped out and was received by a welcoming committee from Gomera.

"Welcome to La Gomera, Admiral." The noble who spoke to him curtsied with a sweeping motion of his plumed hat. He was none other than Alfonso Fernandez de Lugo, present governor of La Palma in the Canarias. Here was a nobleman recognized for his services to the crown, among other valiant war campaigns. Columbus felt elevated by his presence.

Columbus bowed to him. "You do me great honor, Don de Lugo."

"Doña Leonor de Bobadilla is waiting for you in San Sebastian's house. She has been governor of La Gomera since her husband died."

"My compliments to Doña Leonor de Bobadilla. As you well know, her sister Doña Beatriz was instrumental in influencing the queen on my behalf. I'm in their debt."

"We'll all be in your debt for the gold you'll find for España." Don de Lugo slapped Columbus's left arm jovially.

Columbus replied, "This is my goal after winning millions of souls for the church."

"Of course, of course." Don de Lugo agreed with Columbus. "Spain also needs this gold badly. The wars have been hard on the realm's coffers. You're Spain's savior."

Columbus nodded with modesty but remained silent.

They had reached San Sebastian's manor, which sat on a terraced hill that followed the contour of the mountain. Columbus and his men followed Don de Lugo through the gate's portico and ascended the steps to a grand hall. Doña Leonor stood at the end of the hall in a finery of brocade robes. She advanced toward them, and her beauty struck Columbus immediately. She had a fine chiseled face capped by lustrous black hair under her bonnet; and she had large soft eyes and fleshy round lips.

"Bienvenido a Gomera, Almirante." She then took his arm and led him away from the reception hall to a small dining room with a table laden with food.

Juan de la Cosa locked eyes with Columbus with an appreciative glance and smile at the spread before them. His physician; Juan Sanchez; Diego de Arana; and Rodrigo de Escobedo, his secretary, followed him.

When they all sat, Doña Leonor de Bobadilla gave orders for the wine to be poured.

"Where is the rest of your party?" she asked, her magnificent eyes looking straight at Columbus sitting to her right.

"We depart early tomorrow, and I want them sober at their post," Columbus replied.

"Does this mean you won't be drinking much?" Doña Leonor addressed him, her eyes singling him out again.

Columbus stayed mute for a moment, befuddled as to what she meant exactly. "How can I refuse your hospitality, my dear governor?"

A cajoling laugh was Doña Leonor's reply. "I see that you are a politician as well as an explorer."

Columbus felt his face reddening under the compliment. He nodded appreciatively.

As he feasted on the watercress soup called *potaje de berros* and *almagrote*, a paste from goat cheese, and *vieja* fish, Doña Leonor's eyes rested on Columbus frequently.

"We want to wish you a successful voyage, Admiral." Don de Lugo raised his wine glass.

The all raised their glasses in a toast to Columbus.

"You know, my dear Columbus, if I hadn't been commissioned by the queen for the conquest of Tenerife, soon in the offing, I'd join you on this voyage. I can't imagine what you will find—the land, the people, and the treasures."

"We're all in awe of the queen for permitting this costly voyage," Columbus said. "My all-consuming thought is the Christian kingdom we will establish in the lands of the heathen."

"Hear, hear." De Lugo approved by raising his glass again and emptying it.

Columbus got up from the table. "My dear hostess." He turned to Doña Leonor to take leave from the noble assemblage. "We're awaiting word from Gran Canaria on our two ships being repaired as we speak. I will bid you a good night." He stood up and bowed with accentuated chivalry.

Doña Leonor smiled at him and nodded.

When Columbus returned to the *Santa Maria*, his pilot, Sancho Ruiz, took him aside.

"Sailors unloading their caravel from El Hierro Island said they've seen three Portuguese caravels. The rumor was they came to capture you, Admiral."

"Why would anyone want to capture me?" Columbus said with surprise.

"Because you sold your services to Spain instead of Portugal?"

Columbus didn't reply. He nodded pensively. "Thank you for this information, Ruiz." Before walking away he turned back to Ruiz. "I have a plan to thwart theirs."

To Ruiz's raised eyebrows, he said, "We'll hoist Portuguese flags on our masts."

Ruiz burst in laughter and walked away still laughing

Columbus went to his cabin, his hands slightly trembling. *I can't let anything get in the way of this voyage*, he muttered.

7

Berbers at Sea

CUDDLED IN THE HOLD BELOW the deck, Rivka, now ill and seasick, tried to wet her two young sons' hot foreheads; they were also sick with the same fever. She touched Mica, the youngest, and his skin dripped with moisture from humidity and the fever ravaging his body. Guerson lay sleeping and moaning periodically. Her older sons, Leon and Avram, were in deep sleep. Miguel and Isabella were the only ones absent and spending time on the deck above them. Rivka turned to Isaac, pleading with her eyes.

Isaac raised tired eyes to Rivka's plea. He got up from his cross-legged position on the floor, and went to Mica and lifted him off his blanket. The youngster didn't stir.

"I'm taking him above for fresh air."

Rivka nodded, then lay down next to Avram and Guerson.

Isaac carried Mica's light and thin body, then climbed the ladder to the upper deck. The rarefied air that greeted him strengthened him. He looked for an empty corner where Mica could be sheltered from waves spraying the huddled masses.

"Uncle? Uncle?" He heard Miguel's voice from above on the quarterdeck. "Bring him up."

Out of breath, he joined Miguel and Isabella seated near the mainmast. He gently put Mica on the wood beams of the deck and sat next to him.

⚜

"How is Mica?" Isabella asked Isaac.

"Still feverish." Isaac moaned. He then leaned back against the railing's wall with his eyes lost on the horizon.

Isabella bent down to Mica and cradled his head in her lap. She then sang to him.

Bre, Mica, bre, ojos tienes tu
mansana de comer!
por mi vida el Dio me los dio.

"Where did you learn this song?" Miguel asked her.

"From my dada Hannah. She sang it to me when I was little."

"My mother also sang this song for my brother, José, when he was little." Miguel's voice broke.

Isabella lifted her head to Miguel's almost crying voice. "You must be thinking about your brother. You know he's safe in my father's house."

"Thank you, Isabella. I know your father will care for him. I do miss my brother terribly."

Isabella raised her hand and caressed Miguel's face. "I know we'll get out of this."

A loud scream was heard on the lower deck. "Pirates!"

"Oh no, not again!" Miguel screamed in agony. He looked up to see a fast-approaching pirate ship.

Mica suddenly woke up, and Isaac came out of his trance and went to lift Mica in his arms. He turned to Miguel and Isabella. "Quickly, let's go back down!" He then made his way toward the open hatch, but the masses of men, women, and children on the decks prevented all three of them from descending.

Loud screams were heard from the passengers sitting on the deck floor. They stood up all at once and looked to the captain for protection.

Miguel had to fight his way against the wall of bodies preventing him and Isabella from reaching the open hatch. A large thud was heard from the menacing large caravel bumping into their ship, with pirates hanging from the rigging and shrouds. No sooner had the two caravels rubbed against each other than a horde of Barbary pirates descended on the decks. The captain voiced his displeasure with a booming voice. "By all laws governing these waters, you're in violation!"

The Berber pirates laughed at those words, and a multitude of boarding hooks flew over their guardrails to land on their ship and secured the pirate ship alongside them. All at once, a horde of turban-coiffed men sporting tangled dark beards and several cutlasses and daggers inside the red sashes at their waists spilled onto the deck. The passengers recoiled in horror, seeking refuge toward the captain of the ship on the quarterdeck. The pirates put up a fight with the sailors on hand, slashing and fighting their way on the main deck, and several sailors fell bloodied onto the planks; others were mortally wounded. Next, the pirates began pulling from the crowd young and able-bodied men and women.

Isabella, Miguel, and Beneluz, who was still holding Mica, felt trapped on deck, and embroiled by the sheer mass of passengers forming a wall in front of them. Miguel pulled Isabella's scarf around her neck to cover her grimy face. When the pirates came close to them, one pulled Isabella with a satisfied smile on his face.

"I've got a good one, by Allah!"

Miguel reacted without a second thought and jumped on the back of the pirate who was holding Isabella's hand in a vise grip. The pirate swiveled on his heels and hit Miguel with the head of his cutlass. Miguel felt his head where blood began to pour out and collapsed on the deck, under the feet of the terrified passengers fleeing away from danger.

"Miguel! Miguel!" Isabella yelled for him. Miguel tried to get up on his knees and reach for her, but the pirate holding her prevented him by kicking him hard. Miguel fell again and again with renewed effort to stand up.

"I've got me one." The pirate holding Isabella laughed and attracted the attention of another of his co-pirates. "Grab this one! He's strong." He pointed at Miguel's sheer resistance despite his bloody head.

The other pirate reached his long fingernails and stubby hands for Miguel, then dragged him to one side of the deck, where other young men were cornered.

Isabella, meanwhile, found herself alongside other young girls, all crying their eyes out and hugging each other for protection.

Isabella signaled to Miguel, telling him not to resist by waving her hand back and forth.

Beneluz had watched the struggle and stood frozen and unable to help one or the other.

The pirates had gathered a small amount of jewelry and coins from passengers who had hoarded their last precious possessions from the previous raid. They were in tears, beating their chests and holding their heads in their hands, while rocking their bodies to and fro in grief. Others who had escaped the pirates' mortal blows helped the wounded sailors, while other sailors lay on deck without stirring.

The captain stood on the quarterdeck with two pirates holding his arms behind him. He hung his head low without resisting, acknowledging his lost ship to the pirates.

All at once, the pirates, without any communication among them, retreated with their meager loot to the ropes holding the ships together and began to drag their prisoners with them. Miguel and Isabella were transported to the pirate ship and pushed down to the pirates' deck. The girls snatched from the ship renewed their crying and wailing. One pirate came over and smacked each of them successively on the face.

A long cry was heard from all the young women on the pirates' main deck. They were moving away from the passenger ship. Isabella and Miguel saw Isaac Beneluz retreating with the ship with one of his arms holding his young son and the other outstretched to them, trying to reach through the divide separating them.

Miguel realized this must be the last time they would see him. Who knew what misery awaited them now as slaves?

8

Island Magic

MORNINGS ON LA GOMERA ISLAND were perfumed by a profusion of flowers and scented citrus fruit. A gentle breeze awoke Columbus each morning by six, and by seven he was having his first meal of the day with Doña Leonor de Bobadilla. They were now well into mid-September, and the entire voyage held captive to the *Pinta* and *Niña* being repaired in Gran Canaria. He sat distracted in the large dining hall in Doña Leonor's sprawling house.

"Admiral Columbus? Admiral?"

Doña Leonor's words reached his ears. He shook himself from his reverie and looked up at her lovely face. She was adorned with sumptuous robes for the early morning. Her hair cascaded down to her waist in black curly waves. He remembered her sister Doña Beatriz de Bobadilla in Madrid attending to the queen. She, too, was a beautiful woman. He'd heard the rumors that King Ferdinand had been reproached several times by the queen for his admiration for beautiful women. He had heard, too, that Doña Leonor had been married in a hurry to Don Peraza and shipped to La Gomera to keep her away from King Ferdinand.

A smile appeared on his lips.

"I'm glad I made you smile, Admiral."

"I was absorbed in my concern for the voyage. My apologies for my lack of attention to your hospitality, Doña Leonor," Columbus said.

"Never mind, Admiral. I want to show you the island today. All is prepared." She smiled seductively.

Columbus nodded. "It will be my pleasure."

Doña Leonor got up from the breakfast table, and Columbus followed her to the outside of her large house. Outdoors, the sun shone at them with brilliance in the early morning on this tropical island. Below the house, two Guanches natives waited for them to lift them up in portable chairs.

They were transported first down the terraces on the island, then the climb began into the heights covered by laurel rainforest. A mist coming down the peaks encircled them as they climbed. After a two-hour climbing elevation, their porters arrived at a plateau, where they stopped.

The first thing Columbus saw, as the mist lifted, was a panoramic view of the island unfolding before his eyes. Behind him was a volcano caldera with a plume rising from its center. In front of him the hills descended with lush vegetation and pines to black sand beaches. Straight ahead was Tenerife's ominous volcano still spewing fire and ashes. Below in San Sebastián's harbor he saw the *Santa Maria* moored and swaying gently on the blue cerulean waters.

He turned to Doña Leonor and smiled with admiration. "You've brought me to paradise, my dear Doña Leonor."

"Wait, it isn't over yet," she said mysteriously. She turned around to the porters and maidservants and nodded. The servants unloaded baskets full of provisions and food and set them down on a colorful wool blanket sprawled on the grassy plateau.

The meal consisted of dough containing viands and onions and was tasty to the palate. Doña Leonor poured wine into two goblets. Columbus then bit on a glossy yellow fruit and found it soft and sweet. He raised admiring eyes to Doña Leonor.

"We call this fruit *caqui*, and La Gomera exports it to Madrid and other cities in Spain. It brings us much revenue." She then turned to one of her maidservants. "Bring me the stalks."

The servant took reddish stout stalks from a basket and presented them to Doña Leonor.

This is cane sugar. It's also sweet, I will give you more to take with you to the Indies to plant them in my name."

Columbus bowed his head. "It will be my honor."

Doña Leonor continued to pour more wine for him. He felt uplifted and lightheaded. She got up and extended a hand to him. He followed her away from the picnic site, and they climbed a short hill to a rock outcrop. They were now hidden from the rest of the party by a curtain of pine trees. On the face of one cliff, a cavern opened up before them. She led him into it. He was surprised to find blanket coverings on the fine sand floor. She led him to that spot and came close to him. He embraced her full red lips offered to him and sank into the dizzying sensation of her body scent. His world became distilled into this beautiful woman making love to him.

João Treves sat at leisure on *Santa Maria*'s deck watching his mates playing Tavla. The game deeply absorbed them, and grunts occasionally rose from their lips. One sailor threw his die over the game board and chuckled with glee.

"You lost, Alfonso, and I win!"

"But it wasn't your turn, Gomes!"

"Yes, it was," shouted Gomes. "You've played the last hand, Alfonso."

Alfonso lamented, "But I didn't. I didn't, I tell you!"

Hernán came to Alfonso's defense and said, "He's right, Gomes. You played the last turn."

Gomes swiped the few maravedís off the deck, and they disappeared into his pocket. "I won and that's that."

The two sailors looked at each other confounded.

"You cheated!" Hernán yelled.

João smiled at his mate's serious confrontation. He looked yonder beyond the ship moored in San Sebastian's harbor to La Gomera's mountains rising with majestic height. The crew had been waiting now for two weeks in this harbor, and the men were getting antsy. Tempers flared from time to time, and their games were becoming querulous. Patience was wearing thin, and fights tempted the men who were getting bored.

"Hey!" João shouted at his mates. "Tone it down!"

"You tell this cheater"—Hernán pointed at Gomes, who silently got up and strolled on the deck and away from the men—"we won't play with him any longer."

"Then don't play!" João said. He got up and went to the railing to observe the scenery in front of him. The weather had been most clement to the ship and the crew, and calmed by San Sebastian's harbor nestling them from the elements in its cusp.

His thoughts returned to the admiral and his prolonged absence from the ship. He'd heard the rumors of the beautiful Doña Leonor occupying the admiral's time on the island. The neglect of his duties was most troubling. Word came yesterday from Gran Canaria that the *Niña* had been re-masted, and the *Pinta*'s rudder and tiller had been repaired. Why the delay? That could only mean that the beautiful widow Doña Leonor's favors included an amorous liaison with the admiral.

Not only was the admiral oblivious of his duties by pursuing a love affair with the lady in question, but also precious time was running out. He clenched his fists on the ship's railing. He had forewarned his sister Sarita many years ago that the man she had fallen in love with would leave her. It was beyond doubt that Columbus was the same man his sister had adored.

While this voyage was being delayed, an imminent danger threatened the Spaniard Jews. Would the future bring more grief and loss to the children of Abraham? Another land faraway and safe for their generations needed to be found soon, or they might disappear into the mist of time.

9

Adrift

THE BOW PARTED THE DARK waters with white foam lines trailing behind the ship. The few lanterns lighting the deck on the pirate ship faintly drew the prisoners sitting in semidarkness, revealing long faces among the crowd. Not far from the chief pirate's cabin, all the young women abducted from the passenger ship sat forlorn, some still sobbing in low murmurs. Once in a while, a pirate would climb the quarterdeck and slap a few on their cheeks to stop their whining. That act renewed their lamentations.

Isabella sat among the rest of the women wondering about Miguel and her fate. He was wallowing in the hold with the other young men. What wouldn't she give to get a glimpse of him? Would she be sold to the highest bidder or kept for the pirate chief? She shuddered with fright at what awaited her. Where was the pirate ship headed? No doubt, an isolated island or coast where the renegades would unload their cargo. She must not despair. She hoped to be strong for both of them. She hoped that somehow Miguel and she would be sold together in the slave markets. These thoughts swirled in her head, while at the same time kept her from despairing.

The dark figure of a pirate passed in front of the wretched women who were tied up with chains by their feet and hands in a long row. He was carrying a bucket from which he drew a gruel that he dished into wooden bowls. The chains being long enough, the hungry women reached for it and consumed the food with their fingers. When a bowl was passed to Isabella, she turned her head away.

"¿No comer?" The pirate chuckled.

She then regretted her gesture. It was foolish to have attracted the scoundrel's attention. "I'll eat it." She reached for the bowl, and took one look at the gruel then sighed. The young women attached to her by the chains groaned with displeasure at the chains being pulled.

"You not hungry, you dine with captain," the pirate said in a broken Spanish dialect. He reached for her chains and unlocked both ends, then locked them again on the remaining women.

Free from her chains, Isabella rubbed her sore wrists while fear made her legs weak as she stood up.

The pirate pulled one of her arms and dragged her across the deck to the captain's cabin. After a few knocks on the door, an angry voice said, "What is it?"

"A *jameela* wench for you, Captain. A real beauty!"

A grunt was heard; heavy steps approached the door, then a bearded face appeared in the doorway. "What have we here?"

"This woman doesn't like her food, my captain," the pirate said.

"That's not—"

The captain grabbing Isabella's arm and pulling her into the cabin cut her off. He threw her across the cabin, where she hit her right shoulder against the wall. She let out a cry. He then slammed the door.

The bushy face of the rotund captain raised his eyebrows at her, and he smiled. "Don't you be afraid, dear *habibti*."

Isabella, rubbing her sore shoulder, noticed at that moment his perfect set of teeth in a soft and dark hairy face. "I'm not afraid of you or anyone!" She confronted him with both hands on her hips. Inside, though, she quivered with a new fear.

"Calm yourself. You calm," the captain replied in poor Castilian and a softened voice. He turned his back on her and went to a cupboard to retrieve two tumblers and a wine carafe, and filled the two glasses.

Isabella stood plastered against the wall, her thoughts swirling, her hands feeling the smooth wooden planks and finding nothing to hold on to or grasp. She concentrated on her predicament, a calm descended upon her and she became lucid.

The captain brought her one of the glasses, and she took it shyly.

"¡Beve!" he said in Spanish, then raised his glass and emptied it. He then refilled his tumbler.

Isabella also raised her glass. When the captain threw his head back to gulp down his wine, she poured hers into her dress. She felt the liquid sloshing down between her breasts and puddle around her waist. Her dress now began to show a few wet spots on the front bodice.

The captain meanwhile poured another two glasses and drained them both. He belched, wiped his wet lips, and approached her, belching again. She cringed as he came near. He wrapped one arm around her shoulder and tried to kiss her. She recoiled and stood rigid in front of him.

"What's the matter?" The captain stood back. "The lady wants to eat too?"

She remained silent.

He came nearer still. "I bring food," he said with a seductive voice. His hands were over her, caressing her breasts, waist, then her hips.

Isabella pulled further back. "It isn't that," she said calmly.

"What is it?"

She hesitated again. "You see, I carry the disease," she uttered in one breath.

"The disease? What disease? By Allah, what disease can a young girl like you carry?"

"When you came upon the ship, my uncle was carrying his son sick with fever."

He raised both eyebrows.

She repeated again, "Most of the passengers on that ship were sick with the fever. I also have it." She kept a straight face.

The captain moved away from her, his eyes probing hers.

She used that moment to shuffle to a chair and collapsed on it.

In a sudden motion the captain ran to open the cabin door. "Send me another wench!" he yelled through the open door at the pirate standing outside. The pirate stood still for a moment.

"Take this one back! Throw her in the hold!" He ran to Isabella and pulled her by the hair.

"Aaaaah!" Isabella screamed under the pain. The other pirate grabbed her by the arm and dragged her across the deck. He loosened the bolt and opened the trap door to the hold and threw her onto the rope ladder. She lost her balance, but grabbed the rope and steadied herself. Above her, the pirate closed the hatch and ran the chains across the top. She was left in darkness, swinging from the ladder. Slowly, she descended the rungs in darkness and finally touched the floor in the hold.

She let her eyes get accustomed first to the darkness filling the hold for a few moments. Dark forms sitting on the floor were revealed as she came closer. There were men and young boys attached by chains; some were moaning, while others slept soundly. She walked alongside one wall while trying to discern the faces in front of her. Then she saw him. Miguel lay back on the floor with his eyes opened. Her heart skipped a bit.

"Miguel, Miguel?" She came close and yelled at him while shaking him by the shoulders.

A scream escaped his lips. "Isabella!" He grabbed her, the chains pulling and waking his other tied mates, and kissed her over and over on the lips.

"Hey! What's going on?" one man said as he woke up to the sound of joyful cries by Miguel and Isabella.

"Go back to sleep," Miguel told them. He turned to Isabella and asked anxiously, "Are you all right? You're wet and smell of wine."

"Yes," she said. She then told him of what had passed between her and the captain. Miguel exploded in relief and laughter. He kissed her again and again.

The men on either side of them grunted, then went back to sleep.

She returned his kisses, then snuggled up in his chest. "I long to arrive wherever the ship will take us."

"So do I," Miguel said. "Meanwhile, we're together at last. I was sick worrying about you."

"So was I. Now we will wait together for what may happen next."

Miguel didn't reply to Isabella. He held her tighter, their hair and breath mingling.

10

Sailing into the Unknown

September 6, 1492

JOÃO STOOD ALONE ON THE main deck watching the dawn rising in the east with a whisper of orange light. As the light grew stronger, the sea turned from dark green to azure shades. He inhaled deeply, filling his lungs with one breath and smelling the salt in the air. He sensed that the sun was guiding a path on the ocean, illuminating his way to that unknown land that would welcome his beleaguered brethren—Jews and Conversos. A small flutter of hope rose in his chest, but he controlled it, calming himself by breathing rapidly in and out in succession.

A whistle sounded by Maestre Diego, the boatswain responsible for odd jobs on the ship—including cooking for the whole crew—waking everyone to rise. Sailors rubbing their eyes and slapping their cold shoulders stood up on deck and began manning their posts. The young ones who were quick on their feet climbed to the mainmast, foremast, and mizzenmast and began to unravel the square sails clewed to the yardarm. With majesty, the square sails inflated and vibrated under the breeze. Sailors ran across their stations and fulfilled their duties, unraveling the ropes and making sure that none of the cable-laid cordage was torn, all bonnets securely laced to the foot of her courses, and all rigging secure. João joined his shipmates, Hernán, Alfonso, and Gomes, shoving and heaving on the heavy cordage and ropes.

The sound of several carriages arriving at San Sebastian's dock raised a fine dust and stopped their work. The crew ran port side to see Admiral Christopher Columbus alighting from his carriage, and turning around to help Doña Leonor down the metal steps. For a few moments, Columbus held both her hands in silence while looking intently into her face. She stood facing him with a smile. He then kissed her hands, bowed, and took leave from her. Behind Columbus's carriage, Juan de la Cosa, the owner of the *Santa Maria*, followed with the pilot, Sancho Ruiz, and the physician, Maestre Alonso of Moguer.

The party met on the docks with other crew of the *Pinta*. Included were Martín Alonso Pinzón of Palos, captain of the *Pinta*; with his middle brother Francisco Martín Pinzón, first mate; and Gomez Rascon and Cristobal Quintero, both owners. The *Niña's* crew included Vicente Yáñez Pinzón, the youngest of the Pinzón brothers as captain, who was also part of the larger group meeting the rest of the party of navigators. They all stood around Columbus waiting for him to address them.

"My dear compatriots and sailors, you are now the bravest and most illustrious men of all. You and you alone will sail these waters on this voyage of discovery. No one, I repeat, no one in our history has yet made this voyage to the Indies by sailing west. We will be the first, and the first to discover this shorter route to the Indies. Gold will be our share of riches for our travails, and España will gain millions of new souls for Christendom."

"To Admiral Columbus and to the voyage!" They all cheered.

"Let us give thanks to the Lord and ask him to protect us on this voyage," Columbus said.

They all genuflected on the docks, and each sailor murmured a prayer with their eyes closed. The low voices carried as a wave over the small crowd of people, who then crossed themselves and fell to their knees in silent prayers.

The attending priest, waving his incense, raised his palm over the heads of each sailor and blessed them.

Each party of sailors and masters then headed for their own ship. Columbus ascended the plank to the *Santa Maria*, then stood with his hand on the railing. He waved one last time to Doña Leonor, and she waved back.

"¡*Que Dios los acompañe!* ¡*Vaya con Dios!*" The few inhabitants from La Gomera Island who came out to watch the departure cheered to the three ships and their sailors.

All three anchors were lifted with loud metal sounds scraping their decks. A great rumble was then heard as all three ships pulled away from San Sebastián de la Gomera and gently glided outside the port toward the wide Atlantic sea. Shouts were heard from all three ships as their sailors manned their stations and quartermasters yelled their orders at them.

João turned to his mates and smiled widely. "We're on our way."

His mates didn't reply, but each had a serious look on his face, one that questioned what he might find at the end of their journey They all attended to their chores while watching the shores recede.

"A whale! A whale is following us!" a voice sounded.

João and his mates followed the cry with their eyes, dropped the ropes from their hands, and ran to the railing.

A short-finned pilot whale glided in the waters and kept pace with the *Santa Maria* with a few bottlenose dolphins keeping abreast of it. Several yellow-legged seagulls flew above them with their plaintive calls of *ha-ha-ha-ha*.

A booming voice sounded from above the men assembled at the railings on the bow. "Get back to your posts!"

João and the men raised their heads to the quarterdeck to see the admiral signaling for them to return to their chores. He rejoined his shipmates back at work as the men glanced at each other, and he hoped this admiral would be kind to his crew. Nevertheless, the men kept on working throughout the day while keeping their eyes turned to the sea.

After the hour of meal, they all knelt for Compline prayers at seven o'clock in the evening, and with the sun low over the horizon, the sea began to turn dark. The lanterns were lit, and the aroma from the sandbox with protected walls where the food was cooked spread across the ship's deck.

João sensed fear beginning to creep into the men's hearts. They had left behind the only world they had known—family, country, their entire life. In front of them were the unknown, peril, and immensity of the great sea; it was beyond anyone's imagination. Murmurs began to rise from the sailors, who then shed some tears. Soon the entire ship was awash in lamentations coming from the terrified men.

João tried to reassure his closest shipmates. "Come on, mates. We have much to look forward to." His words went unheeded.

When the cries became loud enough, Columbus came out of his cabin on the quarterdeck to see to the disturbance. He called Juan de la Cosa, his second in command. "What's going on?"

"Admiral, the men are turning yellow and now fear the sea!" Juan said out loud for all to hear him.

"I will speak to them," Columbus said.

From his perch, he addressed the men standing in clusters. "I hear you have doubts about this voyage?'

"We'll never see our families again!" one sailor shouted.

"We're never coming back!" another yelled at Columbus.

"Now listen to me!" he thundered from the upper deck. "You know why we're going on this voyage? To gain souls and land for Spain! To find a passage to Cathay and the Indian Islands! There will be gold and silver for everyone, and precious stones and spices! Don't tell me you don't want these?"

A silence fell on the crowd below. Then, one by one, the sailors began speaking in a crescendo of voices.

"Yeah! Gold! That's why we're here!"

"We'll be rich! So will our families!"

"Yeah!"

"All right. Go to sleep now." Columbus gave the order to the men who walked away searching for a protected corner.

João went to a spot near the mainmast and lay down on his blanket. He had witnessed a crew that had lost faith momentarily, and had questioned Columbus's seamanship and authority. It didn't bode well for a voyage in which staunch belief in their leader would pull them through thick and thin on a cruel and vengeful ocean. *God help us if the admiral loses his men's trust.*

The voyage had begun on a bad note, Columbus mulled. He should allay their terrors periodically. Perhaps, their true sea progress ought to be hidden from them, in case the voyage takes longer than anticipated.

He turned to his cabin servant, Diego de Salcedo, an older man, yet a sturdy and seasoned mariner, and said, "Go and bring Juan de la Cosa to my cabin."

Diego left and returned to the cabin accompanied by De la Cosa.

"Admiral?"

"I want you to send an order to the other two ships that if somehow we get separated, they should sail westward and log up to seven hundred leagues," Columbus said. "That would put them in proximity of land."

"Now, Admiral?"

"Yes, now."

"Yes, Admiral. I'll dispatch the boat right away.

11

La Rábida Monastery

THE SMALL PARTY OF MEN and horses climbed the trail on a steep hill toward La Rábida Monastery. The looming monastery, sitting high on a bluff above them and once a Moor's stronghold, dominated the landscape between the Tinto and Odiel Rivers, and Guerida led his soldiers riding horses as they swayed to and fro on the strained animals. Occasionally, he looked behind him to the small mule carrying José. The lad's hands were unbound, and he seemed resigned to stay with his traveling companions. Guerida went over in his head the reception he might receive from Father Antonio de Marchena, the Franciscan, and the leading friar. He was familiar with the friars' hospitality. Wasn't it the same monastery that had sheltered Christophero Columbus and his son Diego for many years when the admiral was a pauper? How the poor and the insignificant make their way in life, he reflected. He was still a poor inspector, even though he was chief inspector of Castile. There was no nobility in his family; their progress in Spain had been won by hard labor and by earning a pittance for their livelihood. The nobles in España had it all. If it were up to him, he'd gladly have arrested Don Obrigon and had the whole household thrown into jail. But Don Obrigon was a noble, related by his dead wife, a distant cousin, to Queen Isabella and King Ferdinand.

"I'm thirsty," the lad said. His face was sweaty under the late September sun still beating down.

"We're almost there," Guerida replied. "Another hour."

José furrowed his brows and lowered his head.

Finally, the small party came to a halt in a dusty cloud. Before them the monastery stood in whitewashed stucco stones with its elevated cross on the church building. They all alighted off their mounts, including José, who looked shabby in his dirty clothes. The visitors entered the Moorish doorway of colorful bricks and were shown in by a monk who received them by crossing himself before them. All the men crossed themselves afterward, as they entered the vestibule of the church area.

"Please wait here," the monk said, and disappeared in a doorway leading to the outside.

Within a few minutes, a friar came in and acknowledged the visitors by nodding at them.

"Welcome to the house of God, my friends," he said. "I'm Father Marchena. What can I do for you?"

Guerida advanced to the friar and said, "We're here to deliver this boy to the monastery, Father."

Marchena first looked at the lad, then made a circular inspection of the trembling boy. "He's very skinny. How old is he?"

Guerida was stumped at first. "Twelve or thirteen?"

"I'm ten years old!" José's small voice shot out from his skinny neck.

"Oh, he speaks," Marchena said in a playful tone.

"Dear Father," Guerida started. "This is a Christian boy, baptized at birth. We thought, under your wing, he'd learn all about our Savior and become a choirboy."

"That is indeed a worthy enterprise. I myself will see to his education. What is your name, boy?"

"José, Father." José spoke inaudibly.

"I can't hear you, my boy," Father Marchena said, cupping his right hand behind his ear.

"José!" he shouted.

"All right. No need to shout, José. You're welcome here at La Rábida. I'm sure we're going to get along very well, the two of us." He then took the lad's hand and turned to the men surrounding them. "Say good-bye to these good men, my boy?"

José stood mute at the request.

"Come on, my boy," he urged him.

José let go of Father Marchena's hand and yelled at the top of his small lungs. "I hate this man! I hate him! He told my brother and me that our mother was dead! I hate him!"

To the men's and Guerida's astounded expressions, Father Marchena raised his eyebrows. "I'm not going to quiz you on that boy's accusation, but go with God on your journey."

Guerida nodded and made a sign for his men to leave. They all exited the church grounds, mounted their horses, and left the monastery.

～⌒⊙⊙⌒～

Father Marchena stood by the entrance and followed the horsemen with his eyes as they descended the hill, then disappeared behind a rocky bend in the path. He turned to the monastery and began to search for the boy. He found him under a tree branch that projected into an open arcade in the cloister. The boy was in tears, sniffling and wiping his eyes on his dirty sleeve.

Marchena approached him. "We must do something about your clothes. You know that cleanliness is close to godliness, don't you?"

José nodded his head between minor sobs.

"Let's head for your room, where you'll wash."

He took José's hand, and quietly the two of them shuffled on the redbrick floor toward the end of the arcade.

12

Landing in Morocco

THE HEAT IN THE HOLD was sweltering, and the sweat dripped from the prisoners' faces onto their dirty clothes. Chains and shackles were removed from their hands and feet, and they were free to roam in the hold. Isabella, who found herself within a cavernous room full of young men, feared for her safety. She sat near Miguel for his protection. No one until now had threatened or touched her. Most of them sat weary and fearful of a gloomy future—more hardships or backbreaking labor in a mine off the coast of Guinea or Africa. For now they had escaped being killed by the pirates, and their gruel and water was brought once a day, leaving them somewhat nourished and alive.

The hold was divided into two compartments: one where they sat on the floor and the other behind a sturdy mesh wall hiding the provisions. A bolted lock forbade them to attempt any pillage of this food staring at them throughout the day.

"When we land, I want you to save yourself and run," Miguel said.

Isabella looked at him absentmindedly. Her mind was far from landing—more in the past. She'd give everything she'd possessed in the past to be back at her ancestral home with her dear father and her nanny. Though, on second thought, Miguel was now her world, one that was dear to her. That still left an ominous fate tearing her away from her roots—perhaps never to return. And what were her roots? Was it Spain or a new land for Miguel and her? And what about her search for her real parents? This thought brought her back to the present.

She looked at Miguel and said, "I won't leave you. I won't."

"But you must. If you escape, I'd be content that you were safe."

She shook her head. "I can't promise anything right now. I can't be without you."

Miguel gave a sigh. "At least do it for my brother José. So that I'll know that the two people I love most in this life are safe and sound. You can look for him if you ever return to your father's house . . . if it's safe," he quickly added.

She nodded. "Let's get a good night's rest."

⚜

A large thud awoke Isabella with a jolt. She raised herself on her elbows to listen for any signs of danger. All she felt below the floor was the rocking motion of the sea. A second thud, this one larger than the first, woke Miguel and other men around them.

"What's going on?" voices murmured near them.

"Are we there?" another anxious voice asked.

The hold was pitch dark. There were no portholes to reveal that land had been reached when the sound of moving chains being loosened from above made all the prisoners stand up.

Miguel put his arm around Isabella's shoulder and pulled her closer to him.

Isabella was shaking, but she tried to conceal her fear. "Don't be concerned about me," she whispered to him.

He pulled her to him still tighter.

The heavy hatch was pushed aside, and two pirates holding lanterns peered into the darkness.

"Start climbing!" The order was given to the wretched mass below.

One by one, the men climbed up the rope ladder and surfaced from the hold.

Both Miguel and Isabella looked up and saw the stars above them in a black velvet sky.

Miguel whispered, "Stay behind. Maybe they forgot about you."

Despite the gravity of their situation, Isabella broke up in a forced and low chuckle. "How can they forget about me after what I did to the captain?"

Miguel didn't reply. He stood silent. He then started moving toward the rope ladder. Taking a last look at Isabella, he turned around and began the climb. Isabella, meanwhile, was hidden by the partial darkness in the hold. Her breath came out fast and shallow while she clung to a wooden column. Her eyes then spotted a metal rod on the floor near the column. She picked it up and waited.

Suddenly a pirate's head popped in from above the hold's opening, and his eyes pierced the darkness below. "That's it!" The heavy door began to slide over the hold, when a shout was heard.

"No, wait!" The door slid open again, and a pirate's raggedy legs climbed down the ladder. When his foot hit the floor of the hold, Isabella hit him on the head with the small rusted bar. He fell to the ground but was still conscious. He raised his hand to his head and found blood on his fingers.

He then saw her. "You'll pay dearly for that, bitch!" He pounced on Isabella and slapped her face back and forth.

Isabella stoically didn't scream, but felt her face becoming hot and prickly. The pirate pulled her by her long matted hair and dragged her up the ladder.

"Ahhh!" Isabella screamed as her hair was pulled painfully from above as he hoisted her. When they reached the ship's deck, the pirate threw her down. All prisoners' eyes were fixed on her.

"Leave her!" Miguel cried.

"No, Miguel!" Isabella screamed at him. "Don't!"

One of the pirates attending to the prisoners hit Miguel on the head with his sword's pommel. Miguel fell to the floor unconscious.

Isabella ran to him. "Miguel, Miguel! ¡A*vla*! ¡A*vla*!" She shook him by the shoulders.

"I'm all right, Isabella," he said in a faint voice.

"Enough!" the captain's voice came booming from the upper deck. "Put the chains on them!"

The pirates got busy tying all prisoners, including Isabella, by their hands and feet.

A voice shouting from the crow's nest alerted the chief pirate. "I see the coast!"

All pirates on deck scrambled about and became busy with tackle and gear, preparing for a landing.

Isabella and Miguel craned their necks over the rails, but only a dark sea prevailed. Two hours later, as the dawn lit a faint line on the horizon, it revealed shimmering sand dunes against a dark-blue Mediterranean, and a coast rapidly advanced toward them.

With chains tied at their ankles, they were packed into two boats. The moving waves made Isabella lose her footing when descending into the swaying craft. Luckily, Miguel held on to her. One false move and the long chains tying them together would precipitate them to their death into the ocean's depth. The paddling and armed pirates faced them while they rowed, allowing no possible way to rid themselves of their captors. A thump shook the boat, and it scraped the sand, stopping its momentum forward.

Isabella, helped by Miguel, jumped onto the beach. The sand raised by a small wind pitted against their faces while blurring the edge of the beach where the palm trees began. In the foreground, a series of padlocked bamboo huts held men and women, and judging by their motley appearance and matted hair, she thought they looked no better than they did. Isabella now felt they were trapped between the ocean, the sand dunes, and the pirates behind them. *What will become of us?*

13

Double Truths

Friday, September 7, 1492

COLUMBUS SAT IN HIS SMALL cabin deep in concentration over his daily log. So far their voyage since Palos had proceeded as he had hoped. He now felt reassured, as they had passed El Hierro, the last island in the Canarias. He had dreaded seeing the Portuguese caravels, but none showed up to chase and arrest him. His conviction that the Lord was looking after this voyage was deeply ingrained in him. There was, of course, the delay due to the *Pinta* and the *Niña*, but now all was in order with those ships. The sea remained calm, the evenings were silent, except for the sounds of the gromet—a young ship boy—calling out each half hour, and the reckoning and recording of time on a slate for each half hour by the captain and master. His men fulfilled their duties as he expected them; the decks were scrubbed with seawater, the sails were checked for tears and repaired right away, and the watches proceeded smoothly every four hours.

Juan de la Cosa, master and owner of the *Santa Maria*, took the first starboard watch at three in the afternoon, while his pilot, Sancho Ruiz, took the port watch at seven, the sunset hour. The graveyard hour followed from eleven to three in the morning. This way each man alternated with four hours sleep and alternate nights with others of his men on board.

"The hour is seven in the evening by the *ampolleta!*" the gromet cried.

Columbus knew the half-hour sandglass had just been turned over by the ship's boy. Time came for Compline, as he had done it so many times at the monastery in La Rábida. He got up from the table and went to genuflect in front the crucifix hanging on the wall of the cabin. After crossing himself, he offered his prayer to Christ.

"May almighty God grant us a quiet night and a perfect end . . . amen. In peace then I will sleep, and I will rest, for thou, O Lord, alone, hast settled me in hope . . ." He continued his prayer in silence, then said, "Amen." He had just ended his twenty-minute prayer and made the sign of the cross, when a knock on the cabin door was heard.

"Who's there?" he asked.

The voice of his servant, Salcedo, sleeping outside his cabin, sounded. "A sailor to see you, Admiral."

"What does he want?" Columbus asked.

The muffled voice of one of his sailors came through. "May I speak with you, Admiral?"

It didn't sound like Juan de la Cosa. *Who might this be at this hour?* He grabbed his lantern and went to open the door ajar and lifted the lamp. The light illuminated João Treves's features.

"Go back to sleep, Salcedo," he said.

Turning to the sailor, he asked him in a dry voice, "What do you want, Sailor?"

"My apologies for disturbing you, Admiral. I want to talk to you."

"We already talked," Columbus said.

"Please, Admiral, only a few minutes."

Columbus stood silent for a moment. "Come in." He then let João in. He took furtive glances down the quiet main deck and shut the door.

"You must stop badgering me. I've been patient with you. So what is it you want?" he said while placing the lantern on the table.

João bowed from the waist. "If I may, Admiral, I'd like to explain why I'm here."

"You mean in my cabin."

"No. I mean on this ship."

Columbus waited patiently to hear him out.

"I joined this voyage because it's my, or should I say *our*, salvation."

"What do you mean?"

"Besides me, there are two more sailors also looking with me for a safe haven."

"We're all looking for the kingdom of heaven."

"Yes, we are. But this haven I'm looking for is for all Jews to find a safe land."

Columbus listened quietly.

João continued. "That's why I came on board. When we find this route to the Indies, all my fellow Jews can come to safety."

Columbus tried to understand João's statement. "There aren't any more Jews left in Spain," he said. "If you mean the Conversos, you're wasting your time. The ships are watching for them leaving from any ports." He tried to see any trace of disappointment on João's face, but instead a mocking smile was there. He knew that João himself must have converted, because Sarita was a Jewess when he knew her. Thoughts of Sarita suddenly flooded him. He chased the thoughts away. "What exactly do you want from me?"

"All I ask is your cooperation to allow Conversos to sail on your next voyage."

"You know I can't do that! The law is stringent and forbids it!"

"We'll sneak them on board without anyone noticing. I also can forge false papers of *Sangre Pura*."

Columbus shook his head. "I can't break the law to help your cause. That would jeopardize my position as representative of the crown."

João stood silent in front of him. He then said, "I remember when you visited my sister. You weren't that stubborn then."

Columbus was taken aback, his heart skipping a beat. Sarita's name flashed again in front of his eyes. He felt a cold sweat. Was João blackmailing him? If anyone knew of his origins, he'd be finished! *I must tread easily with this man.* He decided to make a false promise and delay the inevitable. Once back in Spain he would denounce him.

"Look. We just left twenty-four hours ago. As soon as we hit land, we'll talk about it some more." He looked at João's face for a reaction, but he had stepped backward and away from the lantern's light.

"Until we find land then." João walked toward the cabin's door. Turning back to him he said, "We'll then see." With those words, he closed the door behind him.

Left alone, Columbus tried to calm his racing mind. *He's bluffing. I know he is.* He remembered when visiting Sarita near Sintra, João never missed an occasion to bribe him out of a few *escudos*, and the last time he'd seen Sarita, she had told him that João had been arrested and was in prison. She begged him to help her brother, but Columbus was unable to help him. Sarita threw him out and told him never to return. He was trapped during those days and torn between his ambitions and his loyalties. Now these times were coming back to haunt him.

He went to lie down on the small bunk, much too small for his large stature. He tossed throughout the night with nightmarish visions of a coffin being lowered into the ground as he heard the gromet calling the hours. At the wee hour of dawn he fell asleep.

14

The Bazaar

MIGUEL WAS AWAKENED WITH A jolt by the pommel of a sword on his leg. The Berber shook him by the shoulder with his hand reaching through the cage,

"*Oum*! Wake up, dog!" a pirate yelled at him.

Miguel rubbed his eyes and moved away from the hand shaking him. He looked around him and saw other unfortunate young men like him waking up from a rough night.

Another of the pirates came into the cage and began to flog them.

"Move, dogs!"

Miguel was led with the other men outside their holding cage into the sunlight glaring from the beach's white sand. His stomach growled, and he looked around him for food. He suddenly thought of Isabella, a prisoner, too, in the women's holding cage. The women were waiting outside their cages, and some of them were crying and moaning quietly. He spotted Isabella and felt relieved to find her sulking but quiet. They exchanged glances, but no words passed their lips.

Suddenly, their guards brought over a large bronze cauldron with steam escaping at the top. The other guards pushed them again, this time toward the food. Each male prisoner was served first, with the women following next. In the wooden breakfast bowls that were handed to them was a thick concoction of grain that tasted rough to the gums and palate. That grain wasn't fit for a dog! Miguel spit out part of a mouthful remaining uneaten. He quickly regretted his action. In Arab hospitality, you ate whatever was served to you: good or bad food, poisoned or a heavenly tasteful dish. He saw a guard beginning to walk in his direction with a swinging wooden stick.

"Make room, make room!" A great noise was heard as mounted men on Arabian horses came galloping over the sand dunes and stopped their mounts in front of the prisoners.

A large man, dressed in a white caftan, black boots, and a cotton headdress topped by a black bun to hold it in place, slid down his horse and approached the line of men.

He spoke words in Arabic to the guards, then turned around and inspected each prisoner. Miguel felt as if he were a cow being checked for its fat. He looked over at Isabella standing with the women and noted the same procedure taking place. Cries and screams escaped from the women's mouths as they were examined and patted on the cheeks and buttocks, and their teeth were scrutinized.

"*Imshee!*" The order was given to all prisoners to walk behind several mounted horses leading the pack. Several guards walked along the tied-up men and women, watching them for any attempt at escape.

The caravan of horses, men, and women walked in single file across the hot sand dunes with the sun beating down on them. After two grueling hours, demands rose from the prisoners.

A young lad approximately fourteen-years-old said, "Give us some water. We're parched!"

The prisoner, who was walking near Miguel, received a quick blow to the side of his head with the pommel of a guard's sword. The guard then walked away. The youth stumbled against Miguel, who caught him before he fell to the ground. He then screamed loudly, which brought back the guard.

"Keep quiet or I'll chop your head off!" The sword was raised above his head, and the young boy cowered and became silent. His hands and entire body trembled.

Miguel, who stood near him, grabbed hold of one of his hands and held it tight. The youth raised teary eyes and nodded.

Meanwhile the march continued, and everyone became absorbed in putting one foot in front of the other with no more complaints uttered.

After what seemed hours of crawling through the hot sands a sudden murmur rose in the ranks. Miguel raised his sweaty face and saw that they had arrived at a small city. The caravan of tied-up and tired prisoners entered the narrow streets, where open drainage in the center of the street brought out fetid smells in its running sewage. Camel excrement lay in the street, and above their heads latticed windows adorned whitewashed adobe houses. Shuffling their feet, they emerged into a plaza. There the colorful awnings and tents were spread in a market fashion with crowds milling about and wandering to and fro from each vendor stall. In the center of the hubbub a large fountain offered a cool environment where tired travelers washed and filled their clay gourds with water while their camels sipped water from the trough. The smoke of frying food and grilled meat on wood chips rose from dozens of fires being fanned by their vendors.

"Kef!" A guard yelled to the prisoners. He then untied their hands but left the chains around their ankles. Dragging the first one in line, the guard pushed the prisoner's face into the water trough. The thirsty man drank to his heart's content until he was stopped abruptly.

"Next!' the guard ordered. One by one the men prisoners drank, then the women's turn came afterward.

Miguel saw Isabella swallow large amounts of water until she was stopped. She looked up to Miguel with a slight smile to convey all was good with her.

Next the guards lined up all women in front and the men in back of them. One guard raised his voice to the public beginning to gather in front and listening.

"Listen up! Listen Up! Who'll give me top *dirhams* for these beautiful women?"

The crowds became focused on the women displayed before them. The men looked carefully at the faces, the feet and hands, and the hair exposed to the elements.

Several men paraded back and forth in front of the women displayed in the first row. Miguel stood behind the first row, his hands gripped into fists and unable to breathe. His anger and fear were paramount and rising to a pitch. He then burst his mouth open uttering words of Hebrew, hoping that the Berbers would recognize their Abrahimic cousins.

"*Baruch Ata Adonai Eloheinou Melech Haolam.*" He repeated the prayer again, "Blessed Are You, Lord our God, King of the Universe."

There was a silence among the spectators, but one of the guards came close to Miguel and hit him several times with a whip.

Isabella stood trembling and pinched her lips tight, smothering a cry.

"What are you saying, dog?" the guard demanded.

Miguel protected his face with his hands. "*Aasef! Aasef!*" Miguel burst out in Arabic learned from his stay at the Alhambra.

The guard lowered his whip and looked at him as if he were an animal suddenly gifted with speech.

"I will buy this woman!" A man in the crowd yelled. "Ten dirhams!"

"Ten dirhams is too little. Who'll give me twenty?"

No one seemed to reply. A small voice rose at the back of the crowd. "I'll give you twenty-five!" The spectators turned around in the voice's direction and saw a small man dressed in a white *djllabiyah* with a black caftan on top. The lower part of his face was partly covered by his wrap.

"Who gives thirty?" the auctioneer asked.

No one replied, and the Berber pirate said, "Take her. She's yours."

"No! No!" Miguel ran toward Isabella but couldn't reach her. "You can't take her. She's my wife!"

The short man looked on silently. He then said, "I'll take both for thirty dirhams." He walked to the pirate and said a few words in his ears. The pirate raised a surprised face then stretched his hand to the stranger, concluding the bargain. The stranger gave him a bundle that the pirate examined. He looked up at the prisoners and said, "Listen, all you wretched dogs! You're now the property of this man. Go with him, and may Allah forgive you!"

Miguel looked gratefully at Isabella. At least now they would remain together.

15

Winds of Change

Saturday, September 8, 1492

THE WAVES CRASHED ON ALL three ships from winds coming from the northeast. The wave heights kept getting higher, and the rocking and swaying motion of the *Santa Maria* made the sailors sick for the first time on their voyage. So far their sails had obeyed the motions of the wind powering and leading the ship in a westerly direction. This morning, though, those canvases were taking a beating with the whistling wind coming at them in a nonstop stream. He quickly ordered the mainsail with the clews hauled up to the yardarm, and instructed to make sure the lifts were securely holding through the leech lines.

Columbus himself felt unsteady with a queasy stomach. The planks under his feet moved in a jerky fashion, and he tried to steady his hand at dead reckoning as he plotted a new course west on his magnetic, dry-card compass. He kept the compass in a binnacle box nailed on deck where Juan de la Cosa could keep an eye on it. A second compass was housed in its wooden box by the tiller, for Ruiz to check periodically that they were on course.

He plotted a few more points on his map then went to make contact with his pilot. The decks were drenched with seawater washing the tack and cordage lying in heaps. He held on tight to the drawn rope stretching from bow to stern as he fought his way on the slippery deck, and reached the rudder cage, where Sancho Ruiz was hard at work holding the tiller with all his strength. He rushed to him and gave him a hand. The tiller was being pulled starboard, while the wind wanted to steer it northeasterly off their course.

"I hope the tiller doesn't break like it did on the *Pinta*!" Ruiz hollered.

"The *Santa Maria* is strong. Nothing can break her!" Columbus yelled back.

"Thank you, Admiral! I can manage!"

"All right," Columbus shot back. He left the rudder cage and worked his way back to his cabin on the main deck. His drenched men were holding on to their stations while battling the wind and the sea waves crashing on decks. He looked behind the *Santa Maria* for the *Pinta* and the *Niña*, and they, too, were battling the elements. Reassured that the vessels were keeping above the waves, he climbed to the quarterdeck.

When he reached his cabin, the wind suddenly slowed down to a minor storm. The sea, though, kept its high-peaked waves, then it, too, began to gently fall back to less menacing swells. Seeing that the elements were cooperating, he entered his cabin. He removed his soaked overcoat then wiped his face and wet hands on a cloth towel. On his table, his logbook was still open, but the quill pen had fallen to the floor by the sea's violent motion. He picked it up and returned to plotting his course. He corrected his course west again, hoping for a calmer sea ahead.

The morning had advanced, and they had lost valuable time. He mustn't let the crew know of any delays. *Perhaps I ought to keep any delays to myself and tell my second-in-command what they want to hear. The log should then be falsified.* He then thought of keeping two logs, one with the accurate leagues undisclosed, and one for the crew and his other ships.

A knock on the cabin door brought him back to his feet. He went to open the door to Juan de la Cosa.

"Admiral, may I have a few words with you?"

Columbus quickly closed his logbook and raised inquiring eyes to Juan. "I'm listening."

"Dear Admiral. This is not to alarm you, but you ought to watch out for Pinzón."

Columbus looked at him inquisitively. "Why?"

"Pinzón is a very proud man and very jealous."

"Why should he be jealous? His family has practically risen to nobility through their generations of ship building, and they're powerful all over Palos."

"That's why you must keep watch on him. You have taken the spotlight away from his navigation goals, and he'll try to beat you at the first sight of land."

"The monarchs promised ten thousand silver maravedís to the first man who sights land."

"You should watch that too. He might try to beat you at this honor," Juan warned him.

"I made a promise," Columbus said solemnly. "I can't break it."

Juan nodded silently and left his cabin.

Alone now, Columbus felt his chest constricting. *There will always be an invisible enemy working against me to thwart this voyage.* He'd be wise to heed De la Cosa's wisdom and advice.

16

Sands of Labor

THE MORNING BEGAN WITH THE prisoners eating their breakfast. Then the man who owned them made them stand in front of him. He was of average height, sporting a black beard and a white hooded caftan that covered his head and whole body. Isabella found it strange for him to be wrapped from head to toe when heat was rising early. She fared no better; her long dress was soiled with rips in the fabric, the sleeves were torn in tatters, her hair was matted and dirty, and she yearned to wash her face and feet. She looked at Miguel and they exchanged glances.

"Everyone listen!" an assistant to the slave owner shouted at them.

The prisoners raised their heads from the food they were eating and waited for their host to speak.

The owner began speaking in a flawless Castilian dialect. "I'm your owner now, and I won't tolerate any disobedience. Runaways will be flogged. You'll do as you're told. That's all."

Isabella looked in Miguel's direction, and his face showed bewilderment that reflected her state of mind. Was the owner a Morisco—a converted Muslim? So far, he had treated them with no reprisals, but that remained to be seen.

Thus, following the morning meal, the prisoners left for an unknown destination by foot while their masters traveled on horses. *I wonder where they'll take us.* Her thoughts then turned to her own predicament: What would they do with the women?

The answer came with the arrival of a female wearing a black caftan that enveloped her from head to toe. "All women follow me."

They were led to, individual, enclosed huts with open roofs. To her surprise, Isabella discovered that copper pipes were attached overhead to a wooden tower dispensing water. She undressed immediately, and the warm water flowed through her hair and caressed her body with its cleansing power. She then found a bar of castile soap, made with olive oil and scented with frankincense, and began to lather and wash off the layers of dirt and dust from untold days. When finished, she was about to put back on her soiled clothes, when she spotted a white cotton garment that had been thrown over the hut's top. After dressing, she left the hut and was stopped by a guard.

"*Imshee!*" The threat to walk came with a saber slicing the air.

Isabella knew best not to resist the order and walked with the guard behind her. At the sight of a tent decorated with colorful tassels and sporting guards in front, her legs went weak with fear. She was pushed inside the tent. A luxurious interior greeted her. Sheepskins lined the beaten sand floor with a profusion of pillows strewn about. Tapestries hung from the walls depicting Arabic symbols, and seated on the floor was the same man who had spoken to them earlier. Now her legs buckled with growing fear. She cringed. *This time she wouldn't be playing Shesh Besh all night.*

"Please sit down." The owner spoke in Castilian.

She remained standing and frozen.

"I won't harm you. I give you my word," he said.

She approached hesitantly to the center of the tent, and sat down in a crossed-legged position.

He offered her a filled goblet that she took from his hands. She touched the rim of the goblet and wet her lips with wine, then raised a surprised face to her host.

He smiled at her bewilderment. Turning around he clapped his hands, and several women came into the tent with trays of food. Isabella recognized many of the dishes she had eaten in the Alhambra. The taste of warm lamb, sweet rice with raisins, and garbanzo paste on a side dish left indelible sensations on her tongue. She might as well enjoy the food right now while alive. Who knew what tomorrow might bring?

"Did you like the food?" he asked.

"Yes."

Then as if on cue, her host unraveled his hood and turban and presented his full face to her. She sat bewildered by his action.

"I know you're wondering why I'm revealing myself to you."

She didn't reply, still confused.

"You see. I'm someone you've met before."

She scrutinized him and recognized a slight resemblance to someone she'd seen before. She shook her head.

"Do you remember the ride we took to the Alhambra?"

She looked at him again and was jolted! He was the driver!

He nodded to her expression of shock and surprise.

"Yes, it's me—Benvenide Matigoro. The driver who took you to the Alhambra."

"But it can't be! You can't be a Moor and a Converso too!"

"I'm not a Moor, but I'm still a Converso."

"But what are you doing here?"

"That's why I asked you here to my tent. After I brought you to the Alhambra, I returned to Seville, and through a Jewish woman, Ana Saraual, I was introduced to a wealthy and great man who hired me to supervise his operations in North Africa, especially the slave market.

"What's his name?" Isabella asked.

"I can't reveal his name, but he'd been a great supporter of Spaniard Jews when the Alhambra Decree was forced upon them."

She felt a pang in her heart at the recollection of so much suffering brought upon the Jews. She remembered as well Téresa, Miguel's mother, revealing that Isabella had been adopted. "I remember this too well. But is this why we've been brought here to this godforsaken place?"

"My benefactor hired me as a scout to find Jewish slaves and buy them from pirates."

"Are we to remain here?"

He nodded his head. "Only for a few days, then you and Miguel and others from the ship will be transferred to one of my benefactor's ships."

"And where will it take us?"

"Portugal."

She sat astonished. She tried to process the information he'd given her and the good fortune happening to them. In his power, God was looking after her and Miguel. She thought of offering her thanks to God at the first church she'd come across. Then, as an afterthought, she thought perhaps her prayers would now be more appropriate in a synagogue.

"When are we leaving?" she asked.

"As soon as I get instructions. We must be careful. For all intents and purposes, we must continue with slave transactions. Keep quiet about what you've heard. The same goes for Miguel."

She nodded with a long sigh. She then raised her questioning eyes to him. "There's something that puzzles me. You must've known my uncle João Treves, didn't you?"

Matigoro remained silent for a few moments. He then said, "He only wanted what was best for you."

She stopped herself from blurting out that her origins should've been left buried in the past. But then she wouldn't have known great happiness in marrying Miguel.

"We looked for him in Seville's port when all the ships left that day. He wasn't there." Her voice broke.

"That's because he was hired on a ship in Palos and left with the three ships commandeered by Christopher Columbus."

She let out a cry of despair. "Now I'll never know who my parents were."

"I know about your mother."

She asked with a trembling voice, "Who was she?"

"Your mother was called Sarita Treves. She lived in the town of Komar in Portugal before she moved to Sintra."

"And we are going to Portugal!" Her voice rose with hope.

"Soon. Be patient."

She looked at him for a long moment, afraid to speak up.

"What is it?" he asked her.

"I don't know if I should be telling you this. But Téresa, Miguel's mother . . . is dead."

His face turned ashen. He sat there silent without words. He then spoke again in a whisper. "She sacrificed her life to protect you."

Isabella felt a rush of emotions and thoughts whirl in her head. She felt no more ill feelings toward Téresa. After all, she herself had fulfilled her birth mother's request—to marry her within the Jewish faith. She had carried out that request by a twist of fate when Miguel crossed her path. Her adoptive parents had agreed to that promise, and yet they failed by encouraging then blessing her betrothal to Juan Escobar de Santilla. Now though she felt her adoptive mother dying as a heavy burden.

17

Sailing forward

Tuesday September 11, 1492

"H. Columbus jotted down in his secret logbook his salutation to God, *B'ezrat Hashem,* in a Hebrew phrase he particularly favored: "And if it pleases God, 'Our help is in the Name of the Lord, who made heaven and earth.'" He only used this blessing for his Jewish friends.

He opened his personal logbook to the place where he had jotted down his progress and read his previous notes:

Sunday September 9–Today we made nineteen leagues. At night we scored thirty leagues, or one hundred twenty miles at twelve miles per hour.

This is a total of forty-nine leagues, he thought. In his second, public logbook, he reckoned forty-five leagues.

Monday September 10–This day and night we went sixty leagues at ten miles per hour.

Again he reckoned down only forty-eight.

He continued writing. *Tuesday September 11–As of this day we have sailed one hundred and fifty leagues from El Hierro with God's help. All is calm, and I don't anticipate too much trouble or disturbances ahead. Barring any more fears or disobedience from the crew, all is well.*

"Admiral! Admiral!" Juan de la Cosa's voice reached his ears.

What is the matter now? Bursting out of his cabin onto the deck, Columbus called out, "What's going on?"

"Admiral, you must see this!" Juan called out as he pointed to the sea in front of them. His men were bent over the railing, gesturing in great excitement.

Columbus ran down the three steps from the upper deck to the main deck. He looked over the railing and saw a tall mast that must've been part of a large vessel, larger that the seventy-ton burden of the *Santa Maria*. The mainmast was discolored from its long stay in the seawater, and a shredded canvas sail still attached floated with cordage scattered about. The crew saw this wreck as a portent of ominous things to come, as if the sea itself was barring them from sailing any further.

Columbus ran back to his upper deck and hollered at his men, some hanging on the railing and others perched precariously by one arm from the ratlines, while the waves partly muffled the sound of his voice.

"Listen up! The *Santa Maria* is a sturdy ship. Its round-hulled bottom has been tested in the waters in many voyages, well before we sailed with her! Now go back to your work and wipe this mast from your memory!"

The men muttered words over the whistling sound of the wind propelling the ship.

Columbus reentered his cabin again with impatience weighing him down, anxious to take readings on his map and to plot the next day's course.

18

The Court in Lisbon

THE CHAMBER WAS FULL OF attendants and petitioners to King John II, also called João II. The majority of courtiers were there for economic reasons—the merchant marine wealth and the fleets of goods coming in from the western coast of Africa, and particularly the Elmina mines in Guinea, were at the heart of their concern. The courtiers milling around knew that their own wealth and pocketbooks were at stake, and they vied to be the first to address their complaints.

"Your Majesty, We are about to lose our gold mine to the Spaniards with their explorations."

"Yes, Majesty." Another courtier bowed before King John. "Their spy, Columbus, is at this moment sailing west. He will then work his way south down the coast to seek our gold in Elmina."

King John listened with calm, deciding on the best course to follow. "This man or admiral—Columbus—why was he not intercepted as he sailed off our coast?"

"We did try, Your Majesty, but he escaped us through Hierro, by draping his ships with the Portuguese flag."

"But where did he get hold of these flags? He must've had knowledge of our flags, customs, and coastal regulations, yes?"

"Your Majesty, may I speak?" A courtier advanced to the throne. He bowed deeply and presented himself. "I'm Alvoro Gonçallvez with the merchant marine in Belmonte, Your Highness." He then waited silently to be acknowledged by King John.

The king nodded for him to continue.

"Your Highness, Cristóvão Colón, or Columbus as some call him, fom the republic of Genoa, lived right here in Portugal in 1479 with his brother Bartolomeo Colón. He was a cartographer, and a good one if I may say so, with the customhouse in Lisbon. He then married a noble woman, Filipa Perestrelo e Moniz, and lived in Porto Santo until his wife died and he left for Spain."

King John was dead silent. He then spoke. "I'm familiar with that man. I now remember he came to court in 1484 to request assistance with a voyage to the Indies."

A voice came from behind the assembled courtiers. "And we turned him down, Your Highness."

All in the court turned their heads to see the man who spoke.

"Advance." King John engaged the man.

The courtier advanced toward the throne and bowed. "I am Porto Santo's governor, Bartolomeu Perestrello II, Third Captain of Porto Santo, where Columbus lived with my sister before she died."

"Continue." King John encouraged Bartolomeu.

"Columbus lived in Lisbon and went by the name of Cristóvão Colón. I can vouch for Colón to be a man of integrity, a noble man who married my sister and who only wanted to help your crown, my king."

King John bowed his head, deep in thought. He then spoke. "We have made a mistake in letting this man slip between our fingers. He should've been made to sail for the Portuguese crown. Now, though, we can't let Spain conquer any new territory, especially if it's in our dominion waters." He turned to his scribe and said, "Draft a letter for Pope Alexander VI to divide the waters between us and Spain. And make haste!"

The scribe followed the order.

Meanwhile, the courtiers raised their voices. "What do we do in the meantime, Your Majesty, if Columbus invades our waters?"

"The Pope will see to that by proclaiming our sovereignty over these waters," King John pronounced, then dismissed his court.

19

The Wide Sea

Wednesday, September 15, 1492

ADMIRAL COLUMBUS SAT AT HIS table marking his log. They'd been at sea for only about ten days, but his sailors seemed restless. As he passed by them, he imagined hearing a low murmur coming from the men. He tried to attribute these thoughts to some of the fears he was concealing within himself. What if they didn't find land? No! It couldn't happen. He had gone over and over his calculations, and seven hundred leagues separated the shores of Portugal from the Indies. It must have been his imagination, or his men's fears that were transplanting themselves into his mind.

He sat down to reckon the leagues sailed for the past two days.

Today we have sailed thirty-three leagues.

In his second notebook he jotted only thirty leagues.

He continued writing. *Thursday September 13. We are continuing our voyage westward and made thirty-three more leagues.* Again he marked four less leagues.

Today we had to push against strong currents. We were northwest by compass. We are now at least two hundred leagues from Hierro, where we left. I noticed a shift of the North Star about one-half point from north. Curious. I'll keep an eye on it.

Friday September 14. We made twenty leagues today.

He reckoned down less in his second logbook.

Then he wrote: *The* Pinta *and the* Niña *reported seeing a jaybird and a ringtail. We also saw a tropical bird. These birds stay close to land. Saturday September 15. We have sailed westward twenty-seven leagues on this day and night.*

He felt a glimmer of hope. Again, he showed less in his other logbook. *The North Star shifted again. I must keep it from the men. They scare easily.*

He was about to continue, when he heard a knock at the door. "Come in!" he called out.

Maestre Juan Diego, his cook, popped his head in the doorway. "Do you have a moment, Admiral?"

"Yes, yes, come in." Columbus closed his logbook.

Diego entered with a limp, holding his cap bashfully.

"Well, what is it?" Columbus asked.

"Admiral, I was given the task to monitor the food supplies."

"Yes?"

"Well, this afternoon I took a count, and we're running low on biscuits, and there's little dried meat left in the barrel."

"Have you alerted the boatswain, Bartholomé Garcia?"

"I have, Admiral. It was he who sent me to you."

Columbus put down his quill on a closed logbook. "Are you sure of your figures?" He got up from his chair and came around his writing table. He towered over Diego, who took a limping step backward.

"I checked them over and over, Admiral. We're running quite low on food supplies."

"Yes, I'm aware of that now. Let's go down into the hold to check one more time, eh?"

Diego looked about to protest, but he kept quiet and followed Columbus as he descended the upper deck to go into the hold.

As he passed the men working on deck, Columbus felt pairs of eyes following him. He then spotted João looking directly into his eyes. He turned away from him and descended into the hold followed by Diego.

In the dark hold, Columbus raised his lantern lit by a candle. Followed by Diego, and wading in their boots in the bilge water sloshing on the bottom of the floor, they bypassed elevated crates piled up and containing additional glass *ampolletas*, crates with baubles and trinkets to give away when they landed in the Indies. Then they arrived at last at the barrels in the driest part of the hold with food supplies.

Columbus counted a total of five barrels bound with hoops containing dry biscuits or hardtack; two barrels of lard wrapped in linen; five barrels dry salted cod, salted sardines, and anchovies; ten olive oil and olive jugs; and ten large barrels of wine. Dry goods composed of chickpeas, lentils, beans, and garlic were still plentiful in the provided casks. The brine barrels were leaking, and the barrels containing salted meat and pork were down to only two. Molasses, honey, raisins, and cheese looked plentiful. He inspected the dried goods and found that no water had leaked in. Water barrels were aplenty.

"We're not doing poorly yet. According to my calculations this morning, we have another week or ten days at the most until we see land."

"What about the five chickens in the crate on deck? Do you want me to use them instead of meat?"

"No. The chickens still give us eggs. Keep them alive till we land."

Columbus turned around and climbed to the deck. He was surprised to see the men gathered at the opening and looking down into the hold.

"What are you doing, loafers! Get back to work!" He turned to Juan de la Cosa. "I'd like to speak with you. Now!"

Juan, who had been milling about with the rest of the men, looked surprised. He followed Columbus without a word.

When they reached his cabin, Columbus turned to Juan with his brows knitted in dissatisfaction. "Why were the men standing about without doing any work?"

Juan shrugged his shoulders. "Their work shift ended, Admiral."

"There are plenty of tasks to do."

"Name them, Admiral," Juan said.

"They can paint the masts. The rigging could use some unraveling, and the decks need polishing."

"They've already done all of it, Admiral."

Columbus looked down and hesitated momentarily. This was the first time he'd been displeased with his crew, and Juan, for that matter. "All right, Juan. I was a bit hasty. Give the men an extra ration of wine tonight after Compline. I want these men to pray for their souls."

Juan nodded. "Admiral, there's something I must speak with you about."

Columbus raised his eyebrows.

"The men are getting worried and antsy. We've traveled for ten days so far. When do you expect we will see land?"

"According to my calculations, another ten days at most. The men knew that the voyage would take at least three weeks. We've got another two weeks to go."

Juan nodded again. "I'll go and tell the men, Admiral."

When the door shut on Juan, Columbus remained thoughtful for some time. He decided to send the boat for Martin Pinzón tomorrow to come over to the *Santa Maria* and have a talk with him. He may be dealing with a mutinous crew on his hands. *I wonder what the men on the* Pinta *and the* Niña *are thinking right now.*

After he did his Compline prayers on the upper deck while making sure his men did theirs, he retired to his cabin.

To Salcedo waiting to help him undress, he said, "I won't need you tonight."

Salcedo nodded and went out.

Columbus then looked over his calculations for tomorrow and felt satisfied. If everything continued without another hitch, the voyage might be uneventful and quick, he hoped.

His eyelids grew heavy and his bunk bed drew him in, so he undressed down to his night chemise and tried to get some sleep. He tossed on his small bed and had begun to doze when he heard a commotion.

Dressing feverishly, he ran out of the cabin. His crew was genuflecting on the lower deck and crossing themselves over and over.

"What's the noise about?" he asked Juan, who was at the foot of the stairs below deck.

"The men, Admiral, are spooked and afraid."

"What do you mean?"

"The Pole Star has moved, Admiral!"

Columbus looked at the fixed star in the black velvet sky above him and saw a hint of space where the Pole Star should have been.

A sailor's voice rose. "We'll be lost without the Pole Star! Admiral, what shall we do?"

"We won't be able to find our way back!" another voice pined.

The voices from his crew came to his ears as lamentations. His grown men were truly scared.

"Now listen!" he commanded the trembling men below his deck. "What you're seeing is only a variation of the movement of Polaris or the North Star. Like all heavenly bodies, they shift slightly." He looked at his men's postures in the flickering light to detect a change in their demeanor. They were listening attentively as if he were their salvation from a baffling situation, one of which they had no comprehension or understanding of its meaning.

"It's not the compass needle that is fixed on an invisible point that is correct." He continued. "It's in the nature of the sky and movements of the stars."

A low murmur reached his ears. His explanation must have satisfied and allayed their fears for now. They shuffled back to their spots on the deck and lay down to sleep.

Columbus felt extremely satisfied with the explanation he gave to his men. He knew that his calculations were correct in his assumption of the stars' revolutions. He then returned to his bed and lay down restfully.

20

Passage to Portugal

*A*S PROMISED BY MATIGORO, ISABELLA, Miguel, and the other captives were now marching through the hot sand dunes to get to a hilly alcove by the sea where they would be rescued. Isabella, walking in front of the column, felt the hot sand penetrating her torn moccasins and chafing her feet. At least now her clean and white caftan protected her from the hot sun still burning in September. For some reason, she thought back to the coolness in Seville and her parents' garden. Where had this time gone? So much had happened to her since she left her room that fateful day that perhaps she had imagined this enchanting and protected life she had lived in the past.

No, it was not a dream. She had, it seemed, changed from the inside out. Her trust and beliefs had shifted completely, and she wasn't the same person she'd been a year ago. She knew, though, to proceed with caution regarding what to expect from the near future. Meanwhile, as soon as Miguel and she found this haven in Portugal, they'd both be able to live contentedly well into their old age. She smiled at that last thought. A vision of Miguel and her seated under the shaded trees of their home, surrounded by their children and grandchildren, came to mind.

"Tell me what you're smiling about." Miguel's voice pulled her out of her trance.

"I didn't notice you were walking near me," she said to him with surprise.

"So who were you thinking of?" he asked her again. "Should I be jealous?"

Isabella laughed. "Of course not! I was thinking of you and all the children we'll have."

"How many?"

"Well . . ." She felt herself blush under the caftan's hood. "Perhaps five."

"Five!" Miguel exclaimed. "I'd have to work hard to support them all." He laughed, then his voice took a serious tone. "I still can't believe what you told me about Matigoro and the other benefactor."

"I couldn't believe it myself at first," Isabella said. "It's thanks to him that we're free from danger."

"Still, I—"

"Ma hatha!" A loud voice from one of the guards watching them put an end to Miguel's words. The same guard ran toward Miguel and Isabella and grabbed Miguel by the arm. *"Ta'ala!"* He pulled him back to his group composed of men.

Isabella had remained silent the whole time. She knew that their guard had no knowledge of where they were going, let alone of their freedom. Miguel knew this much too. Hopefully, the men on the vessel they were bound to would treat them better.

The sun had now risen above he horizon, and the heat came down at them with burning fire. She avoided the hot sand on her feet by raising each foot slightly as she walked.

"Imshee!" The guard this time yelled in her direction. She was slowing down the line of men and women walking toward the sea.

Suddenly a breeze came their way from the sea that refreshed her cheeks and forehead dripping with sweat. *Thank God we're here.*

She then saw in the distance a caravel swaying gently offshore, and a boat moving toward them with two men paddling their oars. Within a short time, the boat pulled onto the sandy beach, and the two men jumped out.

They went to speak to their two guards and shook hands with them.

"¡Vámonos!" They ordered the captives to get into the boat.

The twenty captives, including Isabella and Miguel, climbed into the large boat, and the rowers paddled away from shore.

Isabella, now cooled by the sea breeze, looked at the receding sand dunes and heaved a sigh of relief. Miguel, sitting on a bench across from her, smiled with relief too.

Miguel addressed her. "Now we can start breathing."

The rowboat arrived at the ship, and one by one, they climbed the ladder; as sailors waiting for them at the top pulled them over the railing. When all came on board, the captain addressed them.

"*¡Bienvenidos*! The women will sleep in the hold and the men on deck. Food will be given to you at mealtime."

Isabella quickly moved closer to Miguel and held his right hand in hers. "We mustn't be separated," she whispered.

He turned his head to her, but a sailor came between them and pulled Isabella away.

"What are you doing?" Isabella snapped.

"Leave her alone," Miguel said.

"Women and men will not mix!" the sailor said.

"But she's my wife!" Miguel cried.

In the meantime, the sailors kept pushing the women down the hold; some fell to their knees, while others began to scream.

The captain came on the scene and thundered from above. "You'll do as you're told! We're in pirate territory, and we can be can be exposed to an attack at any time. The women will be safe down below."

All calmed down by the announcement, and Isabella waved at Miguel standing on deck. "Don't worry!" she yelled. She turned around and went down the ladder.

21

Changing Parameters

Wednesday, September 19, 1942

WORKING DILIGENTLY WITH HIS COMPASS and quadrant, Columbus prepared his course for the following morning. So far the sea gave him no trouble at all. The *Niña* and the *Pinta* trailed behind him at the prescribed distance, and the crews playfully tried to catch some of the terns flying high above them. He then turned to his logbooks to read the previous days' notes.

We are now almost at midpoint in our voyage. Plowing forward in a westerly direction we saw green seaweed. We must be getting very close to an island. The weather is very pleasant, like spring in Andalusia. Breezes are light and refreshing. We all had a special Mass on deck with the men praying for a calm and speedy voyage. We sailed thirty-nine leagues.

He reckoned only thirty-five.

Monday September 17. The weeds around the ships are thick and green, and the men found crabs in them. It seems they came from rivers. We must be approaching land, at least another seventy-to-eighty leagues where crabs are found. Our ships are sailing fast, racing among each other. The

Niña's *men caught and killed a dolphin. These signs must come from God's hands leading us to victory. I trust we will soon see land. Today we went fifty leagues.*

Again he reckoned only forty-seven leagues.

He wrote: *Tuesday September 18. We sailed fifty-five leagues.* He noted only forty-eight.

He continued, *Today the sea is . . .* when voices rang from below deck.

"Admiral! Admiral!" the crew voices called out. Fearing another disastrous sighting in the water by his men made him dash on deck. The men below were pointing forward in a westerly direction. Columbus scanned the horizon and was surprised to see the *Pinta* ahead. Pinzón was racing again. Columbus went down to the deck below him and waved at Pinzón.

"What's the meaning of this?" he yelled at the top of his voice.

Pinzón, standing on the stern, yelled back to him. "We've sighted a large flock of birds! We'll see land tonight!"

Juan came near the railing. "That's what I've been telling you, Admiral. He plans to get the prize money for himself," he warned him. "We're the flag ship. We have precedence over Pinzón."

Columbus replied without quitting his gaze on the *Pinta*. "This money is for anyone who sights land first. With God's help, we're nearing land. I see to the north a large gathering of clouds on the horizon. That's a sign!" He turned his head slightly to Juan's face and noted him frowning. "Be patient, Juan. I know we're close."

The next morning, the sea was calm. No land had been sighted yet, but Columbus was confident they were nearing a landmass. The sea was as calm as a mirror, and they only sailed a distance of twenty-five leagues; then again, he reckoned down twenty-two in the public book. They sighted more birds; this time they were blue-footed booby birds. The men caught a few of them landing on deck.

"Admiral, we got us some *estúpido* birds. They're so stupid, they landed in our laps!" His men were delighted with the easy prey they had caught.

"We'll feast tonight!" The men brandished the dead birds in their raised arms.

Columbus smiled at them. He was glad his men's morale was high. These boobies were signs that land was near. He knew from his sailing experience that boobies dwelt on islands and coasts and dove for fish in the sea from great heights. He was certain these birds didn't fly further than twenty-five leagues from land.

I sense there are islands to the north and to the south, he thought. *There is plenty of time. For, God willing, on our return voyage we shall see everything when we return.*

Before nightfall, Juan entered his cabin after knocking. "I have readings sent by the other ships, Admiral."

Feverishly, Columbus unrolled the parchment's readings handed to him, and brought in a bucket on a rope line by pulleys between the ships. The pilot of the *Pinta* recorded they had reckoned 440 leagues since they had left the Canarias. The *Niña* reckoned 420 leagues. He looked at his figures from the pilot of the *Santa Maria* and there were 400 leagues. His heart fluttered with excitement. With God's help they were near land!

He genuflected to do his Compline prayers before going to sleep.

22

Treacherous Seas

OTH ISABELLA AND MIGUEL SAT in their respective corners on the Portuguese ship: Isabella in the hold and Miguel on the deck above her. Isabella paced the hold back and forth while her female companions sat looking grim. The sea was storming with wave heights reaching the top of the deck, forcing seawater to percolate into the hold. Even though the heavy cover to the hold was shut, water seeped through the cracks and washed down upon the unfortunate women. Some of the women began to throw up from motion sickness. Isabella thought with dread that Miguel had to be drenched to his bones. She yearned to take a peek at him. Suddenly an idea took hold in her head.

She walked to the ladder and climbed it to the top. At the last rung, she tried to dislodge the heavy plank, but it remained shut. A few of the women raised their heads, their curiosity aroused by her efforts. Then one of them got up and climbed to her level.

"What're you doing?" a young woman of about eighteen or nineteen years of age asked her. She had black hair and coal-black eyes and a dark complexion.

Isabella looked down at her from her vantage point and replied, "I'm suffocating in here. I want fresh air."

"Hold on tight. I'll try to stand on your rung. With effort and with incredible dexterity, she positioned herself on the same rung with Isabella. Their feet in their moccasins were touching side by side with no room to spare. "Now, at the count of three push the lid with all your strength. I'll keep the rope ladder from swaying."

Isabella did as she was told at the count of three and applied all her might to lift the lid, but to no avail. "I can't!" she moaned.

"Let me try," the young woman said.

This time, Isabella used her strength to keep the ladder straight while her companion used both her hands to push the lid. A sudden light appeared through a crack. She pushed the lid sideways, and it moved, letting the salty air whoosh in.

"You did it!" Isabella screamed with joy. "Try to move it again."

The young woman tried, and this time half the lid left an open gap to the outside.

Isabella grabbed the edge of the opening and lifted herself with the woman's help. With great effort she emerged from the hold to face all of the men, including Miguel, sitting on deck. They were soaked, as she had suspected. She ran on the tilting deck to a surprised Miguel and embraced him. He held her tight in his happiness.

"You disobeyed the captain's orders. And you'll get soaked, too, with this surging sea."

"I don't care if I get wet now that I'm with you."

Isabella looked up to see none of the sailors in sight. She figured they must've been occupied in another part of the ship. When she looked up she saw one sailor in the crow's nest, trying to hold on for dear life.

Suddenly, a cry was heard. "Pirates! Pirates!"

Out of nowhere, the ship's crew came out in droves and hoisted their Portuguese flag on the highest mast.

"Quickly, Isabella, go back to the hold!" Miguel begged her.

Isabella cringed, but resigned to follow his instructions. She let go of his hand and ran to the open hold. Before she reached the last rung, she saw the lid pushed back into place. She went to sit down near the women, who were now trembling with fear. Isabella caught the eyes of the young woman who had helped her, and smiled at her gratefully. And then they waited.

23

Hopeful Signs

OÃO WORKED AT THE RIGGING while watching the admiral's cabin above his deck. Since the last time he spoke to the admiral, he hadn't crossed paths with him, except a glance or two as he passed him by. João anticipated seeing land as much as everyone on this ship. He, too, tried to pray, but had forsaken religion many years ago when caught in the Inquisition's web. Years had not erased houghts of revenge for the prison torture he suffered. But most of all they were years of lost hope.

"What's weighing you down?" Hernán Çavallos asked as he worked near him while trying to unravel the rigging on the deck.

"What? Oh no, it's nothing," João said

"If it's nothing, why aren't you talkative like before?"

"I said it's nothing for you to be concerned about!"

"All right, *amigo*. Only asking."

Alfonso Sabatin also working alongside his two mates turned to João. "Don't you trust us?"

João stayed silent for a few moments. "I've asked the admiral . . ." He stopped when two other sailors approached their working station.

"Hey, you're holding the line!" Francisco de Huelva snapped at them.

One of João's old workmates, Gomes from Palos, stood aside working in silence.

"Hey! We're working as fast as we can," Hernán replied.

"You know that I can report you to the master, Juan de la Cosa," Francisco warned them.

Francisco's threat didn't affect João. What could they do to them? Throw them in irons into the hold? They needed all hands on deck for this voyage, especially if a storm broke over their heads.

"We're sorry," João said to Francisco. "Agreed?" He turned to his mates. Both Hernán and Alfonso nodded.

"All right. Back to work then," Francisco said.

When Francisco left them, João said, "Let's get together tonight."

After a moonlit meal and prayers, João took his mates aside by the stern and confided quietly to them, "I thought of a sure way to find land for Jews, and the admiral will help me find it."

"And he agreed?" Hernán said with astonishment.

"Let's just say I'm making a bargain with him," João said with a smile on his face that the moonlight hid from his mates.

"You mean you're blackmailing him?" Alfonso asked.

João remained silent.

After a few minutes' silence he said, "Remember our agreement last year in Téresa's house?"

"You mean, to find a homeland for the Jews?" Hernán said.

"Exactly. Even though all Jews have left España now, they're still scattered in lands where harm can reach them."

"But, will the admiral agree?" Alfonso asked.

"I have a sure reason for him not to refuse." João's voice sounded firm.

"Can you tell us the reason?"

"I will, but not yet."

The two men kept silent. João knew they trusted his judgment, and why they followed him on this voyage. And he trusted their secrecy. As soon as land was sighted, he'd confide in them.

24

fierce Battle

ISABELLA SAT ON THE FLOOR of the hold, huddled together with the other women, her hands trembling and her heart beating fast. No sounds came from above on the deck where Miguel and the men anticipated the pirate ship to dock alongside any minute. They heard the deafening explosion of a Lombard cannon. This was followed by another volley of deafening bursts from their ship. Then, in the distance, they heard a similar reply from the pirate ship. All the women let out a moan.

The young woman who had helped Isabella climb to the deck blasted at them. "Silence! We don't want to alert the pirates of our presence!"

"It's easy for you to say. Gypsies have no fear."

A silence reigned suddenly among the women, while the young woman in question shrugged her shoulders, undaunted by the comment.

Isabella moved closer to her and said, "I'm glad you're here. I'll follow your example and brave those bastards!"

"Call me Juanita." She smiled at Isabella.

Outside above them the volley of cannon bursts increased, then a silence took place while everyone in the hold held their breath. They heard footsteps on the deck sounding as if a hand-to-hand battle was taking place.

Meanwhile, it seemed as the sea itself was offended by the human sacrilege of its waters, and the ship began to toss under turbulence caused by strong waves.

The women began to utter again their fears in small cries. A young girl of about fifteen stood up and began to scream, then ran wildly back and forth in the hold. Juanita got up from the floor and went to catch her. She slapped the young girl several times and forced her to sit down. The girl, now calmer, cried silently to herself.

Feeling pity for the young girl, Isabella got up and went to comfort her. "Why did you hit her?" she asked Juanita.

"She was hysterical and might've revealed our hideout."

"I doubt anyone heard her screams with all the thundering and blasts above," Isabella replied.

Juanita fell silent. She went to sit down, and the women moved away from her.

Now Isabella felt sorry for Juanita. She left the girl still sobbing and weeping, and weaving her way back with the swaying of the ship went to sit by Juanita. "Why are these girls avoiding you?"

Juanita looked at her. "They're ignorant women. Because I'm a gypsy they think they're above me."

A grating of the hold's lid interrupted Isabella. All heads looked up, and the cover slid sideways, and a pirate's head slipped in.

"The devil found us!" All the women except Isabella and Juanita began to scream and retreated at once against the hold's walls.

In no time, several pirates descended into the hold and grabbed the women roughly. The screams from the women now rang louder while some fought back to no avail. Isabella and Juanita let themselves be overpowered and pulled up the rope ladder. When they emerged, Isabella saw the deck crawling with pirates. The foremast was lying down on the deck trapping some men beneath its weight. Bodies of sailors lay in pools of blood. The pirate ship was docked alongside theirs, and the pirates were loading the booty from the ship. Miguel was nowhere, which set her heart thumping loudly and caused her legs to weaken under her.

She cried out for him. "Miguel! Miguel!"

"Silence!" The pirate holding her slapped her on both cheeks.

Stunned, Isabella quieted down. *He must be here; he must!* By now all the women had emerged from the hold and were handcuffed in irons and joined by a chain, including Isabella.

Miguel suddenly appeared, crossing the plank between the ships. She tried to wave at him, but the chains prevented her. Behind him a pirate held a sword at his back. When he jumped onto their ship, Miguel bent down and lifted some of the booty in a crate filled with silver dishes and turned around to retrace his steps on the plank. He suddenly turned his head around to look for Isabella.

"Miguel! Miguel!" Isabella cried out to him.

Just then the pirate following him put the tip of his sword against Miguel's throat. Miguel nodded and followed orders.

A sudden loud cannonade began anew in the distance. The women's ears perked up, and a wave of wailing and crying started again.

"We're cursed! More pirates coming!"

Isabella looked at the horizon and saw a caravel heading in their direction. All looting and sporadic fighting ceased at once. The remaining pirates on their ship retreated toward the plank bridge and began to run to their vessel.

Isabella panicked that Miguel was nowhere in sight. "Miguel? Miguel, where are you?" she yelled. The pirates were now back on their own ship. The plank had been pulled back, and their ship was pulling away while cannon shots were being aimed, but missed at her bow. The pirate ship receding broke Isabella's heart. Miguel was lost to her.

She collapsed on the deck in tears, pulling down her mates still attached by her chains, and cried her heart out. Juanita tried to console her, but Isabella's ears were closed to her words.

"¡*Mira*! They're not pirates. It's a Portuguese ship!" a sailor alerted everyone.

They all looked to the new ship arriving and let out a sigh of relief at the blessed sight of the red square flag with seven yellow castles, and in its center five blue shields containing bezant disks.

Isabella, who had looked up like everyone else, hung her head down in grief. Pirates had taken Miguel away. Nothing else now had meaning in her life. Her shoulders shook with renewed sobs. Juanita tried to calm her, but Isabella remained prostrate in her grief.

The Portuguese ship, with its signature name *Liberação* posted on its stern, came alongside their ship, and their crew then placed the plank between the ships. The sea had now calmed, and the Portuguese sailors began to cross over into their ship. Leading them was a distinguished man dressed in rich clothing and sporting a gleaming sword at his side. He landed on the deck and was approached by the captain of their ship, who had now been freed.

The visitor bowed before the captain, then a few words were inaudibly exchanged.

Isabella had followed the arrival of their liberators and became suddenly agitated. She got up and ran to the leader.

She curtsied before him. "*¿Señor? ¿Por favor? ¡Ayúdame!*"

The nobleman looked at her and became concerned by her request. "How can I help you, señorita?"

"The pirates took my husband away. Please, please help him."

The captain fixed his eyes on the nobleman and shook his head at him. The visitor turned back to her.

"My dear, we can chase after the pirate ship now, or later try to find him by other means."

"Now! Now! You must find him now!" she screamed at him, not wanting to believe his words.

"A man overboard! Man in the sea!" a sailor screamed from the crow's nest.

Everyone's eyes turned to the wretched man fighting the waves while swimming toward the ship. They all ran to the railing, and a sailor threw a rope to him.

Isabella, engulfed in pain, was impervious to the commotion on deck. She moaned, "I can't live without him." The noise and sights around her became a humdrum to her ears, and she felt faint.

"Mi querida. Mi Alma?"

She heard those words pronounced as a prayer. She looked up to see Miguel take her into his wet arms before she lost consciousness.

25

Signs

Thursday, September 20, 1492

THE *SANTA MARIA* AND HER consorts, the *Pinta* and the *Niña*, sailed west-by-north that day, and even though the winds were moderate, they accomplished eight leagues west, one quarter northwest. Several birds were sighted: boobies, terns that were river birds (some were caught on the ship), and a couple of singing birds. These sightings revealed to Columbus that they were closer still to land. They were perhaps no more than twenty to twenty-five leagues from shore. These birds fed upon the sea, then return to land at night.

Later on at dawn a few of his men spotted the waters thick with weeds.

"Admiral, Admiral?" Sancho Ruiz, his pilot, called out. Pretty soon, his crew screamed excitedly to a point in a northerly direction.

Columbus followed their gaze and saw a whale. That was a definite sign that warmed his heart, for whales did not venture far from the coast.

His men joyfully screamed, then slapped and hugged each other. "We'll see land soon!"

Later on by the second watch at three p.m., Columbus stood on the quarterdeck taking measurements on his compass wind rose. According to the magnetic needle pointing to the fleur-de-lis, or north, he counted two major wind points in the thirty-two points compass. They had been sailing previously in a northwest direction, and had now veered away from their course about thirty leagues west. Columbus flared his nostrils and ground his teeth. He had given Ruiz specific instructions to stay the course northwest. Heading the wrong way could deplete their provisions with fateful consequences. Columbus had to be alert at all times, and mishaps couldn't be tolerated.

"What made the ship lose its true direction?" he asked Ruiz.

"Admiral, I've been at the tiller for the last four hours and nothing was amiss to indicate veering off. I can't explain it." He looked as bewildered as Columbus.

"Go get some rest. We'll figure it out later. Wake Juan for the next watch," Columbus told him. He then took over the tiller and steered the rudder back to north until Juan de la Cosa replaced him for his night watch.

Right afterward the winds died down for the next several hours, and by dusk he heard the crew grumbling. He stepped out of his cabin to see to the commotion.

"What are you complaining about?" he asked, his arms flailing in the air.

The crew, still respectful of their admiral's authority, lowered their heads.

"The men are afraid, Admiral." João said. This was the last man he wanted to hear from.

"What are you afraid of? We've bridged more than five hundred leagues so far. We've not encountered stormy seas or winds to blow us off the waves, and we're all safe!" His voice had risen to a pitch. He knew that when his men saw him angry, they would fall silent. Although, he still needed his crew's support and complete obedience. Without it, all would be lost.

"But, Admiral," João answered back, "without the winds in those seas, we can't go back to Spain."

"Hear ya, hear ya." The men standing around him approved by nodding.

Columbus threw João a murderous glance as if his eyes were darts. *This man is my nemesis.*

Suddenly, as he was about to reply, a strange occurrence took place. The sea rose with great waves without the wind powering them. The crew looked at each other's faces, and some of them fell to their knees with fear and crossed themselves.

Columbus was astonished to see such great waves without the proper wind to push them forward. *These waves are what we need. No such thing has been seen or recorded since Moses led the Jews out of Egypt. This is indeed a great sign!*

That evening he recorded their westward progress of twenty-three leagues in one logbook and nineteen in the other.

26

Arrival

AS SOON AS THE COAST of Portugal came into view by noon, voices rose with relief. They all gathered at the railing, standing on their toes and waving their arms as if someone on the shore waited for them. The captain also stood by observing the coastline through his cupped hands to avoid the glare. The steep coastline alternated with white sand beaches and dotted by a green canopy of luxuriant forests.

"We're home at last!" Isabella sighed.

Miguel, standing by her side, pulled her close to him. "Once we find shelter, you will rest, my dear."

"I'm really fine, Miguel. That fainting spell was my despair over losing you. But now that you're near me, I've nothing to fear."

He smiled at her with tender eyes.

Meanwhile, the shore approached nearby, and Isabella looked for a dock or pier, but none existed to moor the boats. Instead, the ship's anchor dropped in deep waters, near a bay nestled at the foot of a cliff.

"Lower the boats!" the captain called out to the crew. The nobleman who had come on board before was standing by his side, and it seemed that the captain took orders from him.

Both Isabella and Miguel looked in his direction. Isabella saw that he was richly dressed in blue linens and an open red silk overgown fastened across his chest with ribbons, and he wore a chaperon hat. His white beard came down to his chest. Their rescuer and benefactor must've been an illustrious nobleman.

By that time, the boats had been lowered. Their benefactor went down first then the rest of the young men and women came next. Isabella slipped into the boat with the other women and sat near Juanita while she watched Miguel descend into the next boat.

Juanita took her by the arm and smiled at her. "We're free!" she said, overjoyed.

"Thank God!" Isabella returned Juanita's smile. "When we land, I want you to stay with us."

Juanita looked surprised. "Thank you, Isabella. I'll try to be helpful."

The rowers now paddled across the shallow waters to slide into the wet sand on the beach. No buildings or fishermen milling about their work were to be seen. This seemed an abandoned shore devoid of population around them. That was strange indeed.

After they all left the boats, they waited for instructions.

The nobleman stood in front of them and spoke gently. "You are now in Portugal, where you'll find shelter. My men will instruct you next where you'll dwell." With those last words, he mounted a horse waiting for him and galloped away on the beach until he became a small dot disappearing in the distance.

"So far, so good," Miguel said in a low voice as he neared Isabella. She reached for his hand, which he took and pressed into his.

"Vá!" One of their guards gave the order to walk in the direction of the tree line.

"There will be no horses for us." Isabella sighed.

Miguel said, "At least we're now free of pirates and the Inquisition."

"I hope never to see sight of them again!"

"Amen," Miguel replied.

They walked from the beach to a stand of trees along the cliffs. After broaching the tree line, they found the forest thick with trees connected to each other by vines and vegetation growing wildly at their feet. Birds jumped on felled trees lying in their path and frolicked in the highest branches. Their two guards riding two donkeys led them and the rest of the caravan on foot.

After what seemed an hour's march, Isabella's feet and legs began to ache, and her throat became parched for water. Her stomach growled, and she began to feel faint from the heat and humidity. Both Miguel and Juanita, who walked alongside, supported her by her shoulders, trying to keep their pace with the entire group.

"I'm feeling sick again, Miguel. Can't we rest for a moment?" Her throat felt constricted.

"*¡Parar!*" Miguel called out to one of the guards.

The guard approached and took one look at Isabella, then signaled the other guard, who came running to them. "Place this young woman up front on one of the donkeys."

"But . . . which one?" the guard asked.

"Yours, of course."

The guard asking the question was none too pleased to cede his mount, but he obeyed the man who seemed his superior.

Isabella, helped by Miguel and one of the guards, was lifted onto the donkey, and the entire caravan continued on their march with Miguel walking alongside Isabella.

Within the hour they arrived at a secluded plantation surrounded by high and white walls. One of their guards rang a large bell by the gate, and a gatekeeper came forward. After speaking to the gatekeeper, they were let in. All around them were fruit trees and several pools in a row leading to the main house.

One of the guards turned to Miguel and Isabella and said, "You stay here." He faced the others, giving them an order to follow him. *"Senhores, senhoras—vindes!"* Both guards called out to the column of twenty men and women, and led them away toward a cluster of wooden huts in the distance.

Miguel and Isabella continued toward the house and as they reach it she collapsed on her mount by the front entrance. Images in front of her eyes began to blur; the house and Miguel twirled around her before she lost consciousness.

⚖️

She awoke at the sound of her name. "Isabella? Isabella? *Me oyes?*" Miguel's voice rang in her ears. She opened her eyes to see an unfamiliar woman's face. The woman's forehead was creased, looking with concern.

"What happened?" Isabella asked. She felt a bit stronger even though her voice was weak, but she was surprised by the concern over her.

"You fainted again," Miguel said to her. He, too, had the same worried look on his face.

"I feel fine now. No need to worry about me. Where are we?"

"You're in Dom Fernandez de Carvalho's estate. Your host," said the woman as she turned around toward the new arrival. The same man who had helped them on the ship previously appeared before them.

"How are you feeling, senhorita?"

Isabella looked at his long beard and comforting smile, and she knew that he would protect them continually from now on wherever they may be. "I'm much better. *Gracias.*" She then saw that Juanita was absent. "There was a young woman by the name of Juanita. Please, Dom Carvalho—can she stay with us?"

Dom Carvalho stared, but nevertheless he nodded. "We'll see that she comes back." He then turned to the woman standing by and said, "I see you have met my cousin Ana."

At the name, Miguel flinched. Isabella looked at him with surprise, but he kept silent.

"Let's go into the dining room and partake of a meal," Dom Carvalho said.

Miguel helped Isabella to her feet, supporting her. She now felt safe and protected as if she were back home with her mother and father, and as if the nightmarish memories of the past year had not happened.

27

Anticipation

Tuesday, September 25, 1492

COLUMBUS WOKE UP FEELING A portentous event about to unfold. If land appeared in his sight, it would fulfill a prophecy for him. He remembered in the recesses of his memory a recurring theme in particular that was prevalent. He had the vague notion, a wisp of a thought, that continually crept into his mind. He recalled shreds of words and images that were unconnected. One was an empty beach in front of him. The other was a blurry, but soft image of a dark-haired woman running to him. A voice calling out said, "You'll be a star in the firmament." What did it mean? He searched his memory, but came up with a blank.

He picked up his quill to record a position on one of his charts, when he remembered he had lent it to Pinzón three days ago. He quickly wrote a message to Pinzón, then told Salcedo to call his shipmaster, Juan, to his cabin.

"Send a message to Pinzón in the *Pinta*," he told De la Cosa. "Ask him to return the chart with islands I had marked." He handed him the note scrawled on a rolled parchment.

"*Si*, Admiral. Right away."

Columbus followed him on deck to see Juan carry out his instructions. First, Juan signaled the *Pinta* of an oncoming message by raising a red flag alert from the mast. They waited for the *Pinta* to come starboard to the *Santa Maria* then Juan threw a metal hook attached to a cord to the Pinta's railings. Through a pulley, the basket containing the rolled chart with Columbus's instructions reached the *Pinta*.

From their side, the *Pinta* retrieved the basket, and Juan saw his counterpart on their caravel take it to Pinzón. He reappeared shortly, and the chart made its way back to Columbus on the *Santa Maria*.

The note from Pinzón read, "Admiral, you are right that we haven't yet hit those islands because the ships were driven by currents running northeastward."

Columbus went to meet Ruiz at the tiller by the stern. "Adjust your course from west to west-southwest. We need to catch up lost leagues by morning."

"*Si*, Admiral."

"Oh, and the master Juan de la Cosa will relieve you at the sunset watch."

Sancho nodded.

Columbus returned to his cabin to jot down the day's reckoning. In his true log he wrote: *Today we sailed west-northwest. So far we have covered fifteen leagues.*

He recorded only twelve in his other, false logbook. Especially since they had lost time northward, the men were bound to complain they were running out of time and provisions.

We've seen many petrels by the ship today, and the men caught several boobies. The men's morale is good, and they're anticipating seeing land any day now.

"Admiral! Admiral!"

Columbus heard excited voices coming from his sailors, and he ran on deck to see to the commotion. The first sight that greeted him was Pinzón standing on the poop of the *Pinta*.

Pinzón was jumping and shouting excitedly on the *Pinta*'s deck. "I have a gift for you, Admiral!" In his hands Pinzón held a small package wrapped in linen and red bows.

"Why?" Columbus hailed at him.

"We have sighted land!" Pinzón said. Thereafter, the men on the *Pinta* fell to their knees, while a man on the *Niña* confirmed seeing land.

Columbus's heart skipped a beat. He, too, fell on his knees, followed by his men.

Immediately, the hymn *"Gloria in Excelsis Deo"* giving thanks to God rose from every mouth and into the sea air above the ship.

Columbus then got up and ran on the heaving deck to his cabin to look for his astrolabe. He felt sure that a landmass was about to appear before his eyes.

Throughout the night he and a few of his men kept a vigil, for a landmass, though most men had fallen asleep. The soft humming of their chests rose and fell with each breath during sleep, while a few snored along the walls on deck. At the four a.m. watch, Columbus ordered Juan to change course to southwest.

During the following morning the *Santa Maria* and her two consorts kept sailing southwest. By midday, Columbus began to suspect that the landmass was none other than dark heavy clouds on the horizon. He, as well as his men, were disappointed, to say the least.

He stood on the quarterdeck and spoke to them. "We are near, I tell you. You've seen the birds, the fish coming in more numerous each day, the green weeds against the side of the ship. Land is nearby. Keep faith in God that by week's end we will land on terra firma. To show you that we're near, I'll allow you to take time off from your duties for the next two hours."

The men remained silent without smiling or cheering. He knew that his foreman in Palos had chosen the right men for this voyage. They still, somewhat, believed in him.

"Let's swim with the fish!" one of his sailors yelled.

Shaken out of their downcast mood, the men disrobed and jumped naked into the water, then frolicked around the ship by splashing each other with seawater. If his dignity as admiral wasn't at stake, he, too, would jump into the cool and refreshing waters, but preserving decorum and authority was preferable. The sea was now calm with numerous large gold fish swimming around them. Some of his men on the ship fished for them, and Columbus could almost smell the aroma from the grilled fish on his table tonight.

28

Peaceful Days

SABELLA HAD REGAINED SOME STRENGTH following her ordeal through the nightmarish voyage to two continents, northern Africa and back to Europe. Portugal had always been a fictitious country for her. Her geography tutor had explained over and over the monarchies, and how they were united at one time with Spain in the Visigothic times, but her mind would wander to childish pursuits, then to matters of the heart. Juan had been her only love until she had met and known Miguel. Miguel's strength of character, perseverance, and sense of justice had created a bond between him and her. He now was and would remain her only love.

The household ran smoothly in Ana's able hands, and Juanita had been brought back to the estate. Everyone saw to Isabella's comfort and well-being. She relished in her good luck, but still sensed an uneasy feeling tugging at her.

The day began with a warm sun that lit a valley behind Dom de Carvalho's estates and vineyards. It seemed that the house and its surroundings was the only habitable dwelling for kilometers in every direction. They were isolated yet protected from pring eyes. She got up from the marble bench among the citrus trees and walked up a cliff to a promontory overlooking the sea. A green plain lay below the cliffs, showing the workers picking grapes from the many rows of vines. She squinted from the glaring sun to look for Miguel and spotted him loading grapes into barrels in front of him. Dom de Carvalho had employed all of the young men and women who were freed from the captive ships to help with the harvest. Here was a pool of workers for the estate, thought Isabella. This, nevertheless, was a better alternative than being slaves to the ruthless and pitiless pirates.

She looked down again and saw Miguel waving at her. She waved back and threw him a kiss. He threw one back and did a sudden fandango dance. She burst into laughter, then waving again at him, she turned around and proceeded to go down the cliff, when without warning a dizzying spell overtook her. She reached for a rock near her and sat down with wobbly legs. *What's happening to me?* Then all of her morning meal was regurgitated. She vomited until she had nothing left to throw up. Shaking, she wiped her mouth and lifted herself from the ground. She made her way back slowly to the house, when Ana caught up with her.

"What's matter, *filha?*" She ran to her and helped her walk to the house, then sat her down on the front porch.

"I was sick. My whole stomach turned inside out," Isabella said.

Ana held her arms across her chest, then burst out laughing.

. Isabella looked puzzled at her.

"My dear child, it's great news. You're with child!"

Isabella held her breath under the shock. "I'm with child. . . with child?" she repeated, not knowing at first what to do with the thought. When it became clear, she, too, burst into light laughter. The two women hugged each other with joy.

Ana turned to the house and called, "Juanita, Juanita?" When she appeared in the doorway, she said, "Go and tell Miguel he'll be a father."

Juanita's face broke into a large smile and she went to hug Isabella, and ran to the hill.

"Now, you mustn't strain yourself. You must rest, eat, and be peaceful," Ana said.

"I wonder how Miguel will take the news," Isabella said softly, but with a twinge of worry in her voice.

"He'll be delighted," Ana reassured her. "All prospective fathers are."

"But you don't understand," Isabella said. We've no home, and Miguel plans to go back to España to look for his brother."

"That's the most foolish thing I've ever heard. You escaped with your life from the Inquisition, then pirates—and now he wants to go back?"

Isabella remained silent to the admonition. Ana was right. But then, what about her search, the quest for her real mother and father? And would she ever again see her loving adoptive father? This was all too troubling.

"Isabella!" Miguel's voice shook her out of her thoughts. She hadn't seen him running to her, but he hugged her with joy. "My sweet and precious wife. We're going to become parents! I'm so happy!" He kissed her over and over.

"You're not worried about staying here in Portugal?" she asked him with concern.

"Why should I be worried? You made me the happiest husband!"

"What about José? And finding my real parents?"

The happy expression on Miguel's face lessened. He became reflective. "Now we have a new child that will come into the world. On that child we'll concentrate our efforts. But someday we will look for my brother and your parents."

She hugged him, her face snuggled next to his.

29

Open Secrets

OÃO SAT ON DECK WITH his shipmates after hours. Hernán and
Alfonso stood not far, next to the mainmast, balancing themselves on
the rigging and the ropes descending from the sails and shrouds. The
voyage so far had been uneventful, except for the false hope that land had
been sighted ahead, and that had sparked a rush of excitement. That land
turned out to be cloud formations, which left the men deeply disappointed.
He'd even heard rumors from the sailors that the admiral had wasted their
time, or perhaps their lives. Fear was beginning to course through their
conversations and whispers.

Everything now was calm: the sea, the men's mood, and more so his
companions. Since the day he'd announced his plan to find land for his
Jewish brethren, Hernán and Alfonso hadn't questioned him any further.
Neither had Gomes, who checked for secrets between him and his two
mates. Someday Gomes might find out all about their mission. By then it
would be too late for him to join them. Besides, rumor had it that Gomes
was an ex-convict that had been pardoned by the queen to make this voyage,
without being allowed to leave the ship. Then, on the other hand, João
thought, hadn't he, himself, done prison time too?

"Hey, *amigo*, what's with the thinking?" Gomes's voice blasted behind him, followed by a slap on his right shoulder.

João turned around with surprise. "Where did you come from?"

"Why, I came from the king's palace!" his voice mocked. He continued. "I was at the tiller with Sancho. Hmm . . . look at these beautiful stars," Gomes said as he turned his face upward to the black velvet sky studded with brilliant points of light.

João raised his head, too, to admire the firmament dotted with sparkling diamonds, like jewels in their box. "We're lucky to have seen these same stars in España. Now they're guiding us with the hand of God." João crossed himself.

Gomes stood quietly without invoking God.

"What's the matter? God isn't good enough to pull you through?" João said.

He saw Gomes make a move toward him, but he stopped short. He snapped back, "Who are you to question my faith? You're a make-believe Christian!"

João cringed at the insult. "I'm as good a Christian as you are!" His rising voice brought Hernán and Alfonso from their location.

"What's going on?" Hernán asked.

Gomes turned to João and blurted, "I happen to know that you're a converted Jew, and you're looking for a new land."

Both Hernán and Alfonso made a move toward Gomes, but João, who was stunned by this accusation, motioned for them to stay put. All his efforts to keep his plans as quiet as possible were now known to Gomes. "You must've heard me talking to Hernán and Alfonso."

"I heard more than that." Gomes had his arms on his hips, goading João, who now felt blood rising to his face.

João didn't reply. He remained watchful and waited for Gomes to strike the last blow to his secret plans. He finally asked Gomes, "Well, what more have your heard?"

This time Gomes remained silent. "Never mind," he said. With those last words he walked back to the stern, where Sancho Ruiz was piloting the *Santa Maria*.

"We must do something or he'll spill the beans," Alfonso said in a quiet voice.

"Yes. He will." Hernán seconded Alfonso.

João, still shook up by Gomes's accusation, thought with concern that Gomes would hold this information above their heads, ready to use it at any time. "We'll keep an eye on him and find a reason to disqualify him in some way. Pardoned or not, he's still an ex-convict. So who would believe him?"

Hernán and Alfonso nodded and seemed reassured by these last words.

30

At the Vatican

T HE VAST CHAMBER IN THE Vatican hall was nearly empty of cardinals and bishops, and only the camerlengo, Cardinal Raffaele Riario, was present by Pope Alexander VI, Rodrigo Lanzol Borja. Two other cardinals—Cardinal Oliviero Carafa, the office dean and suburbicarian bishop of Sabina, and Cardinal Ascanio Sforza—were also seated near him; these cardinals were the Pope's closest advisors and confidants.

"Your Eminence. Before you is a great conflict in the making," Cardinal Riario said.

"Please explain," Pope Borja replied while adjusting his white silk tunic, and with deep concentration on the buttons and ties on the garment.

"We have received a request from Portugal's King John II. He asks for a new papal bull charter to separate them from Spain in territorial waters."

"I thought we'd done that when the two sovereigns signed the Treaty of Alcáçovas."

"Yes, but you have Spain bent on a voyage that will interfere with Portuguese sovereignty. If Spain ever breeches the Treaty of Alcáçovas, there will be more wars between them," the camerlengo said.

Pope Borja stared into space while mulling over Riario's last words. "The peace has lasted so far between these two. I don't foresee any conflicts."

Pope Borja turned his head to the camerlengo's determined eyes, and knew that Cardinal Riario made his reputation by diplomacy and counsel to the papal throne, and that he wouldn't give up easily.

"What exactly do you suggest, Cardinal Riario?"

"We must further divide the ocean seas."

Indeed, Pope Borja fell into the pleasant thought of separating the oceans as Moses had done in Egypt with the Red Sea. He then reprimanded himself. Isn't that, though, one of the seven capital sins? To seek vanity through greatness? He wasn't ready to do penance and obtain absolution yet, so he pushed the vain thought away.

"You must tell us how this may be done," Cardinal Sforza said with a slight smile on his lips.

"We used this strategy before with these two. In the Treaty of Alcáçovas, we divided the Atlantic Ocean and overseas territories into two zones." He paused momentarily then continued. "With the treaty, Portugal gained control over the gold mines in Guinea, the islands of Madeira, the Azores, Cape Verde, and future lands in the kingdom of Fez." The camerlengo stopped again.

"Continue," Pope Borja said.

"Spain gained the Canary Islands, but is restricted to this sphere, while Portugal can trade south of the islands and can possess all lands discovered now and in the future."

"What are you getting at?" Pope Borja asked.

"Well, what if other lands are discovered west and beyond the treaty boundaries? We should set a new demarcation line between the two countries and push the boundaries westward."

Pope Borja pondered in silence for a moment. "I see where you're going," he said to the camerlengo. "But nothing's been discovered yet. We can't assume new discoveries until they happen. Meanwhile, we should monitor Columbus's voyage, and see if he brings results. I thank you, Camerlengo, for your wise thoughts and for trying to keep the peace between those two countries. Meanwhile, as a Spanish Pope, I must be careful how I tread between them lest I'm bound to favoritism. That would be a sin for the Pope."

With that last remark, Pope Alexander Borja raised his two fingers in the peaceful termination of his council.

31

feverish Pitch at Sea

Wednesday, October 3, 1492

STARTLING SEA SUDDENLY WOKE up from a long slumber and churned with foaming white-crested waves. The ships were scudding before the wind. Today the ships had bridged forty-seven leagues, but Columbus reckoned forty in his false log. As usual the *Pinta* and *Niña* would give him their readings to compare, and he would falsify those, too, to agree with his leagues. He must keep the truth from them a bit longer. Soon they were bound to see land. So far, they'd left behind many signs, coming from the north, of green weeds and many more birds and petrels. A seagull came to the ships, giving more weight to the evidence of land nearby. He had marked these presumed northward islands behind them on his map, but the ships had to go forward south-southwest. Now the ships were also speeding with the winds being favorable to them. He knew and sensed the Indies were near.

He checked again his previous readings on the astrolabe, and they seemed accurate for this quadrant of the sea, and for their position in leagues. They were now closing in on the seven hundred leagues he'd estimated to arrive at the Indies. He looked over Martin Behaim's sheepskin chart where the distance for the Indies lay, and was satisfied that they were nearing it. From the island of Hierro, where their voyage began, a series of pinholes had been pricked on the chart. He then pricked another hole on the chart at the corresponding distance. Next, he directed his attention to Zacuto's tables, *Almanach Perpetuum*. The tables instructed Columbus to follow the sun's rise and setting with the movements of the stars to measure lunar and solar eclipses. By converting time into arc, he would come up with longitude or distance in leagues from point of departure to the Indies. Next to Zacuto's tables was his most prized possession, a copy of *Imago Mundi*, by Pierre d'Ailly where he had made important notes for the voyage in the margins. From this source came the conception for this voyage into the great unknown—to go forth and find the Indies.

Compline had started, when he heard the *ampolleta* ship boy call out the half hour of eight thirty. He got up from his creaky wood bench by the table and went to genuflect in front of Jesus's crucifix on the wall. His lips moved quietly as he prayed while listening to Pedro de Acevedo, his able helper, ringing the bell repeatedly on the quarterdeck for Compline prayers. Since boyhood, Columbus had been taught to observe these hours and the prayers for silence during the night. Saint Basil the Great had instituted the hour, emphasizing spiritual peace till morning. By then Tierce service began between eight and nine o'clock.

He closed his eyes and again that same vision of a woman calling him startled him. *What did it mean?* Before he had the chance to give it anymore thought, a knock on the door was heard.

He got off the floor with some difficulty and went to open it. Salcedo, flanked by his boatswain, Bartholomé Garcia, stood before him. "Admiral, may I speak with you?"

"You know that after Compline I adhere to silence till morning, unless there is cause for speech."

"There is cause, Admiral. I came to you before about the food situation, and I come to you again about it."

"Come in, Bartholomé."

"Our food supplies are now dangerously low. I tried to keep it quiet from the men, but they see everything." He stopped there as if to prepare him for the worst. "We're almost finished with all dry meat. We used the last sardines today. We still have anchovies left for another week or so. There's also plenty of flour left for bread and garlic too. Salt biscuits are still plentiful."

Despite his vow of reverence and silence for the hour, Columbus began laughing hard. When he finished laughing he said, "Then we are blessed! We're better than all the beggars on Seville's streets. Tell the cook not to worry so much and get a good night's rest."

"But, Admiral," Bartholomé protested, "the men are saying such awful things about you and the food. They're saying you're eating too much and they have so little."

"Then tomorrow give them my rations, if that's what they want. Now go to sleep, old man!" Columbus commanded him.

Bartholomé stood frozen, then turned and left his cabin, and Salcedo closed the door.

Left alone, Columbus smiled at the past scene. *These men have no faith and no trust in my ability to steer them to a future filled with hope and riches. All we need is more signs for land.* He fell back to his knees and uttered a prayer. "Santo Christo. Give me the strength to be your bearer and the salvation of the faith. To bring all heathens to you, to baptize them in your name."

After he crossed himself, he lifted his sore, arthritic bones and went to lie down on his small and cramped bed. He tossed many times before falling asleep.

32

Quiet Days in Paradise

MIGUEL SPENT HIS DAYS WORKING for his master and benefactor in the vineyards, cutting wood for the kitchen and fireplaces in the many rooms of the house, and handling various other tasks for the estate. This morning he concentrated on splitting logs and adding them to the firewood pile. His forehead dripped with sweat from this early morning work, and the humidity in the forest oozed with sunlight through the conifer trees, offering a naturally lit cathedral. Above him yellow-throated warblers flew in the canopy between the cork oaks, pines, and old thuja firs, looking for their nested brood. Higher in the crested trees, a couple of eagles circled in and out.

He paused to take in the sights and wiped his face with his cotton wide-sleeved shirt, then went to take several sips from his water gourd hanging on a low branch. As he went to replace it, he saw a horse rider advancing at a slow trot toward him. Miguel put his hatchet down near a granite boulder rock and waited for the traveler to dismount. A quick glance revealed the traveler was a *fidalgo* by his rich attire of velvet, and brocade overgown, and breeches complemented by a silk vest and brimmed hat.

"*Bom dia, senhor*, how may I help you?" Miguel said.

The nobleman bowed his head. "Senhor, are you the owner of this estate?"

Miguel shook his head. "No, senhor, it belongs to my master Dom Fernandez de Carvalho."

"I'd like to talk to your master, young man."

"He isn't here at the present time, but you can talk to someone else. Please, senhor, follow me," Miguel said.

The traveler pulled on the reins, leading the horse behind Miguel, who was walking through the forest to a clearing that led to the sprawling estate on elevated ground. They both entered the grounds and approached the front of the house.

"Please wait here, senhor." Miguel turned to the visitor. He quickly went in to alert Ana, who was cooking in the kitchen. She raised her head from kneading her dough when she saw him.

"What is it, Miguel?" Ana asked him.

"There's a man waiting to talk to Dom Carvalho. He's waiting on the porch."

Ana wiped her hands on a towel and followed Miguel outdoors.

"I'm Ana, the manager of this estate, senhor. How can Dom Carvalho help you?"

The visitor bowed his head to Ana. "*Com muito prazer*, senhora. My name is Dom Joam do Allgarve. I represent the king's tax collector from Lisbon."

"Right now Dom Carvalho is traveling. What exactly is your request, senhor?"

Dom Allgarve hesitated to speak. "I'm . . . sent to collect taxes. We have no records of any taxes paid by Dom Carvalho."

Ana seemed perturbed, but she didn't let it show for long. "I'm sure Dom Carvalho has paid his taxes. I'll send an emissary to Lisbon to verify his payment to the king."

"But, senhora, the records do not show having paid taxes because there is no Dom Carvalho on the tax records."

This time Ana paled slightly. "I repeat, senhor. When Dom Carvalho returns, he will send word to Lisbon." With that she walked to his tied horse, turned around, then bowed to Dom Allgarve, who had followed her reluctantly. He mounted his horse and galloped away from the premises.

Miguel looked at Ana silently, not wanting to question her about what had taken place. "I will return now to my chores, but first I'll steal a kiss from Isabella," he said.

Miguel's comment made Ana smile with relief. "She's resting in the back garden."

Miguel ran to the back of the house and stopped to gaze upon Isabella seated on a wooden bench surrounded by rows of lavender, jacaranda blossoms, and calla lilies. She raised her head and smiled when she saw Miguel.

"You look beautiful in this setting, as in a painting." He lovingly kissed her lips.

She returned his kiss. "What took you away from your work?"

"A tax collector for Dom Carvalho."

"Why, hasn't he paid his taxes?" She laughed in her crystalline voice.

Miguel turned reticent. "Nothing for you to be concerned about, my jewel."

"Is there something you're not telling me?"

"How's the future mother of my child?" he asked with a contented smile while hugging her in his arms.

Isabella patted her tummy, where there was no visible paunch. "I'm feeling so much better. No more sickness in the morning and sleeping better."

"I know," he said with a mocking grin. "You don't snore lately."

She raised her hand to slap him gently on the face. "That isn't fair! You snore plenty!"

He was about to reply, when Ana made her appearance and approached her. "You must come in now, Isabella. Too much sun isn't good for you." She then fussed over Isabella, helping her rise from the bench.

Miguel said, "I'll leave you now, senhoritas, to get back to my work." He stole another kiss from Isabella's lips and returned to the forest. On his way back he mulled over the incident of unpaid taxes. *I hope Dom Carvalho paid his taxes, for our sakes and for the peace he gave us.*

33

Low Rumblings

Thursday, October 4, 1492

THEY'D BEEN SAILING NOW FOR twenty-five days, and the men were restless. There were many men assembled on deck, and low murmuring among the crew turned silent when Juan de la Cosa or Sancho Ruiz passed by them. Columbus noted the rumblings coming from his men and felt unable to alleviate their fears. *All I need now*, he thought, *is a rebellion on my hands.* He must distract them, give them extra food rations and wine. *But then, what good will it do if they run out of food completely?*

He went to look for Ruiz at the tiller. "Keep the course set westward."

"Yes, Admiral. I think it's best too. I've been seeing lots of petrels and a booby bird, oh . . . one of our boys hit the bird with a stone. I gave it to the cook."

Columbus smiled. "That will please the men, I'm sure." He then left to find his boatswain, Bartholomé Garcia. Bartholomé sat in the hold of the *Santa Maria*, counting the food crates. He lifted his head from his work as he saw him descending the rope ladder.

"Oh, Admiral. I was coming to see you."

"I don't want to hear any bad news, Bartholomé."

"I'm afraid I have no good news."

"All right. How many more days?"

Bartholomé hesitated at first. "Ten more days total, Admiral."

Columbus felt a chill go down in his bones. "You can cook the remaining chickens for lent this Friday. That'll put them in a good mood."

"Si, Admiral. It will appease their hunger for now."

"Meanwhile, give them an extra ration of biscuits today. And wine too."

Columbus then walked away to resurface on deck with Bartholomé behind him. At that moment, a white gull landed on the railing in front of the mainmast. One man standing and working nearby threw a serving mallet, hoping to catch him. Scared, the gull flew away. The mallet fell and disappeared into the waters, swallowing it up.

"Look what you've done!" Columbus screamed at him. "Wasteful! You'll be docked on your pay," he threatened him. "What's your name?"

"Pedro de Villa. Please, Admiral, I thought it'd be good for supper."

Meanwhile, the men stopped their work and gathered around Columbus and Pedro. They stood silent with grim faces.

Columbus hailed Diego de Arana, his master-at-arms who oversaw supplies, and who stood nearby, also attracted by the noise.

"Mark down one serving mallet on this man's account." Columbus pointed at Pedro. He then made his way up to the cabin as the men moved silently to let him pass. When he entered the cabin, he noticed his hands shaking and his legs weak. He tried to control the shaking, but had to sit down and collapsed on the chair. What was happening to him? Why should this incident affect him so? Why had he become so angry?

He suddenly sprang up from his seat and went to genuflect in front of the crucifix on the wall with his hands in prayer and his eyes searching for an answer.

"Dear God, I have sinned." He lowered his head. "I have mistreated this man badly. Please forgive my sin." His lips moved in prayer while reciting the *mea maxima culpa*.

I confess to almighty God
and to you, my brothers and sisters,
that I have greatly sinned,
in my thoughts and in my words,
in what I have done and in what I have failed to do,
through my fault, through my fault,
through my most grievous fault.

He then beat his chest three times.

Getting off the floor slowly, he walked back to his chair and sat down in front of his logbook. He wrote: *Today we have sailed at least fifty-three leagues.*

He reckoned forty-three in the second public logbook. *The sea is especially calm now, thanks to God. No weeds were to be found. I know and feel strongly that we're close to land.*

34

An Opened Door

L IFE CONTINUED WITH SLOW DAYS for Isabella and Miguel, culminating in peaceful evenings with Dom Carvalho's household members and with Ana's help. They had a room of their own with a balcony that overlooked the sea. Many times, Isabella sat in front of the opened French doors of the balcony, the woolen draperies drawn, enjoying the cool breeze coming from the beach. She was surrounded with comfort: carpeting in front of the heavy walnut bed; sheets and comforter made of fine linen; and Juanita's help with washing and dressing. Each morning, she would find Miguel had already risen early and was waiting for her in the dining room.

"Buenos días," Isabella told Miguel and Ana one morning as she sat down.

Miguel flashed a smile at her, and so did Ana.

"You're looking radiant, my dear," Ana said. "Motherhood becomes you."

"It's thanks to you, Ana, for taking care of Isabella," Miguel said.

Ana waved her right hand. "I'm only following Don Carvalho's orders. That's all."

"Nevertheless. I feel wonderful, thanks to you," Isabella insisted as she ate her gruel.

"And when will we see Dom Carvalho to thank him properly?" Miguel asked.

"He should be arriving next month, I'm told."

"I'm curious how he made his fortune," Miguel ventured. "I hope I'm not being impertinent."

Ana took a few seconds to reply. "Not at all. As a matter of fact, he's very proud to mention it whenever he gets a chance. He'll probably let it be known, especially to young men making their nests." A motherly smile appeared on Ana's lips.

"I'm sure Miguel will provide for all three of us," Isabella said as she patted her budding stomach.

Miguel said solemnly, "I will."

"Meanwhile, you, too, can take a break from life's hard living and enjoy yourselves."

Having finished eating, Isabella leaned against the table as she got up. "I will go into the garden now."

Miguel also stood up and followed her with loving eyes.

❧⊙⊙☙

When Isabella left, Miguel turned to Ana and observed her silently. After a few moments while trying to avoid his staring, she finally said, "All right, what's on your mind, Miguel?"

Miguel swallowed first, then said, "I know that we've met before, Ana. Do you remember me?"

Ana kept quiet. "Yes, I do," she finally said.

Miguel's triumphant voice rang out. "I knew I was right! You used to come to our house when my mother had those meetings, right?"

Ana nodded her head but didn't say anything.

"Weren't those meetings to organize a voyage for all Jews and Conversos?"

She nodded again.

"Come on, Ana." He urged her. "I used to listen in on those meetings, and I knew more than my mother wanted me to know."

"And what happened to your mother?" Ana asked suddenly.

Miguel felt his heart about to split in two. His eyes began to moisten, and he resisted shedding tears. "My mother died in Torquemada's dungeon!" His hands turned into fists.

Ana looked startled by the news. She began to weep. "Your mother . . ." she said between sobs, "was a courageous woman. She braved the authorities by having those meetings and by taking Isabella to Granada." She took a cloth out of her dress pocket and wiped her eyes.

"So you must've known about Isabella's kidnapping. I blame her uncle for that! He put her life in jeopardy and my mother's too."

"But your mother wanted to help. Your mother had vengeance in her heart for what they'd done to your father."

Miguel stayed quiet, remembering a buried pain.

"Besides, that's history now. You and Isabella were destined to meet, fall in love, and marry. That's what matters."

"Where is João now?" Miguel asked.

"I believe he left Palos last August on a voyage."

"The same voyage he convinced the men to take at that meeting?"

Ana nodded again.

"Did you know that my brother, José, is lost to me now?"

Ana startled. "I didn't know. What do you mean by lost? Where is he?"

Miguel told her how José had been left in Don Obrigon's care, and how they could not go back to Seville, with Guerida on the lookout for them. "That's why I must go back to find him," he said.

"You poor boy. You must miss your brother." Before Miguel could answer that new stirring pain in his heart, she said, "I'll have Dom Carvalho look into it. Going back, for you and Isabella, will be a disaster. You'll fall as easily into Guerida's hands as ripe plums."

"How did you get to know Dom Carvalho?" Miguel asked her suddenly.

"He's my employer, and that's all I can tell you now."

"Yet, he's been spotted for not paying his taxes?"

"That's all a mistake. When he returns, he'll get it all cleared up."

Miguel didn't reply. He felt a strange and pressing question on his mind. Why was Dom Carvalho being investigated? But for now, for him and Isabella, he planned to concentrate on living with this temporary peace and enjoy it while it lasted.

35

A Rebellious Gang

Friday, October 5, 1492

THAT MORNING, COLUMBUS WOKE UP with a slight headache. He rubbed his temples with his fingertips all the way down to the back of his neck, where his muscles felt stiff and tight. Walking to a jutting alcove from his cabin, he opened a curtain that revealed a chair with a hole in the seat and another hole in the floor exposing the sea beneath it. He relieved himself, then walked to the credenza holding a bowl with a jug of water. He washed his hands with soap, then splashed and rubbed his face and neck with the salty water until he felt clean enough. Afterward, he pulled on a bell attached at the top of the door that rang for Salcedo, his servant, sleeping on deck.

When Salcedo appeared in the door, Columbus waved him in. "You can bring me breakfast now."

Salcedo stood by without moving.

Columbus raised his voice. "Haven't you heard me?"

"Admiral . . ." He hesitated. "There's no food ready."

"What do you mean, not ready? Go and get me Maestre Diego right away!"

Salcedo hesitated again.

"What is it now?" Columbus felt ready to explode.

"Admiral, he's indisposed."

"Indisposed—what do you mean by that?" Columbus didn't wait for Salcedo's reply; he stormed out of his cabin and went down the steps to the main deck and up three more steps to the cook's corner. As Salcedo had explained, the fire in the sandbox wasn't lit, nor was there a cauldron containing food hanging above it as usual. He looked around him and saw the men still sleeping and snoring on deck. He ran down the hold to find his cook gagged and tied by chains to the wall. Poor Diego fought hard to free himself as he arrived.

"What's the meaning of this?" Columbus yelled.

Diego shook his head, unable to speak. Columbus ran to him and untied the bandana placed tightly across his mouth and nose. Diego panted and took a long breath.

"What happened?" Columbus asked again.

"I don't know, Admiral. The men went crazy and shoved me here last night! I don't know what's got into them."

"We'll see about that." Columbus began to rush out, when Diego called him back.

"What about my chains, Admiral?"

Columbus turned around and found the chains locked. "Where's the key?" he asked Diego.

"They have it."

"All right. You'll tell me all about it when I come back." With that he stormed up the ladder and surfaced on deck. He was surprised to see his men at work. *They sure got up quickly!*

"Stop what you're doing!" he bellowed to the crew.

Immediately they came from all sides of the ship, including his man in the crow's nest, as well as the ones perched on the shrouds. They all lined up, waiting for him to speak. From the corner of his eye, though, he saw João Treves, the man who had cornered him before, standing aside with three of his mates.

For a moment words failed him, then a torrent escaped his mouth. "We're on a voyage of discovery. The world hasn't yet seen the feats we'll accomplish! Now, if anyone on this ship would like to keep us from finding the new route to the Orient, the trade we'll reap, and the monies we'll earn, please advance forward and make yourself known!"

All stood in silence. A few turned their heads around to look for the bold one who might come forward, but no one moved outwardly.

"Anyone who would like to confront me with their complaint—now is the time!" Columbus scanned the faces in front of him, and in doing so he turned his back seaward, and saw the men also assembled starboard on the *Niña* and the *Pinta*, trying to understand why his men were standing at attention on his flagship, the *Santa Maria.*

He faced his men, and one in particular came forward. This man was a sailor chosen back in Palos by Martin Alonzo Pinzón, the captain of the *Pinta.*

"Speak!" Columbus said to him.

"I'm Rodrigo de Jerez, Admiral. The men here"—he turned around to catch the men's eyes, and they all nodded together—"are united in their fears. The fear that we will never find this land you're calling the Indies. We will sail forever until we are dead before we run into any land at all. Our skeletons will only tell the story of our demise." He stopped to look for a reaction from the admiral.

Columbus listened to him without a stir.

Rodrigo continued, "We've all agreed that we must turn back now."

"Listen again." Columbus's voice was quiet but strong at the same time. "We already have bridged six hundred leagues. We're very close to our goal and mission. God knows we're so close, I can smell a different air around us. I've been a sailor all my life since I was fourteen years old, and this air is different from all the other breezes I've breathed until now. I tell you, we're almost there. Trust me, I'm telling you the truth! If we don't find land in five to ten days, we'll turn around. We have enough food and water to sustain us for the voyage back." Columbus looked at the men standing silently to see if his words had swayed them. He was glad Diego was tied up in the hold and not bringing up the dwindling supplies.

"I say we wait a bit longer. We've come so far; let's continue." The man who spoke was his tiller man, Sancho, who stood aside from the other men confronting him. Sancho wasn't a noble or owner of any of the ships;

he stood to gain nothing but his pay for his services. The man was truthful and wise when it came to choose which decision would serve them all.

"I say we wait too," Francisco de Huelva said.

Another of his countrymen from Huelva, Ruiz Fernandes, said, "We wait."

"We must wait!"

Columbus looked at João, who had spoken. *I'm sure his reason is as valid as my own for reaching the Indies*, he thought with relief.

One by one the men came forward and lined up by Columbus to show support. He also recognized João's friends—Alfonso, Hernán, and Gomes—all hired in Palos and also through Pinzón.

Columbus tried to control his sigh of relief and said, "You're all wise to wait." He commanded them. "We'll have extra rations of wine for you tonight." He turned around to leave, then turned back and faced the men. "As soon as you release your poor cook, Maestre Diego."

The men roared in unison.

A weary Columbus returned to his cabin and breathed a deep sigh of relief.

36

Revelations

$\mathcal{A}$S THE NOON HOUR APPROACHED, Isabella leaned on the banisters on the front porch to look for Miguel, when she saw a black horse with its rider advancing toward the house. She wrapped the shawl tightly around her and waited until the rider came closer, then turning around she hurried into the house to call Ana, who was busy in the kitchen. She found her stirring a big cauldron of soup on the fire in the vast chimney.

Her pallor startled Ana. "What is it? Are you feeling all right?"

"I'm fine, but there's a traveler on his horse getting close the house," she said out of breath.

Ana dropped her ladle and ran to the front with Isabella behind her walking at a brisk pace. She cupped her hand around her eyes to see who was the new arrival, when she started laughing.

Isabella looked at her with relief. She always feared someone would chase her and Miguel, and she was ready to be arrested at any time.

"It's only the master, Dom Carvalho, returning home."

Isabella took a good look at him. She recognized the same man who had rescued them from the pirates at sea. He had a distinguished look with his white beard and colorful rich attire of brocade and silks. He wore a sword at his waist that rubbed against the flanks of his Arabian horse. No doubt he must be returning from Africa and his slave hideout, she surmised.

Dom Carvalho, in the meantime, had descended from his horse and kissed Ana with affection. "How is my dear cousin?" he asked Ana.

Ana looked furtively back to Isabella, but Dom Carvalho stopped her from speaking. "It's all right, Ana. There's no longer need to hide my true identity."

Ana nodded. "If that's what you want. I know these young people will keep your secret."

Isabella standing aside nodded at Dom Carvalho, but wondered what he meant by his comment.

"We will discuss this matter further when your young man is here with us. In the meantime, I'm thirsty for your cold *bissap* hibiscus drink."

Ana left them, and Dom Carvalho led Isabella into the house and to the sitting room. He gently held his arm around her shoulder.

"And how is the young, expectant mother?" he asked with concern and affection.

Isabella, hungry for paternal attention, responded in kind. "You're most gracious to have us in your beautiful home," she said to him with genuine admiration.

"Did you know I knew your father, Don Obrigon?" Dom Carvalho said. "He is an old friend of mine."

Tears came to Isabella's eyes.

"Now, now, I made you cry. Forgive me," Dom Carvalho said.

Isabella wiped her eyes on her sleeve. "Please, Dom Carvalho. You have nothing to be forgiven for. On the contrary, both Miguel and I are extremely grateful; you saved our lives. I'm sure my father will be, too, when he hears of your generosity."

"Let's adjourn to the dining room. I'm sure Ana is waiting for us."

Ana appeared in the doorway holding two goblets filled with red liquid.

"Thank you, Ana. Bring them to the dining room."

Ana followed them to the dining room and placed both goblets on the table. Dom Carvalho sat down and gulped down the refreshing drink. Isabella smiled at the way he relished the hibiscus drink with mint. She, too, had learned to enjoy Ana's drink.

"I've learned to appreciate this drink myself, and . . ." She stopped and questioned Ana with her eyes.

"Don't worry, your young man is on his way," Ana told Isabella with a smile on her lips.

At those last words, Miguel entered the dining room and went to bow down, then shake hands with Dom Carvalho. "I'm very pleased to see you back in your home, Dom Carvalho."

"You don't know how pleased I am to be back home, but sit down, sit down." He patted the seat next to him, and Miguel sat at his request. From across the table, Miguel smiled sweetly at Isabella. She returned the smile.

Ana left for the kitchen to bring in the food that she and Juanita had helped cook.

"As soon as Ana joins us, I'd like to talk to you all," Dom Carvalho said.

Isabella eyed Miguel, but he kept his eyes down to the table. Isabella wondered why Miguel wasn't making eye contact with her. Perhaps tact for the host was in keeping, she wondered. Nevertheless, she felt tightness in the pit of her stomach. What was so important that their host wanted to communicate to them? She took another sip from her drink.

"Here we are," Ana exclaimed as she entered the dining room, followed by Juanita laden with aromatic plates containing lamb, rice, flattened bread, and various other side dishes.

"It's as if I haven't left Granada," Isabella spoke out loud.

They all stopped serving to look at her.

Ana sat down and looked at Isabella with curiosity. "You must tell us everything you know."

"I'd rather not think about it," Isabella said.

Miguel raised his hand in the air. "This brings many sad memories for Isabella. She prefers not to dwell on them."

"I can understand your reluctance, my child," Dom Carvalho said with a soft voice. "In the meantime"—he rubbed his hands together—"let us partake of this delicious meal!"

They all ate silently; the tasty food placed on their plates appeased their hunger. Afterward, Ana called Juanita in, and Dom Carvalho waited until she put the empty dishes on a tray and left the dining room, closing the doors behind them at his request.

A sudden silence fell on the room as Dom Carvalho sat without stirring. He looked at all of them and said, "It's time you learned of my identity. Dom Carvalho is the name I took to hide my true identity." He paused for a moment. "I'm Don Isaac Abravanel, and I'm wanted both in Spain by the monarchs and here in Portugal by King John."

Both Isabella and Miguel let out a small cry of surprise and fear.

Don Abravanel—as Isabella now correctly thought of him—raised his hands in an arresting motion. "You have nothing to fear. You can remain in my home as long as you want. I must leave you, though, and join my family waiting for me in Naples. The authorities have already started their search and are getting closer every day now. But first . . ." He stopped then continued. "Let me assure you that I haven't committed a crime for them to seek me." He rested for a moment.

Ana sat silently, her features showing despair at her cousin's planned escape. She looked at her cousin and said in a trembling voice, "We'll take good care of your estate and lands."

Don Abravanel nodded his head. "I know you will, especially with Miguel here. I have all confidence that he can take over my duties on the estate."

Miguel also nodded his willingness to oversea the estate's daily operations. "I'll be your right-hand man."

"I know you will be," Don Abravanel said. "To get back to what I was saying. It all started when I was a close friend and confidant to the duke of Braganza, who was accused of plotting against King John II of Portugal. The duke was executed, and I believe he was innocent. This all happened a long time ago. But because of my association with him, I became a suspect and was accused of having connived with the duke. I was warned in time, and that's when I fled to Castile in 1483. I've also angered Queen Isabella, and written her a nasty letter. In it I poured out all my anger for the expulsion that she and Ferdinand orchestrated. I'm wanted by Spain and Portugal. Now I'm fleeing again from Portugal to Naples."

All three of them—Ana, Isabella, and Miguel—looked aggrieved. Isabella felt conflicting emotions.

Having escaped the Inquisition, she now had to fear Portuguese agents of the king lurking in the background. And what about Miguel and her unborn child? Will they suffer too?

"There's one more thing I want you to do for me, Miguel," Don Abravanel said. "I'm leaving behind the estate and my other businesses. Two of my ships have already gone to Naples and Venice. I'm leaving the third one to find and purchase more Jewish slaves in the markets of African countries."

"I'll help in any way I can," Miguel said. "But how am I to purchase them, and where do I transport them to safety?"

"Aha!" Don Abravanel raised his index finger and nodded his head at the same time. "I will leave funds in a safe to make the purchases. The young women and men purchased at the same time with you have been placed in good homes throughout Portugal. I will instruct you how to find those homes. For the new slave purchases, you will get an envoy bearing messages from Matigoro, my overseer in Morocco."

Ana spoke to Don Abravanel. "We'll carry on your charitable work."

"Thank you, Ana and Miguel. And now I must prepare myself for the lengthy voyage, my friends." A deep sadness veiled his face. "I'll miss very much this corner of Portugal."

He bent down to Isabella on his right and kissed the palm of her hand, then placed his hand on hers. "May the Lord protect you for an easy delivery." He then turned to Miguel. "Follow me into my study."

Miguel got up from the table and followed Don Abravanel outside the dining room.

Left alone, Isabella turned to Ana. "I'm worried about Miguel," she said in a low plaintive voice.

Ana got up and went to sit next to Isabella. "There's nothing to fear. I won't let anything harm you or your unborn child."

"I'm worried about Miguel," she repeated. "He'll be gone on those voyages where pirates may intercept his ship or . . ." She didn't finish her sentence.

"The ship he'll be taking is sturdy, and Don Abravanel has had mercenary soldiers working with him for years. They'll be armed to defend the ship."

Isabella didn't answer those comforting reassurances Ana put forward. She kept mulling over how she'd live without Miguel. Her chest felt tight, and she took a deep breath.

37

Three Ships Race West

Saturday, October 6, 1492

FOR THE LAST TWO DAYS, Columbus saw Pinzón sail one league ahead of the *Santa Maria*. He signaled for him to slow down and look out for the *Niña*. He refused. Pinzón had passed them once before, but then regained his place in the small flotilla. Juan de la Cosa had warned him before to beware of Pinzón, but Columbus disregarded the caution. Now Pinzón made clear his intentions: he'd be on the lookout and the first one to sight land.

His men on the *Santa Maria* felt the pitch of excitement generated by murmurs and betting on whoever spotted land first. The official reward for seeing this anticipated land was a silk doublet and ten thousand maravedís per year and for life.

The breeze was light, caressing the ship as an amorous partner. Petrels followed in the waters, some of them flying straight into the ship. Columbus sent a message on a line to Pinzón that their west sailing was making their voyage lengthier. Pinzón's reply came back in the basket through the pulleys: correct the course to southwest by west. *That is the course for Cipangu,* he thought. As attractive as this thought occurred to him, he rejected it. *There will be plenty of time to visit Cipangu. I will continue my course west.* He then stuck to his decision. He sat down and looked over his reckoning for the past two days.

His logbook recorded: *Thursday October 4. Today was a good day. We went thirty-two leagues.* Only twenty-five were reckoned for his men in his public book.

Friday October 5. Fifty-seven leagues we went with a good wind on the starboard quarter. Forty-five were reckoned in the public book.

Saturday October 6. Today we sailed forty leagues. Thirty-three leagues were reckoned in his public book.

He closed both logbooks and placed his secret book under his pillow, while the other one remained on his table. Working late into the night, he took out the copy of the travels by Marco Polo. He had thoroughly studied Marco Polo's descriptions of his voyage to Cathay. He looked over the margins where he had made notes, and according to Marco Polo, by sailing west he could reach the Orient and bypass the horn of South Africa. Columbus knew that if he closely followed Polo's recommendations, he was bound to touch the Indies.

He raised his head from his book and found himself transported as he softly pronounced with fervor the words, "The Lord saw fit for me to travel and find my destiny."

He then listened to the ampolleta boy turning the sandglass every half hour and a total of eight sandglasses to each watch. The young gromet announced:

"God help that passeth,
and good that cometh,
seven is here and floweth,
it shall be with God willeth,
that makes this voyage happeneth."

Then came the change of the watch. Both Sancho's and De la Cosa's voices came to his ears over the sound of the waves being parted by the ship, and over the rolling and pitching, as he knew they saluted each other on deck.

"Fourth place, fourth place, we sailors finished the fourth watch; wake up, wake up, wake up all," the gromet announced.

Another night had gone by, and Columbus had been awake till the wee morning hours. Feeling that his destiny was in the hands of God, he disregarded his lack of sleep and stepped out of his cabin into the morning sun.

38

Spies Gone

ISABELLA WOKE UP WITH AN oppressive feeling that was overbearing, and her gown was wet with sweat from the humidity in the room. She felt for Miguel, but he wasn't there. She got up, went to the commode in the room, poured water from the jug into the bowl and washed her face. She grabbed a towel and looked outside the open window into the sunshine while drying her face.

The gardens below were empty. The center fountain percolated its gentle waters with its dripping sound. Birds frolicked in the trough, washing themselves in the cool waters while calling to their counterparts that the water was fine. Neither Miguel nor any of the other workers were tilling or gardening the grounds. *He must've started early in the fields*, she thought. She changed to a fresh cotton gown and slipped on leather sandals.

The house was quiet except for slight noises coming from the kitchen. She followed the sounds to where Ana was kneading the dough for the day. Juanita was busy cooking the noon meal.

Isabella stood in the doorway admiring this tranquil scene, but underneath she felt unsettled.

Ana raised her head and smiled at her. "I didn't want to wake you so early."

"You should've woken me. I can't seem to find Miguel."

Ana wiped her hands on a cotton towel and came around the worktable. She put her right arm around Isabella's shoulders and led her away to the dining room. "I've prepared breakfast for you. You must eat if you want your child born healthy."

Isabella let herself be pampered and sat down at the dining room table while Ana served her cooked eggs, grain porridge, and a glass of fresh milk. She started to eat, then stopped suddenly.

"But where is Miguel?" she asked again.

Ana sat down next to her and said, "He had to go on a short voyage early this morning."

"A voyage?" Isabella said. "But where to?"

"Don Abravanel met with him at dawn and gave him instructions for the voyage."

"I don't understand," Isabella answered back. "I didn't know anything about traveling now. Miguel didn't even say good-bye." She felt a sudden panic, and her lips began to tremble, even though she tried to contain the tears on the verge of spilling out in a flood from her eyes.

"There's nothing to fear," Ana reassured her. "Miguel will return to you from this short trip and be with you again."

"And what will I do in the meantime? I feel completely useless in this household. You take care of me and I sit all day. I must do something to forget Miguel isn't here with me." Isabella took a long breath.

Ana took both her hands and said, "How about some light chores to do around the house?"

Isabella nodded and remained silent, almost brooding.

"Come on," Ana urged her. "It isn't healthy for your unborn child for you to be in a sullen mood."

Isabella didn't reply. Instead she reached for the freshly baked bread and began to eat with a pensive look.

"That's it!" Ana encouraged her. "You're now thinking of your child."

39

At Sea

MIGUEL STOOD AGAINST THE SHIP'S railing, his eyes fixed on the shore that diminished, then faded away from his sight. On that shore he had left Isabella still sleeping when he parted from her. He gently kissed her lips while her face squinted at the touch. Silently, he had walked backward to the bedroom's door as he kept her image in his memory.

He knew that Don Abravanel gave him this mission to oversee his operations in Morocco and the north African coast because he had trust in him. Miguel had to honor this trust. Above all, both Isabella and he owed a debt to this generous man. Miguel would now supervise Don Abravanel's operations to rescue and redeem Jewish slaves. He shivered thinking what would've become of them had they fallen into cruel Berber hands.

He turned away from the now-familiar sight of Portugal's coast to the job at hand. The vessel he was captaining was a small caravel with square sails that propelled the ship southeast toward Africa and Ceuta. He also knew, from his engineering and sailing studies, the current created by the strait would raise turbulent seas. Not only was he now a full-fledged mariner, he also had to learn fast how to command a ship.

He smiled at the thought of being a captain. He'd been suddenly propelled into this profession, and barely nineteen, he had climbed to the apex of a mariner. His mother would be proud to see him now. His eyes misted at remembering his mother's constant encouragement for him to acquire a profession. She made sure that Miguel wouldn't follow in his father's merchant occupation. She'd told both him and his brother José that their father had jeopardized his life and that of his family by bartering his wares in Granada.

"Raise the sails!" The shouts from the men tore him out of his reverie. He stiffened up and forced himself to see to his duties.

"Master Miguel?" his pilot, Fernando said. "We're close to the strait now. We need to brace ourselves for turbulence."

"Thank you, Fernando." Miguel tried to lower the tone of his voice. "Hey, um . . . make sure the bonnets are secured and properly folded. We'll need them in good sailing weather."

"*A la orden, mi capitan.*" Fernando left him for the tiller below the stern deck.

Ahead of the ship was one of the most feared straits advancing rapidly toward them.

40

Fears of Starvation

Sunday, October 7, 1492

THE SEA HAD NOW CALMED to a smooth mirror, and the men were turning morose again. Columbus noted that they were neglecting their chores and had to be told over and over to inspect the sails again for tears or loose rigging. He constantly relayed his displeasure to Juan de la Cosa with the effect of alienating the master and owner of the *Santa Maria*.

"*Almirante*, the men are truly tired of no news. They're also beginning to show signs of fatigue."

"I can't see why they're tired. Their chores are light: sew up tears in the canvases, clean the decks, and check the rigging."

"You seem to forget, Admiral, that their rations have been cut in half. They're not getting meat as before, and it's only biscuits and dry sardines. And we have water left for only another week."

Columbus received the news with a blow. *That can't be*! He must see to it that water would not run out. "Cut their rations of water."

De la Cosa stayed silent.

Columbus knew the men were powerless to rebel. Without water, no one would remain alive to make the voyage back. Sailing forward was their only choice; they would die going back. He controlled them. After all, wasn't he the admiral?

A bell rang on the main deck by the gromet calling all for Lauds prayers at the hour of seven thirty in the morning. The men slowly drifted to the center of the main deck and went down on their knees. Columbus led the prayers above them on the quarterdeck; and since they had neglected to bring a priest onboard, he officiated as their religious leader. "In the name of the Father, and of the Son, and of the Holy Spirit," Columbus began after making the sign of the cross.

"Amen," the men responded in unison.

"Glory to God in the highest, and peace to his people on earth. Lord God, heavenly King, almighty God and Father, we worship you, we give you thanks, we praise you for your glory."

"Amen," the men repeated.

"Lord Jesus Christ, only son of the Father."

"Amen," the men repeated again.

"You alone are the Most High, Jesus Christ, with the Holy Spirit, in the glory of God the Father. Amen."

"Amen," the men repeated in unison.

Columbus now prayed silently with his eyes closed, his lips moving with slow methodical opening and closing. He felt that each man assembled on deck prayed, too, with reverence, on his own. Columbus continued the silent prayer for ten minutes longer, when the gromet boy called the half-hour glass turn and broke his concentration. He opened his eyes and crossed himself again, then waited for the men to do the same. As each one got up from the deck's flooring, Columbus hailed them. "Wait!"

All faces turned to him on the quarterdeck.

"I want to announce that it's a matter of days or hours before we see land."

Grumblings were heard from a few mouths. The sailors, who had uttered low words of discontent, turned their back to him and looked at the sea.

"I know how much you've waited for the day when we touch land. I'm confident in the Lord that this hour is near." He saw a few men cross themselves.

"I beg your pardon, Admiral."

Columbus looked to the man who spoke. It was João.

"Speak," he urged him.

"We would like to know how many leagues we have done so far."

"Hear ya, hear ya." The comment came from many of the men on deck. João seemed to be leading them as he smiled to them.

"We have reckoned so far more than six hundred and seventy leagues. According to my calculations, when we hit seven hundred leagues, we're bound to see land."

"And if we don't?" The voice came from Gomes.

This man had done time back in Palos and had been pardoned by the queen to make this voyage. *If it weren't for his devotion to Queen Isabella, he might've done without him altogether.*

Columbus looked directly at him and said with a sure voice, "We will." His voice grew strong. He became animated and waved his arms in the air. "We're so close that I can feel it in the air, as the saltwater on my lips."

"How come we don't feel it or see it this way?" Gomes came back at him.

"Because I've been a mariner longer than you have and sailed many seas. That's where I draw my knowledge of those—" Columbus was interrupted by the sound of guttural squawks from a flock of birds. They were flying from the north and headed southwest.

"It's a sign!" one man screamed. "We're near land! They're flying south to escape winter!"

At the cry, all men went down again on the deck's floor and started praying.

Columbus felt triumphant. The Lord was aiding him in his hour of need. He, too, said a silent prayer from where he stood.

At that moment, the *Niña* and the *Pinta* sailed alongside to join them. The *Niña* had hoisted a flag at its masthead, and a Lombard was fired from its cannon on the starboard. The men on the *Santa Maria* hailed them by removing their caps and waving it at the ship. The *Pinta* remained silent, but her sailors came to the railing too and hailed them.

The remainder of the day was spent by all the sailors on the three ships looking for the first sign of land. Noon came and went. Vespers were read. Then Compline took place again on deck. So far, no sign of land was detected.

"Another false alarm," De la Cosa said to Columbus standing on the quarterdeck.

"I don't believe so," Columbus said. "But I know we're close now. Set a course for west-southwest." He then went into his cabin and sat at his table.

We have sailed twenty-eight leagues, he jotted down in his secret logbook. In the public book he reckoned eighteen. *The Niña fired a Lombard, but no land was seen yet. Soon we will see land.*

41

Morocco

HE *LIBERAÇÃO* GLIDED INTO THE Moroccan port of Tangier with her Portuguese flag hoisted on the starboard yard. Miguel waited for the goods and crates to be unloaded, and went down into the empty hold to check on the workers. He saw that all the wine jugs, sheepskins, and olive oil had been properly unloaded onto shore. He climbed back up on deck to find Lourenço da Sintra, his second in command, waiting for him.

"All cleared, Captain," Lourenço said.

"Good work!" Miguel said. "Now we wait for the goods to be loaded."

"I'll see to the merchants when they arrive."

"Thank you, Lourenço. We'll meet up with the ship in two days' time in the prescribed waters."

Lourenço nodded at the instructions.

Miguel left him and disembarked from the *Liberação*, then searched among the crowds. The din that greeted him coming from the docks caught his attention while he skirted crates and bales waiting to be loaded onto the ships nearby, and avoided the metal hooks swinging dangerously near him. He kept searching until he spotted Matigoro waving at him.

"I'm so glad to see you, Matigoro!" Miguel said, embracing him with joy.

"And I am pleased to see you too." He slapped Miguel's shoulders with a wide grin. "I wasn't sure if you'd make it to the end of your voyage. I see you're alive and well." Matigoro lifted Miguel's canvas bundle and flung it over his right shoulder. "Follow me," he told Miguel.

After navigating through the crowded bazaar and narrow streets, they arrived at a whitewashed building skirted by a wall surrounding the property. Matigoro led Miguel inside the building, where an old servant greeted them.

Matigoro addressed him. "Help our visitor to his room, Bernal."

"Please follow me, signor."

Miguel looked back to Matigoro who said, "Return back to the dining area."

Miguel nodded and followed Bernal to a comfortable room with a large bed, throw rugs on the floor, and a view of a back garden. He opened the doors to the garden and was surprisingly greeted by the scent of jasmine growing in profusion. *Ahhh, this must be paradise.* He reentered the room smiling at Bernal. "Thank you, Bernal."

After the servant left, Miguel washed the grime from his face with water from a bowl changed his clothes, and returned to find Matigoro seated at the table.

"Come," Matigoro urged. "You must be as hungry as a camel!"

Miguel laughed. "Thank you, but I was fed on the *Liberação.*"

As Bernal brought the traditional dishes of hot lamb and rice, Matigoro kept silent. When the doors to the dining room were shut on Bernal, Matigoro said, "Tomorrow, we'll make a purchase of slaves in the market. So eat and rest, my friend. We'll have a long trek through the desert tomorrow."

Miguel remembered his and Isabella's ordeal as they had walked through the hot desert to Matigoro's hideout. From there, his ship would pick up the slaves to deliver them to freedom.

"We're very lucky that we are under Portuguese authorities here in Tangier. We can trade in goods and slaves and live here peacefully."

Miguel said, "Is this why you decided to live here?"

"After we left Spain, I was contacted by Don Abravanel to find and purchase Jewish slaves caught by pirates."

"And we are extremely grateful to you and Don Abravanel for bringing Isabella and me to Portugal. Otherwise, I dread to think what would've happen to us."

"We were here for all Jews that were captured. We also try to help other non-Jews fleeing the Inquisition's snare as they, too, are escaping to Morocco."

"Who are these unfortunate souls?" Miguel said.

"There are many: gypsies, Moriscos, who are converted Moors persecuted by the Spaniards, and those who objected to the Inquisition on moral grounds and couldn't bring themselves to live in Castile any longer."

Miguel sat, struck by Matigoro's revelations. The cleansing and purity of España reached to the core of its citizens regardless of whether they were Jews or not.

42

Empty Days

SABELLA PACED THE FRONT PORCH up and down, then when tired she stopped to scan the horizon for Miguel. Three weeks had gone by, and no signs of the caravel appeared. She yearned for Miguel's touch and his presence near her in bed. Ana constantly reassured her that he would be back soon, but she still looked for any signs of ships on the horizon.

Since he had found out she was with child, Miguel had hovered over her with plenty of concern and affection. At night, alone in their bed, he had held her close until she fell asleep. The paunch growing steadily made the life growing inside her evident. She rubbed her hands against the small bulge in her abdomen when she felt movement. They were slight, single taps as if the child inside her was knocking to be let out. Marveling at this sign of life, she gently rubbed her abdomen again.

"You sweet little one," she said to it, and laughed out loud. "As if you can hear me."

Her thoughts immediately came back to Miguel "Why did he take this mission?" Isabella uttered. "Oh, *Dio*, now I'm talking to myself!"

She turned away from the porch and went to the kitchen, where she always found Ana.

Ana raised her head from the table and smiled at her. "Come and keep me company," she said.

Isabella came close to watch her line up clay pottery on the table. Ana then took a large wooden spoon and dished out a concoction from a large cauldron cooling off near the chimney.

"What are you doing?" Isabella said, intrigued.

"I cooked grapes with sugar and lemon, and now I'm putting this jam in pots to be sold."

"I never knew where the jams on my parents' table came from," Isabella said.

"We prepare these jams from the remnants left at the harvest. The best grapes go to Lisbon to be sold in the market."

"Please, let me help you," Isabella begged.

Ana hesitated for a moment, then pulled an apron from a cupboard, attaching it high around Isabella's bodice. "All you do is spoon the jam and fill the pots."

Isabella watched her and proceeded to help. Meanwhile, Ana turned her attention to the clay bowls on the table filled with blue grapes, dishing them into another cauldron hanging above the fire in the chimney. She then joined Isabella at the same task.

They worked in silence for a while, and Isabella turned to her. "Will Don Abravanel ever return to his estate?"

Ana looked her in the eyes. "He said his good-byes before he left. I don't believe he'll be returning at all."

"Why didn't he clear this matter of taxes?" Isabella asked.

"As you heard him, the taxes were a way to find him. King John's men tracked him down here, after finding out his true identity."

Ana caught Isabella trembling. "My dear child, are you unwell?"

Isabella didn't respond right away. She then said, "I'm also afraid we might be found out."

Ana began to laugh. "There's nothing to be afraid of or concerned about. You are far away from Castile, so they won't be searching for you here in this hideout."

Isabella did not feel reassured by Ana's words. She tried hard to erase the fear from her mind. She asked Ana, "Is Don Abravanel rich?"

Ana laughed hard this time. "My cousin is immensely rich. He owns ships in every port in Europe, has many estates, and is also a prince among princes."

To Isabella's baffled expression, she hastened to explain herself. "Our family is descended from the great King David." Again she stopped and smiled at Isabella's surprised expression. "The only thing is," Ana continued, "my family was poor, but my cousin helped generously."

Isabella remained silent while trying to digest the information.

"So no more worries about your safety. My cousin allowed us to live here indefinitely, and no one will find you or Miguel in these remote parts."

Isabella's thoughts returned to Miguel. She feared for his life on the high seas with pirates—or worse, with Guerida probably still looking for them. She concentrated hard on chasing away that ominous thought from her mind.

She took off her apron and turned to Ana. "I need to get some air."

"Go ahead. I'll call you at mealtime."

Isabella left Ana in the kitchen and returned to her post at the sea lookout.

43

Scents of the New Air

Tuesday, October 9, 1492

THROUGHOUT THE DAY THE MEN worked with a feverish pace but remained silent. They labored in short fits, now and then stopping to check the horizon. Back and forth communication with the *Pinta, the Niña,* and the *Santa Maria* went on intermittently. The men would raise their right arm with the left arm placed perpendicular to the inside of the right elbow if they saw anything that looked like a wisp of land. Its opposite—the left arm raised with the right forming a rectangular box—meant nothing had been seen on the horizon. Several times from the crow's nest on the *Pinta*, then on the *Santa Maria*, came a cry of land, but that, too, turned out to be thin lines of clouds or bird flocks flying near the horizon. Meanwhile, the ships were headed south by west, making slow progress.

Columbus then changed directions to head west by north.

He knew that the men were stretched with anticipation mixed with fear. They prayed inward and silently for land to allay their fears that death may be a possibility. Once or twice, he saw several men go down on their knees and pray with eyes closed in deep fervor. He also followed his prayer ritual among the men on the deck floor at sunrise with Lauds, morning prayers at seven, followed by Middies at twelve in the afternoon, Vespers evening prayers were conducted at five in the late afternoon, then Compline by seven in the evening. Each time, the gromet and ship boy turned the half-hour glass, Columbus made an extra short prayer that the next half hour might bring the coveted announcement.

As he said the last word for Compline, he heard a commotion followed by hundreds of birds chirping and flying above ship.

"Admiral, Admiral, we're near! We are!" The voice of his cabin boy rang in his ears.

Columbus got off the deck floor and followed the birds with his eyes. They were headed in a west-southwest direction. He went to look for Juan de la Cosa at the tiller's nook.

"Tomorrow I want to head west-southwest throughout the day. I feel and sense we should stay in that direction. I know now we're near. I can smell the air of land."

De la Cosa looked at him strangely as if he had gone a little mad. *No matter, they can think whatever they want.* He knew he was right in his calculations. Land was near. He went up to his cabin and opened his logbook.

Today we made some progress of eleven leagues and fifteen by seven o'clock, and we still have the night for approximately twenty-six leagues.

For his men's measurements, he reckoned seventeen leagues.

He closed the logbook and called Salcedo into the cabin. His servant helped him remove his overgown and undress to his linen gown, and pulled his boots off.

"Thank you, Salcedo," he said.

After Salcedo closed the door to the cabin, Columbus got into bed. Throughout the night he felt at ease as he heard the squawking of birds flying constantly over the ship, and the sleep that usually eluded him till the early morning hours came quickly, and he fell sound asleep.

44

An Expected Sight

AFTER BREAKFAST THAT MORNING, ISABELLA made her way to the front porch and sat down on the wooden bench for her watch. For the last week, she'd been standing at attention throughout the day to spot any sign of the ship. Ana tried to convince her that no matter what, the ship would come and she'd see Miguel. But Isabella refused to budge.

"I want to see the first sign and prepare myself to greet him."

"My dear Isabella," Ana said. "He'll come to you as soon as he disembarks."

Isabella still shook her head and prepared for the long watch.

"You'll make yourself sick that way. Come into the house or sit in the back garden. I know you enjoy it."

Isabella didn't reply. She stared at the ocean, her hands gripping the porch's wooden banister.

"All right," Ana said, resigned. "I'll bring your meal as planned, like yesterday."

Isabella turned her head toward her. "Thank you, Ana." She looked at Ana disappearing into the house and returned to her contemplation of the ocean.

How vast and powerful is the ocean, she realized with some fear mixed with awe. Miguel must cross these leagues to get to her without falling into the hands of nefarious pirates or Castilian ships in those waters. Her thoughts went back to her father now protecting José from Guerida's men. Someday, when events permitted, she would return with Miguel to visit them. But wouldn't it be dangerous or forbidden for her to return to Spain?

She shivered under her light silk dress even though no winds were blowing yet for October. Portugal seemed to have similar weather to her native Spain, she noted. Heat waves may last well into the fall season. She looked up again to the sea and saw the same line at the horizon, as straight as a thread. No clouds marred its rigidity, except . . . *no, that can't be*?

She strained her eyes toward that line breaking now and then until she saw a small dot. *Must be a bird*, she thought. She concentrated on that growing dot until it became clear with masts and sails. She got up with anxiousness and called for Ana.

"Come here, Ana. Come here!"

Ana ran out, her face expressing fear that something had happened to Isabella. "What is it?"

"The ship! I told you—there it is!" she cried excitedly at Ana, and went to kiss her on both cheeks.

Ana laughed hard. "Don't you get all worked up. It may be another ship."

"No. It's Miguel. I know."

The wait now became unbearable for Isabella. She ran into the house and changed into another silk gown. This one was loose and didn't show her figure. She hurried back outdoors to regain her watch place.

"Now, young lady. There will be another two or three hours until this ship comes close enough for anyone on boat to come ashore. We can eat our meal in the meantime."

"No. I'll eat right here."

"All right. I'll have Juanita bring you a tray." With that Ana reentered the house and shortly sent Juanita with a tray of food and drink. Juanita laid it on a small table and served Isabella.

"Thank you, Juanita. I'll be fine now. Please go back in the house."

Juanita looked at her hesitantly, then turned around to attend to her chores.

Isabella ate her food slowly, without losing sight of the approaching ship. A small breeze began to blow, and she hoped it would propel the ship faster to her.

The ship now appeared closer on the horizon with its tall masts, and Isabella jumped to her feet with a pounding heart. When the sailors on the ship became visible, a rowboat was lowered and many came down. Tense, Isabella paced the porch. One of the men on the boat waved at the house near the shore, and she knew it was Miguel!

Before long, he was running toward her, embracing and showering her with kisses. She laughed wildly and returned his kisses. "I was so afraid . . . you wouldn't come back!" she said with an admonishing voice.

"Well, I'm here now." He held her tight. He then looked down at her abdomen with surprise. "I thought you'd be as big as this house," he teased her.

Isabella blushed. "I *am* big. It's the dress that's loose."

"Now, don't I get a kiss too?" Ana's voice came through as she stepped out on the porch.

Miguel ran to her and kissed both her cheeks. "I missed all of you," he said. "I consider this my home now."

"You are home," Ana said. "Come inside. I want to show you something." Her face was mysterious.

Intrigued, they both followed her into the sitting room and watched her retrieve a document from a desk. She waved it in the air. "This document signed by Don Abravanel provides handsomely for you and Isabella to remain on this plantation for the rest of your life."

Isabella didn't understand. She turned to Miguel, who looked confounded.

"But why? We're no blood relatives of Don Abravanel," Miguel said.

"True," Ana replied. "But Don Abravanel has immense fortunes and is always willing to help his brothers and sisters in need. He wanted to provide for you and Isabella. You'll supervise all his operations here in Portugal as he instructed you, and you'll benefit from the income from the proceeds of the land."

Miguel looked stunned. Isabella went to him and gently grabbed both his arms. "We have been blessed by the God of your fathers, and mine too," she added. "We can live now without fear or having to flee constantly for our lives."

Miguel didn't seem convinced. He grabbed the document from Ana's hands and read it. He looked stunned. "He bequeathed us the whole estate, the lands around it, and the *Liberação* too."

"Of course, this windfall includes me." Ana laughed. "One share is for my old age and to remain with you in this house."

Miguel stepped out of his daze. "Of course. You're also our benefactor. It's your home too."

"This is a cause for celebration," Isabella said.

"I'll bring wine right away." Ana left the room.

Miguel looked at Isabella and went to hold her.

"We can grow old in this beautiful house and never worry again about anything."

"Yes," Isabella said. "We can bring your brother to live with us, and maybe my father too."

They both sat down on the divan, their hands clasped while a great sense of peace descended upon both of them.

45

A New World

Thursday, October 11, 1492

FTER THE HOUR CALLED BY the gromet and the morning prayers, the men began their daily routine on the *Santa Maria*. The decks were washed with saltwater, sailors climbed to the bonnets on the masts to inspect them for tears or unraveling, and the rigging was checked and rechecked. Their first course to the west went at the rate of five miles per hour as the wind propelled the sails. A few of the men sat right on deck sewing and repairing holes in the sails, while others threw a net overboard to catch some of the petrels swimming around them. This idyllic and peaceful scene seemed satisfying to Columbus.

Columbus stood on the quarterdeck, feeling confident as his intuition assured him they were near land. He had already taken various measurements following breakfast, and they coincided with his projection that shores were beyond the horizon, when he overheard low voices rising from the lower deck below him. He glanced down over the railing to see and hear three of his sailors working on mending the sails. Columbus stood silent and unseen by his men while their voices came up to him.

"We're in for trouble," one sailor said as he grabbed a roping needle from the tallow bullock's horn. "Mark my words; we're headed for our graves."

The other sailor sitting next to him on deck stopped threading his needle with hemp thread, and shrugged his shoulders. "The way I see it, we either die or return home. We need to face the admiral."

"Who's going to do that? I'll be thrown in chains and starved in the hold."

"Nobody's going to throw you in the hold! You'll be dead long before that!" The third sailor laughed with a roar.

Columbus then noticed João joining the threesome working on the sails and sat on the floor near them. João watched them repair the sails and joined them in the work. He grabbed a torn sail and cut away a patch from the canvas fabric with a crude pair of scissors. He then fashioned a square piece from another piece of fabric, then placed it on the hole in the canvas. He sewed it quickly, finishing the work with speed, then cut away the damaged area from the other side of the sail, leaving a single layer of strong cloth with just an overlap.

The men around him stopped their work to watch him.

"By *Santiago*! You can make a fast patch. Where'd you learn that?"

"I've been a sailor all my life," he quietly said.

"You're João, aren't you?"

João nodded.

"What do you think about our end, João? Is this the end of life for us?"

João hesitated to speak at first. He then calmly said, "Perhaps we're headed in the right direction. I can tell by the air, the birds, and the current."

One of the men whistled. "You sound sure of yourself."

João shrugged. A commotion on deck prevented him from answering. Ten of the men suddenly stopped their work and went to face Columbus, who was standing on the quarterdeck and looking in the distance.

"Admiral? Admiral?" they called out to him. "We want to speak to you." The voices were strong and sure. The men put their hands on their hips and nodded in each other's direction.

Columbus looked down at the men assembled below. "Who wants me?" he asked, searching the three rows of men looking up at him.

"Admiral. We're tired of sailing. We need to turn back," one of the men ventured forth.

"We're sick of this long voyage!" said another.

"Aye, aye. We are!" all the assembled men cried in unison.

Columbus didn't say a word to them. He crossed his arms and shook his head.

De la Cosa had joined the conversation on deck and tried to order the men back to work.

"No!" Columbus ordered him. "Let the men speak!"

João, who had kept silent till now, faced the men. "I for one say we push a little longer." He looked up at Columbus, who dropped his arms alongside his body in surprise.

"Yeah! I, too, say we continue. We may be dead either way. At least I want to know what's on the other side!" This was one of the men working on the sails.

The men facing Columbus retreated due to the contradicting comments coming from their mates. They paced silently.

"Listen!" Columbus shouted down at them. "It's no use complaining. I know we've reached the Indies, and with God's help, we'll be there shortly"

"How can you be so sure, Admiral? We been hearing it for weeks!"

"You must trust me! Remember the riches and gold we'll discover!"

The men below grumbled.

"To prove to you that we're near, you'll get double rations tonight. Why would I do that unless I was sure?"

More grumbles were heard.

"You can also have double rations of wine too."

At that announcement the majority of the men cheered, while a couple of them stood aside discontented. The crew quickly forgot their objections to the voyage.

"All right!" Columbus said. "Get back to work. I want volunteers to keep an all-night vigil for any signs, any signs," he repeated. "For land, birds, or anything out of the ordinary to report to me or your captain right away."

A sailor shouted from the *Pinta*. "Admiral, Admiral!" The voice was faint, but the rest of the crew on the *Pinta* had assembled alongside the starboard facing the *Santa Maria*. One sailor brandished a stick above his head that they clearly saw to be a fashioned tool.

"Admiral! Here!" Another man from the *Santa Maria* this time pointed to a mass of land grasses under the surface of the water.

The *Niña* sent another call to the *Santa Maria*, brandishing another stick covered by barnacles.

Columbus crossed himself. The Lord was sending these messages to them not to turn around and face a sure death.

"We begin the watch now. The first one who spots land receives a reward of ten thousands maravedís per year!"

The men below cheered, throwing their caps in the air. A feverish pitch followed, each man rushing to finish his chores and be on the lookout. When supper was served, the men ate standing up, disappearing now and then at the poop deck hole when nature called.

After sundown, many of them were exhausted by the day's tribulations. With eyes tired from being fixated on the horizon and sometimes from the hallucinations that made them think they'd seen land, the men began to drop one by one. They looked for their favorite spot on deck and fell asleep on their blankets.

The remaining die-hard creatures were Columbus himself and Juan Rodrigo of Triana in the crow's nest on the *Pinta* sailing close by starboard. Juan de la Cosa was at the tiller, his head emerging now and then to take a peek into the darkness. They had now sailed twenty-seven leagues by sunset, and had bridged ninety-two miles.

Columbus went down the deck to speak to Juan. "Adjust the course to west as before."

Juan looked up from the tiller's hole. "Aye, aye, Admiral."

He then left Juan for his watch post on the quarterdeck. He felt tired and sleepy, when the *Pinta* sounded their Lombard.

Columbus squinted but saw nothing in the darkness of the night. Only the stars above him shone and twinkled. It might've been a false alarm. By ten o'clock under a quarter moon, he stood on the stern-castle and thought he had seen a light. He rubbed his tired eyes, and the light was gone. It suddenly reappeared as a small wax candle and as a candlelight flickering on and off. He looked up to the crow's nest and heard no reaction from

Fernando. *Probably asleep?* Columbus grumbled. He went to wake Pero Gutierrez, the steward of the king's dais, who sailed on the *Santa Maria*, and asked him to come to the lookout.

Pero looked into the dark night and saw nothing. He then screamed, "Yes! Yes! I see something!"

They both looked for Rodrigo Sanchez of Segovia, the comptroller sent by Ferdinand to supervise the gold they hoped to find, and who was deeply asleep.

"You must come with us," Columbus ordered him.

Rodrigo rubbed his eyes, got off his blanket with slow movement, and followed Columbus to the watch post on the quarterdeck. He looked for a while and said, "I see nothing."

"Come on!" Columbus prodded him. You must see it! Pero did and so did I."

In the darkness, a light flickered again like the flame of a wax candle going up and down—this time seen by all three of them.

"Wake the men!" Columbus ordered.

The men staggered on a dark deck, their eyes still filled with sleep. After a number of minutes, when the word traveled through the ranks that land had appeared, all hands on deck were now awakened, all speaking at once, excited and energized.

Columbus spoke to the assembled men. "You'll now witness the most wondrous event in all your lives. Land is awaiting us!"

Even though Compline hour had passed, Columbus felt an additional prayer was necessary. He went down on his knees and sang the *Salve*. "*Salve Nobilis Regina, fons misericordiae . . .*"

The men crossed themselves, repeating after him. After the prayer, the watch began in earnest. Silence reigned on deck, a cough sounding now and then, followed again by silence.

By two o'clock in the morning, by the ampolleta, a faint line appeared on the horizon.

"Take down the sails!" Columbus's voice trembled as he spoke, his words strangled. "But leave the mainsail on. *No need to crash so close to land.*"

"Heave to!" Columbus ordered the vessel to sail close to the wind with her sails adjusted. The vessel rolled and pitched in a laying-to position and in silent waters. The men down on deck kept their vigil by the stern's forecastle, checking the horizon for telltale signs of land.

A voice suddenly pierced the darkness.

"¡*Tierra*! ¡*Tierra*! Land! I see land! Admiral, Admiral, land ahoy!" Juan Rodrigo de Triana's hysterical and excited voice came across from the crow's nest on the *Pinta*. Shortly afterward the *Pinta* fired a Lombard, bringing all the men to attention. They all ran forward starboard and held their breath as the faint line on the horizon grew into light sandy beaches reflected by moonlight, and with palm trees and flocks of birds flying from their heights. Each man on deck gripped the rigging, the mizzenmast, and ratlines on the shrouds, holding silent and mesmerized while all three ships lay to, close-hauled, and there they waited until dawn.

Columbus, standing on the quarterdeck, was struck by an overwhelming thought and his legs went weak: *At this precise moment they were leaving behind an old world and standing on the cusp of a new dawn!*

Friday morning, on October 12, the land appeared in all its glory. The rising morning cast a luminescent light, bathing the land before them as it revealed a beach of pure white sand and a profusion of emerald palm trees framing the beach. From high on the quarterdeck, Columbus saw a small village with hut roofs in a distant clearing among the trees.

A crowd of naked men suddenly appeared on the beach, as naked as their mothers bore them, talking and gesturing toward the ships.

"We're going ashore!" Columbus gave the order that went to the other ships too.

Columbus went down the Jacob's ladder into his boat along with his men armed with crossbows and *espingardas*—the muskets fashioned from a bronze tube attached to a wooden stock. After them, Martin Alonso Pinzón and his brothers, Francisco Martin Pinzón and Vicente Yanez Pinzón, followed him with their men from the *Pinta* and the *Niña*.

Columbus then raised a royal standard with the royal initials of F and Y for Ferdinand and Ysabella, while the natives retreating from the beach watched behind the palm trees. Two other banners brought onshore by Pinzón and Vicente were raised with the green cross in the name of

Christendom. He then gave the sign, and everyone went down on their knees to say Mass and thank God for his mercy and salvation that brought them to the island.

After the prayers, Columbus stood and called his master-at-arms. "You may now distribute our gifts to the people."

The crates were opened, and the naked men and women rushed from the line of trees with curiosity to see what they were doing. Colored glass beads, mirrors, red caps, and hawk's bells were given away to the natives. They first looked at them and screamed in delight to see their reflections in the mirrors. The women tried to adorn themselves with the glass beads as well as the men and attached them to string around their necks and ears. They placed the caps on their heads and took them off over and over. They delighted as children with the bells and were greatly pleased.

Columbus noted their handsome features similar to the Guanches of the Canaria Islands—Their skin color was darker than the Spaniards and the rest of Europe, but lighter than the Africans from the western seaboard. Their hair was coarse like horse's hair, and short, straight, and black, except longer in the back and over their eyebrows. Their foreheads were flat and high. Some natives painted their faces or bodies in white or red. They were not carrying firearms. All were young, no more than thirty years of age, with well-built and healthy bodies. Women were beautiful and also naked. A little girl was the only child on the beach. The Indians were very poor, but they gave Columbus and others some cotton balls, shells, and carved wood trinkets.

Columbus noticed, too, that the natives had only spears carved from wooden sticks to a sharp point. One Indian came close to Pinzon and touched his sword.

"Show them your sword," Columbus told Pinzón.

Pinzón detached his sword from its sheath and showed it around. One of the natives pulled the sword with his hand and cut himself on the sharp blade. He stood motionless, watching his red blood run on his hand.

"Mynu! mynu!" the Indian yelled.

"He must be saying 'blood,'" Pinzón said as he pulled back the sword from the Indian's reach.

Columbus also noted a few men with scars on their bodies that were healed. He called Luis de Torres, his interpreter.

"Ask them how they got those scars."

Luis de Torres approached one of them. "*¿De dónde sacaste esta cicatriz?*"

The native man looked at de Torres with a blank look on his face.

De Torres then pointed to the scar on his side below the ribs and repeated his question.

The native man became excited talking in a gibberish tongue that no one from the Spanish side understood.

"*Carib! Carib! Taino pyrywa kyto! Moco bouroulourebo!*" he yelled as he pointed east. After a few moments he tapped his chest with the word *lucayos*. Extending his arm in a semi-arc motion he said, "*Guanahani.*"

"It seems a people called Carib came to their island and inflicted those wounds," De Torres said.

Columbus nodded and remained pensive. Meanwhile, the natives encircled Columbus and came close to him. They observed him up and down and looked in his eyes, then touched his red hair. He tried to remain still with a smile on his face. One of the natives speaking in his own tongue pointed into the distance, to which another native ran to their round huts.

I hope I didn't scare him.

"Rodrigo Escobedo and Rodrigo Sanchez?" Columbus called his royal secretary and his comptroller for his fleet. "Write these words down. Know that you're my witnesses, that I've taken possession of this island for the sovereigns."

"On this blessed day in the year 1492 of our Lord, Friday, October 12, we have found the Indies and one of its islands called Guanahani by their natives. I take possession for the crown of Spain and name the island San Salvador. We have also found many friendly Indians.

"My wish is that they might feel our great friendship, and I know that they would be converted to our faith by friendship rather than by force. The Indians are friendly and gave us the little they possessed. They are intelligent, saying quickly what is said to them. I believe they will make good Christians and have no religion that we observed. At the time of our departure, if it pleases the Lord, I will take six of them to Your Majesties so that they may learn our language. No beasts are seen on the island, except for a dog or two, who did not bark, and many parrots. These are my words for this blessed day, where we found salvation from our Lord," Columbus concluded.

The secretary and the comptroller put their quill pens away and rolled the parchment to be quickly dispatched to the queen when they first touched land in Spain.

"We will now go back to our ships," Columbus said to everyone.

46

The Slave Market

MIGUEL WOKE UP AT DAWN, unable to sleep with the humidity in the room. He parted the white mesh curtains around his bed and went to look out of the window. The village was waking with the sounds of roosters, then with camels and mules braying nearby. He found his situation and good luck extraordinary. A short time ago he had been a slave about to be purchased, and now he was a purchaser of slaves and endowed as the captain of a sizable merchant ship. At the age of almost nineteen, his fortune was made. Isabella and he were indeed lucky to have found Ana and Don Abravanel. He finished dressing as these thoughts ran through his mind.

"How's the captain this morning?" Matigoro's voice startled him as he entered the room.

"I'm ready," Miguel said.

"We ought to leave now. Breakfast should wait," Matigoro said.

"That's fine. I'm not hungry yet," Miguel replied.

After adjusting their camel mounts, they led them through the narrow streets of Tangier, being the first buyers arriving at the market. No slaves were displayed, nor market goods in the vendor stalls.

Miguel leaned forward on his camel and was surprised not to see Berbers roaming the alleys or in the marketplace. He was further astounded to see Portuguese merchants trading with a few Muslim slave owners.

Matigoro watching him, smiled at his puzzlement. "Portugal has controlled this city for more than seventy years. You can feel at home now without Spaniards."

"I'm pleased."

"We'll wait here until they begin," Matigoro said.

Miguel nodded and looked around him at the people busy in their open stalls, preparing to display their wares. Colorful pottery dominated all the other products such as skins, sandals, caftans, and rugs. Beads and jewelry were guarded, with entire families looking out for robbers.

In a stall, across the plaza, Miguel detected a man in a Spanish, military uniform, scrutinizing the crowds. He then made a gesture that brought back painful memories from the past. This man was none other than Guerida!

Miguel turned to Matigoro. "Watch out for the uniformed man standing across the plaza," Miguel said in a low voice. "I believe it's Inspector Guerida."

Matigoro turned pale. He said, "Let's move away from the plaza where he can't see us."

Miguel wrapped the white shawl he wore around his neck to cover part of his face. He followed Matigoro, leading the two camels away from the marketplace, and positioned himself behind the building.

Miguel spoke low. "What's he doing here?"

Matigoro shrugged his shoulders. "Perhaps he's looking for renegades or Jewish slaves that escaped him back in España."

"Why would he want them?" Miguel's voice came up with anger. "Isn't it enough they were driven out of their homes—now he wants them back?"

"No. That's not what he's after. He's probably looking for Conversos or New Christians marked by the Inquisition, who may have escaped on the ships." Matigoro looked at Miguel with insistence.

Miguel looked back at him. "Why are you looking at me?"

Matigoro nodded. "Miguel, I know your mother was baptized and accepted Catholicism to save you and your brother. I was part of the rebel group, remember?"

Miguel lowered his head, remembering too well when their mother sent them to Conchita's house. He had caught a glimpse of the men and women arriving at their home, some wearing a cross, while others wore the cursed red star on their sleeves.

"Don't worry," Matigoro said. "He can't do anything. Even though Portugal rules Tangier, he is a Christian stranger among the Berbers and Muslims."

"I don't— "

Miguel heard noise and sounds of feet walking toward the market in the plaza. From one of the streets a column of African men and women following behind came to a stop in front of the vendors and men waiting for purchases. Those slaves looked tired and scrawny, perhaps starved and driven by the whip.

Matigoro said, "We won't be purchasing any Jewish slaves today."

"Wait!" Miguel said. He had noticed that one slave in particular hid his face in his *bournous* hood, looking down at his feet periodically. There was something familiar about the young man and his mannerism in wrapping his cloak around his body.

In a flash Miguel recognized his cousin Avram Beneluz. Confounded by the discovery, he turned to Matigoro. "We have a problem."

Matigoro raised questioning eyes.

"You see the young man at the end of the third row, on the left?"

Matigoro looked in the direction Miguel pointed. "What about him?"

"That's my cousin Avram Beneluz."

Matigoro fell silent. He then said, "This *is* going to cause a problem."

A loud voice rose from the market. "Today we have strong and young bodies to work in your houses and fields. Who'll give me ten dirhams."

The sale of slaves had begun, and he and Matigoro stood by the sidelines.

"We can easily slip him through by distracting Guerida," Matigoro said.

"How?"

"Wait here," Matigoro said. He left him and disappeared into a nearby house. He reappeared shortly with a young Moorish boy.

"You do exactly what I tell you," Matigoro told the boy. The young boy nodded and ran toward the market, then veered to the stall where Guerida stood. He approached him and tugged at Guerida's sleeve, while his other hand begged for *backsheesh*.

Guerida first ignored him, but when he became insistent, he flashed the boy a whip. Suddenly the marketplace became silent. All heads turned to Guerida and the boy, who was crying and holding his arm.

A Berber man walked up to Guerida, addressing him. "Why did you whip the boy?"

Guerida first looked him over. "I didn't whip him. He pestered me for money."

"You shouldn't have whipped him," the man replied.

"I tell you, I didn't whip him. Look at his arm—there's no mark there!"

The Berber grabbed the boy, who was still crying, and uncovered his sleeve. The Berber man took one look and called out for everyone to hear, "The boy has a slash mark on his arm!" He turned to Guerida and said accusingly, "You're a lying man. You're a guest in our land and you whip our children!" The Berber's voice bellowed at Guerida, who shrank away from the tall and furious figure.

Many other Berbers came close with anger showing on their faces. "Let's whip him!"

"Yes, whip him!" other voices came in a chorus.

By now Guerida was trembling while trying to explain his action. The tall Berber grabbed Guerida's whip and struck him on his side, then on his back, slashing him across his body.

"Stop! Stop!" Guerida yelled.

A strong and bellowing voice came through the crowds. "What's going on here?"

A man dressed in fine Moorish clothing surged through the market masses. Upon seeing him, the crowd let out a hushed cry. "The Pasha!" They went down on their knees bowing to the ground.

Observing the scene from their hideout. Matigoro pulled on Miguel's sleeve and forced him to bow down on his knees like the others.

"Come here, boy," the Pasha called.

When the young boy approached, the Pasha tousled his hair. "Is this true that this man here whipped you?"

The boy nodded and turned his eyes away.

"Seize this man!" The cry came from the Pasha's lips, and many Berber soldiers fell upon Guerida, pulling him away from the scene.

Guerida yelled and tried to free himself as he was led away. "My government in Spain will not be pleased!"

"Yes. They won't be pleased with you!" the Pasha said, and turned around to smile at the boy, then left with his guards and servants through an alley.

The boy ran to Matigoro and tugged at his sleeve. Matigoro took two dirhams from his pocket and slipped it into the boy's hand.

Miguel said, "How did you get the red mark on your arm?"

The boy smiled and replied, "I tied my arm with this rope." He showed the rope in his *jalabiah*.

"You clever boy!" Matigoro slapped him gently on his backside, and the boy ran away giggling. "Now, let's get back to our business here."

The sale of slaves picked up speed now that the merchants were focused on their picks. "Going once, going twice, going—"

"I'll double the last offer!" Matigoro yelled at the auctioneer still standing with his hammer in the air. Followed by Miguel, Matigoro advanced rapidly through the crowd and grabbed Miguel's cousin by his left arm, startling him.

"How did you know he was about to be purchased?" Miguel said in a low voice, hoping not to be overheard.

"I have many eyes, young man, and you should have the same in this business."

Miguel smiled.

Meanwhile, the outspent bidder walked away disappointed, and Matigoro went to pay for his purchase. When all three moved away from the marketplace, leading their camels, Miguel came close to Avram.

"Don't you recognize me, Cousin?"

Avram's astounded eyes took one look at Miguel's revealed face and burst into tears. "Yes. I'm glad it's you, Miguel. Thank you."

"You can thank Matigoro, who did the bidding. We'll talk about it later. Meanwhile, let us get away from here."

Matigoro smiled at the two young men as if he were their father.

47

Exploration

Saturday, October 13, 1492

BY EARLY MORNING, AT THE first sign of sunrise, Columbus gave the order to lift anchors. A chorus of voices stopped him in his tracks. Many canoes, some made from one piece of a dug-out tree and containing forty rowing men, along with other canoes rowed by only one man, paddled toward the three ships. The rowing men hovered around the tall ships and offered gifts to the *Santa Maria*, the *Pinta*, and the *Niña*. The natives also gave them balls of spun cotton, spears, and colorful parrots. Columbus noted that some of the Lucayo Indians wore small gold rings through their noses, and another one wore gold bracelets on his arms and legs.

"*¿De dónde sacaste los anillos de oro?*" Columbus, bending over the railing, asked one of them by touching his own nose.

The Lucayos became excited and pointed south around the island. They signed with their hands to say, "*A great king has lots of gold!*"

"You." Columbus pointed to one Lucayo Indian. "Come with us," he told the poor man trying to understand Columbus's meaning by pointing to the ship.

The Indian shook his head several times, then sat in the canoe with his arms crossed.

"Cancel and drop anchor!" Columbus bellowed to Juan de la Cosa at the tiller post and still in his morning watch.

With surprise, the crew lifted their heads from watching the Indians to look at Columbus.

"We will stay put on the island for another day to explore the other side," Columbus said.

Columbus descended from the ship with some of the crew into the boat and rowed ashore. The Indians followed them with their canoes, shouting and waving with excited gestures. At the shore, other Indians were there to greet them with the same exuberance as before, and many more showed up.

The crew and Columbus walked away from the beach, and he noted that the palm trees were bursting with green leaves, and red flowers mixed with vines at the edge of a forest. A great lake in the center of the island reflected the strong sun, and the terrain was flat, with no mountains showing in the background. Behind him the surf rolled gently on the beach, and in the distance his three ships swayed in the water. Reassured that all was well, he waved his hand to move forward.

After an hour walk in the hot sun, sweat beads appeared on Columbus's forehead. He stopped to take a drink from his leather gourd.

"How long should we march?" his secretary, Rodrigo Escobedo, said.

"A while longer. I want to understand the island length and breadth."

"Most certainly we can't do that in one day," Rodrigo Sanchez, the inspector, said.

"No, but I'm searching for higher ground. From there I can view the whole island."

The other two men nodded.

They kept on trudging through the jungle forest, when the ground became higher. By now all three of them were sweating heavily. Columbus stopped to remove his heavy overcoat, and the march upward continued. When they reached the top of the hill, they had gained a slight elevation over the beach and were able to see above the treetops. The whole island was flat without mountains or valleys. They descended the small hill and rejoined the crew on the beach.

"Tomorrow we sail around the island," Columbus said.

48

A Painful Tale

M IGUEL SMILED AT AVRAM WHEN he came in the dining area. Avram looked rested and wore clean clothes that Matigoro had given him, and sat down without a word. A tired look veiled Avram's face with creased lines that Miguel didn't recall him having before.

"You can feel at ease now," Matigoro said to him.

At those words, Avram broke down in tears.

Both Miguel and Matigoro looked at each other with surprise and waited for Avram to quiet down.

"I'm sorry," Avram apologized. "I'm grateful to you both." He wiped his cheeks, and a hard look set on his face. "I lost my mother and two of my young brothers on the ship. And I don't know where my father and other brother, León, are."

The news of his aunt and young cousins missing or dead pained Miguel. He still remembered her warmth when he, his brother José, and Isabella were guests at their uncle's home.

"What happened?" Miguel asked Avram.

Avram pulled himself out of his grief, and with an angry voice told them how they had died from their fever and lack of food and water. How another pirate took his brother León away, and his father's whereabouts were still unknown.

"When did you last see your father?" Matigoro asked Avram.

"It was on the boat that brought us to Morocco. The bodies of my mother and my two brothers were buried at sea, and right after that my father disappeared."

Matigoro remained silent, and Miguel felt the horror of an unspeakable deed.

"Did they do a search on the ship?" Miguel asked.

"Yes, but nothing turned up." Avram fell back into silence.

The door to the room opened, and two Berber servants came in with food. They placed it on the table and left quietly.

Matigoro said to Avram, "You're now safe and can stay with me as long as you like."

Avram nodded.

"I think Avram can come back with me on the ship. I'm sure you want to see your cousin Isabella."

Avram's face lit up at the news. He then directed his attention to the food on the table.

A peaceful silence descended on the room, and Miguel rejoiced at the thought of seeing Isabella back at home.

49

Guanahani Island

Sunday, October 14, 1492

AT DAWN, RIGHT AFTER EARLY Mass, Columbus ordered all three ships to lower their boats to explore the island. They rowed in a northeast direction to the other side of the island. The same scenery greeted them as they skirted the shore and the beaches. Within an hour they came to a village where the inhabitants came running to shore as soon as they saw their boats.

Also naked, and with the same characteristics as their neighbors to the south, many young Indians came to them. They had strong legs and flat stomachs, looking energetic and willing to approach the boats. Many of them gave thanks to God by throwing themselves on the ground, then looking up to heaven. The Indians called out to them to land, but Columbus feared the large rocks might break their boats. Nonetheless, it was a natural port with deep water, and where many caravels might find shelter for the night. Instead of waiting for them to land on the beach, the Indians braved the reefs in their canoes and came to them with offerings of food and water.

"Admiral, we can reach the shore a few leagues up the coast," Pinzón told him.

"This is a good port, and we may be able to build a fort there, but these reefs concern me greatly," Columbus replied.

"Then, perhaps, we'll find other suitable landings," Pinzón said.

"Let's continue our exploration of the island," Columbus said.

The boats continued their rowing around the island, finding many shelters and coves. More villages came into view with their inhabitants waving for them to land.

"Admiral, we should stop here to talk to the natives," De la Cosa said.

"No. We must continue without stopping."

By then several natives jumped into the sea and swam to them. One of them came close to Columbus's boat, then pointed at him, then to the skies.

"What is he saying?" Columbus asked his interpreter, Luis de Torres.

De Torres smiled at the gesturing native. "He's asking if we're from heaven."

Columbus nodded to the swimming man, who took off immediately and swam ashore.

"These are God-fearing creatures. They're gentle and obedient. They will convert to our faith easily," Columbus said. "So far, the island measures approximately twenty-one kilometers in length. Let us return to the ships."

50

Return to Portugal

MIGUEL AND AVRAM STOOD ON the deck of the *Liberação*, which glided smoothly through the Atantic waters and in view of Portugal's shores. Since their departure, Miguel didn't probe Avram about details in his aunt and cousins' deaths. He remembered his gentle and sweet aunt, who had made them comfortable in Cordoba while sheltering them from Guerida and the Spanish militia. He chased the painful thought away from his mind and concentrated on the ship.

Miguel gave the order: "Lower the mainsail!"

He turned around to see admiration in Avram's eyes. Miguel felt at ease that Avram and he were no longer rivals back in Cordova and vying for Isabella's attention. In the end, Miguel had won her.

The shores came into view, and he looked for the forest of eucalyptus and pines where the house was nestled. Smoke from a fire rose up through the chimney, and his heart warmed at the thought of seeing Isabella.

"Wait until you taste Ana's food," Miguel said.

"Is it that good?" Avram said. His face held a fleeting smile that hadn't been there since they'd left Morocco.

Miguel nodded with a large grin. "Drop the anchor and lower the boat!" he called out to his crew.

Avram helped with unloading the boat and rowing to shore. Miguel remarked that he would be a good helper on the property.

"Miguel! Miguel!" The voice calling him was Isabella walking with measured steps toward him.

He grabbed her as she approached and held her tightly. A kiss on her lips brought back the honey taste in them. "You can't imagine how much I missed you." He released her from his tight embrace and held her at arm's length. "I see he's growing well." He patted her stomach.

She smiled with pleasure. "He is," she said, caressing her growing abdomen. "My heart hurts from missing . . ." Her mouth suddenly fell open when Avram took a few steps forward. Her voice rose. "Is that you, Avram?"

Avram smiled timidly. "Yes, Cousin. It's me."

Isabella hugged him with affection. "How thin you are!" She held him back, studying his gangly appearance and bony face. "Come!" she said to Avram, pulling him by the arm. "Ana will fatten you up."

Miguel glanced at Avram, and the two laughed with relief.

51

Many Islands

Monday, October 15, 1492

AT THE CALL OF FOUR o'clock by the gromet, Columbus ordered to lift the anchor. The crew awakened in darkness from a deep sleep, moving sluggishly, but they climbed on masts and ratlines to lower the sails. With a thud the sails were lowered and swelled with the strong breeze from the stern. The dawn began with a wisp of orange glare on the horizon, growing steadily to a strong sun by five.

Down on the beach, Columbus saw a few native men run to their canoes and start to paddle them to the ships sailing away. Within a short time, Columbus saw the lit torches attached to the canoes become smaller, then disappear from view as the *Santa Maria*, followed by her consorts, the *Niña* and the *Pinta*, entered the high seas.

By then the next watch took place as scheduled. De la Cosa exchanged places with Sancho Ruiz at the tiller post. The morning crew began to wash the decks with saltwater, and Maestre Diego fanned the wood chips in the sandbox for the morning meal. When Diego rang the bell, the crew, assembled in a row, was eager to eat the hot gruel.

Satisfied that the voyage began smoothly, Columbus went to his cabin and sat down to record his latest reckonings and sights.

So far we saw simple men devoid of firearms but wielding bows and arrows. I believe they can become good Christian subjects. I will carry captives to Castile. After they learn our language we can return them to Guanahani. They can be made to do all we desire. I saw beautiful orchards and very green trees like those in Castile in the spring. Water was found everywhere. The natives told me with signs that there are many islands. So many I cannot decide which one to sail to. I'm now headed for the largest island.

He put down his quill and left his logbook open on his table, then stepped out on the deck.

The sea gleamed with teal reflections, and the sunlight hit the small crested waves in pure white. His crew now inspected the sails for any tears, the decks were freshly scrubbed, and the whiffs of cooked food for the noon meal came to his nostrils from the sandbox. *No doubt Diego is cooking something tasty.* The natives had supplied them with fresh water and plenty of fish and turtle meat. *The Lord has seen fit to bequeath us these islands with rich sustenance.*

By midday, Columbus went to confer with Juan de la Cosa and compare his readings with his.

"How many leagues have we sailed?" he asked De la Cosa.

"By my readings, Admiral, we bridged two leagues so far. We should be getting close."

"Your measurements coincide with mine, Juan. We should be there by evening," Columbus replied.

He then left him to inspect the rest of the ship down in the hold. He sidestepped the ballast bags filled with coarse gravel used to steady the ship, then reached the provisions well stacked against the walls on two rows of scaffolding, and above the wet floor. He counted all the remaining barrels and crates and walked to the ladder, when he noticed two sailors from his crew hard at work on the sludge built up near the bottom. They were using a wooden pump to draw up fetid waters and filled buckets to be emptied into the sea. The overpowering pungent smell coming from these stagnant waters was perfume to Columbus's nose. The *Santa Maria* was tight by the stench of the bilge. If these waters smelled fresh from the sea, there would be a dreaded leak or hole in the hull.

"Good work!" Columbus said.

The men raised their heads from their labor, their foreheads and noses wrinkled by exertion and sweat.

"What are your names?" Columbus asked, still hard at learning his crew's identity.

"Hernán, Admiral," said one of them.

"Alfonso, Admiral," said the other.

"Where is your sailor friend?" Columbus asked without revealing the true nature of his question.

Both hesitated at first. "He's doing his watch in the crow's nest, my admiral," Alfonso then said.

"How well do you know him?"

Hernán wiped his forehead with the collar of his shirt, straightened up his back, and said, "We boarded the *Santa Maria* in Palos."

"I know that," Columbus replied with impatience. "How long have you known him?"

"We worked on the docks to refit the *Santa Maria*, then on the other two caravels, the *Niña* and the *Pinta*," Alfonso said.

Seeing that the two sailors wouldn't supply any more information, Columbus waved his hand for them to continue their work. He strolled on deck, seeking fresh air for his lungs. Looking up to the crow's nest on the mainmast, he saw João looking down at him. *He must be watching me.* He waved his hand in front of his face to chase the thought away.

After Compline and the sleep hour announced by the gromet, Columbus remained on deck to watch for signs of the large island. He now feared the island was further away than predicted. His readings showed five leagues made by the *Santa Maria*'s flagship and no island in sight. By morning, Juan confirmed they had gone six leagues, and by midday a large island appeared in their view. Further to the west a larger island appeared, but it was inaccessible at the present time.

"Stand by to lower the boats!" Juan ordered.

All three ships came closer to shore, but remained in deeper waters while the boats were lowered. When the shore was reached, the entire armed party went down again on their knees to pray.

"I christen this island Santa Maria de la Conception," Columbus pronounced while the men crossed themselves.

Columbus then pulled aside the six men he had forced to come on the ship from San Salvador, and asked them by signs where the gold was they had told him. The taken natives shook from head to toe with fear showing on their faces.

Columbus's voice rose in volume. "Did you lie to me?"

Puzzled, the Lucayan Indians fell down on the beach, trembling before Columbus.

"It's no use, Admiral," Juan said. "They're children with fables to tell."

Columbus tried to conceal his disappointment, when the natives from the village on Santa Maria de la Conception began to stream to the beach carrying baskets with fruits and foods. None of the natives wore any gold jewelry as was predicted before.

Juan laughed. "At least we won't be starving."

"There's nothing here to keep us," Columbus said. "Let's return to the ships and sail west toward the larger island."

When they neared the ship, one of the taken hostages jumped in the ocean, then swam to a large canoe moored by the *Niña*.

"Seize him!" Juan ordered.

"Don't!" Columbus rescinded the order. "He's afraid of us, and we shouldn't force him any longer. We still have the remaining Indians, who'll show us where the gold is."

Juan threw a surprised look, but remained silent. "Hoist the sails!" he ordered.

The three ships departed with a southeast wind on the stern.

52

Harvest

EACH MORNING A BELL ON the estate's premises rang after breakfast for the workers to begin their work. By now, Avram was familiar with the day's procedure through Miguel's instructions: first the cook had to be wakened, an hour before dawn, then the workers would come in one by one with their wooden bowls to be served gruel and freshly baked bread from the estate's kitchen. Avram saw that the entire workforce was fed regularly twice a day with periodic breaks for water.

It seemed that Miguel was a good master. How had he acquired the wealth displayed before him, and the ship and mastery over all operations was a mystery? When he asked Miguel how he came by his money, Miguel told him vaguely that a generous man had bequeathed it upon him and Isabella. Avram then asked for this incredible patron's identity, but Miguel changed the subject. *This is extremely curious*, he thought.

The men working now under a setting sun ended a fruitful day of labor by the sound of another bell. All of them packed their water gourds, wiped their sweaty brows, and walked back to their cabins on the estate.

Avram walked to the shed given to him by Miguel, and washed off the grime and sweat of the day. On his mind was the vision of Isabella, growing larger by the day, and of her beauty that brought a sigh to his lips. He knew that he'd never possess her, nor dream of ever being favored by her. She was now married to Miguel and expecting a child. For some reason he looked forward to that child's birth. When the time came, he'd see that her child was protected and cherished while Miguel was on his travels. All he hoped to receive in return was a grateful look from Isabella.

"There you are!" Isabella said when Avram came into the dining room.

Avram replied with a faint smile and took his place at the table, where Miguel and Ana were serving themselves food.

"How did the harvest go?" Miguel asked Avram between bites of bread and lamb stew.

"We finished all rows on the south side. Tomorrow we begin from the north side of the vineyards."

"Good. We can begin stomping the grapes by next week," Miguel said.

"That's good," Ana said. "I'd like to prepare the jams before the end of fall." To Avram's inquiring look, she added, "The remnants left from rejected grapes are excellent for my jams."

Avram nodded.

Miguel said, "You should've seen the shoppers lining up for your jams, Ana. They cleaned me out at the market in Lisbon yesterday."

Pleased with Miguel's praise, Ana laughed with pleasure.

Isabella threw Avram a glance. "You're silent tonight."

"I'm just tired. That's all." He then quickly added, "Please, never mind me. I feel satisfied with today's work." He lowered his head to look at his food on the plate. He felt no hunger.

"I'm glad," Miguel said. "I'd hate to think that I'm putting too much of a burden on you."

Avram raised his head. "I've never complained so far."

Miguel remained silent to Avram's comment. He turned his attention to Isabella. "How are you feeling, my dear?"

Isabella was still looking at Avram when Miguel spoke to her. "I'm feeling very well, Miguel."

Miguel threw a glance at Avram sitting quietly and playing with his food. He asked Avram, "I see you're not too hungry, Avram?"

Avram said, "I'm finished eating, thank you. With your permission, I'll check on the men in the cabins and the gates on the property." He then got up from his chair, nodded to all three, and left the room.

⤞◦◦◦◦⤝

Miguel sighed, while Isabella showed a perplexed face. Ana silently ate some of the fresh fruits placed on the table.

"What is wrong with Avram?" Miguel asked.

Isabella looked at Miguel. "Maybe he misses his family?"

"That's right," Miguel said. "It was insensitive of me not to think of it."

"Perhaps it's because you're preoccupied by your duties." Ana's voice was conciliatory.

"I'm worried about him. We must keep Don Abravanel's identity secret from him," Miguel said.

"Sounds like you don't trust him," Isabella said with doubt in her eyes.

Miguel moved on his chair with uneasiness. "It's not that. I don't know if he understands the seriousness of our situation."

"Maybe you still remember what happened in Seville," Isabella said without reproach in her voice.

"What happened in Seville?" Ana asked.

Miguel told her the entire incident, how Avram had betrayed them, how he had alerted Guerida as to their whereabouts, effecting their capture.

Ana remained silent a few moments. She turned to Miguel. "Indeed, this is serious news. How can you trust him now?"

Isabella interjected before Miguel answered. "We must trust him. He's a repented young man. I know he feels conflicted by what he's done. It's all in the past now. He works hard at his job, atoning for the past."

"I hope you're right," Ana said.

Miguel remained silent.

53

A New Island

Tuesday, October 16, 1492

AS EXPECTED, THE NEWER ISLAND was much larger than the previous two. It was noon, the hour of Middies, and they couldn't see the bottom, so Columbus feared losing the anchors in deep waters. He decided not to land and instead to stay put. They spent the day and night on the ships until the next morning at low tide. Then several canoes, paddled by the inhabitants, came to the ships, bringing barrels of water. They climbed on board with wide eyes and mouths making yelping sounds while pointing fingers around them.

"Give them molasses," Columbus told Maestre Diego, his cook.

Diego limped to the hold and reappeared with a bowl filled with the thick, sweet molasses. He put the bowl on the deck, and all the Indians dipped their hands and fingers in the amber paste. When they finished licking the sweet taste of molasses off their fingers, Columbus gave the order for his crew to leave for the island. The Indians followed their boats with their canoes, paddling furiously toward the beach.

Upon disembarking, Columbus christened the island Fernandina. They were eight full leagues from the island of Santa Maria de la Conception and southwest of San Salvador, where they had landed blissfully.

The natives came running to them with the usual gifts of foods. An Indian gave a ball of cotton as a gift to a sailor, but Columbus forbade him to take it.

Another Indian gave Columbus some large green leaves with a sharp aromatic scent and with long slender white flowers. He quizzed the native with gestures to the leaves. The Indian took part of the leaf and chewed it.

Heartened by this gesture, Columbus put a piece in his mouth, which gave him a bitter and sharp taste. When Columbus made a grimace, the native laughed with everyone around him. The Indian then ran to a fire burning near a hut and came back to Columbus and the party standing with him. The leaf in his hand was brownish, rolled, and burning at one end. He sucked on the other side, and red cinders with white smoke appeared at the lit end.

"It's black magic!" one sailor of his crew shouted while crossing himself against evil.

Columbus turned to him and shouted, "It's not! These people are welcoming us by sharing their culture and lore. They're not evil!"

To prove to his crew and those of the *Pinta* and the *Niña* it wasn't black magic, he took the rolled leaf from the Indian's hand and tried to suck on it. Immediately, the smoke made him cough several times. The Indians laughed. Columbus took another whiff, and a light sensation took hold of his head, but he didn't faint. He turned to the Indian and smiled at him, upon which all the natives jumped up and down shouting and gesturing with joy.

Martin Pinzón, standing next to Columbus, slapped his back. "You made friends with the natives, Admiral."

"Give them the baubles we brought," Columbus said.

The glass beads were distributed with brass timbrels, worth a maravedí back in Castile. The natives greatly rejoiced in receiving the gifts.

Columbus then noticed an Indian with a gold anklet. "*¿De dónde sacaste este oro?*" he asked.

The Indian first looked at Columbus, then pointed northwest on the island.

"Let us sail around the island now," Columbus ordered.

The three boats followed the contour of the island southerly, to discover that it surpassed the eight leagues' distance from the Santa Maria gulf to extend to a full twenty leagues. Columbus was told that the island of Samoat contained much gold, which is what the Indians from San Salvador and Santa Maria had told him. The Indians of Fernandina had the same jet-black hair—straight and long in the back. Their legs were sturdy, and they were all young. He found that these Indians had more manners, as they wore a cotton cloth on their heads, and the women used it to cover their genitals. Everywhere on the island were green trees of deep emerald with leafy fronds. These trees were different from the ones he knew in Castile, and he was amazed to see different leaves on the same tree. No animals were seen except many different and colorful birds, such as parrots, and lots of lizards. These Indians were not known to practice any faith, and he thought again they would make good Christians. They were gentle and obedient and would make good workers.

54

Voyage Time

SABELLA FOUND A PEACEFUL ROUTINE within the fruitful labor done by all on the estate. Both Miguel and Avram oversaw all aspects of farming and growing crops. The harvest was now completed, and Ana was busy creating her jams for the market. The new-season grapes were stomped in large vats and the wine stored in barrels and jugs in the basement under the house. The grounds around the property were filled with fragrant flowers and shaded trees. In the gardens, at the back of the two-story house, a profusion of lavender grew wild along with cultivated water lilies in the pond, bougainvilleas in flaming red, morning glories, laurels intertwined with clematis, and calla lilies, which spread a perfume in the air. Their scents raised her mood while she sat in the reclining chair built for her by Avram. He had added a mattress pad to the chair that made it most comfortable. She thanked him, but stopped short of effusive compliments, and short of comparing him to his missing brother León, who was an excellent woodworker. She wanted to avoid at all costs stirring unpleasant memories of his lost family, afraid it might put him into a somber mood. The life inside her was growing as well as her body, now showing a visible paunch. She was now beginning her fourth month of pregnancy, and the morning sickness had long passed. All around and inside her life was bursting to come out and spread its wings. She looked up to see small clouds gathering high in the blue sky, but they were only a whiff in the day's sunshine.

"You look much at peace," Miguel said, shaking her out of her reverie.

"I am, my love." She raised her head to receive his firm lips upon hers. He rubbed her neck with abandon, and kissed her again.

"How is our son?" Miguel asked while gently rubbing her abdomen.

"She may instead be our daughter."

Miguel laughed. "Whatever we receive from our God will be loved immensely. Boy or girl."

She nodded with a smile.

"My dear Isabella . . ." Miguel started.

She looked inquiringly into his eyes.

"I don't want to alarm you, but I've received a letter from Matigoro."

She fidgeted on her chair and took deep breaths. "What does it say?" Her voice came out strangled.

Just then a rumble was heard, and they both looked up to more gathering clouds above their heads.

"We must get you inside. There's a signal for the approaching winter." He helped her get up and held her by the arm, and they made their way inside the house as a few drops of rain began to fall.

When they entered the living area, Ana was seated, knitting near the hearth. She looked up from her needles and smiled. "Just in time, with the rain coming," she said.

Avram was stocking the fire in the fireplace and kept working without acknowledging the new arrivals.

Isabella supported her weight on the armrest and sat down. She arranged and rearranged her dress, then smoothed her lustrous black hair painstakingly.

Miguel watched her without a word. He turned to Ana and said, "I wanted to announce my next voyage."

Avram stopped his work and looked in Miguel's direction. Ana stopped her knitting and put the pink and blue wool garment into her lap.

"When will you be leaving?" Ana asked.

"Tomorrow. The *Liberação* is standing by to sail for me and Avram."

"Again? So soon?" Isabella said while she fidgeted nervously and plucked at her dress. "You've just arrived one month ago." She felt heat flushing through her body.

"I know, my darling." Miguel took on a sad look. "There's nothing more I'd like to do than stay here for the rest of my life. You know the duty we swore to."

Avram looked at Miguel with questions in his eyes, but he remained silent.

Miguel continued without elaboration on his last sentence. "We'll leave early."

Ana nodded her head in agreement. "If you must, then you must leave tomorrow."

A moan escaped Isabella's lips. She lowered her head onto her chest and remained quiet. Miguel got up and went to sit by her on another chair, then took her hand silently.

Ana threw Avram a glance, and they both left the room quietly.

"It pains me to leave you in your condition, and I want nothing more than to return quickly to you." He stopped, grabbed both her hands, and caressed them. "You know I swore to Don Abravanel to look after his estates. Part of that oath was to buy back and free Jewish slaves. It's our duty not only to Don Abravanel for his generosity and the wealth he showered on us but it's also to our brethren, who may die in captivity."

Isabella let out a pained cry. "It pains me more to see you go while I'm sitting here helpless."

"You're not helpless. You're contributing to our future, to our new and growing family." He moved his chair closer to her and held her tightly. "The distance between us cannot separate us. It isn't about how much time we spend together, or being close to each other. We are and will always be close in thought and mind wherever we are. "

Isabella raised her head to him and kissed him on the lips. "Come back to me soon."

55

Maravillas

OÃO STOOD WATCHING ALFONSO AND Hernán fishing at the railing. The many colored fish of yellow, blue, red, and orange looked so different from the ones back home in Castile, they were afraid to harm them.

Alfonso marveled at them. "I've never seen so many colors in fish."

Hernán stood by with his mouth open in amazement. He then said, "They're like a rainbow."

Only João remained unfazed. He cracked his knuckles now and then and kept pacing back and forth. He felt jumpy and couldn't rest.

"Hey, João. You're scaring the fish," Hernán warned him. "What's eating you?"

João stopped pacing and grabbed the railing, looking over the fishing lines in the water. "We're wasting time in those godforsaken islands."

"You can look upon them as paradise," Alfonso said as he gently taunted the fish with the hard biscuit attached to his line.

"Paradise is where our brothers and sisters can breathe free from evil men!" João then unleashed a string of curses.

"Whoa! Take it easy, João. You must be patient. When we get to the Indies, you'll have your land. What you been waiting for, eh?" Hernán said.

"Apparently, this is as close to the Indies as we'll get. It's a faraway land. One that we'll never reach." João looked down at his knuckles turning red.

"Then perhaps we ought to remain behind on one of those islands?" Alfonso said casually, as if remaining behind was up to him.

"The admiral may have other plans for you," Hernán said, lifting then throwing the line back into the water.

João shrugged his shoulders. "The admiral will agree to all my demands."

"To what demands will the admiral agree?" Gomes's voice dropping between all three startled them.

A silence fell in which only the sound of waves lapping the hull was heard. Gomes turned to each one of them, coming close to their faces to look for a sign. Not one replied.

"All right. Since I'm the only one not in on your secret, I'll have to report to the admiral."

Alfonso jumped at Gomes and grabbed his shirt. He came close to his face and said, "You do that and you'll have me to reckon with." Alfonso also stood a head taller than Gomes.

Hernán seconded Alfonso's remark by pulling his lower lip forward, and his eyebrows knitted close together.

"All right. All right," Gomes said. "But if you're keeping me in the dark, you must be plotting something behind my back."

João spoke calmly. "No one is plotting anything. It's nothing to do with you or the admiral, or the *Santa Maria* for that matter." He fell quiet.

"Then why didn't you take me into your confidence? My lips are sealed."

João took a long look at him, mulling over his question. "All we want is to find a land on which to rest our heads. We're tired of sailing, storms, and the uncertainty over whether we'll live or die in a liquid tomb."

"Why didn't you say so in the first place? Those are exactly my thoughts too. There's no gold to be found on these islands. The little that I've seen won't bring a ducat. If they find any, it won't be for us."

Alfonso looked puzzled. "Then why did you come on this voyage?"

"The queen pardoned me to go on this voyage. The pay is good, and who knows—perhaps prison will be my lot upon my return."

Another silence fell between all four men.

"Listen," João said. "As soon as proper land is in the offing, we'll leave the ship."

"You mean escape?" Gomes said.

"No. We'll do it with the admiral's blessings," João replied. Before Gomes asked again, João silenced him with a finger to his mouth.

Gomes nodded.

I hope this will suffice to keep him quiet for now.

56

fernandina

Wednesday, October 17. 1492

THEIR PROGRESS SLOW, THE THREE ships sailed now in a north-northwest direction around the island. As they sailed, Columbus admired the vibrant and vivid colors of teal-green palm trees in profusion, the white sands, and flowers of paradise shouting in bright reds and whites as pure as those in Castile in May. At each village they stopped, the natives looked the same as the ones on the islands of San Salvador and Santa Maria. They wore long black spiky hair in the back and short bangs above their foreheads. Strong legs and lithe bodies were the norm.

With a favorable wind on their back, they came to a large harbor that could hold close to one hundred ships at least. In the center of this vast expense was an island looming in front.

"Sound the waters!" Columbus called.

Several sailors, with one leadsman to count the marks, lowered the sounding rope into the waters with a plummet coated with tallow in its concave cup.

"By the mark two, by the mark three, by the mark five . . ." The sounding rope with knots at intervals was brought back up, and the leadsman checked the inside of the cup. "No sand or pebbles, Admiral."

"Try again," Columbus urged.

" . . . By the mark thirty . . . We're in deep water, Admiral. Almost sixty meters."

"Lower the boats!" Columbus gave the order. "We'll leave the ships in the harbor."

Three boats were lowered respectively from the *Santa Maria*, the *Pinta*, and the *Niña*. Within thirty minutes the boats hit the sandy beach. From all directions, natives ran to them, speaking excitedly, their arms bearing baskets of fruits and fresh fish.

"¿Dónde está el agua?" Columbus asked the natives by sign language, and showing them empty wooden barrels and small wooden pails for water.

The natives grabbed the barrels and pails then ran with some of his crew to the village in the distance.

While he waited for them to return with drinking water, Columbus walked to the line of trees offering a canopy of delicious shade and coolness. The palm fronds interlaced their branches above his head in various deep shades of mint green. Other trees were similar to those in Castile in the month of May, and some were different from what he'd ever seen. The lime-green grasses below his boots were up to his mid-calves, and fruit fallen from the trees abounded among them.

"The natives are coming back, Admiral!" one of his men called out.

He rejoined his crew, and the men helped the natives carry the water. His eyes fell immediately on one native with a gold ring attached to his nose. Columbus was surprised to find that the natives had in their possession broken wooden porringers his men had given them in exchange for spears.

Columbus stood akimbo, his high stature planted with his legs wide. "Why didn't you trade for the gold ring in his nose?" Columbus's voice rose in volumes at his translator Luis de Torres.

"But, Admiral, I couldn't do such a thing! Beside, one of the crew already tried, and the native refused to trade."

Columbus was sweating profusely. He removed his heavy velvet overcoat, then rolled up his cotton long-sleeved shirt. He breathed and exhaled with relief the sweet breeze coming at him from the rolling sea and cooling him off. Now he understood why the natives dressed minimally, letting their skin breathe free in the sunshine. Seeing the admiral disrobe gave his second in command, De la Cosa, the liberty to follow his example. Perhaps these natives had discovered the fountain of youth. *Go with your instincts and live unencumbered.*

Columbus suddenly felt sorry for having admonished Luis de Torres. He turned to Luis. "Please forgive me for my outburst just now. I'm anxious to find the gold, which is the main reason for this voyage of discovery."

Luis smiled and nodded, giving him his friendship's absolution.

"Let us return to the ships and feast on the offerings showered upon us."

57

Back to Morocco

M IGUEL STOOD AGAIN ON THE *Liberação*'s deck with his eyes fixed on shore and the white house receding on the horizon. He sighed when it disappeared altogether. Each voyage he made to retrieve and buy back Jewish slaves kept him away from Isabella. How he wished to never leave and hold her in his arms forever. But he had a duty to render, which his conscience dictated must be fulfilled.

He turned to Avram and found him entranced in a gaze at the disappearing shore. Was he still in love with Isabella? *Poor Avram.* He had everything taken away from him—first Isabella, then his entire family. No matter. He would find someone for Avram who would love him and be his constant companion. Both couples would then live with the happiness and richness of growing families. He smiled at his wish list. *I must be getting soft. Danger is ahead, and I must concentrate on the task at hand.*

"Hoist all sails!" Miguel gave the order to his crew.

"Aye, aye, Captain!" His twenty men deployed the mainmast and foremast sails, and their canvases stretched under the wind power, swaying majestically to and fro. When all sails were properly hoisted, the men went back to their usual chores of scrubbing the decks with saltwater, and checking the rigging and ropes and for any tears in the sails.

Presently, the clouds began to gather on the horizon, looking dark and ominous. The caravel was gliding in smooth waters but was nearing toward the Strait of Gibraltar, and Miguel braced himself for pirate ships. As it was, all caravels were safer without sailing that route. He knew that Berber pirates were still lurking around Casablanca and Agadir, preferring to steer the ship toward Tangier on the northern coast of Morocco.

Avram's voice behind him startled him. "All's well with the ship."

He turned around to Avram. "Thank you, Cousin, for your help. Don't know what I'd do without you."

Avram displayed a faint smile but remained silent. Both men leaned against the railing facing the straits, which loomed larger, without saying another word.

Avram suddenly broke his silence and said, "I'm still thinking about my father."

Miguel looked at him. "I can understand that. My father died when I was ten years old. He's often in my thoughts."

"I can't believe my father's dead," Avram uttered. "If he were, I'd know." His voice was sure.

Miguel didn't want to kill his hopes. He said to him, "Chances are he may still be alive. But where would you search? The sea is large. So are the continents."

Avram didn't reply; his voice quivered. "Someday I'll find him."

"Look, Avram," Miguel said. "My brother is also lost to me. Even though Isabella's father is looking after him, the reality is I can't go back. It would mean instant arrest by Spanish authorities. I'm hoping that José is safe," Miguel said as an afterthought.

Avram remained silent.

"Let's get ready for the perilous strait," Miguel prompted Avram.

By now the winds had picked up speed, flapping the sails with force. "Reef the mainsail!" Miguel hollered over the hissing sound of growing winds. The men rushed to the mainmast and began to roll and clew the topsail to the yardarm. "Leave the foresail up a while!" Miguel hollered again.

The crew followed his orders, when one man yelled down to Miguel, "Captain, we'll lose the foresail if we don't take it down!"

"Take it down then!" Miguel yelled back.

While some men were busy with the sails, Miguel, followed by Avram, went down in the hold and saw that the bales and barrels were strongly ballasted by sacks of pebbles to prevent them being thrown across the empty space. They reappeared shortly, and Miguel went straight to the tiller and took the rudder from his sailor. He held the tiller with both wet hands and tried to pick a path between waves. The small caravel hit the waves at twenty-degree angles, and the bow cut through without getting knocked back.

"Avram, to the tiller!" Miguel yelled at Avram, who rushed to take it from his hands. "I must see to the crew and the rest of the sails!"

Miguel made a dash for the men still working on clewing the sails. They were finishing tying all ropes and clambered down from both masts.

"Good work!" Miguel said.

The soaked men replied by saluting him.

Then Miguel strode to the sandbox that held their meal. His cook was trying hard to reignite the fire under the cauldron.

"See that the men get a warm meal soon. They're soaked to the bone."

"Ay, Captain," replied his poor cook, struggling against the wind shutting down the fire each time it was lit. After many attempts, the cook finally succeeded in preventing the fire from going out. He secured the tinplate screen around the fire and waited for the brew to boil.

Satisfied that the ship was taken care of, he returned to the rudder. "Give back the tiller to the pilot," Miguel told Avram.

Both men braced the wind to return again to the upper deck, when a voice from the mast called out. "A ship ahoy!"

Miguel looked beyond the crested waves to a distance of two kilometers and saw a ship closing in on them. The ship wavered among the waves, trying to prevent their hull from being hit head-on. As it came closer still, a dreaded call rang out. "Pirates! A pirate ship!"

"Oh no!" Miguel yelled with desperation. "Bad weather and pirates too!" *Our luck has run out*, he grumbled. *But we'll have to teach them a lesson.* "Prepare the cannons!" He gave the order for taking out the cannons belowdecks.

His men scrambled below to the starboard side and removed the canvas tarps on the row of four bronze cannons. The iron balls were neatly stacked below on the deck floor, and wadding and gunpowder were poured down the vent while the fuse waited to be lit.

The pirate ship came closer still, and Miguel could clearly see the wet pirates' grim faces and cutlasses held between their teeth. The sea was churning in white foam and preventing any chance to hit them in a straight line. Their caravel rode the waves with men, cannons, and everything else as little and insignificant crafts on a gigantic sea meant to swallow men and ships.

Miguel's right hand grasped the hilt of his sharp sword, and his eyes were fixed, waiting for the pirate ship to approach them by starboard. Now the pirates' eyes were clearly seen, and they held a fierce look in them.

"Fire!" Miguel stood arched in attack mode as he sent the order.

The fire exploded from the cannons, then the blast followed as it hit its target. The mainmast on the pirate's ship immediately went down, thundering on their deck with the cries of men caught beneath it.

"Fire!" A second wave of cannon balls exploded with the same violent force as the pirate ship hit them. *The Liberação* shuddered with a panel by its port side splintering near the tiller.

"Check for damage!" Miguel shouted at some of his men, who ran down into the hold. A young boy returned amid another blast to communicate that a slight leak had occurred down below, but his men were quick to stuff rags and pour bitumen between the large cracks.

Just then the pirate ship tried to dock alongside but succeeded only in scraping their ship and was thrown back by a large wave soaking everyone on both ships.

"You're out of luck!" Miguel shouted over the renewed blast coming from the pirates operating their own cannons. Between the flames from the cannons, the black smoke lingering around the vessels, and the cannon balls hitting men and ships, chaos reigned.

Another blast from the pirates hit their mainmast, and it withstood the shock by sheer luck, splintering here and there but standing still, the metal ball only grazing the wood.

Miguel turned around for an instant and saw another attempt at invading his ship by the pirates. Their grappling hooks were laced over the railings and the rigging, drawing them in, while some daring pirates hanging on to the yardarms jumped over onto their ship.

"Brace for attack!" Miguel gave the call to all men.

The battle that ensued spilled onto the main deck. Several of his men were pierced by the pirates' swords and went down mortally wounded on deck. Miguel took on one of the attackers by waving his sword and another small blade in his hand. In the hand-to-hand combat, the pirate sword cut him across his right upper arm. He winced in pain, but held the combating pirate until he saw him crumple in half and collapse bloodied on the deck. Miguel looked up and saw that Avram stood above the dead pirate with a bloody sword in his hand.

Miguel shouted at him, "Thanks, Cousin!"

No sooner had he yelled in his joy than a tight grasp around his neck by a muscled and large forearm kept him in a viselike grip. "Don't you wiggle, young man? You'll choke faster."

Avram, meanwhile, was wincing, as he was caught from behind too. Miguel saw his cousin being dragged across the deck and tied with ropes to his other men.

"Halt!" The cry out of a grim and fearsome bearded man standing in front of a mass of pirates. "Search for booty!"

Miguel watched the pirates scurrying across deck, down to the hold, then reappearing shortly with their provisions, wine, and other goods to be sold in Morocco. He trembled with rage at the sight and braced his body in the vain wish to release his bindings, but they were tight and made his skin raw.

"Thieves! Robbers! Wretched men!" The cry escaped his lips. The next thing he heard was a cry from Avram's lips, "No! Don't!"

A blow hit Miguel on the head, and a spiraling blackness swallowed him up.

58

Isabella Island

Friday, October 19, 1492

COLUMBUS SAT IN HIS CABIN and painstakingly tried to recollect the last few days of sailing. They had seen many wonders and surprises as they skirted the island of Fernandina. After they sailed away from Fernandina on the eve of October 17, many more islands came into view.

A tropical rain suddenly pelted their ships, making it more difficult to land on those fertile islands, whereby he gave the order to stay put. On Friday October 19, he made anchor. The *Pinta* was told to sail clockwise around the island and the *Niña* ordered to sail counterclockwise about the island, while the *Santa Maria* followed a southeast course. By midday all three ships were to meet.

The San Salvador native men on Columbus's ship called the island Samoete and it was chosen as a meeting point. With a north wind upon their back, all three ships dropped anchor by a rocky islet.

"I name this island Isabella for our sovereign in Castile," Columbus pronounced while the men knelt on the sandy beach and crossed themselves.

From the looks of it, Columbus estimated at least twelve leagues for the length of Isabella with a cape in the distance he called Cabo Hermoso.

Deep-green tree groves appeared on the northeast and low hills in the background. Water abounded in small lakes in the center of Isabella. Columbus marveled at the rich and beautiful island with the sweetest smell about its flowering trees. He surmised that many herbs could be obtained from those trees and verdure that might be of immense value to Spain for spices, dyes, and medicine. He despaired though of not knowing their exact properties, which gave him much anxiety. He put the details on the back burner in his memory and dwelt on the gold to be found.

On the morning of October 20, he weighed the anchors and traveled in a southwest course to the cape he had seen in the distance the previous day. The water was shallow for the *Santa Maria* and as a large *nao*, or cargo ship, with its rounded hull, she couldn't land, but the two smaller caravels found a suitable spot to drop their anchors. Columbus, still of the opinion that danger might lurk for the *Santa Maria*, decided to sail around the island and reconnoiter instead for deeper waters. With a light wind in its sails, the *Santa Maria* was directed in a north-northeast course along the western side. By morning on the twenty-first, when the light arose along the horizon, he returned to the cape and decided to anchor at a distance away from the caravels already there. After a hurried breakfast, Columbus landed.

"I name this peaceful harbor Cabo de la Laguna."

No village came into view as they landed on the beach except for one hut that he found empty. *We must've chased the inhabitant.* The utensils and animals were still in the round hut.

"Don't touch anything," Columbus warned his party. "This man and his family will come back to find us as friends."

The rest of the men followed Columbus along the beach, then into the groves, where many different types of trees interlaced their branches to form a thick canopy above their heads. The scent of red and white flowers was intoxicating. Orange-red, royal-blue, and bright-yellow parrots with long tails flying in droves between trees seemed to follow them on the trail cleared by two of his men ahead of the party. Many different birds of colorful plumage clung to the branches and entertained them with their tweeting and singing. Columbus felt again the pangs of not knowing their breeds but found them, nonetheless, wonderful in their varieties. He saw many aloes and ordered his men to carry several of them back to the ship. A large serpent, seven palms in length and hidden underfoot in the brush, slid in the open and bolted for a small lake. Alonzo Pinzón followed him and killed it with his spear.

"Save the skin, Pinzón. I intend to bring it back to His Highnesses."

De la Cosa, walking alongside Columbus, kept stealing glances now and then at him.

Columbus turned sideways and asked him, "What is it? You have something to tell me?"

De la Cosa reddened under his sweaty face. His shirt was soaked with sweat. "Admiral, I must ask you a question."

"What is it?" Columbus answered without inflection in his voice. He was sweating as well in the temperate and humid grove, and stopped now and then to drink water from his gourd.

"We've covered four islands in as little as ten days so far."

"So we have," Columbus replied.

"Don't you find it odd that we haven't found any substantial amount of gold so far?"

Columbus stopped abruptly. He wiped the sweat off his face with a cotton cloth, then said, "Whatever we found so far is very little. But these villagers and natives are poor and have very little to their names. When we reach Cipangu, I'll introduce myself to their king and find the gold they have in large quantity."

"What makes you sure he'll share his gold with us?" De la Cosa asked.

"We will cross this creek and bridge when we get to Cipangu. The natives call it Colba, and they've seen large amounts of gold worn by the king. Near this island is another one called Bosio. It's a very large island. I will decide then what to do if we find gold or spices. When we get to the city of Guisay, the letters I carry for the great khan will endear us in his favor and his benefaction."

De la Cosa remained silent to this long speech. Columbus thought he had convinced him. He must have his first mate and all the men under his command trust his judgment. He also knew that this was a sound and proper order they would follow.

They continued their march when they arrived at a clearing near the other side of the island, where many huts were arranged in a semicircle.

The inhabitant natives came out in droves and much chatter as they welcomed Columbus and his party of men. The natives carried with them wooden spears and large quantities of cotton they traded for broken glass beads, hawk's bells, and some leather items. Two of the sailors exchanged pieces of colorful glass for nose rings made of gold. Columbus examined them and found them so small as to be almost nothing to possess.

By morning on Tuesday October 23, Columbus gave the order to lift the anchors. "We sail for the island the Indians call Cubao. I know that it must be Cipango where the great khan resides, and where we'll find gold!" The chains lifting the anchors grated against the mast's post and brought up the rusty iron to land on deck. The sails were hoisted along the three masts of each ship, and the vessels glided free yet leaving behind them a paradise of nature wonderful in its making.

59

The Grim Return

A SPECK OF WHITE AND brown appearing on the horizon sent tremors to Isabella's heart. She ran as fast as she could to the kitchen, despite the extra weight she carried, where she was sure to find Ana. But the kitchen was empty. Only the hearth hummed quietly with a pot of water boiling and steaming.

That's curious. She frowned and rubbed the back of her neck. Perhaps Ana was at the workers' barracks. Out of the door she bolted and walked the few meters to the wooded area on the left side of the house. After a few minutes, she arrived at a clearing where many barracks were lined up. She went to the first one, where the manager usually hung around, but it was also empty.

The next place she decided to check was the overlook at the top of the small hill above the vineyards. Sweating and laboring, she made it to the top. She saw the workers cutting dead leaves and branches of remnant grapevines from the previous harvest, but no Ana in sight.

Anxious and worried now, she took deep breaths to calm herself. She applied her hand gently on her stomach and felt her child kick several times. A laugh of relief escaped her lips.

"Let's go back to the house," she said out loud.

The house was still quiet and no Ana in sight. Isabella returned to the lookout on the front porch to gaze at the ships getting closer.

"Isabella?" Ana's voice gave her a jolt.

She turned around to see a pale Ana standing in the doorway.

"I've been looking for you everywhere." Isabella's speech was rushed. "I wanted to tell you about the ship!" Her body twisted slowly as she turned and pointed at the horizon.

"I was in the back garden, pruning and clearing," Ana said quietly.

"But look at the ship! Miguel is back!" With a smile, Isabella clapped her hands together.

"Yes, I see," Ana said calmly.

"Why aren't you glad?" Isabella asked her.

"I am. Let's get ready for them." Ana helped Isabella get off the low bench on the porch, and they walked arm in arm inside to the sitting room. And there they waited.

⋙∘◦◌◦∘⋘

Within the space of an hour, Avram made his entrance. He appeared disheveled, and tired lines showed on his face. His head hung low.

Ana's hand plunged into her dress pocket as she grazed the letter hidden there. Her heart was skipping beats, and she stood frozen and rigid.

"Avram, we're so happy to see you. Where's Miguel?" Isabella got off the sofa with a large smile on her face.

Avram didn't reply right away. He then raised his head and said, "Miguel isn't here."

"He isn't here? What do you mean? He stayed back in Morocco?" The questions flew one after another from Isabella's mouth.

Avram stayed as silent as a grave. He threw his arms up in desperation. "I did all I could. All I could," he repeated.

"What are you saying? He didn't want to come back now?"

"He couldn't come back to you."

Ana decided to interfere. She went to Isabella and sat her back down. "It means . . . he's not . . . coming back," Ana said, the words strangling in her throat.

"But why?" Isabella's words were a cry of pain and bewilderment. Her face was pale and confused.

Ana's heart tore in her chest. She had held the letter too long from Isabella. It burned her dress as it lay there in her pocket. "All it means is we won't see Miguel for many months. Something happened and he can't come back."

"Is it the Spanish police? I knew he was in danger! I must go and see him. Avram, where is he being held?"

"You can't see him," Avram said.

"Why?"

"Because he isn't in Spain."

Ana looked hard at Avram and raised her hand, trying to stop him.

"Where then?" Isabella asked. "Where? Tell me where!" Isabella got up and came close to Avram, then looked in his eyes.

Avram glanced at Ana and shook his head slowly.

"I must tell her, Ana. I must!"

"Yes, you must!" Isabella yelled at him. "I'm strong. I can take it."

Avram looked her in the eyes and lowered his head. "He's been taken captive by the Berbers." His voice died down.

Isabella gave a great cry. "No! No! It can't be true! No, it isn't true." She collapsed to her knees and broke down in a great wailing cry. "Miguel, oh, Miguel . . . I warned him about the dangers. It's my fault. I should've stopped him." She moaned.

Ana gave a sigh more of relief than of pain. She again grazed the letter in her dress pocket, promising herself to destroy it.

"You mustn't blame yourself, Isabella. You must think of your unborn child." Ana came to her and led her to the sofa. "You'll see, in time, you'll be a mother. That is what you must think of now."

"What are you telling me?" Isabella's voice rose in volumes. "To forget Miguel? I won't! I will search for him to the ends of the earth, if need be! We will buy him back from the pirates. We have the money!"

Ana shook her head. "You'll only make yourself sick." She turned to Avram. "Help me get her to her bed."

Isabella let herself be led to her bedroom like a child being carried in sleep. Ana covered her with her blanket and kissed her on the forehead.

"Try to sleep a little. When you wake up, we'll see what to do."

She saw that Isabella was lulled by her empty promise, and seeing her calmer now, she walked out of the bedroom and shut the door behind her. In the hallway, she grabbed Avram's arm and led him back down to the sitting room. Once there, she turned to him with accusing eyes.

"Why did you have to tell her? Why?"

"Because it's best she knew now than later. She'll never believe our words again. We lied to her."

"When you sent the letter by courier a month ago, I couldn't believe it myself. I made great sacrifices to keep it from her."

"But you still didn't tell her the truth?" Now his eyes were accusing her.

"It would've killed her." She looked him squarely in the eyes. "Now I want to hear the whole story, and don't spare me."

Avram told her about the pirate ship, how Miguel protested, and how a pirate hit Miguel on the head. "He was bloody all over," he said to Ana. "I was tied up and couldn't help him." Avram lowered his head and began to sob.

Ana waited for him to calm down and continue.

"When the pirate who hit him came close, he cut the ropes, dragged him, then threw him overboard . . ." Avram stopped and breathed rapidly. "I jumped to my feet, dragging the others with me, and looked over the railing. I saw him going down into the depths of the sea."

Ana crossed her arms in grief, and with her head low on her chest she rocked herself back and forth. "My poor Miguel . . . poor Miguel." She cried quietly, afraid to wake Isabella.

"I blame myself." Avram's voice was harsh. "I couldn't jump after him, to see if he was still alive."

"Don't," Ana said. "We're not to blame, nor is Isabella. We must keep an eye on her to make sure she never finds out that he's dead."

Avram nodded his head. He got up and left the room.

Ana looked after him and cursed herself for having suggested to Don Abravanel to send Miguel on that path. She thought of Téresa, Miguel's mother, and her death. Now Miguel was gone too, and who knew what has become of José? How cruel was fate. She had to keep this secret deep in her breast and prevent Isabella from ever finding it.

60

In Search of Cuba

Wednesday, October 24, 1492

THE THREE SHIPS SAILED TOWARD the mainland of Cipango, where the khan and gold awaited them. The Indians on the ship told Columbus by signs to sail in low winds in a west-southwest direction to lead them to Cuba, which he believed to be Cipango. He sailed throughout the day, and it rained through the night, so he ordered some of the sails furled. The following day he continued until early afternoon, when a fairly good wind arose. His men were tired, but he called to raise all sails. Most men not on duty grumbled at the task. Columbus heard a few remarks such as "dog" or "His Excellency," but preferred to ignore them. He needed all hands on deck.

"Raise the mainsail with two bonnets! I also want the foresail, mizzen sail, and spritsail up! We need them all while the wind is good!"

The men rushed to abide by his orders, heaving and pulling until the sails filled with the wind, projecting their majestic ballooning, and propelling the *Santa Maria* forward at a comfortable eight miles per hour.

By two o'clock the wind built up with a stronger gale, and he woke the men. "Lower the sails except for the foresail!"

They sailed all day and by evening Columbus came upon small islands under the moonlight, but without knowing which one was Cuba. The waters were deep, and he continued his course of west-southwest without landing at any of them. It began to rain again, and as the wind increased he ordered to take down the main sail. They hardly went two leagues that night. But at sunrise they progressed five leagues.

At morning land appeared at five leagues, then seven to eight islands came in their sight. The waters were shallow, and he anchored at midpoint by the fourth island. He sent the weary men for fresh water, and barely having slept, he entered his cabin to write in his journals.

Friday October 26. Your Highnesses. We have accomplished much since my last report in my notebook. Everywhere we landed, we found friendly Indians who gave us gifts of food, water, and whatever little they had. On one island, the natives fled before us. But the Indians we brought from Guanahani told them we are friends, and they came back to their huts and gave us many gifts. Their huts are round and more beautiful than the previous ones. They are clean with proper furnishings. We found statues of women and some with masks. I don't know if they like them for their beauty or for adoration. The villages are large and have no streets. Again, I ordered nothing to be touched, to prove we're friends. I don't believe we found Cuba yet because these islands do not look like a mainland or Cipangu. We will sail from here to Cuba to deliver your letter to the great khan.

He signed with his customary signature with a sigla at the bottom.

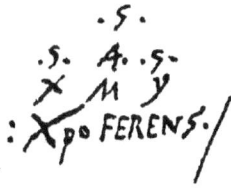

A great ruckus came to his ears, and he rushed on deck to find his men having returned from the island. They were excited and joyful despite having slept little.

"What's the great noise about?" he asked De la Cosa, who had joined on the excursion.

"Admiral. It is with great pleasure that I announce we have found gold." De la Cosa said ceremoniously while bowing low.

A great pang of joy struck Columbus's heart. "Where is it?" he asked, anxious.

"Bring the gold!" De la Cosa called out to one of the sailors.

The sailor was none other than João Treves, the last man he wanted to bring him this news. He stood nonchalantly away from Columbus and walked slowly toward them.

"Show him!" an excited De la Cosa said.

João opened his right hand and showed them a small ingot of gold the size of his pinkie.

Columbus reached for the gold finger and looked at it curiously. He bit on it and found it malleable. "It isn't much!" Columbus said.

"How can you say that, Admiral? It's the first one we found, larger than all the other trinkets," De la Cosa said.

"I still say it's nothing to be joyful about. And where did you find it?" He looked at João with narrowing eyes.

"I was wading through a river, when I looked down at this shiny thing. There it was stuck between two boulders."

"Did you see any others like it?" Columbus said with a forced smile.

João raised his head from the gold and his eyes expressed surprise at the admiral's tone of voice. Columbus saw that he refrained from flying at him. His face had reddened, and his other hand formed into a fist.

"No, Admiral."

"All right. You may go back to work now, João."

João put the small ingot in De la Cosa's outstretched hand and walked away as nonchalantly as ever.

Columbus felt his blood begin to boil. This braggart was taunting him. Why? João had no way of exposing him, and there hadn't been a new request to leave him at any one of the islands. Perhaps he was waiting to get to Cipangu and reveal Columbus's identity? No matter—he'd keep his eyes close on that one.

"Admiral? Admiral?" De la Cosa's voice pulled him out of his thoughts.

"We must find Cipangu next!" Columbus said in an angry voice.

61

Days of Haze

SINCE ISABELLA HAD LEARNED OF Miguel's disappearance, she retreated from her world. Meals went uneaten, her posture sagged, and her whole demeanor was unkempt. Her black lustrous hair was unwashed and looked matted, her eyes looked dull and tired, and worst of all—she rocked herself continuously when seated in the garden. Ana noticed that she hardly enjoyed the flowers' late bloom that still resisted winter sliding in slowly, nor was she making contact with her unborn child. She now sat on the front porch for hours staring at the horizon.

Ana warned her. "You're going to make yourself sick, not to mention your child."

"I don't care what happens to me," Isabella said in a dying voice.

"You can't mean that. You have to care. You must!" Ana's voice rose volumes. "You want to kill the life inside you?"

Isabella didn't answer at first. She then broke out in sobs. "I don't want . . . to hurt the little one inside me . . . I don't."

"Then you must force yourself to eat."

"But what can I do? Miguel isn't here with me. He won't see his son grow up and become strong like him. I'm being punished for deserting my parents, my father . . ." Her voice died down.

"You mustn't say such things!" Ana reproached her while feeling guilty pangs. If she hadn't suggested Miguel for that task to Don Abravanel, he'd be here now with his wife and unborn child. "It isn't your fault the ship ran into pirates. That's a danger no one can predict at sea."

"I knew it was going to happen. I tried to prevent it, but fate wanted to chastise me as a sinner."

"You can't believe this fate nonsense. Jews don't believe in that. We make our own destinies. We can only hope to redress mistakes by not repeating them."

"There's no chance of that." Isabella's lips were pressed tight, her head low on her chest, and she heaved with a moan.

Ana was desperate to lift her mood, but nothing seemed to help. Then words escaped her lips before she could think of them. "Perhaps he isn't dead. Perhaps he swam to escape the pirates?" No sooner had these words passed her lips than she regretted them. What good was it to give false hope? Hadn't Avram described Miguel's final moments as he descended into dark waters? She shivered.

Isabella's eyes suddenly flickered. "Do you really think there's a chance he's been taken by pirates to be sold as a slave?"

Ana's heart skipped a beat. Here was the old Isabella, the one who had laughed in the past, displaying a tough resolve and a stubborn streak when she wanted something badly. Ana had no heart to extinguish this glimmer of hope.

"There's always hope." Ana's voice died down.

Isabella straightened her posture. Her eyes looked feverish, and she moved restlessly on her seat. "I'm very hungry. Let me have some food," she said avidly.

62

Cuba at Last

Sunday, October 28, 1492

AS WHEN THEY FIRST FOUND land, since leaving the Canarias on August 3, the men were quiet on deck. It rained hard that night while the sailors tried to sleep on an unprotected deck, and they were soaked to their bones. There was grumbling and cussing coming from the men, but Columbus noticed they were hopeful at the same time. He had lectured his reluctant sailors that gold was finally at hand and in their grasp. Cipangu was near, and with it the great khan and his gold temples and reserves.

Columbus stood on the main deck with his head and shoulders covered by a spare canvas sail. The rain, nevertheless, seeped into his neck collar and dripped down into his clothes. The mainmast and foremast sails were fully blown by the wind powering them forward. He felt that they had gone a good seventeen leagues in a south-southwest course that would get them to Cuba by early morning.

The faint light rising on the horizon and coming from an eastern sky illuminated a large island without end. They were there at last! Columbus waited for the light to get stronger before landfall. Dangerous shoals were lurking ahead, and he hesitated to drop anchor.

By midmorning the emerald palm trees came into sight with white sand shores. The rain had stopped, and a sweet smell in the air lulled them forward. The *Santa Maria*, was followed by the *Niña* and the *Pinta*, a league behind her.

All three ships veered into a large river twelve fathoms deep, where the water was clear and the anchors were dropped down at a distance of a Lombard shot. All three boats went ashore this time with Columbus, Juan de la Cosa, and the Pinzón brothers; a slew of interpreters and scribes followed the small party.

"I name this river and harbor San Salvador," Columbus said with pride and gravity.

The native huts were again empty. All they found was a dog resting his chin gently on his front paws while examining the men curiously.

"Look, this dog isn't barking," De la Cosa noted. "It probably means the owners are gentle."

Columbus didn't reply, but he noticed again the huts' clean-swept floors, their nets made from palm threads, and harpoons and fishhooks made of bones.

When Columbus reappeared out of one hut, he noted the large trees with fruit and flowers in red blooms and no deciduous leaves or bark at their feet. The birds sang constantly, and tall, soft grasses lay on the floor of the groves. At one point along their march in the groves, Columbus bent down to the grass and discovered purslane with yellow flowers and reddish stems that were used as cooked vegetables back in Spain. In the fields surrounding the huts, he found amaranth grain abounding everywhere they looked, making for a good breakfast source for his men.

"Take many samples of these plants and bring them to the ships," Columbus ordered his men.

The terrain was higher with green trees growing on the sides of the mountains that appeared emerald with a profusion of vegetation. Fresh water abounded from lakes and rivers around them. The men taken from Guanahani had said by signs that many rivers existed on this large island. Their canoes could not go around it in as many as thirty days. The

Guanahani Indians also indicated that gold and pearls were plentiful. Columbus noted that the lack of rough seas made for abundant grasses that grew close to protected shores and were ideal for mussels and pearls. The Indians further told him that the great khan had come with large ships from the mainland, which was a twelve days' voyage.

"Tomorrow we'll sail to the land where the great king dwells," Columbus said.

63

The Search Begins

ISABELLA WOKE UP THAT MORNING with feverishness. She touched her forehead, afraid that a fever had overtaken her, but it felt cool. She got up, washed, and dressed faster than usual, despite the great weight she now carried. She patted her growing abdomen, and a smile fleeted across her mouth. *I must show Mig—* She was stopped short by a pang piercing through her. She was about to succumb to the memory but stood erect. *I'll find him if it takes a lifetime!*

She left her room and went down to the dining room. Ana and Avram were finishing their breakfast.

Ana said, "I just sent a tray to your room . . ."

"Isabella?" Avram said, surprised.

"Did you think I'd hide in my room forever?" Isabella said in a harsh tone of voice. "I have an unborn child to feed." She looked down to her stomach with her hands caressing it soothingly.

Ana looked pleased with Isabella's appearance at the table. She got up to serve her from the sideboard displaying hot dishes. She put in front of Isabella fried eggs, bourekas pastry filled with spinach, and fresh fruit, filling the plate.

"I can't eat all that!" Isabella protested.

"You must and you will," Ana said with a smile.

"Avram?" Isabella turned to him sitting across the table. "I want to see the ship's manifest and the journals from the last voyage."

Avram's mouth fell open.

"What is it you want to know?" Ana asked.

"I want to see it. That's all."

"But you won't understand the mariner's language it's written in," Avram said slowly in a carefully controlled voice.

"I want to see how a ship records its data. I know that Miguel—" She stopped abruptly as both Ana and Avram looked startled. "You can't refuse." She continued. "Miguel was in charge of ship's operations by right. As his widow, I'm entitled to see it."

Both Ana and Avram sat without a word.

Ana then said, "You're entitled, as Don Abra . . ." She corrected herself, "As Dom Carvalho bequeathed his Portugal holdings to you and Miguel as heirs."

Isabella said to Ana, "It's all right Ana. It's time to tell Avram the truth about Don Abravanel." Isabella then revealed to Avram, Dom Carvalho's identity and how both Isabella and Miguel came by their wealth.

For a few moments, Avram sat without stirring. "I'm grateful for your trust in me Isabella. I will keep this information secret."

"We have to keep his identity secret to protect him and his family. Now Please, Avram, have those journals available as soon as possible."

"I'll requisition them this week," Avram said. He got up and left the dining room silently.

Ana looked perplexed. "I still don't understand why you had to tell him?"

"Because secrets among us breeds mistrust."

Ana stayed silent to Isabella's comment.

Isabella then said, "I'm grateful to Don Abravanel and to you for these last months of peace for Miguel and me. Now I want to be useful . . . to stop, for a few hours, the pain . . ." Her voice broke out with a moan.

"I'm sorry." Ana let out a heavy sigh. "Of course, you want to occupy your mind. You can help me with the operations of the house and by going through those journals Avram will get for you."

"Then it's decided," Isabella said, sighing. "Now, I'm going for a walk to the workers' barracks and see if they need anything."

64

foreign Intrigues

THE COURTIERS AND ADVISORS TO Queen Isabella waited for Her Majesty to arrive. A hushed murmur rumbled across the hall, jumping from group to group as they congregated together. Concern and anxiety showed on the courtiers' faces, and some of them shook their heads not wanting to believe the news put to them. Near the throne stood one of Aragon's most illustrious courtiers: Louis de Santángel. He was visiting the monarchs in Castile, where Ferdinand was spending the beginning of winter with his queen.

"The queen and king, Isabella I of Castile and Ferdinand II of Aragon!"

Both Isabella and Ferdinand glided slowly across the room with grave looks on their faces. They climbed the three steps and sat down respectively on their thrones.

"What is the order of the day?" Ferdinand asked.

Luis de Santángel, finance minister to Ferdinand, said, "Sire, we're getting more disturbing news from England. King Henry II has asserted claim to France's throne. Since they tried to invade France on the second of October, their troops are fighting as we speak and have invaded and besieged Boulogne. King Henry has twenty-six thousand men fighting for him and voted in by Parliament."

"Huh! Why would King Henry pursue such a foolish war when they have barely recovered from the War of the Roses?" King Ferdinand shook his head while frowning.

"We're still honoring the future betrothal between young Prince Arthur and the Princess Catalina," Queen Isabella reminded her assembly like a mother hen looking out for the future of her brood.

"That's quite true, my queen. The princess is still young, and so is Prince Arthur," Santángel said

"May I remind you, Counselor, that the princess is bringing a dowry of a hundred thousand crowns when the marriage is performed," King Ferdinand said.

"That is what concerns me," Isabella interjected. "If Prince Arthur's father, King Henry, is squandering his wealth on wars with France, the dowry will be further spent on future wars in Europe."

"That is most wise, my queen." Santángel bowed his head to the queen.

"We must then keep a close eye on Henry and the outcome of this war," Ferdinand cautioned.

De Santángel nodded and bowed to both monarchs.

"On another subject, Counselor." Isabella raised her hand. "Have we any news of the voyage?"

Santángel lifted his head and remained silent.

"Well?" Isabella asked again.

"Dear queen, we wait each day to hear about the great voyage by Columbus. As soon as the word reaches us, we'll advise Your Majesties. We have many spies planted on Portuguese soil to give advance on the ships."

"That is a good precaution, Counselor. We want to know immediately any news that reaches you," Ferdinand said.

Santángel nodded to both Isabella and Ferdinand, bowed, then took his leave.

65

An Education

SABELLA PORED OVER THE JOURNALS provided to her by Avram. In them she learned of the trade conducted throughout ports in Portugal, the south of Spain, and all the way into North Africa. Entries were made in the last five years with details and deliveries of goods and freed slaves. The latter were transported to Portugal for dispersion to the cities of Lisbon, Tomar, and Sintra. Goods of cooked fruits, dried raisins, citrus fruit, and wine were distributed throughout Portugal by ship along the coasts and by mules on land.

Now Isabella understood Don Abravanel's unlimited wealth and why he had bequeathed a small fortune upon them. In a way, she was grateful to Don Abravanel, yet angry at the grief it had brought her. Losing Miguel was a price she was unwilling to pay. What good was it in the end? She covered her face with her hands, about to break down, when Ana came into the room.

Ana frowned. "You must get fresh air. You've been looking at those books long enough."

"Tell me, Ana—how wealthy is Don Abravanel?"

"Even though he was my cousin, I never asked such a question of him."

"But you must've seen his estates and the people he associated with. Didn't you?"

"All I can tell you is that he loaned immeasurable sums of money to the monarchs in Spain for their wars. His estate in Seville was magnificent! So it was no sacrifice giving you and Mi—" She stopped, with concern in her eyes.

"Don't fret," Isabella said in a modulated tone of voice. "I know that Miguel is alive. If he were dead, I would feel it deep in my heart."

Ana gave her a desperate look. She shook her head but no words came forth.

"I know what you're thinking," Isabella said. "But I know I'm right."

"I must go back to my work," Ana said.

"Look, Ana, I want to learn everything there is to know about shipping."

Ana raised questioning eyes.

Isabella raised her chin with determination. "I know it sounds strange to you that a woman would want to learn about commerce. But I intend to know all there is about it, then work at it."

"You don't mean that, do you?"

"I mean it and will pursue it"

"And what about your child?" Ana's voice mocked her as she crossed her arms.

"I'll attend to my child like any mother would. I'll also try to direct and coordinate operations for commerce."

Ana threw her hands up. "I think right now we need to plan the noon meal."

Isabella's lips cracked into a faint smile.

66

Island Enchantments

Monday, October 29, 1492

THE ANCHORS WERE LIFTED, AND the three ships navigated west to find the city where the king dwelt. They sailed two leagues northwest along its coast to another point five leagues east. One of the rivers they found was narrow, and Columbus named it Rio de la Luna, and another river springing from this one was a larger river he called Rio de Mares. The ships turned around to the mouth of Rio de la Luna and measured its depth to be about eight fathoms, and the waters were calm. Columbus saw a village in the distance and sent two of his men and one of the Indians from his ship to translate.

"These villagers fled when they saw us," De la Cosa reported to the admiral. "Although their houses were pleasing to the eyes and better constructed as we came nearer to the mainland. We also found large skulls from cows. "

"We'll dock here for the night and explore the rest of the island in the morning," Columbus said.

That night, Maestre Diego cooked a feast for all the men on the *Santa Maria*. Columbus saw that the *Pinta* and the *Niña* shared the same bounty from provisions on their ships. Fresh fish and sweet tuber plant tasting like chestnut were served, and they ate it with pleasure. An extra serving of wine was served with sea biscuits, satiating the men.

The early morning of October 30, the second day on the island, woke them up with a dizzying smell of flowers and the sweet smell of grasses and verdure in the groves. Fruit from trees everywhere had wonderful tastes. His men went swimming near the mouth of the river and found the water a bit salty. Snails abounded around them, but they seemed tasteless, not like the ones in Seville. Above them the mountains were high, green, and beautiful. One particular mountain had a summit they called the Rock of Lovers, like *Peña de los Enamorados* back in Antequera. It was all lovely and beguiling. Columbus wished they could stay the rest of their lives on the island.

The boats were launched again into the Rio de Mares in a northwest direction. A cape covered with large, tall palm trees was called Cabo de Palmas. Columbus examined the large leaves from the palm trees and saw that they could cover the roof of a small hut. Everywhere he looked, trees, rivers, and huts were bigger and more plentiful than on previous islands. A pleasant breeze blew their way, caressing their foreheads and lifting the hair off their faces.

"Admiral?" One of the *Pinta*'s men addressed Columbus.

Columbus stopped his march to face him.

"Admiral, this man here"—he pointed to one of the Indians who had been on the *Pinta*—"says that after the cape on a river, and after a four days' voyage, there is a large island and city they call Cuba."

Columbus listened carefully. "Go on?"

"Well, the Indian says that the king there is waging war with the great khan of Cathay."

"We will pursue this lead. *Gracias, Marinero*," Columbus told the *Pinta*'s sailor.

Throughout this Tuesday night, Columbus urged his men to continue sailing until the river became narrow and shallow. The wind to the north became too strong to follow their course.

"We must return now to the ships," Columbus yelled over the whistling sound of a powerful wind. He then looked upon the sailors rowing in his boat, startled to find João rowing with the others. Columbus grumbled. *Each time I look around, this man is staring me in the face.*

67

Aboard the Liberação

VRAM PULLED ISABELLA AS SHE tried climbing the rope ladder on board the *Liberação*. Her cumbersome skirts wiped the wet railing, and she stood on deck with a surprised and contented look on her face. Avram couldn't understand her excitement at being on board. To him, being on ship represented nothing but hardship and reluctance. Not to mention the mortal dangers of the sea.

"I want to see everything," Isabella said.

Avram looked at her curiously, but abided by her desire to inspect the ship.

"The ship is seventy tons and can hold great cargo," Avram said. "The hold has a large storage capacity for goods, and we make sure to keep it dry from rain or seawater falling from the hatch above the hold."

"Let me see this." Isabella walked to the central area on deck and peered through the grate. "It's dark down there."

Avram lit the candle in the lamp hooked near the hold and lowered it with a rope attached to it. The light from the candle illuminated barrels girded by metal hoops, casks, jugs, sacks of ballast filled with rocks and pebbles, and two sailors moving crates and barrels.

"Take me now to the captain's cabin," she said with a strong voice.

Avram looked at her hesitantly and remained silent.

"Don't worry. I'll be strong. I want to see where Miguel spent his time."

Avram nodded and led her to the quarterdeck and to Miguel's empty cabin. They walked into the small space near the tiller, and Isabella held her head high. *She's trying hard to hold on*, Avram observed.

"Where are his journals?" she asked.

"Besides the ones you looked over at the house, he kept the rest in this strongbox." Avram walked to a chest near one wall and unlocked it. In it, neatly stacked, were the journals with logs of previous voyages documenting the ship's history. He picked up one up lying on top and put it in Isabella's hands.

She opened it slowly and turned the pages one by one, then gave it back to Avram. "There's lots of information here I don't understand," she said.

"Naturally. It's all for seasoned sailors and learned men."

A pinched expression appeared, and she tapped her foot on the floor. "Why, do you think that women can't understand these sea rules? That it's incomprehensible because we sit at home by the hearth?"

Avram saw that Isabella's tone was impatient, not angry, and he let out a sigh of relief. He wanted to avoid any ill feelings coming from her. It would pain him greatly to add to her grief.

"I didn't mean anything untoward, Isabella. If you like, I can explain these journals to you. My father had me join him when he traveled on his ships and taught me all about seafaring."

Isabella's face looked pleased. She smiled—a rare occurrence these days—and said, "I would be most grateful to you, Avram."

It was his turn to be pleased. A smile from Isabella was heaven for him. But he couldn't show his feelings to her. It would betray Miguel's memory.

"Let us go back home now, "Isabella said.

68

forward to Cuba

Thursday, November 1, 1492

THE MORNING BEGAN WITH A slight chill, and Columbus surmised that winter was lurking in paradise. He stood at the railing on the quarterdeck to admire a heavenly spectacle before him. The island looked the same as yesterday with its emerald-green palm trees swaying in a gentle breeze. The birds tweeted and sang their songs as usual as they sauntered from branch to branch, and the sea was as calm as a mirror. Not a cloud marred the beautiful azure-blue sky with a slight tint of orange where the sun was hiding. The vision of snow gales and icicles on rooftops in Castile's mountains came up in his mind's eye. A shiver went through him. He then delighted in this clement weather on Cuba's island in the Indies.

"We're ready to go to the island, Admiral," Juan de la Cosa shouted from the lower deck.

Columbus waved at him and shouted back, "Pay attention to gold sightings!"

De la Cosa nodded and embarked on the boat, followed by two Indians from Guanahani and two of his sailors. João again was one of them. From the *Niña* and the *Pinta* two other boats rowed ashore in tow, with Martin Pinzón and his brother Vicente manning them.

Barely had the day advanced when the men returned empty-handed. No gold was to be seen, although a silver ring was noticed hanging from a native's nose.

"We scoured every hut in the village and found nothing," De la Cosa said, to Columbus's disappointment.

"Did you make sure no one touched or took anything from the huts?" Columbus asked.

"*Si*, Admiral. I warned the men I'd cut off their fingers if anyone stole."

"That's good. Tomorrow I go ashore with the men."

The following morning, Columbus left the ships in the deep harbor and instructed the men that upon his return in six days they were to run them aground to clean the hulls, but to make sure to collect wood from the trees, which were plentiful. He also made good his promise to search the island further with his men. The boats rowed to the mouth of a river, where another village surged before their eyes, and he ordered them to land on the beach. Many natives came forward to welcome them. *The word must've spread*, Columbus thought, rejoicing. The natives offered them more spun cotton that grew on the island on small trees.

Two of the men he took along to translate were Rodrigo de Jerez from the town of Ayamonte and Luis de Torres from Murcia. Torres was a Converso who spoke Arabic, Chaldean, and Hebrew. If they were going to address the king, they had to be prepared. Along came two other Indians from Guanahani to help translate from the natives in Cuba. Columbus also had in his possession a letter from the monarchs in Castile. A large satchel carried presents for the natives and the king.

Around them the verdant trees, the birds singing, and the sweet air made them all feel giddy in this enchanted paradise. They continued two leagues up the river and found fresh water. The rest of the day was spent on seeing more villages and more natives, and yet, no signs of gold.

On that night Columbus took a reading on his compass. He estimated They had traveled 1,142 leagues since they had left Hiero Island in the Canarias. Therefore, according to his calculations, they were on the mainland.

On the morning of November 3, Martín Pinzón came to him carrying reddish nuts. "Admiral! I found cinnamon!"

Columbus bit on it and declared it wasn't the tasty and flavorful cinnamon he was familiar with. Columbus showed a stick of cinnamon he had carried from Castile to the natives, and they became excited by pointing further up to the southeast where it could be found. He then showed them a gold necklace and some pearls, and the natives again affirmed that in Bohio one could find much gold and pearls, which the Indians wore as earrings, and around their necks and ankles. They also opened their eyes wide and made frightful gestures with their hands, indicating that these Indians cut the throats and genitals of all trespassers.

The natives also brought them a chestnut-colored carrot that tasted like chestnuts and green *faxones*, similar yet different from the green beans back home in Spain.

Upon his return he ordered the *Niña* to be beached while the *Pinta* and the *Santa Maria* were to remain in the harbor for security reasons. Right after examining his ship from top to bottom for any wear and tear while he was gone, the *Niña*'s boatswain, Bartholomé Garcia, came back to him excitedly.

"I found mastic, Admiral! Mastic, I tell you! There were thousands of Arabic gum trees. Do I get the reward?"

"Well, where is it?" Columbus asked, his heart beating fast. He calculated quickly that mastic could procure a thousand quintals per year.

"I lost the sample, Admiral." The boatswain was in tears.

"That's all right. I promised you the reward. Tell my men where exactly you found it." He then sent Rodrigo Sanchez, his comptroller, and Master Diego, his cook, to the trees where the boatswain had found the mastic. They all came back with samples and portions of a tree to be carried back to Spain. Later on, other men from the *Pinta* discovered many aloe plants. Columbus was elated.

That same night, Columbus wrote in his journal:

With blessing from our Lord, the harbor Puerto de Mares is the best place to build a fort for great trade to be conducted with many nations. With the best climate and gentle people, many great deeds will occur to protect the merchants sailing from many countries for trade. We will dwell on this island another few days, then leave for the mainland of Cipangu.

That night he slept soundly, and dreamed of riches that would come down in his path.

69

A Plan

ISABELLA SAT IN THE DINING room, planning and imagining what she would do with the information from the ship. The best plan would be to safeguard the ship itself. But how could it be protected? The *Liberação* was a merchant ship, and as such to be used strictly for storing and retrieving merchandise at other ports. What if the ship were outfitted as a warship? What would it take to garner and load it with armaments? That was knowledge she lacked. Perhaps Avram, or Matigoro in Morocco, could provide the information. Then, on the other hand, she couldn't risk another voyage that might jeopardize the ship or its crew. She had to find another way. The only other way was to join the enemy.

The enemy? Was she going mad? But what if the protection came from the enemy camp, such as the pirates themselves? Perhaps a percentage of the booty would go to the lead pirates, and in return they would leave the ship alone. The question was not how to find them but rather how they might find her.

She got up from her seat with some difficulty now that her weight had increased, and with her hands supporting her growing belly, she made her way to the front porch of the house. In the distance she saw Avram working on trimming the trees around the barracks. She waved at him, but he couldn't see her, as he was busy at his task.

Isabella went down the steps and walked to Avram. He lifted his head for a moment from his work and looked surprised to see her.

"Please, Isabella, you should've called me."

"I did, but you didn't see me."

"What can I do for you?" Avram said eagerly.

"Why don't we sit down first?" Isabella made her way to a wooden bench nearby. Avram joined her and waited for her to speak.

"I want you to know," Isabella began, "that you've been a great help to me and Ana on the estate." She then tried to stop Avram from protesting. "I know you feel that we helped you in your time of need, and why not? That's why Miguel undertook those dangerous travels—to rescue our endangered brothers and sisters."

"I want to help as much as I can," Avram said.

"I know that, and you paid your dues manyfold. But now I want you to help in another capacity." She then told him of her plans.

His first reaction was shock. His mouth slackened and his eyes widened. He got up from his seat and went to pace back and forth.

"What you're asking is folly. You'll endanger everyone and the ship too. Once the ship is taken, you will have lost the best means to save those brothers and sisters from the slave market, and the means to sell your products overseas. It can't be done."

Isabella shook her head. "I'm not asking to befriend the pirates; I'm asking to show them the advantage of leaving us alone, with bribes."

Avram came back to his seat and looked at her suspiciously. "I can't believe my ears. You want to become like them! A blackmailer to the pirates?"

Isabella nodded this time with a smile on her face. "That's exactly what I mean. We can play at their game. We're not joining them in piracy. We're trading money or goods for preventing their raids."

Avram kept silent. He shook his head and tightened his lips. Isabella feared that she hadn't won him to her idea.

"Look," she said. "We can first outfit the ship with more cannons, weapons, and men to defend us if they renege on us."

Avram continued his silence for a short while Isabella's heart tightened. *He won't help me.*

"Look," he said. "Let me think about it. Besides, I'm the one who'll make those voyages, so I'll have to decide."

"You won't have to do it alone. I'll be joining you in the negotiations."

Avram seemed confused. "What do you mean by negotiations?"

"As soon as you find out how to reach them, I'll be there with you."

"You can't! You're pregnant and a woman too."

Isabella smiled. "A woman can learn, and I won't be pregnant for long."

Avram looked away, nodding his head. "I'm not promising anything." He then walked away to the tree to resume his work.

Isabella got up with a smile and a vague inkling that he would see things her way, then walked back to the house.

70

Gold

Monday, November 12, 1492

THEY BEGAN THEIR VOYAGE BY weighing the anchors on all three ships. Then with one ship following the other, they set out to sea in search of the next island where gold was to be found. The sea rolled in small waves, capped with white foam, and seals followed them with frolics. They would perform great acrobatic jumps in the air, followed by crashing into the waters. Columbus watched his men joyfully following the seals and clapping their hands like children. He smiled at the sight, delighting in the scene. He threw his head back with laughter surging deep from his throat and with a liberating feeling of release. His men had confidence in his ability and trusted him to find the rewards promised upon their departure from Spain. Now he needed to come through with that promise.

Their destination for that day was the island of Babeque, as the Indians on his ship told him by signs. The natives there had much gold, which they scoured for at night with lit torches. Columbus turned the prow to the east and sailed eight leagues till he reached a long coast. River after river appeared in their sight, and he bypassed them for the sake of finding Babeque.

"Admiral, we're bypassing these rivers when we should be exploring them," De la Cosa said.

"Yes. I know," Columbus said. "But we must head on to our goal: the great Kahn. I know the weather is clement now, but who's to say what winter will bring?"

"These islands are paradise," De la Cosa replied. "If anything, the weather won't turn at all."

"We can only hope with the Lord's blessings that it won't change. But we must not lose time."

De la Cosa sighed but abided by Columbus's plan.

They sailed forth that day till sunset, then beat about without headway until they saw a gap between two large mountains. Columbus surmised that Cuba was one island and Bohio another island leeward, with a gulf between them.

The following morning and throughout the day, his Indians affirmed again that large quantities of gold were to be found. Columbus saw small villages along the coast and decided to bypass them too, as the wind from the north had increased before him. They passed many islands. On that day they sailed fourteen to fifteen leagues.

On the morning of November 14, and throughout that day, he searched for a harbor for their ships. The wind was strong and the sea just as powerful, making him change plans to drop anchors at one of the inlets. He feared a rocky sea bottom would shred the anchors' cables. Instead, he sailed northwest along the coast that he named Rio del Sol until he found a deep and wide inlet with a safe harbor where the bottom had sand. Before him were innumerable islands covered with deep-green trees and many different types of palm trees bearing fruit of all kinds.

"I name this island La Mar de Nuestra Señora, and the safe harbor Puerto del Principe."

In his journal he noted his impressions for the day and what he believed—that his search for gold was near.

Your Highnesses, the Lord saw fit that I should see these marvels of faraway lands I conquer in your name. No other land can be as beautiful as these; no trees, nor rivers, nor any other birds, fruits, and fishes to be found in the waters can compare with these magnificent islands. I believe much trade can be made here, especially aloes, mastic, and cotton that grow on trees without sowing. The harbors are deep with clear waters, and the natives here are docile. They believe there's a God and that we come from heaven. It will be easy to convert them to our holy faith. I will bring back these Indians to vouch for the gold that can be found here.

He put down his quill and called De la Cosa to his cabin.

"We'll heave-to and beat about the night. It isn't safe for us to land, and there's still much I want to explore on this island," he said to De la Cosa.

"Aye, aye, Admiral. I'll give your orders to Ruiz for the next watch."

When the door to his cabin shut after De la Cosa, he went to get some much-needed rest on his bunk bed.

The following morning and throughout the next days, Columbus explored the island, then made sail for the island of Babeque. He set his course east, toward where his Indians told him much gold could be found. His Indians had also told him that within three days' sailing Babeque could be reached. With a moderate wind, he then sailed all day southeast and found by nightfall that they couldn't land due to high winds and a changed sea. They continued sailing eight leagues along the coast that had many inlets and harbors, but they didn't dare land, and continued northwest and quarter west for twenty-four leagues. Finally, he found a good harbor and decided it was high time to land.

On Wednesday the twenty-first around two a.m., he woke up with a sense of urgency. He forewent calling Salcedo and dressed without his help. When he stepped outside his cabin, he saw Salcedo all rolled up in his blanket and deeply asleep.

Dawn hadn't arrived yet, but the sky's dome shone with myriads of stars above, and Columbus reveled in the magnificence of the Lord's works. The North Star reigned in the firmament as in Castile, and that made him yearn for home. He took in the pure air of the island still sleeping with palm trees waving gently in the breeze.

He turned around from the railing, and to his horror saw that the *Pinta* was gone! But where? He ran to the stern to find Ruiz still asleep.

"Wake up! Wake up, Ruiz!"

Ruiz threw his blanket back, and his head emerged in the darkness on the deck. "What is it, Admiral?"

"The *Pinta* is gone—gone, I tell you!" Columbus felt his befuddlement giving way to blood going up to his head. "Go and find De la Cosa!"

De la Cosa joined him by the tiller in his night chemise. "Admiral, is it true?"

"I'm afraid it is, Juan. He left for Babeque without my command."

"I was afraid of that, Admiral. He's done you wrong, and his avarice for gold led him astray. What's to be done now?"

"There's not much we can do. We'll continue tomorrow toward Babeque." Columbus fell quiet. "In the meantime, Juan, leave a torch burning until sunrise in case Pinzón returns."

71

The Voyage Begins

*A*LL PREPARATIONS HAD BEEN MADE: food, clothes, goods for the Tangier and Moroccan market, and additional sailors hired for the voyage. Isabella made the decision to undertake the voyage despite Ana's protests and crying that she might not return—or get killed along with her unborn child.

"Ana," Isabella told her calmly, "Avram will be there to protect me."

Avram nodded with a grimace.

"But what if Avram is captured?" Ana said.

"We won't be captured. The ship is now outfitted with five cannons, so no one can board it." Isabella said.

"You forget what happened to Mig—" Ana looked furtively at Isabella and Isabella's shoulders dropped.

"I'm sorry, Isabella. I didn't mean to remind you," Ana said.

"It's all right, Ana. Miguel is in my thoughts every day."

"The carriage is waiting for us," Avram said.

Isabella went to Ana and embraced her. "We'll be back soon."

Tears appeared on Ana's creased face. "Send word by caravel that you've arrived safe."

"I will," Isabella said as she walked away out of the house and into the waiting carriage. She waved at Ana, and at that moment felt a strong urge to remain behind, but struggled against the pull. She turned her head away from the disappearing house and toward the road.

"We should arrive under three hours," Avram said.

Isabella nodded silently. "Tell me again the crew's names."

Avram looked surprised. "Why?"

"I need to know who they are and where they come from."

"I'm your first in command, and second is Lourenço da Sintra, The pilot is Joham Alvaro, the cook is Hanrrique, and the first mate is . . ."

Avram's voice grew faint as the image of Miguel rose in her mind. She needed a free hand in searching for Miguel, even if it was for his body. A slight moan escaped her lips.

"Are you all right, Isabella?"

Isabella startled. "I'm all right. Just felt a kick," she said as she held her right hand over her stomach.

Avram smiled. "He sounds strong, like a boy."

Isabella said, "What makes you so sure it's a boy?"

"Just a hunch," he said, smiling.

Isabella didn't reply to Avram, and tried not to think of Miguel. For the next hour she remained quiet, and no other words passed between them. The carriage rolled with bumpiness on the country road, and little hamlets appeared surrounded by their fields of barley and wheat at the foot of the Sintra Mountains. She hadn't traveled to Sintra since they came to live in Portugal, nor had she seen the big city of Lisbon, a place Ana had told her was full of lights and gaiety. Ana also talked of the royal court of John II dictating the fashions, the ladies in their colorful gowns coming and going to court, and of their amorous escorts. The only brush with royalty Isabella ever had was at the court of Queen Isabella. She vaguely recalled being dressed in her fineries of satin and velvet at the age of five and being presented to the queen by her mother Estrella.

"What a beautiful child!" the queen had exclaimed. "And she's my relative!" the queen continued in her delight.

Isabella dismissed the memory as a dream from another life and didn't want to dwell on it. She returned her gaze to her surroundings and saw a large rock jutting into the sea.

"This is the cape of Cabo da Roca," Avram said, disturbing her thoughts.

"It strangely looks like a sail made of rock."

Avram smiled at the allusion.

"It's also called the Rock of Lovers." He rushed to explain. "Because when the men sailed away, their women made a prayer from that rock for them to return safely."

Isabella thought for a moment, then asked him, "When we first landed in Portugal, we landed on a beach far from port. Why not Lisbon?"

"Because the ship carried passengers unknown to the authorities."

"Why, was it illegal?"

"No. Don Abravanel had good business sense. He'd have to pay a heavy tax for each passenger."

The next hour passed in silence between Isabella and Avram, and she felt her mood spiraling downward as thought of Miguel came back to her.

The carriage stopped, and Avram said, "I believe we've arrived."

The hustle and bustle of Lisbon's port came to her ears. Outside, the many masts without their sails dotted the landscape like winter trees in a forest without branches or leaves. The many sounds of merchants unloading their wares on the docks, the foremen yelling at their workers, and captains shouting orders to their sailors were deafening.

Avram helped her alight from the carriage, and they made their way to the *Liberação* swaying gently on the waters. She climbed the plank to the top of its deck.

"Welcome. It's a lovely day for passengers on our ship!" A burly man with white hair rubbed his hands together with glee.

Isabella said, "Let me guess. You are Lourenço da Sintra. Second in command?"

Lourenço stood with his mouth falling open.

Avram hastened to explain. "This is Isabella Obrigon da Costa, captain of the ship."

Surprise and shock appeared on Lourenço's face. His eyes fell down to her bulging midriff, and he shuffled back a step. "My apologies, *minha senhora*." He bowed before her.

Isabella held her laughter in check. After all, she didn't want to insult a most useful man aboard her ship.

"We have much to discuss, Lourenço." She walked up the quarterdeck to take residence in her cabin.

72

Thousands of Islands

Saturday, December 1, 1492

COLUMBUS SAT IN HIS CABIN at work on his journal after two weeks' neglect. The islands were so numerous, so fertile, and so beautiful that he had become entranced by them. His men, too, were becoming less enterprising, less eager to work faster, and less interested in sailing forward. Perhaps the crew had lost their intention to gain their rewards at the end of the voyage? It gave him a shiver, though the weather was temperate and calm. *I must motivate them to regain their original excitement for the quest for gold. I must!*

Your Highnesses, since November 17, in the year of our Lord, we have seen so many wonderful and fertile islands that they are too numerous to tell. I will make an effort to describe them to Your Majesties.

I named Cuba, La Isla Juana of Cuba after prince Juan, Prince of Asturias, your heir. We left La Isla Juana, where we made much progress and sailed many leagues. The islands in the southwest were very fertile and green, with fresh water and many palms along the river and into the islands.

We saw large nuts and crawfish that tasted sweet, like lobsters in Spain. We also smelled a scent of almazique or musk in their forest of many birds.

On November 20, we entered the island of Babeque east-southeast and sailed to Puerto del Principe at twenty-five leagues. The Indians we carry with us from Guanahani were assured that we would bring them back upon finding gold.

It is marvelous how many islands one can sail to on this sea. These islands have the highest mountains, and I believe they have precious stones and spices on them.

On November 21, on this day, Martin Alonso Pinzón took the caravel Pinta *and sailed away without my knowledge. Pinzón has engaged in many insubordinations and injurious acts to me personally.*

Everywhere we landed we placed a cross on the highest cape. These islands have deep waters near the shore, and many caravels can drop anchor there with safety. A fortress can be build to help many ships bring trade. Large snails were found in the waters, but they were tasteless, not like in Castile. The crew found a fish the natives call taso, and it is mean-looking with a hard shell and not much meat.

On November 22, we sailed south quarter southeast with an east wind, and went twenty-four leagues by Vespers. We found ourselves midway between the celestial poles, or about. My quadrant had loose plates and is in need of repair.

By November 25, we were southeast of a large island, and we saw water from a river cascading with great thunder from a mountain. We found in the water shining stones, which were gold. Such are the stones bearing gold by the great river Tagus back home. We carried many stones to bring back with us.

The mountains were very green and covered with pines that would make great masts for our ships.

Today, on November 30, it rained and was cloudy and dark. We stayed on the island so as not to endanger the ships. We did see a canoe carved from a single tree that could hold at least one hundred persons.

I swear to Your Highnesses that all the lands are good and fertile. The weather is temperate, and neither cold nor hot. There is plenty of fresh water and rivers throughout, unlike the rivers in Guinea infected with pestilence.

My crew has been healthy till now without ailments or pain. The Indians can be made into good Christians easily, for they are neither idolaters nor have a god to pray to. A fortress will be built on Rio de Mares. No foreigners can be allowed to enter the harbors, and only Christian traders will set foot here on all the islands.

Columbus closed his journals, stretched his limbs, and felt satisfied for all the good work he put in for the sovereigns and the Lord.

73

A Voyage of discovery

THE VOYAGE HAD PROCEEDED SMOOTHLY so far for Isabella. The sea kept calm, no clouds gathered overhead, and no pirates appeared at the horizon. The previous day, a caravel sent a Lombard shot to warn them, but the vessel headed in a northerly direction never to be seen again. Its mast sported a black flag with markings that couldn't be distinguished due to its distance. Isabella breathed easier when the ship disappeared from view. She didn't want to face unwanted surprises. True, the *Liberação* had been outfitted with additional cannons before they'd left port, and she was fit for battle. Yet, it was too soon to mar the beautiful ship she inherited from Miguel.

Isabella pored over the journals contained in the coffer of Miguel's cabin. She surfaced now and then to take food prepared for her on the quarterdeck. Her second in command, Lourenço da Sintra, used this quiet time to keep her abreast of the navigation requirements and rules of the sea. Words and visions of this moving and liquid world took shape, and she became adept in its unique language. She learned of rigging and cordage, of masts and sails, of the hull, the hold and the required ballast, tiller and rudder safety, of leagues and miles, when to drop anchor, of cannons and their uses, the language of sailors' warnings, of windward and leeward winds, and of quadrants and astrolabes.

By the time the north African coast came into view, she had acquired a solid knowledge of maritime operations. Avram stood aside observing the instructions handed down by Lourenço and did not interfere, but continued his supervision of the men on deck.

"Is it all to your satisfaction?" Avram inquired when he came her way.

Isabella raised her eyes from the quadrant and turned to Avram. "I never dreamed that such a world existed. I had taken it for granted that we sailed on ship as passengers, then disembarked at our destination. This opens up a curious and exciting world."

"You must consider, though, that dangers and perils exist?" Avram said.

"Of course I do," Isabella replied. "That is why I want to minimize them." She fell quiet to observe the African coast on the horizon. She lowered the quadrant still in her hands and pulled away strands of hair flowing in front of her eyes and blown by a gentle wind. "You see," she continued, "our livelihoods—yours, Ana's, and mine—depend on the trade and commerce we bring with this ship. Without it we're at the mercy of poverty and the lords depending on it to keep us yoked. I'm not even including the men and women we employ and who earn a living. This ship must survive the weather, the usurers baiting us, and the pirates. These are the dangers we face."

Avram remained quiet while she spoke. He then said, "My father had to fight the same evil forces, in addition to our religious enemies."

Isabella nodded her head in commiseration. "I'm sorry you've been through a lot of grief."

"I'll never find out what happened to my father . . ." Avram said, his voice trailing in a suppressed moan.

"Captain?" Lourenço's voice came to their ears. Isabella's eyes searched the deck by instinct for the captain.

Avram said with a smile. "He's calling you, Isabella."

A faint smile appeared on her lips. She'd have to get used to being called captain. "Yes, Lourenço. What is it?"

Lourenço approached her on the quarterdeck and presented her with documents. "These are the customs documents for landing."

Isabella had not anticipated this added responsibility. "Can you explain those papers?" she said to Avram.

"I'll be glad to." He explained that cargo had to account for an exact number of barrels and crates. All additional goods would be confiscated by the Portuguese authority in Tangier, never to be returned. All had to be above suspicion, including the captain and crew, with no stowaways.

"Would you see that it is done, once I study those documents?" she asked Avram.

"Right away, Captain," Avram said with a smile.

Isabella followed him with her eyes and felt sad at once. She knew that Avram still had feelings for her, but she could not and would not allow them to take hold in her. She'd remain faithful to Miguel and to his memory. She hid her clenched fists in the folds of her dress. *You've already given him up for dead.* She scolded herself. *Don't forget that this is a voyage to find Miguel, and the search has only begun.* She then entered her cabin to study the customs documents.

"Land ahoy!" the sailor shouted from the crow's nest.

Isabella stepped out on the quarterdeck from her cabin and cupped her hands in front of her eyes to view the coastline before her. Peach-colored beaches stretched under an azure-blue sky that paled over an indigo-green sea. It brought back memories of her previous voyage and leaving these hot sands with Miguel. A sigh lifted her chest that she muffled quickly. *I must concentrate on my task at hand.* Her impossible quest lay before her, and being levelheaded would bring success to this venture, which was to maintain trade on board the *Liberação* with the neighboring countries, and to find Miguel.

"Isabella?" Avram's voice shook her out of her thoughts.

"Yes?"

"We're hitting port shortly. We must present our custom papers for inspection," Avram said.

"I will go and get them ready," Isabella answered, then reentered the cabin.

Within an hour, the *Liberação* glided into Tangier's port. After the ship docked, the customs inspector came on board. He was a short man of Berber origin, wearing a white caftan and a *taqiyah* skullcap on his head. His sported a whip in his right hand to accentuate his orders. His left hand rummaged into his long black beard.

"Where's the captain of this ship?" he called.

Isabella presented herself before him with papers in hand.

The reaction was instantaneous. "What's this? Are you wasting my time?" he bellowed.

Isabella didn't flinch. She stood in front of him with her arms crossed in front of her chest. This posture delineated her bulging stomach, accentuating her pregnancy.

"I'm the captain!" she said firmly, while trying to squelch a tremolo in her voice.

"I don't do business with women. Get me the real captain."

Avram advanced and took the papers from Isabella's hand. He also threw her a sideways glance. "I can speak for the captain."

The inspector turned his back on Isabella and proceeded to check the papers. While he was busy reading the ship's manifest, Isabella tried to contain her anger at being rebuffed. *A fine beginning*, she fumed inwardly.

"These are in order," the inspector declared. "Let me see the hold."

Avram accompanied the inspector down the hold, while Isabella waited for them on deck. They reappeared shortly with the inspector carrying a jug of wine under his right arm.

Isabella's mouth fell open, but Avram looked at her sharply. She held back her gasp and shut her lips tightly.

The inspector passed by her without a glance, then descended the plank to the docks.

"What's the meaning of this?" Isabella snapped at Avram.

"You have to give *baksheesh*," Avram said calmly. "That's the way trade is done."

"Do you how much we've lost already?" Isabella said, raising her eyebrows.

Avram raised his right hand to calm her down. "I know, but we can't avoid it." he replied firmly.

"All right." Isabella conceded. "Then we must take that loss into account and charge more for the wine."

Avram looked at her surprised but nodded his head.

"Let us unload the cargo now." Isabella gave the order for the men to lift the various crates, jugs, and barrels containing wine, jams, citrus fruits, flowers, and plants. The lifting was done with pulleys and ropes thrown deep into the hold. The unloading proceeded smoothly with no broken ropes, nor anyone getting injured by barrels tumbling onto the docks.

Below, on the bustling docks, vendors in the market and narrow alleyways chanted about their wares and foods. Noise from rolling carts leaving and entering the small port, and the smells of cooking lamb and grilled meat in open fires, filled the air. Vendors poured into tin cans a juicy liquid through spouts from their decorated brass glass jugs, and highly adorned women sporting veils and nose ornaments on their faces waited in doorways to snag an itinerant sailor hungry for companionship.

Isabella turned her head away at the last sight, then breathed a sigh of relief to see the last barrel roll down the plank.

She turned to Lourenço da Sintra and said, "We'll stay in town for the night." She made a motion of her head toward Avram. "You can find us at Matigoro's house if an emergency comes up."

"I'll take good care of the ship . . . Captain," he quickly added.

Isabella smiled at Lourenço's hesitation. He was getting used to her as captain and commander. She felt a secret pride from the overpowering feeling of her position.

She headed for the plank, lifted her voluminous skirts, and descended slowly down to the docks. An opened carriage was waiting for her and Avram sent by Matigoro. She mounted the two steps into the carriage with Avram following behind.

He sat opposite her on the bench, and called out to the driver on his high bench. "Go on!"

Isabella looked around her as the carriage sped down the narrow alleyways bordered by white, stone houses with flat roofs, and their terraces covered by palm leaves.

"The residents sleep on their roofs during the summer heat," Avram explained to Isabella as she observed the scene.

"Similar to our homes in Spain," Isabella remarked. This time she was riding in a carriage, not walking in hot sands and fleeing from the shores as a redeemed slave. How her life had changed since she was a sixteen-year-old girl living under her parents' benevolent and protected old life. The carriage, meanwhile, turned down several alleys, then stopped at a whitewashed square house with blue awnings.

Matigoro was there to greet them. "Welcome, welcome." He extended his hand to Isabella for support as she alighted from the carriage. "Please come into my humble abode."

Both Avram and Isabella followed him into a large hall with low sofas and cushions spread along the four walls. A low and round wooden table, encrusted with inlaid tile, held pastries and *zarfs*—chalice-like brass ornamental holders for hot drinks.

Isabella sat down with some difficulty, and her hand reached for the *basbousa* desert made of fine semolina and ground pistachio. She licked the honey off her fingers, then looked up to find Avram and Matigoro staring at her. Her face reddened, and she hastened to explain. "I still have urges for certain foods."

"Please, Isabella. No need to explain. It's understandable in your condition." Matigoro sported a large smile. His face suddenly lost its open and lighthearted expression, and sadness appeared instead. "I was saddened to hear of what happened to Miguel." He looked down to his crossed-legged position.

Isabella came to the point. "That's why I'm here. I was left with Miguel's affairs. I'm conducting the trading now. I also intend to enlarge the operations and increase the goods."

Matigoro faced her with a smile and raised eyebrows.

His bemused smile didn't deter Isabella. "This is why we need your help, Matigoro."

"How can I help? I'm already deep in purchasing Jewish slaves from merchants and reclaiming those poor souls."

"Where do those merchants get the slaves?"

Matigoro shook his head. "I don't know. Perhaps from trading with pirates?"

"That's exactly what I want to do. Trade with pirates."

This time Matigoro burst into laughter. He went on for a few moments, then looking at Isabella's stern face, he stopped. "I'm sorry, Isabella, but why would a woman, and a pregnant one at that, trade with pirates?"

"Because these pirates are threatening our livelihood. They're a menace on the seas. It was a miracle we didn't run into a pirate ship. That is why I want to reach an agreement with them."

"How are you going to do that? They might kill you or take you as hostage, then sell you as a slave."

"I will reach an agreement with them. They leave us alone, and we pay them a bounty."

Matigoro remained silent. He then said, "I don't know if it can be done."

"I want you to try hard to put me in touch with the pirates infesting the Atlantic and the Mediterranean seas."

"That's a lot of sea to cover." Matigoro looked at Avram, who had remained silent till now, and asked him, "You support Isabella in this folly?"

"I can't change her mind. She's determined."

"Let me look into it, Isabella. You might have to remain here in Tangier for some days," Matigoro said.

Isabella nodded and looked at Avram.

"It's your decision," Avram said.

The following morning, Isabella, Matigoro, and Avram made for the market in Tangier. Again, the smells of the bustling city came to her nostrils. The tan-colored camels brayed incessantly in the market square along with loaded donkeys waiting to be relieved of their loads. The overburdened beasts took a break now and then, drinking from a wooden trough filled with murky water.

Matigoro walked fast, and Isabella found it hard to follow him. She skirted camel dung lying in her path, carefully picking up the hem of her long dress. She now wore a scarf over her head to hide her black tresses tied in a bun on her head, and the edges hung low over her brows, partly hiding her eyes and her face.

"We're here," Matigoro announced.

They found themselves in front of a whitewashed house girded by a tall stone wall. Fragments of colorful broken glass topped the wall caps to ward off intruders. Matigoro pulled on a rope, and a musical sound was heard from inside the house.

A Nubian servant opened the brass doors and waited for orders.

"Go and fetch Effendy Abdul-Azim. We want to trade with him," Matigoro said. After the servant left inside the hall, he turned to Isabella and said, "Let me do the talking. Berbers don't talk or do business with women. It is forbidden."

"I know." Isabella sighed.

Matigoro went in the house, then returned holding a black *abaya* garment in his hands.

"Cover yourself with it," he told Isabella.

She looked up at Matigoro with quizzing eyes, and he nodded at her. She wrapped herself in the black cotton garment and pulled the hood over her head, through which she could see only through a lattice veil, and waited for an explanation.

"These men don't bargain with women. You must sit quietly and not speak," Matigoro said.

She nodded, and all three went inside the house to a waiting room and sat on the low divans positioned around the room.

A few minutes later, a hooded, cloaked man came into the room and saluted Matigoro.

"As-salamu alaykum. Sabaah al-khayr. My friend!"

"Wa 'alaykum salaam! Sabaah an-nuur" Matigoro welcomed Effendy Abdul-Azim by touching his own chest with his right hand, his mouth, then his forehead.

"You sent for me?" Abdul-Azim said. He then proceeded to finger a necklace of blue agate prayer beads in his hand.

"We need your help," Matigoro said.

Isabella, meanwhile, thought how strange that Christianity and Mohammedan religions had similar rituals.

Abdul-Azim glanced at Isabella covered in her cloak, then turned his eyes to Matigoro.

"Do not fear. She's mute and deaf," Matigoro said.

Isabella ground her teeth but kept silent.

"So what can I do for you?" asked Abdul-Azim.

"We need to reach the pirates pilfering the seas for slaves and booty," Matigoro said.

Abdul-Azim burst into a laugh that boomed to the high ceiling carved with Arabic letters on the wooden beams. After he stopped laughing, he snorted, then faced Matigoro. "That is all?"

"Look, I know I'm asking the impossible," Matigoro said with his right hand in a fist. "Every time we sail our ships, we fear the worst from these vandals. We lost a shipment recently, as well as this woman's husband, who was a son to me." Matigoro turned to Isabella still wrapped in her scarf and hiding part of her face. He lowered his head in grief.

Isabella, too, hid her face. Her grief was genuine, bringing back the pain in her chest.

Abdul-Azim looked with commiseration at Isabella and shook his head. "I'm crying with you in your sorrow," he said honestly to Matigoro. He then said, "I can put you in touch with some pirate who trades in slaves. You'll find him and his crew by the sands of Al-Maghrib al-Aqsá. They unload their prisoners at night, then march them to their hideout."

"How should I approach them?" Matigoro asked.

"All you have to say is 'Abdul-Ahad, servant of the One' and you will be received. Meet me tonight at the bazaar, but don't bring the woman with you," Abdul-Azim warned him.

"*Shokran!*" Matigoro said to Abdul-Azim, who saluted again, then left them.

Matigoro said, "You'll wait for us, Isabella. I will go with Avram to Al-Maghrib al-Aqsá tonight."

Isabella nodded. As a woman, she had no choice but to wait for their return.

By nightfall both Matigoro and Avram had changed their clothing to trousers, long-sleeved shirts, white *jalabiyas*, and dark caftans on top. Their heads were covered by a cotton *keffiyeh*, folded in half and held in place by a roped circlet.

After they left, Isabella paced back and forth in her room, her heart beating fast from worry and anxiousness. What if she was sending them to their deaths? She chased the thought away. Nevertheless, she kept awake the entire night waiting for their return. In the early hours of the morning, she fell asleep with exhaustion.

"Isabella? Isabella?" Avram's voice shook her out of a deep sleep.

"What is it?" she said with a start.

"Be ready to leave in an hour."

She said her good-byes to Matigoro, and he hugged her with affection.

"Avram will tell you all about our meeting."

"*Mucho gracias,* Matigoro. You've been like a father to me."

He hugged her again, and she left the house with Avram. Within minutes they reached the port in Tangier in a carriage and boarded the vessel. In its hold, Jewish slaves hid silently in search of a new haven.

74

Winter in Paradise

Tuesday, December 4, 1492

WHEN COLUMBUS WOKE IN THE morning, he felt a chill. He stood up with a jolt as if he were now in snowy Spain and not in paradise. His heart chilled. *Did I dream this wonderful voyage and all these marvels?* He ran out of his cabin, and with relief he saw a gentle rolling wave break upon the shore. It was raining, but he cared not about that detail. He was in paradise, and that's all that mattered.

He gathered his men, and they carried a pine cross from the harbor to a high promontory overlooking the sea.

"We'll call this harbor Puerto Santo," Columbus said, and all crossed themselves.

The short rain had just stopped, and he turned to his men and spoke to them. "The Lord has willed for us to find these wonderful islands and lands for Spain, the monarchs, and Christendom. This is a good harbor, seven to twenty fathoms deep with clear water and a sandy bottom. In this southeastern part of the harbor, our ships from Spain can enter and find safety from winds. The island has many groves that cover every hill and mountain. We will dwell on this island because there's much I want to learn about the natives."

His men shook their heads, and a low rumbling of voices followed when all fell silent.

"Can someone say what the meaning of this is?" Columbus said.

The same man he detested until now advanced toward him. "João here, Admiral."

"I know who you are." Columbus raised his chin high.

"We were wondering, Admiral, when we'll turn back."

"We'll turn around when we find gold. Have your forgotten why we're here?" His voice rose above the men's heads. Columbus was a head taller than all of them, and he took advantage of this feature.

"With respect, Admiral." This time it was Luis de Torres, his translator from Murcia. "The truth is, we were hoping to be home for Christmas."

Columbus remained silent. He knew for certain the voyage back would be deadly in the middle of winter once they crossed into home seas. It was best to keep that information secret from his men and not worry them any further.

A man by the name of Gomes, whom Columbus knew to be João's friend, came forward among the crowd. "We thought, Admiral, you wanted to discover the Indies. To find a shorter passage to the Indies, wasn't that it?"

"We have discovered the Indies. Now we are close to Cipango, and that's where I intend to contact the great kahn. I carry a letter from the monarchs especially for him."

"Admiral. With due respect," Juan de la Cosa said, "how can we trust we'll find those treasures when we've been outrun by the *Pinta* and Martin Alonso Pinzón? He'll find the gold first, and we'll have nothing to gain."

"In all fairness," Vicente Yanez, captain of the *Niña* and Martin Pinzón's brother, interjected at once, "I know my brother should have heeded the admiral's advice before taking off on his own, and I trust the admiral with his word that we will find gold despite the *Pinta*'s advance on the sea."

Columbus threw him a look of appreciation. He said, "Have I ever given you a word of distrust? Or have I said anything that hasn't materialized so far?"

Most men shook their heads.

Columbus saw that they were easily convinced. At least he still had the authority that was bestowed upon him by the monarchs. He decided to elaborate further on that vein.

"Now listen. I was chosen by the queen and the king of Spain and Aragon to undertake this voyage. Those kingdoms would not have given me the sums to undertake this voyage without their blessing and trust. Would they?"

He looked at the men's faces, but they were looking down at the sand. When they raised their heads, he saw he had convinced them.

"Admiral," Sancho Ruiz, his pilot said, "we trust you that we will find the gold, the precious stones, and all the rest. Let's give a hurrah for the admiral."

"Hurrah! Hurrah!" the men repeated with loud voices.

"All right, men, let's gather our boats and explore the island and search for villages," Columbus said with a smile.

75

Whiffs of the Past

HE WIND CAME AT HER with force, blowing her skirts and her hair. She held on to the railing and rejoiced to see the Portuguese coast. She missed Ana and the great house. She now considered Ana as a mother, friend, and protector. And the home was her anchor now for family and hearth. She had accomplished much in the space of this voyage and couldn't wait to report her progress to Ana.

Isabella turned to Avram standing near her. "Are you sure the pirates will abide by our agreement?"

"I know they will. Matigoro promised the sum of fifty dirhams per sighting. That's worth eleven hundred and fifty maravedís. He also alluded to the extra cannons we carry on the *Liberação*. But the best argument was the bounty sum we will pay them for each voyage."

"I hope it works," Isabella said. "I can't wait to be home now."

"So do I," Avram said with a wide grin on his face. "And I'm especially eager for Ana's cooking."

Isabella said, "I'm also glad to be rescuing these poor souls we're carrying to safety."

"Perhaps it's now time to let them come on deck," Avram suggested.

"Yes. Soon we can lower the boats for them."

Avram gave the order, and twenty disheveled and scrawny creatures emerged from the hold. Their eyes flinched before the strong sun, and their faces held expressions of bewilderment.

Isabella moved in front of them and addressed them.

"You're at the end of your voyage. The boats waiting for you will take you to the coast, where you'll be directed to your final destinations."

One of the men said, "Why aren't we landing at port?"

"You are stowaways. Without papers of identity, the port authorities will send you back to Tangier," Avram said.

Isabella heard a few grumbles. These poor creatures were, understandably, suspicious and fearful after their capture by pirates. Trust had been stolen away from them. She had to reassure them.

"Portugal has declared their country a haven for Jews exiled by Spain. And that is the reason we brought you here. Here you'll find a future for yourselves. I was once a slave like you, sold and bought by slave merchants. We owe a great debt to Matigoro and to a great man who provided for your purchase."

"Who is this man?" the same youth asked again.

"His identity is secret. What's important is that you're saved."

Appreciative voices sounded among the men and women.

"You can descend into the boats now," Isabella said.

One by one they climbed over the railing and descended into the two boats swaying on the ocean. When the boats rowed away, Isabella let out a breath of relief. She had done Don Abravanel's work in redeeming Jewish slaves. She was also continuing Miguel's legacy.

As soon as the boats rowed toward shore, the *Liberação* turned its bow toward Lisbon's port. Already the frenetic pace of the port made its hurried sounds and food smells drift to their ears and noses as the ship glided into the harbor. After docking, the inspector came on board and inspected the cargo.

"It looks in order," the inspector announced, and stamped their papers with a small wooden block dipped in ink. He then climbed over the railing to descend into his boat, when he turned around and said, "Where are your emergency boats?"

Isabella looked at Avram for help.

"We careened them into port to be repaired," Avram said quickly.

"You mean here in Lisbon's port?" the inspector asked.

Avram took a moment to answer. "No, Inspector. We left them in Tangier, and we'll reclaim them on our next voyage."

"In that case, you will be fined for lacking safety measures." He climbed back and issued a document on which he affixed his seal and handed it to Avram.

Avram took the document in silence, and both he and Isabella sighed with relief to see the inspector and his boat row away to other ships waiting to be inspected.

"Isabella said, "Thank God we unloaded them before we hit port."

"Those poor wretched men and women would've been returned to Tangier," Avram said.

"You've been a great help to me, Avram, especially with bargaining with the pirates."

Avram regained a calm composure. "Gracias, Isabella."

Their carriage awaited them in a livery stable by the docks, and they took off for home. Isabella rejoiced as the carriage reached the fork in the road for the estate. A sign pointing in the direction of Sintra suddenly aroused her interest.

"Stop the carriage!" she yelled.

Avram looked at her surprised. "Why?"

"I don't know. I just feel I want to go to Sintra."

"Why Sintra?"

"I told you, Avram. I don't know."

The next half hour was passed in silence as the carriage lurched toward the town. When the twenty-nine kilometers were bridged from Lisbon to Sintra, a few hamlets appeared in their view. Their agricultural field lay far and wide at the base of an old Moorish castle perched on the north-facing wall of the Sintra Mountains. The rectangular towers gave a sense of safety and protection. Soon, the conical chimneys of the royal palace came into view as they entered the small village.

"Stop the carriage!" Isabella said again as the carriage rolled to a stop by an inn.

"Do you want to rest here?" Avram asked.

"Yes, I'm quite tired."

Without a word, Avram descended and gave Isabella his hand. She came down the two metal steps and entered the inn. Inside, they found the innkeeper busy serving an elderly customer. Isabella walked to the other table in the room and sat down.

"*Boa tarde*. Bring us some food and drink," she told the innkeeper when he came to her table.

"We were less than an hour from home," Avram remarked.

"I know, but I felt a strong feeling to stop in this town."

Avram mulled over her remark for a few moments. "Why?"

"How many times must I tell you, Avram, expectant women have strange and sudden thoughts."

Avram smiled at her comment. "You sure do."

The innkeeper, meanwhile, came back with a tray containing several tin plates with fowl, and grain, and wine goblets.

Isabella attacked the food, appeasing her hunger. Avram smiled at her voracious appetite. She raised her head from her plate and noticed the elderly man looking at her. She licked her fingers and wiped her hands with a small cloth she produced from her pocket. Finally, intrigued by the man's insistent stare, she nodded her head in his direction.

The elderly man got up and approached Isabella and Avram.

"*Senhorita*, my name is Juan. Are you from this part of the country?" He stood hesitant in front of them, fingering his hat's brim.

Isabella hesitated at first, not wanting to be too forward. *"Sim,"* she replied in Portuguese.

"Forgive me, senhorita, but are you related to Sarita, a local woman who lived here?"

A shock hit Isabella; she dropped the cup of wine in her hand. The red liquid spread on the table, and the innkeeper rushed to wipe it with a rag.

Her words shot out. "Who's this woman and where is she?" Her hands began to tremble, and her heart raced out of control. She tried to control her fast breathing.

Avram became alarmed. "What's wrong, Isabella?"

"She lived in a cottage by the sea. She died many years ago, but you resemble her so much," Juan said sadly.

"*Por favor*, sit down, senhor. Can you tell me more about her?" Isabella whispered in a faint voice.

"She lived not too far from Sintra"

"Can you show me where this cottage is?" Isabella felt her skin tingle. She wiped her forehead with her hand.

"I'll be glad to show you," Juan said. "Both my wife and I live in this cottage."

Isabella got up and turned to Avram. Please wait for me here."

"But, Isabella—"

"Wait until I'm back."

Avram's face still looked pleading.

Isabella flashed a wide smile. "Don't worry, Avram. I've waited a long time for this. Please pay for the meal."

Avram became resigned. "If you're not back in one hour, I'll come and get you."

Isabella laughed. "We'll be back soon." She took Juan's arm and led him out of the inn and into the waiting carriage. She whipped the horses, and the carriage lurched through the narrow alleys until it came to the last house in the village.

"Stop here," Juan called out.

The small thatched house had blue awnings with flowerpots hanging from the two windows. Juan knocked at the door, and a small old woman opened it.

"*Boa tarde*, Juan," the woman said with a smile. Her soft blue eyes then fell on Isabella, and she blanched.

"And good afternoon to you, Estrellita," Juan replied.

Isabella stepped backward in surprise. *This woman's name is singularly the same as my adoptive mother's: Estrella.* Was it the hand of fate?

"Come in, come in," Estrellita said with her eyes fixed on Isabella. Estrellita shooed away a cat sleeping on a chair. "Sit down."

Isabella sat, while Juan took the other chair. Estrellita went to the window seat to sit down.

Juan spoke first. "This senhorita is anxious to find out about Sarita, who lived in our cottage."

Estrellita turned to Isabella with a sad look. "Yes, your mother lived here."

Isabella put both her hands on her chest to quiet her racing heart. "Please tell me about her."

"You look just like her. She was like a daughter to us, and I helped bring you into this world."

Isabella leaned forward, sitting on the edge of her seat while feeling elated with bursting energy. "What was she like? How old was she when she had me? Who was my father?"

"*Mais devagar!* I'll answer all your questions, *meu menininha*." She said smiling.

Isabella felt endeared to be called her little girl. "Then tell me everything you know."

"Your mother was a beautiful young woman when she met your father. He was a redheaded sailor with blue eyes and a great stature. Your mother was deeply in love with him, but he was a dreamer. He only wanted to sail and explore. I know because your mother told me."

"But why did she give me away? Why?" Isabella's voice broke.

"*Meu menina.* She died giving birth to you. Your father was on a voyage at that time, but he never came back. I don't think he knew he had a daughter."

Isabella muffled a cry in her throat. She lowered her head with sadness. "He didn't know my mother was pregnant?"

"No, he didn't," Estrellita said.

"But what about my uncle? He was here. Wasn't he?"

"Yes. Your uncle João Treves took you away. He told me a little bit about your adoptive parents. And I share the same name of Estrella. Your uncle thought it was a good omen."

Isabella sat stunned with the sheer volume of information that had come her way. She had wondered for an entire year about her real parents, and now it had all been explained in the space of one hour. How strange and fortuitous. Suddenly, relief, sadness, and disappointment all rolled into conflicted feelings, and tears came down her face.

"My poor child," Estrellita exclaimed. "I made you sad telling the truth."

Juan said, "Please don't cry. We loved your mother very much. She was like a daughter to us."

Isabella smiled amid her tears. "I'm glad she had friends who cared."

"Now wipe your tears and let's look forward to the future."

At that mention, Isabella broke out in renewed crying.

"What is it?" Estrellita asked with confusion.

"There's no future for my child . . ." She sobbed. "His father is dead." Her chest shuddered under the grief.

Both Estrellita and Juan were greatly pained by her grief.

"Don't cry. We can be your family now," Juan said.

Isabella wiped her tears, then calming down said, "I have obligations to others, and I must leave now."

"Please come back soon," Both Estrellita and Juan begged her.

"I will," Isabella said, and took leave of them.

Back in the carriage she felt a great load had lifted off her chest, and when she met Avram at the inn, her composure was calm and without a trace of the secrets divulged to her. She kept silent the rest of the way home; all her thoughts now were with her adoptive father left alone in Castile.

76

Shades of Gold

Thursday, December 6, 1492

THE FOLLOWING DAYS ON THE island of Puerto Santo, Columbus explored the coast and its surroundings, then continued further up the wide river by a harbor he called Puerto Maria. The cape on its south tip was named Cabo de Estrella. Several other capes lay to the east, and fifty-five miles from where they stood was another cape southeast he named Cabo del Elefante. Between Cabo del Elefante and another cape he called Cinquin, an arm of the sea lay, which he called Isla de la Tortuga. He wanted to sail to all those capes and explore them, but time was now pressing to push to Babeque Island, where the gold was waiting for them.

During the night, fires were lit throughout Puerto Santo, and smoke columns appeared by early morning. Columbus asked his Indian translator, Rodrigo de Jerez, what it could mean. Upon asking one of the Indians on his ship, he immediately grimaced with fear and fell to his knees, while his arms were thrown to the skies.

"What is the meaning of this?" Columbus now asked Rodrigo.

Rodrigo questioned the man over and over, but the Indian burst out in short grunts and cries of fear. Rodrigo turned to Columbus and said,

"Admiral, this man is terrified. He said that the Caribs on the island of Bohio have one eye in their forehead; they're cannibals and wage war with many killing weapons. The people they took with them never came back and were eaten alive."

"Ask him if the Caribs have gold," Columbus said.

Rodrigo translated with sign language, and the Indian returned with affirmative motions.

"Yes, Admiral. But he also said that you will not live long enough to enjoy it."

Columbus smiled with his hands on his hips. "I'll decide that for myself. Tell him not to fear that the Caribs are intelligent people since they possessed weapons, and tell him that the people did not return because they're captive."

Rodrigo translated again with sign language. "They're still afraid and want to go back home now."

"Tell them they will return to their home shortly. As soon as we explore the island and as soon as we find some gold."

When Rodrigo translated, Columbus saw the Indian's face become long and sad. *They must trust me*, he thought, thereby ignoring their fears.

He then ordered to set sail for south-southeast and sailed along the coast. They passed many inlets and small harbors, but they pushed on all day. By the hour of Vespers they came into a harbor one and a half leagues wide. The depth was measured with a cord at fifteen fathoms with clear waters and no shoals. He named the harbor Puerto de San Nicolao on this day of St. Nicholas. He then saw a promontory on the southeastern point that could be used as a lookout fort. The boats were lowered, and they rowed to a beautiful and pleasing beach with all sorts of trees. Columbus found them to be nutmeg and spice trees, yet could not identify them correctly. After locating a village they contacted the natives, but they fled again from fear of strangers. They found their many *fustas* canoes carved with fifteen benches like those in Africa.

By dawn the following morning they set sail from Puerto de San Nicholas and headed along the coast in a southwest direction with the wind about two knots. They found a small promontory southeast of Cabo de Estrella twenty-four miles away. Forty-eight miles toward the east lay Cabo

Cinquin in high land. He found evergreen trees of oak, and strawberry trees like in Castile. At an opening in the mountains, he discovered a large valley planted with barley fields. Thirty-two miles to the northeast lay Cabo de la Tortuga, and where Cabo Cinquin lay at a Lombard shot, a rock stood high in the sea that could be seen from afar. By midday the skies turned dark, and the wind blew hard at the stern, heralding rain. They entered a new harbor they called Puerto de la Conception and landed near a small river by the end of the harbor. Fields of great beauty lay on either side.

"We will anchor here for the night," Columbus said. "Take out the nets and find fish."

The men were delighted to find many fishes such as mullets and soles that were in the waters near Castile. The sailors' mood turned joyful with grilled fish for supper. The rationed wine elevated their mood higher, and they sang of their Castilian señoritas waiting for them back home. The nightingales sang magically throughout the night, and Columbus thought he'd been transported back to Castile.

77

Anticipation

ECEMBER AND WINTER CAME QUICKLY. A fine rain fell, and a chill enveloped the entire house. Ana had stoked the chimneys in all the rooms with wood that kept everyone warm. She piled wool shawls on Isabella and constantly worried about her health.

"Are you warm enough, Isabella? Do you want something hot to drink? What about something to eat?"

"Please, Ana, I'm fine. I'm more than well. My only problem is boredom. We can't sail in this weather, and we're stuck here in the house."

"Spring will come quickly, you'll see," Ana reassured her.

"Yes, but in the meantime, what's happening to the poor slaves? I hope Matigoro can keep them until we can sail to get them."

"You're not going back there! It'll be madness so close to the end of your confinement!"

"Don't you fret about me, Ana. I'm very strong." Isabella let out a giggle—a rare occurrence now, since she came back.

"You speak as if you already had many children," Ana said. She then covered her mouth, and redness crept across her cheeks.

"Don't worry, Ana. This only child will probably keep me busy for years. I know because he'll be spoiled rotten."

A smile appeared on Ana's face. "I'll help spoil him or her."

"Meanwhile, I ought to get ready for this blessed event." To Ana's questioning look, Isabella added, "The baby's clothes and crib."

"Of course," Ana said, and ran out of the room. She reappeared shortly with a box she put on the table in front of Isabella. She took out various knitted blankets, long cotton gowns, and bonnets for the baby.

Isabella smiled with marvel at the clothes displayed before her. "When did you do all this?"

"While you and Avram were gone."

"All we need now is a crib."

Again, Ana left the room in a hurry and returned with Avram carrying a wooden baby rocker.

Isabella's mouth fell open. "We just got back from our voyage. When did you build this?"

Avram gave her one of his rare smiles. "I've been working on this for some time." He put down the rocker in front of Isabella.

Isabella got up and went to hug them both. "Thank you, Ana, and thank you, Avram. You're spoiling me."

They looked pleased with Isabella's delight. "We'll store them in your room." Ana piled up the clothes in the rocker and signaled Avram to take it to Isabella's room.

"Now I must talk to you about an important matter," Ana said seriously.

"Why the serious face?" Isabella said, laughing.

"Please listen to me. Your confinement will end in a few months. I have brought many babies into the world. So you must listen to me."

"¡Avla!" Isabella said.

Ana talked to her of resting and eating, how to walk supporting her stomach, not jumping or get excited, the approaching labor . . .

Her voice became faint. In front of Isabella's eyes the image of Miguel surged. His tender gaze, his affectionate voice, his passion for her and caring for others became acute and alive. She slowly caressed her crossed arms, longing for his touch.

78

Española

Sunday, December 9, 1492

IT RAINED HARD FROM THE northeast that day. Columbus found the weather the same as October in Castile. When they landed on shore, the villages were deserted, the inhabitants having fled before them. All around them the lands were cultivated with root plants similar to theirs in Spain. The fields and mountains were magnificent like those of home, and he found two large rivers near the deep harbor. The waters there were deep and sandy bottomed, and he called the island Española.

On the following morning, he sent six of his men inland to find the villagers. By night's end the men came back to describe the many wonders they had seen. The women, he was told, were whiter than all the other ones they'd seen so far. They surpassed their women in Spain by their beauty. The huts were large, and they had wide roads. His men carried mastic plants and told him there were many to be found.

On December 11, all the men stayed on the ships with strong winds blowing through the harbor and on land. Not far from the harbor they saw a large island parallel to Española. His men told him the natives called it La Tortuga. Columbus decided to remain on Española, one of the most beautiful islands so far with tall mountains, rivers and valleys, then go to Tortuga. The Indians on his boat said that south of Española Island was Babeque Island and Bohio Island, which were larger than Juana, called Cubao by the Indians. Again the Indians described a land behind Española they understood to be a continental land or mainland they called Caritaba, where its inhabitants lived in fear of habitants of Caniba.

"This Caniba must be where the great kahn resides and where his ships capture them."

"Is this why they fear the men are eaten?" Juan de la Cosa said.

"Yes. Since they don't return them, the natives believe they are boiled."

Juan de la Cosa laughed. "These are very ignorant men. The great kahn is a civilized ruler."

Columbus agreed. "I feel, Juan, that the Lord has shown us the way to these islands. That we're near our goal of finding gold."

"Amen, Admiral. We can then go home."

"We are close."

By the following morning, Columbus, seeing that the rain let up, sent men to the island. There they found a great deal of fish in the waters of the harbor and the two rivers. The nets were filled with golden salmon, silver fish called pampano, mullet, shrimp, and lots of sardines. They brought it all on board along with more aloe plants.

In the afternoon, Columbus placed a large cross on a hill by the harbor. "Your Highnesses now own this land in your name and in the name of Christianity," he said.

From the trees and bushes surrounding them they heard a great commotion made by many naked men and women who ran away in fear. His men chased them, but they fled fast down the hill. Two of his men caught a beautiful young woman and brought her back to Columbus.

Columbus noticed the woman's gold piece dangling from her nose.

"Don't fear," he told her by sign language. He grabbed a cape from one of the sailors and covered her body. He then gave her some beads and hawk's bells. The Indians from his ship talked to her in their own language, which she understood. She was told not to be afraid of them and to go back home.

Columbus spoke to his Indian interpreters. "Tell your people we come as friends and in peace."

The young woman nodded, then ran back to her people as fast as she could.

This island must have gold, Columbus noted.

79

Echoes of the Past

ISABELLA SAT BY A WINDOW in the large sitting room, watching a downpour fall on the estate. All harvesting had stopped, the workers had been sent to their homes, and the *Liberação* sat grounded in Lisbon's port. Some days, the cloud cover tore to expose a blue sky above. That was when all nature woke up for the day, to sing to life; birds twittered in from the trees, their two horses were exercised outdoors by Avram, and she also took a walk around the property to smell fresh scents coming from the earth.

Her thoughts then went back to discovering her birth mother's origins. She pictured her living near Sintra in the cottage by the sea, meeting with her father, and their love for each other. Why did her mother have to die giving birth to her, and why hadn't her father returned to her mother, Sarita? And why hadn't her uncle looked for her father? These were disturbing questions that crossed her mind. Meanwhile, her plan to search for Miguel had been thwarted by the winter weather. Since their last voyage from Tangier, sea travel had been curtailed. Avram refused to sail due to the weather and Isabella's condition.

He said, "I know that I'm your employee, and you can't do without me—"

Isabella tried to interrupt him, but he continued. "I also know that you won't get rid of me, so I won't sail until the bad weather stops."

Isabella kept silent at his comment, knowing by now that when Avram made up his mind, nothing would budge him.

"I won't force you to do anything against your will," Isabella said. "I'm only anxious that our trade is at a standstill. Our jams haven't reached the markets in Lisbon, let alone in Morocco."

"That's why we trade two-thirds of the year and rest the last third," Avram said.

"Look, Avram, I'm very grateful for all your help these past months since Miguel's disappearance..." She stopped when she noticed Avram shake his head slightly and turn his eyes away. "I'm also convinced that Miguel is still alive."

Avram turned back to her with eyes wide and mouth open.

She knew that in Avram's heart, Miguel was dead and buried at sea. It was understandable. Only she had the capacity to feel Miguel's love in her heart. And in that heart, she knew he lived, but she also knew that she couldn't convince Avram, or Ana.

"Perhaps we can find a new source of trade in winter right here in Lisbon?" Isabella said.

"What did you have in mind?"

"I noticed on our return trip, while we were in that last town, the scarcity of foods available to the townspeople."

Avram encouraged her. "And?"

"And we can market those wonderful cakes that Ana makes and sell them on market days. Of course, I already talked to her and she agreed."

"All right, and who will be selling those cakes?"

"I will," Isabella said quickly.

"Here you go again. You'll endanger your child traveling on those rocky roads to town."

"Please, Avram. I'm responsible for my child. So what say you?"

Avram kept quiet for some minutes. "If Ana sees fit for you to travel and peddle her cakes, then I'll drive you into town, but mind you, not in a downpour," he reminded her.

"You've got my promise," Isabella said with a smile. Inwardly, she rejoiced at the thought of seeing Estrellita and Juan again.

80

Gold

Monday, December 17, 1492

COLUMBUS SAT IN HIS CABIN at the hour of Vespers and spent the entire night filling in his log. He had so far seen wonders and many clues for finding gold. The natives he encountered on each island had led him to this present time, when the precious metal would fall into his hands. His crew cooperated on all the sorties to find this gold, and their mood increased with tension and joyful anticipation. How the Lord worked in his favor and had led them to find the islands, he knew not. What he knew was he had received his protection throughout.

Your Highnesses and most gracious Majesties. It's been two glorious months so far since we discovered the Indies, and the miracles never cease to manifest themselves. With the Savior's protection, I know that we are close to finding substantial gold.

On the blessed day of December 13, we found a young woman who brought an entire village to us. She told the villagers how friendly we were and the trinkets we bestowed on her, and how we didn't harm her but returned her to her people. More than two thousand villagers came to our ships and put their hands on our heads to bless us. They told us again by signs that we must be from heaven. They were offering us friendship. They then went to their huts and brought back many different types of foods. The first food was "niames," a sort of radish they plant with little sticks in the soil. These sticks produce four or five plants. They look like great radishes, and after they toast them in fire, they taste like chestnuts. They brought us many colorful parrots that chatter pleasantly all the time. They also told us not to leave and to stay the night in the harbor. They promised to return the next day and take us into the mountains.

A large river that flows through their valley irrigates all their lands. Many trees were green and carried numerous fruits, and nightingales sang from their branches. Grasses were tall with flowers in them. Their roads were also wide. At night we heard crickets and frogs.

On Friday December 14, we sailed north-northeast with the breeze from Puerto de la Conception to Isla de la Tortuga and saw a great point east-northeast at its end and called it Punta Pierna. And yet another point twelve miles distant that we called Punta Lanzada. The island of Tortuga has high lands and is very beautiful with long beaches. We returned that night to Puerto de la Conception.

The following day we started again from Puerto de la Conception with a strong wind from the east and went to Tortuga. We were not able to land with the high winds. A large river flowed in an extensive valley by their village. I named it Valle del Paraiso, and the river I named Guadalquivir after our river Guadalquivir in Seville. The villagers came on the beach, then upon seeing us ran away in fear. Smoke signals were seen thereafter.

By the hour of Tierce we sailed away east and found a lone rower in a canoe. We helped him come on board with his canoe and gave him hawk's bells and glass beads. We then dropped him in his village sixteen miles away. This villager told how we helped him, and five hundred of his fellow villagers came to see us on the following morning. Some of them had grains of gold in their noses and ears. These men and women will make good Christians, and they now belong to you, Your Highnesses. Their king came on the beach, and upon our telling him by our ship's natives that we came from heaven and were looking for gold, he promised to take us to Babeque, where gold is plentiful.

Their fields are sown with "ajes" that look like carrots, and they make bread from them. I tasted this kind of bread in Guinea and it is the same. All the villagers are handsome and as naked as their mothers bore them. They have no fire arms and can be governed easily. They are not shy, and their skin is whiter than all the other Indians we've seen till now. The king came on board afterward and ate with us, and liked all the food he shared, with his councilors sitting behind him.

On December 16 we stayed all day on the island of Tortuga, which was protected from strong winds coming from east-northeast. The villagers came to us again, and what I believed to be their cacique brought us a gold leaf as large as a hand. The cacique then returned to his village and kept coming back trading little pieces of the leaf for our trinkets and foods. I found him and his people to be very clever business traders. This cacique also told us that on the island of Baneque there is to be found much gold, but he couldn't get more because he didn't have much to trade for it.

I believe Baneque is the main source for gold, and we can reach it within four days' sailing, about forty leagues. The Lord is leading me to this spring, where the gold will be found.

Satisfied with his logbook, Columbus heard the ampolleta boy announcing the hour of two in the morning. He blew out his candle and lay down in his bunk bed to find sleep.

81

The Past Revealed

THE WEATHER HAD COOPERATED FOR Isabella, Ana, and Avram seated in the carriage. At their feet lay a large basket with Ana's bread desserts and a few pots of her best jam made from the leftover grapes from last summer. The scenery graced their ride on the bumpy road, and Ana made frightened gestures for Isabella each time the carriage bounced.

Isabella burst into laughter at Ana's expression. "Don't you worry, Ana. I have a strong constitution."

Ana sighed heavily and crossed her arms. "You're stubborn, Isabella. I'd say you gave grief to your parents when you were little."

Isabella became sad by the remark. Her stubbornness had indeed affected her parents greatly. She overcame the feeling and said, "Dada Hannah was the most grieved of all. I wonder what she's doing right now." She became pensive.

"Here's Sintra," Avram announced.

The vendors and shops were busy with townspeople buying their foods and wares, and Ana hurried to a booth protected by an awning to sell her goods.

"I will go and look for some farm implements. We could use new tools and scissors for the grapevines," Avram said, walking away.

Isabella used this opportunity to slip away and visit Estrellita and Juan at their cottage.

When she arrived, she became disappointed to find the cottage unoccupied and empty of furnishings.

A woman by her cottage stopped feeding her chickens to observe Isabella.

Isabella walked to the woman's cottage and asked, "Where's Estrellita and Juan?"

The woman shook her head, then said, "Estrellita passed away some weeks ago and Juan left town right afterwards."

The news pierced Isabella's heart. Tears came to her eyes instantly, and she sobbed openly.

"My dear child, I didn't know she was close to you. Forgive me."

Isabella shook her head, unable to find her voice to respond to her. She left the woman and returned to the marketplace. She found Ana busy selling her pastries; she tried to help her but couldn't and sat heavily on the chair without speaking.

"What is wrong, Isabella, and where did you go? I was worried about you," Ana said.

Isabella told her of her meeting with Estrellita and Juan, the secrets revealed to her, and the death of the old woman.

Ana looked hurt. "Why have you not confided in me?"

"I'm sorry, Ana. It's all new to me too. Please tell me if you know anything about my real parents or my uncle."

Ana kept silent as if remembering something she'd forgotten long ago. She then said, "I knew your uncle João Treves, and I knew about his dreams and quest."

Isabella looked at Ana curiously. "What dreams did he have?"

"He talked of a new homeland for the Jews of Spain. And his desire to find a land where they'd be free from persecution."

Isabella reflected on the information given to her. "Where could he be now?"

"I believe that he embarked on a voyage. One that would take him overseas to a part of the world where the Inquisition wouldn't find him and where he could help others who have been persecuted."

"Why would the Inquisition follow him?"

"Because he was a Converso. He converted to Christianity and wore a cross to prove his conversion. Those were the ones that were most persecuted and spied upon."

"Is this why you never converted, Ana?"

Ana let out a sigh of relief. "Yes. Although I was forced to leave a land I loved, at least I was safe."

"Why must one religion be hounded by another? What gives them the right to punish and persecute someone of a different faith? Why?"

"If we knew the answer to this riddle, we would've conquered wars. Who knows?" Ana said with another sigh and slumped shoulders. "In our case, the Jews were lucky to have found a haven in Portugal."

"Perhaps the answer to that riddle has something to do with my birth parents. Perhaps they were persecuted and hid their identities," Isabella said aloud.

"Perhaps," Ana replied. "Your uncle, though, never gave up his beliefs and dreams."

"Where can I find clues to my Uncle João?"

"First you must trace him back to the ports where he worked on ships, then work your way forward."

Isabella stayed silent while absorbing the information, when suddenly she felt a strong kick in her stomach that caught her breath. She bent down supporting the weight projecting her forward.

"Isabella? What's wrong?" A concerned Ana came to her support. She helped Isabella sit on a stool by the table.

"I don't know, but he's kicking his way out." She tried to laugh, but her lips were strained.

Ana grabbed the remaining goods on the table and proceeded to return them to the basket. "We're going back! It's an order!" Ana said resolutely.

Just then Avram returned with new tools in his hands. One look at Isabella and he could tell they had to return in a hurry. The return to the estate was in silence, Ana keeping her eyes fixed on Isabella. She helped her rest in the sitting room when they arrived and said to her, "From now on, you'll do exactly as I say. No more trips for you, young lady."

Isabella could only nod and left her care entirely in Ana's capable hands.

It was the end of her searches and voyages for now. She promised herself that she would concentrate on the life inside of her—Miguel's child. A nagging thought, though, kept reemerging now and then. Visions and names from the past came back with her memories, what her parents and dada Hannah knew of her origins. She tried hard to erase them, but they kept coming back in all hours of the day and night. The burning need still remained—to find Miguel, who she strongly believed was still alive, and to continue to probe for a father she'd never met. Then her thought went back to her adoptive father in Seville. Was he sitting now and pining to see her, or was he occupied by Miguel's young brother, José, living now in her old home? She thought of his tender age of ten and missed him as well. She relished the thought that Guerida and his men were far away from them.

Avram entering the room interrupted her thoughts.

Ana said suddenly, "What is it, Avram? You look pale too. Have you seen a ghost?" she said with a slight mocking tone.

Avram threw himself down on a chair and stared at Isabella and Ana. He then nodded his head.

"I saw a man lurking outside on the grounds. He was a commoner, wearing poor clothing and unshaven."

"Did you try to accost him?" Ana said.

"I was in my barracks, and he didn't see me. When I ran out, he seemed to have vanished."

Ana's face looked anxious. "Avram, keep an eye out to see if he returns. And you, Isabella, stay indoors even when the rains stop."

Isabella was about to reply but stayed mute. She'd have to follow Ana's warning.

82

A Mirage

Tuesday, December 18, 1492

COLUMBUS WOKE UP EARLY, AND with the wind scarce that day, the *Santa Maria* and the *Niña* caravel remained anchored near the beach on Tortuga Island. He sat abaft, near the stern by the forecastle, and enjoyed his breakfast while watching the island before him. A sudden commotion was heard from the beach, and soon at least two hundred men, some lifting the king, made their way for the *Santa Maria*.

Columbus slowly got up from the crate he sat upon, and waited for the young king to climb on the ship and join him by the stern. The king took one look at Columbus's plate then turned to the *Santa Maria*'s Indian translators, signing that Columbus should finish his food. Columbus sat back and offered him various morsels from his plate and ordered more to give to the king. As he tasted each of the foods brought to him, the young king took a bite, then passed the food behind him to his councilors and governors. Afterward, the king gave him two thin pieces of gold.

"Please follow me," Columbus signed to the king. They entered Columbus's cabin, and the king immediately smiled at the linen red cover draped over his bed. Columbus removed it and offered it to him. He grunted and smiled with pleasure, wrapped it around his shoulders, then went to his councilor and said a few words.

"What's he saying?" Columbus asked his Indian translator.

The translator, familiar with a few words of Spanish by now, said, "King give you all on island." He pointed to Columbus.

"Juan, bring me more beads," Columbus said.

Juan reappeared shortly with a handful of colorful amber and green beads that he put in the king's hand. Columbus also pulled from a small purse an *excelente* piece of gold, worth at least eight hundred maravedís, and gave it to the ruler.

Columbus then pointed to the image of His Highnesses on the coin and said, "King and queen of greatest land o- earth."

The cacique king laughed with pleasure. He turned to his people and gave the order to leave with a grunt and a shout. The king's canoes left for shore, where two hundred of his people and a litter waited for him.

Columbus gave the order to salute the king as a sign of respect. "Fire the Lombards!"

The following morning on December 19, Columbus and some of his crew erected a large cross at the center of the village and watched the Indians fall on their knees before it.

He wrote in his log that night to the monarchs that these islands and their entire population could become Christians for the glory of God.

The ships left the island that night and made sail through the gulf between Española and Tortuga. By daytime a strong wind from the east pushed them to and fro, catching them between the two islands in the gulf. Their ships tossed on the waves all that day without making headway. When nighttime came they couldn't make land or reach a harbor. The waves were brutal and overpowering. Columbus was stunned that here in paradise they were being tossed upon the sea and in mortal danger.

"Raise and clew the sails! Strengthen the main and foremast with ropes!" The orders were shouted through the crash of waves on all decks and the creaks in the vessel. The crew rushed to carry the orders, tying themselves with ropes to the masts. When done, and soaked to their bones, they clambered down on deck and made their way to safety by holding on to a rope extended down the length of the ship.

By morning the sea was calmer but still choppy. Columbus spotted upon the nearest island a promontory where a village lay nearby with high mountains as a backdrop. He named it Dos Hermanos for the two mountains in proximity to each other. Tall and deep-green pine trees covered their flanks. Further down a cape he called Cabo de Torres, he saw a small island he called Santo Tomas because the next day was his devotional watch and religious feast with prayers. Still further down the coast a cape jutted into into the sea that had a low and high escarpment. He called it Cabo Alto y Bajo. On the east and southeast another mountain overtook all other mountains by its unusual height, appearing as an island unto itself, and he called Caritaba.

By sunset on the night of December 21, the ships entered the harbor between Santo Tomas and Cabo de Caribata. All along the entrance many protruding rocks in the sea blocked their path with many shoals lurking below the waters. The depth of the water was seven fathoms. Further beyond the harbor, he saw on land many villages with smoke escaping from their huts.

"We will moor on this island for several days to meet the natives," Columbus said determinedly.

83

A Visitor

WINTER DAYS PASSED QUIETLY FOR Isabella anticipating her child to be born by spring. The season had progressed with daily rains and temperatures falling down. Ana draped warm sweaters and woolen shawls on Isabella, who tried to remove them one by one. The extra weight she carried gave her a closed feeling. The breezes were chilly, and Avram was in charge of filling all the holes that allowed cold drafts to penetrate into the house. Once in a while the clouds parted to reveal a blue sky, but the mist upon the sea came back and clung as a heavy gray cover. She tried to glimpse at the waves on shore, but they remained invisible. She now longed for spring to arrive and with it this new life in her belly. Ana had taught her to knit clothes for the baby, and she busied her fingers on a long knitted gown for the arrival.

They worked in the kitchen by a warm fire in the hearth while Juanita helped cook the afternoon meal on another table in the vast kitchen.

Ana said to Isabella sitting by the table, "You look a bit pale today."

"I haven't been out in weeks," Isabella said while struggling with her needles. "Any more waiting and I'll disappear."

Ana, kneading a batch of dough on the table, stopped to look at her. She sprinkled more flour on the wet dough and said with a smile, "You can't disappear, Isabella. Just your eyes will glow in the dark."

Isabella forced a smile. "I'm so bored with winter, rain, and being confined."

"Now, now, Isabella. You should look forward to that blessed event."

"I truly do. I'm just not used to being idle." She missed a loop in the knitting and tried to catch it. "Heck! I'm no good at this!" She dropped the needles with the yarn onto her lap.

Just then Avram entered the kitchen and sat quietly at one of the chairs around the pine table.

Ana looked at him curiously. "What's the matter? Looks like you've seen another ghost." Her voice held a mocking tone in it.

Avram said, "I saw another man prowling around the estate. He rode a black horse and was dressed in fineries."

Isabella's heart gave a jolt. "What did he look like?"

"He wore a black cape and hood that covered his face partly. I walked toward him, but he took off on his horse."

Ana blanched slightly. "Do you think it's the same man who came last summer?"

"I couldn't identify him. But it doesn't bode well. We must keep our eyes open."

Isabella's anxiety rose. "What could it mean?"

"I don't know, but Miguel had told me the stranger who came last summer was a tax agent for the king." Avram looked up at Ana. "You remember he wanted to find Don Carvalho about back taxes?"

"It was all settled," Ana said, waving her hand covered by flour. "The proof is he hasn't come back since then." She wiped her hands on her apron and went to check the bread baking in the hot hearth. She turned around and said, "We will keep our eyes and ears open. Meanwhile, we should be thinking of Hanukkah coming soon."

To those words, Isabella tried to look forward to experiencing this holiday. As a new Jewess, she wanted to delve into the religion of her mother, Sarita, and the father she'd never known, but sadness engulfed her. Notwithstanding Ana and Avram, she felt alone in the world. Everything she loved had been swept away from her. Her mission now was to love her unborn child as a mother and a father, and attend to the task of bringing up that life with care, devotion, and protection.

84

A Brewing Storm

Saturday, December 23, 1492

THE WIND BLEW STRONG ALL night with unusual force. Between the gales coming from the sea and the whistling wind, the crew couldn't sleep throughout the night. The ships stood in the inlet formed by the two islands and at the mouth of a river. By dawn, Columbus, having not slept a wink, stood on the main deck supervising his men unfurling the sails while shouting orders.

"You left the bonnet clewed up on the yardarm!" he shouted to Pedro, his new cabin boy and now a thirteen-year-old, young apprentice. He could see him hanging on the mainmast above the bonnet and trying to climb further up, but he hung frozen with fear, not advancing or descending the mast.

"João! Bring Pedro down!"

João gazed at the admiral, then looked up at Pedro's small body and legs wrapped around the mast's slippery surface. He tied a rope around his waist and secured it around the base of the mast on a large hooked nail. With small movements, he raised himself using other hooks along the surface of the wooden mast. As he closed in on the youth, he kept extending his arm, but the lad was still too far from reach. After sliding upward a few more times, he at last grabbed Pedro's leg and pulled him down toward him, but the boy remained still.

"Come on, Pedro!" João shouted at him over the din of the wind. "Come on! Don't be afraid!" João could see the boy's eyes fixed on his hands grasping the mast. Below them the waves churned and heaved. João pushed himself up one last time and grabbed the youth by his shoulders.

"Come on, Pedro! Come on, lad!" The voices of the crew assembled below on deck kept exhorting him.

"Listen to me! I will tie the rope around your waist! Follow me down the mast!"

The youth finally let go of the mast and slid downward after João until they reached the deck.

"¡*Viva*! ¡*Viva*!" The men assembled around the mast cheered both João and Pedro.

The cook, Maestre Diego, rushed to hug the still-scared Pedro. "You gave us a scare!"

"All right now—back to raising the foremast sails!" Columbus gave the order. He then turned to João and said, "I want to see you."

What could he want now? João thought. Nevertheless, he climbed to the quarterdeck behind Columbus and faced him.

"Thank you for helping Pedro," Columbus said.

Surprised, João didn't know what to say. He then said, "It was the least I could do, Admiral."

"You can go back on deck now," Columbus replied.

Just as they were getting close to the river's mouth, a large wave of seawater rolled into the river waters. The ship lifted slightly and careened forward, but stopped short of grazing the bank of the river.

Columbus looked at an angry sea advancing inland with waves after waves. "Stop!" he shouted to his crew. Clew the sails back up!"

The men grumbled, then after a higher wave hit the ship again, they scrambled on deck to follow his orders.

"We'll dock here for the night!" he shouted to the crew.

Throughout the night the sea roared, and the river rose and fell while the ships riding over the waves leapt forward and backward at the mouth of the river. The beams on the *Santa Maria* creaked along with the thunder caused by the sea.

In the morning on Sunday, after Mass, when both sea and wind calmed down a notch or two, Columbus thought it best for the ships to remain moored by the river on the island for the remainder of the day. The native chief or cacique, as the inhabitants called him, sent a servant in a canoe to their ship holding a large mask made out of beaten gold that had large ears, a nose, and a tongue, and was attached to a belt made of strong wrought cotton.

Columbus received the present and communicated to his Indians to thank them and their chief. The natives spoke to the Indian translators and pointed to the island.

"What do they want?" Columbus asked one of his Indians.

The Indian translator indicated by signs that the cacique wanted to see him to give him more gold.

"We ought to see their chief right away," he told Vicente Pinzón.

With the wind still unabating, Columbus, along with Rodrigo Escobedo, his royal secretary; Rodrigo Sanchez, his comptroller; his two translators both named Rodrigo—one from Jerez and the other from Murcia—and ten of his men, including João, Hernán, and Alfonso; entered the two boats and went ashore to the cacique village.

The march against the wind coming from the east was testing their abilities to push forward inland. Columbus thought that the chief asking for their presence signified an important request. As much as he honored the chief's request, he was reluctant to leave, since Sundays were reserved for prayers. These natives, though, would become good Christians in time, Columbus reminded himself.

When they arrived at the chieftain's tent, followed by hundreds of villagers, the leader got up from his highly decorated chair, took Columbus by the hand, and told him to sit down close to him. The chief had many colored feathers on his head attached by a bolt of twisted cotton wrought into a belt. He then gave Columbus small pieces of gold, and to his men bolts of cotton.

Columbus turned all gifts that had to be accounted for in to his comptroller, Rodrigo Sanchez. He also knew too well that his Spaniard men were greedy and would take advantage of these good and innocent souls.

The colored glass, baubles, and hawk's bells were then given to the natives in return.

Afterward the villagers brought many foods for them to eat, including bread, sweet cooked yellow roots, and three fat geese. In return, Columbus gave the chief a leather belt with an iron buckle, for which he showed he was very pleased by displaying a large smile and uneven teeth. Colorful parrots were then presented to Columbus, and he turned them in to Rodrigo Sanchez to check them.

"Kynoro," The chieftain said with a smile.

Rodrigo said, "Admiral, I think he means the parrots."

The chief then gave him bread to eat. Columbus took a bite and relished the taste. "It tastes sweet."

"Taino caçábi. Aawu kijere sikai. Amoro arepa ekeiko." The chief then showed him a tuberous plant. A native brought in a stone bowl, and the chief put the tuberous plant in it and rubbed it against the bowl back and forth with a pumice stone to grind it. He then repeated the same procedure with a long yellow fruit that had small seeds.

The chief said, *"Mahiz."*

The chief then transmitted by signs that in the land of Española much gold was there to be had. Columbus tried to get more information regarding how far the island lay and in what direction, but his Indians couldn't report any clues from the natives or the chief. They only pointed southeast with their fingers.

"Civao! Civao!" the chief repeated as he showed another piece of gold in his hand.

"¿La Isla de Cipango?" Columbus asked the chief.

The chief nodded and repeated again, *"Civao."*

When the meeting was concluded, hundreds of villagers carried the gifts on their heads through muddy rivers and followed Columbus's party to the ships moored on the river. All was done for them, for they believed that Columbus and his men had come from heaven.

When the ships appeared before them, so did hundreds of canoes that had moored while they were away. Many natives came on board, carrying bread, fish, and earthen jars containing water. They also gave Columbus seeds and spices and threw them in a porringer containing water, then rubbed their stomachs with a smile, saying it was good for health.

By the afternoon the winds had not only abated but died altogether, as if the storm from previous days had never taken place. The skies were deep blue with flocks of geese flying in groups over the ships. There was an inland breeze and the anchors were weighed in. Their course for that day was the sea of Santo Tome, heading toward the island of La Amiga—a flat island with no considerable mountains except one tall one within one league Columbus named Monte Caribatan.

Outside the island Columbus noted several shoals at a Lombard distance from La Amiga. The lead line was dropped in the waters and measured at seven fathoms with a gravel bottom. Further up in the sea another reef and lots more shoals extended far within two leagues of a cape. Columbus decided to drop anchor at the first sign of a large harbor. The *Santa Maria* and the *Niña* docked all day, and the men looked for fish in the harbor of La Amiga.

At sundown, the *Santa Maria* and the *Niña* came alive. Columbus ordered several more torches to shed the festive yet reverent light of Christmas Eve. Vicente Yanez, captain of the *Niña* and Martin Pinzón's brother, came on board the *Santa Maria* to pay his respects to the admiral as was customary.

"A most auspicious year, I might say, Admiral."

"Indeed," Columbus said. "We will see the fruit of our labor when we reach Civao or the mainland. That's where our luck and good fortune by the Savior will show by his will."

"I agree, Admiral," Vicente replied. "I'm only sorry my brother Martin isn't here to witness it."

"You know, Vicente, that I don't hold grudges. Your brother must come back before we sail home. Otherwise, I'll be forced to report him to Our Highnesses for insubordination."

"He'll come back. I know it," Vicente said with confidence.

"Meanwhile, let's celebrate and give thanks for this amazing voyage." Columbus crossed himself, and Vicente followed suit. "Let us celebrate this Christmas Eve and the birth of our Savior!"

The men who had waited for this signal jumped up from their seated positions on deck and ran to a makeshift table set up by Diego, who had been cooking all day under the most difficult conditions. The breezes coming across his sheltered corner kept extinguishing the flames in the sandbox. Although his cooking corner had an iron back to prevent flames from dying out, Diego had to rekindle the fire several times. In his cooking cubicle, he was able to fry mullet fish in his hot skillet with olive oil. He cooked the three geese given by the cacique chief, and the tuber plant that tasted like chestnuts was baked under hot ashes. Wine and sweets were given to all, and Columbus told Diego not to spare the rations. By midnight the men were sound asleep; exhausted by revelry and satiated from plentiful drinks, they slumbered drunk and snored loudly on deck.

Columbus, who hadn't slept in two days, went to look for Juan de la Cosa at the tiller. "I'm going to lie down and get some sleep. Wake me at the next watch."

"Go and rest, Admiral," Juan said. "Don't worry—the ship's in my hands."

Columbus walked the length of the ship to his cabin. He stood for a moment on deck to take in the view of a silver waning moon that lit the sea and bathed it in an eerie calm. The islands they passed along the way were illuminated by moonlight, showing their contour and the heights of their mountains, but they kept secret what treasures they might hold. Comforted by the lull of the ship gliding through a dark sea, he entered his cabin and found sleep immediately.

By one o'clock in the morning he was shaken out of his sleep by his cabin boy shouting on deck. He jumped up and ran out on deck in his long chemise. What he saw brought a jolt to his heart. The *Santa Maria* had run aground onto a shoal and lay athwart in the sea.

"Wake up! Wake up!" Columbus yelled at his first in command sleeping on deck. "Wake up, Juan!" Columbus slapped him on the face over and over until he opened his eyes. "The ship ran aground!"

"What! Where?" Juan shook like a leaf by the light of torches still burning on deck.

"Launch the boat at the stern! And cast an anchor there!"

His crew scuttered in their bare feet on the wooden deck, then launched and piled into the boat at the stern but neglected dropping a second anchor to steady the ship lying on its side. The boat led by Juan rowed toward to the *Niña*, half a league downwind of the *Santa Maria*.

Columbus, who saw them flee and disobey his orders, was beside himself. "You forgot to drop the anchor!" His voice was lost on the men rowing to safety.

Within minutes, the ship took on water. Columbus screamed at the remaining men on board. "Cut the mast! Cut the mast!" he yelled at the top of his lungs. João, Gomes, Hernán, Alfonso, and Alvaro rushed to cut the mast with picks and axes. When the mast crashed into the sea with all the attached sails and cordage, it raised a wall of water onto the deck, stunning the men, but the ship buoyed up, relieved of its weight. The *Santa Maria* carrack was still lying sideways and taking on more water as the seams split. The vessel, though, stayed intact and didn't break apart.

Columbus then sent the remaining canoe with João, Diego de Arana from Cordova, his alguacil or constable, and Pedro Gutierrez the royal scribe to the cacique king on the island. When João returned with the empty canoe, Columbus sent the rest of his crew to the *Niña* for safety, and felt relieved the *Santa Maria* lying on its side was in no danger of sinking.

The delegation composed of Diego and Pedro returned in an Indian canoe to convey that the king wept when he heard that the ship ran aground. Hundreds of his people were sent with canoes to unload the cargo on the ailing ship. The goods were stacked along the beach with the king's armed guards watching them.

When the king returned to the *Niña*, now crowded by the *Santa Maria*'s crew and her captain, his eyes were tearing. He indicated by signs that all the cargo and goods had been transported to two vacated houses in the village. He reported that everything would be at the admiral's disposal.

Columbus thought how gentle and giving these people were. They had shared everything they owned with them and promised more. His soul lifted from the deep mood he found himself in by the loss of his flagship, and he bowed deeply to the king.

85

More Ominous Signs

NA RAISED HER FACE FROM peeling vegetables and turned pale. What she saw made her put down the knife in her hands. Isabella turned her head around to see what had attracted Ana's attention. The sight at the front door made her feel faint. She held on to the edge of the table for support and was glad she was sitting in her chair.

A man wearing a long fur-lined coat in embroidered fabric stood erect by the door, his black-feathered hat in his hand. Avram stood next to him with an ashen face.

At the stranger's sight, Ana stood up. "To what do we owe the honor of your visit, Senhor . . .?" Her voice fluttered but remained controlled.

The visitor bowed slightly, then standing up said, "Senhoritas and senhor." He turned to Avram. "Dom Joam do Allgarve. I'm here at the request of King John of Portugal." He stopped and examined their faces, one by one.

When Ana recovered from her shock, she said, "What can we do for His Highness? We are humble people living by the sea."

Dom Joam looked away, then turned his head back at them, his face tight and brows drawn. *"Pequena nobreza.* You're very modest. With your estate and horses, you're well-to-do. And that's why I'm here."

"If you're taking about the taxes due, we've taken care of it. It's all paid off." Ana waved her hand.

"No, I'm not talking about taxes. We want to know where your wealth came from," Dom Joam replied.

Isabella felt stunned that their wealth was being questioned. Ana's face reflected a gamut of shock, surprise, and anger, one following the other. Avram sat silently without uttering a word.

"We have never been asked this question before. Why do you ask?" Ana said.

Dom Joam took his time answering her. He walked to a chair and sat down with his hands clenched together on the table. "Before you all moved here to Portugal, there was another man who owned the property. We're looking for him."

Ana jumped in. "We know nothing of him. All we know is the property was sold through an intermediary. If this is the man you want, he left the country."

"Where did he go and what was his name?"

"We don't know of his whereabouts."

"But you do know his name. Is it Dom Carvalho by any chance?"

Ana's face went white.

Isabella bent her head down. Her nightmares were reoccurring over and over.

Avram spoke for the first time. "We're honored by your visit, Dom do Allgarve. But you are upsetting my wife. She's with child, and she mustn't be disturbed any further. Please leave us now."

Isabella was about to let a cry of surprise, but she held it in check.

Dom do Allgarve shifted in his chair while shaking his head. He got up and bowed to all three, then walked toward the kitchen's exit, when he turned back to them. *"Obrigado e bom dia."* With a quick step he left the kitchen.

"I'll see him out," Avram said in a hurry, then left after the visitor.

Left alone, Ana sat mute, while Isabella covered her face in her hands.

Ana then said, "Don't worry, Isabella. I won't let anything happen to you or Avram. They can't do a thing to us."

"I'm not sure, Ana," Isabella said. "I've seen this kind of inquiry so many times, where they'll hound us until we're caught."

"What do you mean by caught? We're no longer under the Inquisition's whip!"

Isabella wasn't convinced. She closed her eyes and shook her head. "What kind of life will my child have? Will he, too, be hounded? What do they want? Blood?"

"They're looking for Don Abravanel. That's all. He isn't here any longer, so we can't be punished for that."

"I just want peace in my life and for my child," Isabella said.

"You will. You must look forward to the birth of a beautiful child. I can't wait for this blessed event." With dreamy eyes, Ana grasped her own two hands together and brought them close to her lips.

Somehow, Isabella felt a weight lifting off her chest. She would, nevertheless, have to find a way to evade these men wanting to harm her. She would have to rise above these despicable men, and not give in to despair.

Avram came back agitated after seeing the visitor depart.

"What's the matter?" Isabella said, alarmed.

"This man wasn't sent by King John. When he climbed on his horse, I saw him wearing a Spanish sword." To Ana's questioning eyes, he quickly added, "The long sword's pommel didn't have the Portuguese crest and emblem. It was an *espadón* with the Spanish emblem of Castile with castles and lions."

86

Aftermath

Wednesday, December 26, 1492

COLUMBUS SAT DEJECTED ON THE *Niña*'s main deck, looking beyond to the wreck of the *Santa Maria*.

She lay sideways in the water, the waves washing over her port sides where debris was floating, and while all its cargo was being brought to the island with the natives' help. The king had visited him many times since yesterday, trying to console him.

"*Gracias. Mucho gracias.*" Columbus brought his cupped hand to his forehead and bowed his head slightly. He had seen it done with the Moors many years ago and thought it appropriate, to which the king renewed his crying to see him so humble.

Touched, Columbus offered him one of his shirts with long ballooning sleeves, and a pair of gloves. The king broke in a wide smile, exposing his uneven teeth. He slipped them on and admired both gloves on his small hands and felt the shirt's fabric between his gloved fingers as he paraded in front of Columbus. With a roaring laugh he slapped Columbus on his shoulder. He was extremely pleased.

"Chuq! Chuq!" The king exclaimed at the top of his lungs and pointed to several canoes approaching the ship from the seaside.

Columbus got up and approached the railing, watching the canoe, with the king following behind. He turned to his interpreter Luis de Torres to translate those words.

"What is the king saying?"

Luis scratched his temple with a shake of his head. "Hmm . . ." Luis uttered.

Meanwhile, the canoe approached the starboard side, and the natives showed the admiral gold pieces in their hands.

Luis hit his head. "C*huq, chuq* means hawk's bells!"

Columbus shrugged his shoulders and concentrated on the two men in the canoe, one of them signing and pointing to a hawk's bell in his hand.

"They want to trade their gold pieces for hawk bells!" said Juan de la Cosa, the now-deprived master of the flagship *Santa Maria.*

The king put his arm on Columbus's shoulder and pronounced many words that Columbus couldn't understand. He called his Indian translators, who by signs indicated that the king would give him more gold.

Columbus smiled, and the king, pleased, broke out in roaring laughter.

"Civao, civao" The king repeated over and over. *"Bohio, Caribata!"* He held his hands wide to indicate "much gold"—as Columbus interpreted his words and motions.

Columbus gathered that the king was speaking of Cipango and Española Island, where gold was plentiful, or so he'd been told.

The natives that came from other islands on canoes raised four fingers, then pointed to the gold pieces in their hands as they left the side of the ship.

Columbus looked at the Indian interpreter and he signaled for four gold pieces for *chuq, chuq.* "Tomorrow they come back. More *chuq* for gold," he signed.

Afterward the king invited him onto the island, where a great meal was spread for him and some of his men. They feasted on shrimp, fowl, and bread they called *caçábi.*

Columbus showed him a bow and arrows, and one of his crew shot an arrow that pierced a tree nearby. The king's face displayed amazement. Next, Columbus ordered the *Niña* to fire a Lombard. The sound of the cannonball hitting a target on the island made a deafening sound, and all the islanders, except for the king who recoiled with amazement in his eyes, scampered everywhere. The king then quickly brought from his house many jewels made of colorful pebbles with which he adorned Columbus's neck.

Columbus thanked him by nodding his head several times and displaying a large smile to the king. He took leave from the king, and with great fanfare of the natives hitting wooden bowls together, they made their way back to the *Niña*. Upon arrival, he received news of the *Pinta* caravel moored on the island at the head of a large river.

"Prepare for the return home," he told Vicente. "Tomorrow we'll inspect the ships and load up all goods for the voyage home."

Columbus left Vicente and headed for his cabin. He pulled his logbook and sat down to note all of the events that had taken place until now.

To your most gracious Highnesses, it is with great joy and trepidation that I announce we found what we were seeking on this voyage. We met wonderful Indians who are docile and gentle. They will become good Christians because they have no religion.

I regret to bring one bit of bad news to Your Highnesses. We lost the Santa Maria *because it was not properly fitted back in Palos, and due to the master's decision, and his men's, not to draw the ship with an anchor as I ordered them to and deserting ship. Not one bit or nail of her cargo was lost, and a most gracious king transported all to the island. When I return to the island from Castile, with God's will we will find much gold traded from mines with the Indians to the men I leave behind here. It was the will of the Savior that directed our ship to this island for us to find, and within three years Spain will have all the gold it needs for the conquest of Jerusalem.*

87

A Cold Winter

*A*S SHE SAT BY THE window, Isabella wrapped herself in the cotton shawl knitted by Ana. A mist blanketing the sea beyond the estate was wrapped too, in a thick cover, as if nature wanted to protect its fluid asset: its life-giving source of water. She felt her belly and listened for any movement, but the baby was hibernating as well. Outside the house, trees were pelted by rain and wind.

She longed to return to the sea. Since the last two voyages she made with Avram on the *Liberação* to Morocco, she had come to appreciate and love the sea. Sometimes she felt at odds for having been born female while men dominated the sea. She longed, too, for spring to arrive and for her child to be born. This wait for her child and spring made her impatient and cross most of the time. She recalled how her temper burst several times at Ana's pressure to ward against the cold and to eat all her meals. Avram, too, tried her patience when he forbade her to venture beyond the estate on calmer days.

"Stop fussing over me! I'm not an invalid!" Isabella had yelled one day at Avram.

He had stood stunned by her outburst. "Nevertheless, you must take care not to get lost beyond the forest and the road."

"Why would I get lost? I know my way north to Sintra and back south to the estate."

"Even so, it isn't safe for a woman alone on the road, and expecting a child, at that," he replied forcefully.

She covered her ears with her hands. "I won't listen to you or Ana. You're keeping me prisoner in my own home!" She glanced at Avram and saw his shoulders drop with a pained look and suddenly felt sorry for her outburst. She quickly went to him and held his hand.

"I'm sorry, Avram. I know you mean well and care for my well-being and child." She looked for any signs of forgiveness.

A bright light danced in his eyes, and he smiled warmly. "I'm glad you understand me. I only want the best for you and the child. I'd like very much to care for your child and guide him too."

Isabella let go of his hand and fell silent for a moment. "Of course, he'll be glad to have an uncle to lead and teach him," she said quickly.

Avram's smile faded, but he nodded. "I'll be honored to direct his steps, if it's a boy you're having." The smile returned to his lips.

After she turned her back to Avram that day and headed for the house, she had an uncomfortable feeling. Had she given him a reason to hope— hope that she could ever care for him and love him? She wanted to avoid misunderstandings. Still in love with Miguel and his memory, she tried hard to negate the fact that he might not be alive. *No*! It mustn't be so, she reminded herself. She hung with tenacity to shreds of testimony and hearsay that he may have resurfaced and swam to a lifebuoy.

A shiver went through her body, and she got up to stoke the fireplace and add more wood. Reborn again, the flames blazed high into the flue cavity with sparks at the end of flaming tongues. She turned away from the fire and walked out of her room, then went down the stairs slowly to the lower floors of the house.

88

Preparations for the Return

Friday, December 28, 1492

COLUMBUS SAT ON A WOODEN chair alongside the cacique king near his large tent. His council sat around them on ornate milled-cotton blankets with stripes and geometric figures. The king spoke to his audience in an Indian language accompanied by the motion of his hands and guttural sounds.

Columbus called to his Indian translators and asked them to repeat the words to him.

The Indian translated with signs. "The cacique said he will give you much gold to take home with you."

"Please tell the king I'm grateful for his gifts."

After his Indian translated, the king got up and motioned to Columbus to follow him. They walked through the village to two large houses. Inside, Columbus saw all his possessions saved from the *Santa Maria* wreck on elevated platforms. The king then turned to one of his pages and retrieved a gold plate, attached on opposite ends by a rope, that he hung on Columbus's neck. He thanked the king profusely through the translator, and accompanied by the cacique they walked to the promontory where his men were working erecting a fortress. Much of the plank wood used in the fortress's construction came from his beloved *Santa Maria* ship; the massive boards and masts were anchored into the rocky point and fused with the new soil. The sounds of hammers and nails pounded into Castilian wood sealed their permanency in a new land. Columbus felt now a link and a tether to the land he had discovered for the Spanish realm. This land was now blessed with the one true faith.

He left the construction site, and after taking leave of the king, he rejoined the crew on the *Niña*. His two cooks came running to him to request some of his time.

"What is it?" he asked Diego and Pedro.

"We must take more provisions with us," Diego pleaded.

"Isn't what we have enough?" Columbus said.

Pedro rushed to reply. "We counted all the crates, bails, and jugs, and we're short many things."

"What, for example?" Columbus asked.

"For one thing, there's no olive oil. We used the last drop last month. How are we to cook the fish?"

"Don't worry, Diego," Columbus reassured him. "Use coconuts. I saw the Indians do it."

Diego's face looked bewildered. "Then we must load many of these coconuts on the ship."

"Do that. I'll contact the king's brother who promised everything to us."

By sunrise on the following day, a young boy visited Columbus from the island.

"He said that he's the cacique's nephew," his translator said to Columbus.

By signs, the young boy told him that four days east of their island were other islands on which gold was plentiful. He proceeded to name a long list of islands that Columbus jotted down for his records.

"Thank the king from me and tell him that we'll go to the island to say good-bye," Columbus said smiling. His translator explained the words to the boy.

On the following day, Columbus went on the island again to meet with the Guacanagarí king, and five kings from neighboring islands came wearing their crowns and colored fineries of feathers and colorful cotton gowns to greet him. Again the king took him to the largest house, where his cargo had originally been stored after the *Santa Maria*'s wreck. The empty space was filled with the king's council, the other kings, and many villagers. The king then took off his feather crown and placed it on Columbus's head. In turn, the admiral took off a necklace of green jasper bloodstones dotted with bright red spots and placed it around the king's neck, then transferred a silver ring from his finger to the king's. He also removed his own scarlet cloak and wrapped it around the king's shoulders. Two of the other kings came forward and offered Columbus a couple of gold plaques. All kings and the admiral smiled at each other while other officials roared with laughter.

Just then the sailor Columbus had sent in a boat came back, huffing with news.

"We saw the *Pinta* two days ago in a harbor, and they said they're leaving to meet with the admiral!"

"That's the news I've been waiting for," Columbus said joyously. He bowed to all the kings present in the large house and took his leave from them.

Upon arrival on the *Niña*, he found Vicente happy with the news of his brother returning from his voyage. He also greeted him with the news that rhubarb had been found on an island, six leagues away. He showed him the plants that had been collected, still attached to their roots, with large triangular leaves and long yellow-and-reddish stems. Fruit resembling green mulberries were attached to the plant.

"I know it's rhubarb, Admiral. The roots are like pears, and the stems can be used medicinally."

"That's good news, Vicente. How many plants did you collect?"

"Admiral. We're sorry, but we couldn't gather but these few samples. We didn't have a spade with us to dig into the soil for more."

"All right. These will do for now," Columbus reassured the loyal mariner.

Columbus rubbed his hands together, energized by the gold gifts, the supplies in place, and the *Pinta* about to rejoin them. He headed for his cabin and prepared a crew list to remain on the island, and the ones to return on the two remaining ships.

When he finished, he looked at the men staying on the island and was satisfied. He then read the long list of forty-three men again to see if he had omitted anyone.

"Pedro Gutierrez, keeper of the king's drawing room; Rodrigo de Escobedo, of Segovia and notary; Diego de Arana, of Cordova and Alguazil mayor; Alonzo Velez de Mendoza, of Seville; Alvarez Perez Osorio, of Castrojeriz; Antonio de Jaen, of Jaen; Benardino de Taoia, of Ledesma; Cristobal del Alamo, of Niebla; Castillo, silversmith and assayer, of Seville . . .

He kept on reading until he remembered João Treves. *Good. Now, I can finally rid myself of the man with accusing eyes.* He added João's name at the bottom of the list. He then thought, guiltily, how João had come to his help when confronted by his crew, how he had saved Pedro from certain death down the mast, and how he had helped in shuttling the men from the *Santa Maria* to safety. He lifted his quill and crossed his name off the list.

89

Rumors

THE RAINS HAD LET UP for two weeks now, and Isabella used this opportunity to go back to her daily walks. As warned by Avram, she kept to the perimeter of the estate, but as soon as her confinement ended she wanted to return to sea. She couldn't explain this thirst for the ocean and the lure of freedom that the sea gave her. All her life she had been restricted to Seville and her home, as proper señoritas were told to. Her parents, her dada, and teachers who came to the house had supervised her around the clock. This new sense of being free to decide her fate made her drunk with excitement. The anticipated birth of her son would reward her with the freedom of being a new woman.

She caught herself with a smile forming on her lips. *A free woman*? What could it mean? No woman was truly free. She had to account to her father first, then to her husband by marriage, then to her children, to see them safe. What was that freedom that men experienced and endured for? At this moment in her life, she didn't give an account to anyone, except her duty and friendship to Ana and Avram, but they wouldn't restrict her movements.

"Isabella, Isabella!" Ana's voice called from the front of the house.

Isabella turned around from the furthest part of the estate by the front gate and waved at her. She quickened her step to meet Ana, and found her agitated and grasping her hands.

"What is it?" Isabella said.

"Please come into the house."

She followed Ana to the hearth in the kitchen and was surprise to find a peasant woman clutching a basket in her arm. Isabella acknowledged her with a nod.

"Kualo accontisio?" Isabella said.

"Senhora, senhorita." The woman bowed to Ana and Isabella.

"La Senhora Carmo lives in Sintra," Ana said to Isabella. "She's been helping find work for the young people we bring from Morocco."

"Si, Señora Carmo?" Isabella said.

"There's been a serious development," Carmo said.

Isabella raised her eyebrows.

"There was an announcement in the plaza."

"What announcement?" Isabella asked.

Ana asked, "And what exactly did it say?"

"The announcement was posted in the plaza in Sintra by the royal palace that all Jewish citizens need to report to the *Polícia de Segurança Pública.*"

Both Ana and Isabella stood stunned without a word. Isabella sat down, her legs feeling weak.

Carmo broke the silence. "I'll leave you now. If you have another girl looking for work, please let me know. "

Isabella reached into her pocket and gave Carmo a *dinheiro.*

"Obrigada," Carmo said, and left in a hurry.

Ana spoke first. "I'm sure there's nothing to worry about." She looked at Isabella with her head downward.

"Why, all of a sudden? All of a sudden?" Isabella's voice echoed.

"The Portuguese government is probably taking a census for taxes. Who knows?"

"No, it's vague. It reminds me of the Alhambra Decree I witnessed in Cordoba."

"You poor child," Ana said. "You've been through a lot. But don't worry. We are landowners, and nobody knows our true identities."

Isabella shook her head but remained silent.

Ana's strong voice said, "Let's get back to our life now."

Isabella tried to absorb Ana's reassuring voice, bur a small voice inside her told her otherwise. *We're doomed to escape from one country to another. When will it cease?*

90

Homeward Bound

Tuesday, January 1, 1493

COLUMBUS STARED AT THE ISLAND in front of him with the small fort being erected by his men, the lush green palm trees crowning the tops of the mountains framing the beach, the village huts he could see in the distance, and his men on the *Niña* loading the last of the water and provisions, and he sighed. With all his heart and soul he wanted to remain in this paradise to see more islands. He strongly wished he had more time to sail east along the coasts of those islands and assess their importance to Castile. He suddenly imagined all the trade to be conducted for Spain, the Christian souls won for Christendom, and all the gold to be mined. All he had left, though, was this small ship, and he blamed Pinzón for separating from the *Santa Maria* during the voyage.

It was all his doing for leaving him and his men devoid of an additional caravel to explore these unknown islands. Martin Alonso Pinzón still hadn't returned from his excursion inland from the river mouth, and Columbus could ill afford to wait for him any longer. On the other hand, he feared that if the *Niña*'s safety was compromised by a storm, they would sink without a consort to rescue them, and Pinzón would return to the monarchs and spread his lies against him. He sighed with despair. No matter—it was high time to leave now before the sea became a murderess in her fury.

"Admiral?" The voice behind his back came from Juan de la Cosa. He turned around to see him and Vicente, Pinzón's brother, standing next to him.

"Are you ready?" Columbus asked them.

"Yes, Admiral," Juan said. "All that's left now is your benediction."

"Assemble the men on the beach for a last good-bye." Columbus's voice broke at that point. He considered each and every one of his crew as his own son. They had battled the unforgiving sea and obstinate waves as well as the fear and doubts displayed each day before finding land. They had shared meals together. They were all partners in adversity with the sea.

By Middies at 12:05 p.m., for the midday prayer, all forty-three men staying on Española Island were there on the beach to say good-bye to the admiral and the remaining crew of the *Niña* and the *Santa Maria* returning to Spain. He left in charge Diego de Arana from Cordoba as governor; Pedro Gutierrez the *repostero*, or king's keeper of the drawing room; and Rodrigo de Escobedo as lieutenants to govern the island and trade for more gold. To that effect, he left plenty of trinkets to trade for gold, seeds, one year's supply of biscuits, wine, and artillery for protection. The *Santa Maria's* boat also remained in their possession to explore more island coasts for gold. Columbus hoped that upon his return from Castile he would find much gold and the mine it came from. Included in the total number of men were: his *escribano*, or court clerk, to take notes, and the *alguacil*, master at arms, from his vessel, as well as a ship carpenter, a caulker, a gunner, and a physician were also left behind.

The cacique king of Guacanagarí stood aside from the men assembled on the beach with tears streaming down his face. He talked to his court and men around him with a choked voice. Columbus had his translator explain the king's words, and he was told the cacique was sorry he was leaving. Columbus bowed to the king and had his translator tell the king he was sorry too, but that he would be back soon.

"Let us pray to the Lord for a fast and safe voyage, and I wish all the men a safe sojourn on the *Niña*—and the *Pinta*, when they finally get to follow us. To the men I leave behind, a most productive time to trade with the Indians." Columbus stopped to watch the men on their knees in the white sand, praying and kissing their rosary and necklace crosses. A slight breeze rose from the sea, a good omen for their ship to sail. Columbus made the sign of the cross, then kissed his fist.

"In nomine Patris et Filii et Spiritus Sancti. Amen."

The men repeated "amen" in one voice, which prompted the natives to fall down on their knees and bow their heads like the Spaniards.

Columbus received this Indian honor as a sign from the Lord for a protected voyage.

"Good-bye," Columbus told the cacique, and bowed his head in his direction.

The cacique replied by approaching Columbus and hugging him several times to his heart. Columbus was touched by the gesture and turned to his translators to tell the king he was parting from a dear friend. The cacique king lowered his head with reverence, and all his subjects did the same.

Columbus left the beach with all his men following him and entered the two row boats left to them.

"We will sail at sunrise."

91

A New Outlook

*J*SABELLA SAT AT THE KITCHEN table, trying to make sense of her accounts. Whichever way she added the numbers and accounted for the deductions, the balance remained negative. At this rate, all three—Ana, Avram, and herself—were bound for the poorhouse. If this January weather didn't let up and the rains failed to stop, this prediction might come to pass. Already, the surplus reserve of *reales* was dwindling dangerously. The vintage season had just started, and the berries were still green on the vines. They needed two to three more months to ripen.

In a way, she felt that her son would arrive in time, like the ripeness of the golden and purple berries. For now, they had to curtail their expenses in tools and implements for the farm, and wait to the last possible day to hire help.

"Isabella, Isabella?" Ana's voice came to her ears along with squishing and thumping sounds. She looked up to see Ana kneading fresh dough for the morning breakfast. Hot gruel was boiling in the iron pot on the fire in the hearth, where the fire kept them warm.

"What is it?" Isabella said.

"Do we have anything left?"

Isabella took another look at her figures and crossed out a few with her quill pen. She raised her head from the ledger on the table and looked at Ana. "Not much."

Ana stopped kneading dough and looked at Isabella with a pallid face. "How much?"

"We have a few silver reales left, about six hundred dinheiros."

"Then it's time I showed you our reserve. Come." Ana gave a nod and took off her apron.

Isabella got up, puzzled, slowly sliding her enlarged figure between the bench and the table. "Where are we going?" she quizzed Ana.

"You'll see. Follow me." Ana lit a taper, walked to a closed door inside the kitchen, and unlocked it.

Below them steps led downward in darkness. Ana raised her candle and descended the narrow steps.

"Take care to lean on the wall," Ana warned her.

When they reached bottom, the light from Ana's candle lit up a large room that ran under the house. The candle shed light on shelves lined up along the walls filled with clay pots and wine barrels below.

"Come into our treasure vault," Ana said with a satisfied smile on her face.

Isabella was stunned. "How did you accumulate all of this, and when?"

"As soon as I arrived here from Seville, my cousin Don Abravanel revealed the cache to me. He said, "Use it with caution. If the authorities find out, they'll arrest me and take all the supplies."

"So, he did owe back taxes?" Isabella said.

"Yes, but he was overtaxed. Way more than most landowners here in the county of Sintra. He discovered that injustice over the years, that other farmers were paying much less."

"How are we going to move all this merchandise when we're being watched?"

"We will sell a few bottles of wine at a time, and jams each time we go to market," Ana said.

Isabella felt a weight lift off her chest. "Then we can go to market next week!"

"I'll have Avram accompany you to town."

"You've been a treasure to us, Ana. I can never repay you and Don Abravanel for all you've done for Avram, Miguel . . . and me."

92

Heading Home

Friday, January 4, 1493

AFTER WAITING LONG ENOUGH FOR Pinzón and the *Pinta* to show up, Columbus decided it was high time to raise the anchor on the *Niña*. "Raise the sails!"

At sunrise, with the sound of waves crashing and powered by a sea breeze, Columbus saw to the crew carrying out his orders to depart. The master sail was the first to be hoisted, filling with light air, then came the foremast and mizzenmast joining in to move the *Niña* gracefully outside the bank where it had lain for several days. The returning seventeen men from the *Santa Maria* were added to the seven sailors of the *Niña*. He made a silent prayer for the safety of the forty-three men remaining on the island of Española. He felt reassured that King Guacanagarí would see to their protection and well-being. Diego de Arana and his two other lieutenants would see to the bartering and mining of gold on the island, which gave him further reassurance.

Columbus had warned Diego de Arana, "Make sure to treat the Indians with Christian charity and goodness. They're gentle souls and will make good Christians once we convert them to our true faith."

"As mayor of La Navidad, I give you my word, Admiral," Diego said solemnly.

Before leaving, Columbus said to Diego, "Now I want to plant the first sugarcane plants on La Navidad Island, donated by the gracious Doña Leonor de Bobadilla."

Columbus waited for two of his men to plant the first shoots of sugarcane near the mouth of the river.

"You will see that they thrive," he had told Diego.

"I will, Admiral."

"We will now sail home!" Columbus ordered his crew.

All the men remaining on La Navidad had come to shore to see them leave as Columbus embarked on the *Niña*. The caravel's bow parted the waters, its sails flapping in a gentle breeze. He felt reassured that the caravel was filled to capacity with a crammed hold loaded with many varieties of plants, parrots in wood cages, and food provisions. The water barrels were stacked one on top of another as a solid wall reaching the top ceiling in the hold. Other goods were stored in Vicente Pinzon's cabin, graciously ceded to the admiral for the voyage. Columbus had made sure to lock up the gold in a chest by his bunk bed.

Columbus, standing on the main deck, sighed as he watched the shore recede in the distance. He regretted not seeing the other islands further south. If it hadn't been for Martin Pinzon's stubbornness and greed to be the first to find gold, both caravels would be sailing one after the other. Now with only the *Niña* at his command, no mistake or foolishness could be allowed. If, God forbid, they were caught in a powerful storm, they'd be as good as dead.

He had the option, though, of stopping at a few islands on his itinerary home going northeast; nevertheless, he sensed a great rush to return home before storms crossed his path. As the Navidad fort disappeared from view, he knew that he'd come back to build more forts and cities in a new world.

On Saturday January 5, he sailed by the island of Monti-Cristi, two leagues away from Villa de la Navidad. He noted down the bearings for future reference. Monti-Cristi then had to be Cipango, where a great deal of gold could be found, according to the Indian translators taken with him on the ship.

"We will land on Monti-Cristi!" Columbus decided and gave the order as the *Niña* approached the island. First, Vicente sounded for depth and found it to be three fathoms with a sandy bottom.

Upon landing with the boat, he saw many natural rock formations of many colors, and made a mental note for it to be quarried in the future.

"This will be a good quarry to build a church," Columbus told Vicente as they explored the island.

"There are many mastic trees, Admiral." Vicente pointed them out to Columbus.

Columbus turned his head in the direction Vicente was pointing and saw magnificent six-to-ten-foot-tall trees, some of which had beautiful red flowers. The sight made his heart jump with joy. The red berries, still young, would gradually turn green, then brown, and the resin would be ready for harvesting between July first and October thirty-first on his next voyage.

"These would make excellent medicines to aid digestion and for baking biscuits!" Columbus felt invigorated as he visualized the tons of mastic to sell to markets in Europe. "I want to take as many samples as possible from the young trees."

By sunset, when all the plants that could be gathered had been loaded on the deck, Columbus ordered several tarps from the reserve sails to cover the plants from strong winds or lashing rain.

"We can sail now!" Columbus ordered.

"Have a good night," he told his crew after supper, and retired to his cabin to say Compline prayers as the ship pulled out of the harbor.

After sunrise the following morning, on Sunday January 6, the wind was favorable as they sailed, and after Lauds—morning prayers at 7:45 a.m.—he went to his cabin to jot down in his logbook his impressions of the day and the many wonderful harvests the ship would carry back home. In his mind's eye, the vision of praise and gifts from the monarchs filled his head till midday, when the cook, Maestre Diego, brought him with a limp his noon meal.

"Congratulations, Admiral, on a great voyage successfully accomplished!" Diego said.

"Thank you, Diego," Columbus said, laughing. "We couldn't have made the voyage without you feeding and nourishing us."

Diego stood with his hands on his hips, laughing and showing his bad teeth. "I might say, Admiral, the liquor you allowed the men had a lot to do with it."

"Yes, Diego. As much as I don't approve of imbibing, I had to give them some recompense for their hard—"

Shouts stopped Columbus. He jumped from his chair and ran out the cabin to see to the commotion. What he saw brought a smile to his face. The *Pinta* was sailing from the east and heading toward them.

The crew on the *Niña* was ecstatic with joy. They jumped and danced on deck, and waved to their co-sailors on the *Pinta*.

He then saw a boat launched from the *Pinta* and Martin Alonso Pinzón descend into it with four of his crew. The men rowed to the *Niña*, and followed by Pinzón, climbed on deck.

Columbus advanced, reluctantly, toward Pinzón.

Pinzón bowed to the admiral and proceeded to explain himself. "My dear admiral. It was against my will that I separated from the fleet. I wanted to surprise you and find all the gold you needed, with the *Pinta* being the fastest caravel."

"You knew the orders we received before sailing from Spain. We had to stick together and help one another in case of storms!" Columbus tried hard to contain his voice and his ire. "You disobeyed me out of greed to find gold for yourself!"

Pinzón raised his hands in protest. "No, no, Admiral. It was done to speed up the voyage!"

"It was to fill your coffers!" Columbus roared.

"You are misled, Admiral! The Indians from your ship that came aboard the *Pinta* told us of much gold to be found on Babeque. Since the *Pinta* was a light caravel that traveled faster than the *Santa Maria*, I thought it behooved me to go ahead."

"You could've slowed down enough for the *Santa Maria*, and together we might've found more gold."

"But, Admiral, you wanted to spend more time on the island of Juana, and spent many days sailing along the coast of Española Island!"

Columbus ran to his cabin, leaving Pinzón puzzled, and brought back some of the gold. "This is where we found gold on Española! Had you waited we might've had more!" He showed him gold pieces as large as his hand.

Pinzón's face went white. Whether it was envy or shame, Columbus wasn't sure.

"I truly tried to help, Admiral."

Columbus knew Pinzón was lying between his teeth, and he was about to blast him again, when Pinzón lowered and shook his head.

"Admiral, I know I've failed you miserably. I found very little gold."

Columbus stood surprised by Pinzón's admission and contrition, and thought it would be best to push his anger away and concentrate on the task ahead of them. At least now he had another ship as backup.

He turned away from Pinzón and shouted, "Get back to the *Pinta*! We're sailing back to Monti-Cristi for you to refuel with provisions!"

Pinzón bowed to the admiral, and rejoined his men in the boat to take them back to the *Pinta*.

The *Niña* and the *Pinta* following right behind sailed back to Monti-Cristi, ten leagues away.

93

To Market

ISABELLA AND AVRAM RODE TO Sintra at an early hour. Avram had convinced her to take their spacious, four-wheeled wagon, and the pots of jam and wine jugs were stacked and secured behind them. A solid canvas covered the goods, and Avram led the one horse with dexterity, avoiding the rough edges on the road. Every once in a while, when they hit a rough bump in the dusty road, he inquired about Isabella's well-being.

"I'm all right, Avram. Just concentrate on the road," she reassured him. "This was a godsend, all those goods," she said. "We can stretch it now to the next harvest in August."

"That is, if we don't get more rain and mildew," Avram grumbled.

Avram cast a downward note on her rosy outlook. She was determined, nevertheless, not to let it get the best of her. "I can't understand you, Avram. Your father, your mother, and your brothers always used their wisdom to look forward not downward." She then regretted her unwise words.

Avram became moody immediately. He whipped the horse, which lunged forward, shaking the carriage boards and jars.

"I'm sorry, Avram. I didn't mean to remind you of that. Please forgive me."

Avram remained quiet, then said, "We've arrived."

Isabella saw crowds of people milling in the market square of Sintra. Horses and donkeys were being watered at the main fountain, local farmers were lined up behind their wooden tables selling their produce or wares, and children oblivious to their parents' slaps to keep them quiet ran between vendors' tables, nearly toppling them.

"We'll set up by the end of the row," Avram said.

He then helped her descend from the wagon, brought down a small wooden table and two chairs, and climbed back in the wagon. One by one, the jam and wine jugs were unloaded with Isabella helping him. In the following hours, they sold much of the wine and some jams. Isabella kept slipping the dinheiros inside a leather pouch hanging inside her robe by her chest. By noon, she felt fatigued and sent Avram to fetch water and food for the both of them. He quickly left her to walk to the nearest tavern they had seen at the entrance to the town.

Left alone, she realized how useful Avram had been to both Ana and her these past months. They had been fugitives clinging together from the Inquisition, the police, pirates preying on them, and the elements preventing them from living their lives in peace. She owed him a debt for his male presence, protecting two women alone since Miguel had disappeared.

At the thought of Miguel, her mood became downcast, when suddenly she felt a kick in her belly from her unborn child. He wanted to experience his life to the fullest. She smiled as she patted her stomach.

A woman shopper who stood by the table smiled at her. "How long do you have until the blessed event?" said the woman.

"Not till the end of March," Isabella replied.

"Not soon enough, judging by your size," The woman chided her, without malice.

Isabella laughed at the remark. "I do want to be liberated from all the weight, but I also can't wait to see him."

"Looks like you've decided on the child's gender."

"Yes. He must take over after his father."

The woman's questioning eyes didn't give Isabella time to reply. Loud sounds and noises rose from the crowd with people running sideways to let a carriage pass them at full speed. When the dust settled down, Isabella looked to the woman's eyes for an explanation.

"It's only the Spanish queen sending her daughter's emissaries to our King João II."

"Why are the Spaniard emissaries sent here?"

The woman shrugged her shoulders. "Probably to find their widowed daughter a new husband."

"Why? What happen to her husband?"

The woman said, "Her first husband was Afonso, King João's only son. He died mysteriously in a riding accident." The woman's shoulders drooped and her voice broke. She then cupped her mouth and bent down to Isabella's ear and whispered, "But we'll always suspect Spain had something to do with it."

"I still don't understand," a bewildered Isabella said.

"Well, Queen Isabella's eldest daughter is searching for a new husband."

"How will she find one here, if King João has no more sons left?"

"Yes, but he has cousins. So if they married, Portugal could become heirs to Castile and Aragon. That's why!" The woman crossed her arms on her stomach with a satisfied look on her face.

Isabella still couldn't understand these lines of inheritances and countries vying to subdue others for possession of their crowns.

"How will the people benefit from those plots between kings and queens?" Isabella said.

"If Queen Isabella's daughter marries into the Portuguese crown, all faith in Portugal will become one."

"What do you mean by one?"

The woman looked at her as if she were a dunce. "Because, my dear child, your child will be born in a Catholic country. We will rid ourselves of all foreign religions and their influence."

A sharp pain suddenly hit her. She bent down and grabbed her stomach.

The woman's face became white. "My dear child, you couldn't be ready yet?" Concern showed on her face.

With great effort, Isabella sat upright and said, "I'm all right. It was only the strongest kick yet."

"Thank the Lord. You gave me a scare," the woman said. "I'll leave you now. My husband may be looking for me." And with that she turned around and disappeared into the crowd.

Just then Avram appeared holding a flat round bread and some cheese in a linen cloth. "I've got food for us." He produced a jug of water for the meal. He then stopped when he saw Isabella's pallor. "What's wrong?" he said while taking a small knife to the cheese.

"I'd like to go back home now."

Avram stood with the knife in the air. "Then let's head back." He quickly gathered the rest of the goods and loaded them into the wagon. Next, he helped Isabella climb onto the seat up front.

He urged the horse forward. *"¡Arre!"*

Isabella turned to the uneaten food wrapped in the linen and broke off a chunk of bread and cheese and offered it to Avram.

"Do you want to talk about it?" he asked while chewing on the bread.

Isabella took a bite of bread, taking her time to chew and swallow it. "I prefer we wait until we get home and in Ana's presence."

Avram nodded submissively to Isabella's request, and no other words passed between them.

Upon arrival, Ana came to greet them at the door. "You're back so soon?"

Isabella said to her, "I'd like to see you in the kitchen, Ana."

Ana and Avram followed her into the kitchen, where she sat herself down.

"So what's going on?" Ana asked, crossing her arms over her apron.

"Today, I learned that we can't just live in peace in Spain or in Portugal."

Ana's mouth fell open. "Why?"

Isabella told them of what she'd heard in the marketplace. "So no matter where we go, they'll always follow us."

"Now wait a minute," Ana said. "It was King João who declared to the Spanish sovereigns that he welcomed us to reside in his country."

"Until now," Isabella said.

"Look. We *are* far away from the city here and—"

Isabella cut her off. "Until when?"

"Go and wash, children." Ana used this word with Isabella and Avram when she wanted to become motherly. "I cooked a delicious meal for you."

Isabella looked at Avram, and he returned the worried look. He tried to pacify Isabella. "Let's put this behind us for now."

She nodded, but inside a nudge kept coming back to haunt her. Would she have to flee again?

94

Sailing Out

Sunday, January 7, 1493

THEY ALL WOKE UP IN the morning to find out that the *Niña* had sprung a leak. Columbus went down into the hold, sloshing around in one-meter-deep water and ordered the caravel pumped out and caulked. Now they were forced to remain on Monti-Cristi until the leak was repaired.

"Empty and ground her onto the beach, and let's inspect the bottom hull," Columbus said to Antonio de Cuellar, his carpenter.

Pushing and hauling the empty and disabled caravel, they all succeeded in grounding her on the white sand beach. Next, she was pumped out and made ready to be caulked. Columbus sent two of his sailors to the nearest village to trade trinkets for cotton thread to fill the board seams. Meanwhile, he also sent two more sailors to check for more plants.

The *Pinta* men searched the island for fruit and river water for drinking. The entire beach on the island resounded with the noise of trees being felled, the pounding of hammers, and the voices of men calling and shouting their orders to each other.

Columbus, supervising his men near the *Niña*, saw Martin Alonso Pinzón working alongside his men on the *Pinta* hauling the cargo of wood onto the deck, and avoided going near him. "I'd better steer away from him," he grumbled between his teeth.

Before the noon sun was up, many natives from the village, led by their cacique chief had spilled onto the beach, speaking in loud tones. Through his interpreter, Columbus signed a request for cotton, and gave the chief a belt buckle in exchange for it. Within a short time many baskets in the natives' hands filled with cotton balls were passed to the *Niña*'s men.

Antonio had worked all morning on cleaning the old caulk without further chipping or damaging the edges of the wood planks. Under the eyes of watchful natives, he began filling the seams with the new cotton using his raking iron and mallet, tapping the threaded cotton until it disappeared into each seam. Afterward, caulk was applied to cover the repaired seams.

"You might check the whole bottom of the hull, too, for any weak spots," Columbus told Antonio as he walked away.

"Admiral?" The voice of Juan de la Cosa came to his ears. He approached him with his hands loaded with plants. "My men found plenty of aloe and mastic plants!" he said, overjoyed by the find.

Columbus inspected the plants and found them of good stock with large leaves. "Take more men and harvest many more, then load them on the *Pinta*." He now knew that fate had led him back to the island to make sure the voyage would be safe and sound. The Lord was looking out for him. He went down on his knees in the sparkling sand and said his Middies prayer.

The following morning on January 8, Columbus felt a great rush to sail. He went to Antonio and asked him, "Is the repair completed now?"

"I just checked it early this morning, Admiral, and she looks fit to sail."

"All right, men!" Columbus yelled at his crew and the crew of the *Pinta* still slumbering on the beach. He first supervised and watched the *Niña* pushed onto the high tide, where she glided as a queen riding the crested waves with smoothness.

"Now gather up all the wood on the beach, the water barrels, and the fresh provisions, and let's load them up!"

"Hurrah! Hurrah!" the men cried from the beach, hugging and slapping each other on the back.

Making several hauls, the men loaded the provisions from both boats onto the caravels. They were ready to depart.

Columbus looked at the beach covered now with natives who had traveled to see them sail away. Their hands went up in unison with their chests emitting loud cries, and the cacique chief waved his scepter in front of him—all presenting a solid and united front of friendship from the New World to the Old World. Columbus now knew that his work was completed for this voyage. He would be back to seed religion into the natives and bring them the civilized notions of Europe.

95

A New Season

T HE RAINS AND FROST HAD completely abated earlier this year, and the new season for wine had begun. Even the sun cooperated by shining a few hours a day, bringing warmth with the gentle breeze flowing over the hills. Avram looked to the new hired hands from Sintra and the nearest villages, as he managed the supervision of pruning and setting the new crop. The new workers were grafting grape vine cuttings from the old crop, which were resistant to disease, onto the newer plants.

Avram knew these practices since his father had employed him with the nearest vintner near Cordoba. Reluctantly, Avram had gone to work each season for Master Fernando, but questioned his father's wisdom for sending him away entire summers. Beneluz had told his son, "You'll gain immense skills and knowledge when you sell wine to markets." Avram smiled at the recollection. Not only had those skills benefited him then, they were also helping Isabella and Ana now for next year's livelihood. His father had been wise.

He grew suddenly sad at the thought of his father. Where and how could he have disappeared? He recalled the last time he'd seen him. He had been battling a pirate, trying to prevent them from administering a fatal blow to his brother, León. Instead, the pirate hit his father on the head with the sharp side of his cutlass. He saw his father bleed before him, before the pirates carried him away. He moaned softly, afraid to show his deep anguish over the loss of his father.

He chased the thought away and concentrated on his work with the cuttings. His underling, Pedro, worked near him, handing him the shoots that had hardened off, pruned from last season's grapevines, and watched him attach it to the new shoot. He exposed the scion, trimmed it on both sides to expose the core and cranium, and inserted it into the cut trunk, then tied it with raffia.

"You see how it's done. Now you go ahead and do the next one," he told Pedro.

For the next several hours, he watched Pedro faithfully cutting and grafting new shoots into the trunks above ground. Afterward, Avram mounded up each grafted plant above the soil's level to prevent scion rotting.

"Now it's your turn." Avram handed him the knife.

After Pedro finished grafting, Avram slapped him on the shoulder. "You're learning fast. I might keep you on for the rest of the year!"

Pedro's face lit up. "Thank you, Master Avram."

"Just call me Avram."

Pedro nodded. "If I could find shelter on the estate, I would be most grateful."

"We can find you something in one of the sheds," Avram said.

"Anything will be suitable. It will be better than—" Pedro stopped.

Avram looked at him. "Better than what?" he asked with curiosity.

Pedro fell silent.

"It's all right. You don't have to tell me if you don't want to," he reassured Pedro.

After a few moments, Pedro said, "Do you know the ruins of the Castelo dos Mouros?"

"You mean the Moorish Castle overlooking Sintra?"

"Yes. That's where I live. It's a place for the Jewish refugees. It's open to the skies, cold and drafty. And we have no privacy."

Avram jerked his head back. Jews were living in a ruined and abandoned castle, homeless and poor. "Why did you choose this abode? Don't you have family to take care of you?"

Pedro's eyes dimmed. He shook his head, staring down at his hands. "My parents were killed a long time ago. I can't remember exactly when. One day they left for the market and never came back. The family who took me in was Christian, and they saw to my safety."

"So what happened to you?" Avram asked.

The church wanted me to become a priest, and they kept cornering me every chance—"

Avram finished his sentence for him. "And you didn't want that."

"No. I ran away from them. I remember my parents initiating me, at a young age, about my Jewishness and never to worship another God."

"Then your parents gave you their legacy, and you want to preserve it."

Pedro nodded.

"Pedro," Avram said, "we're done for the day. Come with me."

Avram led Pedro up the hill overlooking the dormant vineyards, then they climbed down and made their way toward the main house.

They entered the sitting room, where Isabella and Ana were unraveling yarn and rolling it into balls. They both raised their heads when Avram came in tow with Pedro.

"Are you bringing us a guest?" Ana said, smiling.

"Yes. This is Pedro. He will be staying in one of the sheds."

Ana glanced at Isabella and she nodded.

"Then you're welcome, Pedro. You can join us for supper tonight," Isabella said.

Pedro's lips cracked in a large smile. "*Obrigado*."

"I will show Pedro his new room and be back soon." Avram took the youth with him, then returned alone.

Ana paused from spooling the yarn and asked Avram, "Where did you find him?"

Avram related to Ana and Isabella the youth's circumstances. "I felt sorry for the young lad."

"You did right," Isabella said. "We have enough room and food to spare."

Ana asked, "I'm curious about the Jews taking refuge in the old castle."

"I don't know any more than what Pedro told me. Perhaps on our next trip to town, we can get more information."

"I wonder why . . ." She didn't finish her sentence. Ana had a curious look in her eyes.

Both Avram and Isabella kept quiet at Ana's remark. Avram sensed that something wasn't right. These folks might be refugees from Spain, and as such might have no resources, forcing them to find shelter in the ruins. But then, Portugal had welcomed all exiled Jews to enter the country and contribute to her commerce and population and live freely among the Portuguese. So why were they in hiding? The next trip to Sintra might yield answers to this baffling question, Avram thought.

96

Before the Last Landing

Tuesday, January 8, 1493

THROUGHOUT THE NIGHT THE SEA was as smooth as crystal, and no wind powered the sails. The *Niña* and the *Pinta* floated aimlessly, with slight adjustments to the tiller to steer on a northeastern course. Columbus, still eager to get on across the Atlantic, was stifled by the lack of progress.

"At this rate we will be caught in an unforgiving wintry sea."

"Admiral," Juan de la Cosa said, "we're better off returning to Monti-Cristi or the nearest shore."

"Why?" Columbus threw his hands up. "We're as ready as we'll ever be."

"We could still use more provisions." Juan looked straight into his eyes.

"The hold is full. We'd have to carry them on deck."

Juan tried to sway him. "And maybe, maybe, we might find other plants we overlooked."

After a few moments of silence, Columbus said, "Without the wind, we're stuck." He looked down at his chart and measured how many leagues they had traveled from the nearest shore. "We could go back within the hour," Columbus said, resigned. "Give the men the order to return."

The two caravels returned, in tow one after the other, pulled by the rowing boats toward Monti-Cristi looming westward on the horizon.

Columbus gave the order to leave the ships in deep waters. "We will disembark at dawn tomorrow."

Throughout the night he stirred and couldn't find any sleep. The delay weighed heavily on his mind. All his enemies, including Pinzón and his men, and João Treves, were there to discredit him and bring dishonor to his name and achievements. Eventually, his two sons might suffer in shame. No matter—he would not squander valuable time to punish Pinzón despite all the great honors he conferred upon him to undertake the voyage.

Early at dawn on January 9, he got up from the small bunk bed feeling down and with all his joints sore and inflamed. He dressed slowly with Salcedo's help, and then went on deck to find his pilot. Instead of Juan de la Cosa, he found Sancho Ruiz at the tiller.

"Did you switch at the last watch?" His voice rose volumes.

"It's all under control, Admiral," Ruiz tried to reassure him. "We switched first at midnight, then Juan took his next watch at four a.m."

"You must tell me whenever you alter my orders."

"Yes, Admiral." Ruiz looked at him sideways.

"Sound the bell to the crew. I want to go ashore now."

"What about your breakfast, Admiral?"

"It will have to wait." Columbus was anxious to start right away and not delay an inland expedition.

Followed by some of his crew and another boat filled with Pinzón's men, they rowed to the entrance of a wide river that was a league and a half south-southwest away from Monti-Cristi. The empty barrels were unloaded from the boats and filled from the river waters. As they waded on the river's shore, Columbus noticed shiny reflections in the bottom of the water. He sent for one of his men to bring him some of the bottom sand, and gold flakes caught the brilliant sunlight.

"Gold! Admiral, it's gold!" Juan de la Cosa said.

Columbus examined the flakes that looked more like grains than anything else. "Let's row the boat up the river."

Within a few meters, his men spotted a few gold grains as big as lentils. The rest of the sand contained more gold flakes in larger quantities. This was a good omen. Columbus's downcast mood and ire over Ruiz disobeying his orders turned to joy. This river, so like the Guadalquivir in Cordova, reminded him of home.

"I will call this river El Rio de Oro." Columbus baptized the waters and made the sign of the cross.

"We are now seventeen leagues from the village La Navidad, Admiral. Do you want to return to the fort at La Navidad and tell the men to mine the river?" Juan said.

Columbus mulled Juan's request for a few moments. He then answered, "No. It will have to wait. This sand in the river and all islands we discovered belong to the monarchs. They own the gold in the river. I must hurry home; I long to tell them of my discoveries."

Juan nodded at Columbus's request.

They continued exploring the coast, and having found no other point of interest, the sails were raised with a southeast wind. After sailing sixty miles east of Monti-Cristi, the ships arrived at a projecting point he called Punta Roja where he anchored. Reefs abounded when they came in, making it dangerous and foolish to sail by night.

By morning on January 10, the land in front of them revealed high mountains running east to west, and handsome cultivated fields watered by many rivers, but no natives or huts in sight. Land tortoises littered the beaches, laying their eggs, which the men collected and brought on board.

They further sailed to a river three leagues southeast that he called Rio de Gracia. He found the harbor to be shallow and only two fathoms deep. A better harbor lay further east, but had shipworms that greatly affected the *Pinta* when she had docked there for sixteen days while trading for gold. He had been told by one of Pinzón's men that the master had traded for gold, then asked his men to swear that they had been on the island only six days. His wickedness knew no bounds. Columbus longed to get rid of him.

By Friday January 11, Columbus left Rio de Gracia with a breeze from land and sailed four leagues to where a river with deep waters, he believed, must have contained much gold. All that day he encountered more capes as he explored the surroundings.

"We will be laying-to tonight," Columbus told his pilot, Sancho Ruiz.

"But, Admiral, we could land and have a good night's rest for all."

"Look, Sancho. I know you desire much rest from the tiller. You and De la Cosa will have much rest when we return home."

"All right, Admiral." Sancho lowered his head with a bitter smile.

"It is seven p.m. Let's prepare for Compline prayers and thank the Lord for this great island of Española. We will continue our exploration for the next five days, then we sail home."

97

El Mouro Castle

ON THE NEXT TRIP TO town only Isabella and Ana traveled in the open cart to Sintra to sell more jams and wine. Before they left, Isabella instructed Avram to stay home to supervise the fieldworkers. Since January was going fast, the rows of vines still had to be pruned, and the grafting of young shoots was accelerating. The returning workers were extremely pleased to earn a few dinheiros for their families, and they toiled under a weak sun.

"I hope it was the right decision to leave Avram behind," Isabella said to Ana.

"Yes. It was. You are running the estate affairs with much wisdom. Miguel would be proud of you." No sooner had these words come out of Ana's mouth than she regretted them.

Isabella went silent without replying.

Ana turned to face Isabella. "I'm sorry. I didn't mean to stir up your memories."

Isabella rushed to allay her embarrassment. "No, Ana. My memories of Miguel are still alive. I think of him every day and especially at night."

"Isabella. I know you're still mourning for him and the year hasn't yet passed. But you can't devote yourself completely to his memory. You have to live along with his memory."

Isabella looked at her. "What do you mean *live*? Am I not living and anticipating this child? I wake up every day, look to my duties and the estate, and help as much as my condition permits. Isn't that living?"

"That's not what I meant. You're still so young. You'll have a different future someday."

"Again, you're talking in riddles." Isabella looked in the distance to the dusty road and the elms growing alongside it.

"What I mean is you must think of your future and the need for a father for your child."

"My child will have a mother. He won't need a father. I'll be both to him."

Ana smiled. "For him? You're still sure it's a 'him'?"

"Yes. I know it's going to be a boy."

"Ha-ha-ha!" Ana laughed. "We're here."

Isabella looked down from her perch to see the market full of milling shoppers, colorful clowns entertaining the crowds, cooking pits with sizzling meat that sent aromas spiraling into the air, and sweets attracting all the children around the vendors.

Isabella sighed with yearning. "This smell makes me hungry."

"I will get something to eat for you and your 'boy,'" Ana jested while she helped Isabella down from the open cart. Ana quickly set up a cloth on the table and unloaded the merchandise from the cart.

"You can sell these while I go food hunting," Ana said.

Isabella sat down and waited for Ana to return.

A young girl, not more than nine, stood in front of the jam pots, staring without a word. Her clothes were dirty, and her hair matted and disheveled.

"You'd like to buy jam?' Isabella said. From her looks, she obviously didn't have the means to buy anything, so Isabella opened one of the pots and offered it to the girl. She looked up to Isabella with great big eyes in a small and bony face and timidly grabbed the pot from Isabella's hand, then took off in a hurry.

"You didn't thank—" The girl had already disappeared. *I wonder where she belongs.*

"I brought food!" Ana called as she approached Isabella's staked-out spot. She took one look at Isabella's face and asked her, "What's going on?"

"I just gave a free pot of jam to a little girl."

"Why? If you continue to give it away, we won't make any money today."

"I felt sorry for her. She looked hungry and tired."

Ana dismissed Isabella's comment by waving her hand through the air, then proceeded to split the hot bread and cheese between her and Isabella.

Isabella nibbled on the food, and having lost her appetite turned to Ana. "Why are there so many unattended children?"

"Because," Ana said between bites, "the parents can't or won't take care of them, or she may be an orphan."

"Even an orphan needs someone to look after her."

"Well, apparently she's not an orphan," Ana answered, looking in the direction of the road near them.

A young woman approached them holding a baby wrapped in swaddling in her arm, while pushing the little girl with the jar of jam in her hand.

"I want to return this pot my daughter took from you. I won't have my daughter steal for—"

Isabella noticed the little girl's wet eyes. She had shed tears for what she'd given her. "I gave her the pot of jam," Isabella said with a firm voice. "Please keep it. It's a gift."

The woman's eyes teared, then she broke out in sobs against the infant's head. "I'm sorry for crying . . . I didn't think there were people like you left on earth."

"Shh. It's all right. Here." Isabella went to the little girl and gave her the uneaten food she had left, and watched her devour it. Ana also gave the mother a portion of her food, and they both watched them enjoy eating it.

"Where do you live?" Ana asked.

The young mother raised her head, swallowed, then said, "We're refugees from Spain."

"Where's your home?" Ana asked her again.

The woman fell silent, but the little girl pointed up to the horizon "We live in the castle on the mountain."

Her mother gave her a glance but remained quiet.

"You don't have to be afraid," Ana reassured her. "We're also refugees and lucky to have found a benefactor. Do you have more family in the Mouros?"

The woman looked surprised that Ana knew the castle's name. "No, I don't. Her father died as soon as her brother was born. It's only the three of us now."

Ana looked to Isabella for a sign, and she nodded and batted her eyes back at her. "If you'd like, you can come back with us to our home," Isabella said with a smile at both of them.

The woman's eyes shone with surprise and joy. She broke down again in tears. When she stopped crying, she said between sniffles, "We will. Thank you. Thank you."

"Then you can tell us on the way why you live in such a poor dwelling," Ana said.

The woman nodded. "I'm called Raquela, and my daughter is Sarina and my son Aron."

"You can help us sell our jams and wine, and then we'll go back home," Ana said.

"Please, let me first nurse my son."

"Of course, Raquela," Isabella said with a tender look upon Raquela's baby.

98

Last Landing

Tuesday, January 15, 1493

OVER THE PREVIOUS THREE DAYS, Columbus had pushed on with many landings, discovering new lands to the south. In a sailing route north-northeast he found a cape he named Cabo de Padre y Hijo with two rocky peaks, one taller than the other. Two leagues east of the cape he found an inlet with a wide harbor that would offer an excellent docking port for future settlements. Further east he discovered a rocky and magnificent cape he dubbed Cabo del Enamorado, then further east still, he came upon a more beautiful cape, similar to the Cabo de San Vicente back in Portugal. Of all the lands he discovered that day, he was astounded to find that they all connected as one island. How wide and vast was Española Island!

The following morning the two caravels lay idle in a wide harbor exposed to the elements, but the lack of breeze prevented Columbus from sailing further. He sent two men ashore to look for the tuberous edible plant the Indians called *ajes*.

By noon his men returned with a naked Indian villager carrying a bow and arrows balanced in a sack on his shoulder.

Columbus examined his charcoal-painted face and his long black hair tied behind his head and complemented with colorful parrot feathers. His face was hard-featured and unattractive, and lacked the attractive beauty he'd seen in other Indians. *This must be a Carib cannibal, a man-eater. This island must be separate from the mainland, or I must be mistaken.*

"Why have you brought this man on board?" Columbus said.

"Admiral, we wanted him to speak to you."

"Luis, ask this Indian where the Caribs are."

Luis de Torres approached the man with reluctance. He gestured with his hands and asked him *"¿Dónde son los Caribs, Caribs?"*

The Indian understood the sign language and the word *Carib*. He replied in Taino language with guttural sounds, then pointed east. Columbus showed him a gold piece he had on him, and the Carib Indian gestured with his hands that much gold was there.

Columbus then asked his Indian translators to ask him where more gold could be found.

The Carib then said, *"Tuab, tuab."*

Luis turned to Columbus. "I think he means gold or copper, Admiral."

The Carib went on to utter several words, his Indian translators said, that implied that east of Carib Island there was an island settled by women only, and they had a great amount of *tuab*.

"Admiral, in San Salvador they call copper *tuab*."

"They must be very bold to go to other islands and eat people," Columbus said. "Give him some food, and some pieces of glass and cloth."

The Carib Indian smiled widely at the treasures he received, especially the small pieces of green-and-red cloth.

"Tell him to bring gold with him next time and send him back on land."

When the Carib native returned to the beach in his canoe, close to fifty other natives who were observing them and hiding behind trees waited for him with bows and arrows and heavy long sticks.

"Go on land and see if you can barter for their bows and arrows," Columbus ordered.

Seven men went down in the boat and bartered for several bows and arrows for a few glass beads. Suddenly the natives lifted their bows and arrows and, and holding ropes in their hands, began to attack Columbus's men.

"Run to the boats!" the men watching on the caravels shouted at them. "Run!"

One of his men still on the beach turned around and, lifting his sword, cut one of the Indians on the buttock, and a sailor used the bow and arrow he'd just bartered to pierce another Indian's chest. The rest of the Caribs ran away screaming, some leaving their bows and arrows behind. Columbus came to their rescue by fetching his *espingarda* musket from his cabin and firing several shots at the Indians without hitting any of them.

When his men returned to the caravels, Columbus felt uneasy. It disturbed him that he left forty-three men behind at Villa de la Navidad, and these Caribs were evil men instilling fear in other Española inhabitants. His men, though, were superior and without fear.

Throughout the night, many fires burned into the night at the Carib villages.

At dawn on the morning of January 17, he had the sails trimmed and ordered to leave for Spain. The wind blew favorably from land as he sailed through the Golfo de las Flechas with a west wind, and as he turned his prow east and quarter northeast. The caravels were taking in some water, and Columbus's faith was in the hands of God. The course for the island of Matinino, where women ruled, was postponed; he wasn't sure the Indians on board knew the way.

They sailed in a straight course for Spain, and judging by the sandglass of fourteen ampolletas, each a half-hour, they moved forward twenty-eight miles. Afterward the wind grew in intensity, and ten more ampolletas were turned, and another six before sunrise. They had sailed thirty miles, or twenty-one leagues northeast and quarter east, when a pelican landed on the *Niña*.

"Admiral! Admiral!"

Columbus ran on deck to his men's shouts. "What is the matter?"

"Grass, Admiral. Remember?"

Columbus smiled. They were on the right course as confirmed. Now his men were reassured by seeing the same floating and familiar weed on the water they had seen on the voyage west. It was a good sign, and he felt reassured that the Lord was looking out for them.

He went to see Juan de la Cosa, who had been waiting on deck for his watch to begin. "I want round-the-clock shifts between you, Vicente, and Ruiz at the tiller. Also make sure the water in the hold is pumped out. Assign two men per watch."

"*Si*, Admiral. I was just going to suggest it to you."

Columbus turned away and lingered on the stern watching both caravels leaving a white trail of churned waters behind them. In his mind's eye he pictured a red carpet under his feet greeting him back to Spain.

99

A New Season

THE OLD VINES WERE NOW prepared for the new season. The workers with Avram and Pedro were checking each completed row to make sure all the grafting and the trimming back of the old foliage and trellising were done. The work was slow and hard, and they were constantly pricked on the rusted vines threads or the splintering wood posts. Nevertheless, all they had to do now was wait for the first buds to appear on the new crop of vines.

Avram left the workers checking for missed vines and went to climb the hill separating the vineyard from the estate. From the promontory on which he stood, he could scan the horizon beyond the shore. Protecting his eyes from the glare of the sun, he saw a caravel on the horizon headed south for the Gulf of Gibraltar. He sighed at the sight. Where was his old father now? Was he alive or dead? He was grateful for being alive and having been sheltered through Don Abravanel's generosity, but he longed to return to the ocean.

"I'm finished now."

Pedro's voice pulled Avram out of his thoughts. He turned around to see that Pedro had caught up with him on the hill.

"Let us go back to the house," Avram replied.

When they arrived, they found the three women, Isabella, Ana, and Raquela, working on the noon meal. Sarina, Raquela's little daughter, was sitting on the bench next to Isabella, and both were peeling onions while little Aron slept soundly in his basket. The prickly smell hit Avram's nose and eyes.

"You're back early," Ana said.

"We finished before the estimated time. All the grafting is done, as well as the pruning."

Ana went to the cauldron cooking on the fire, and with Avram's help they lifted it and place it on the wooden table. The aroma of cooked chicken and vegetables came to his nostrils, while Pedro stood with a hungry look nearby.

"Go, Pedro, and call the men from the field," Avram told him.

As soon as Pedro left, Avram turned to Isabella. "I want to talk to you in private."

Isabella looked up at Avram with teary eyes. She took a cloth from her long skirt and wiped her eyes. "I hope my son isn't crying right now."

Everyone in the room broke out in laughter.

"Then he must like my cooking!" Ana said with mirth in her eyes.

Raquela went to feel Isabella's belly and said, "I think he wants to eat with us."

Avram waited till everyone stopped laughing, then asked Isabella again, "Can you talk now?"

"I'm sorry, Avram. Let's go outside."

He followed her slowly to the front porch, and after she made herself comfortable on the bench, she raised questioning eyes. "Well?"

"Isabella, I'm most grateful for Ana's and your hospitality. My work is done here. I want to return to Morocco."

Isabella's face blanched. Suddenly her eyes seemed anxious. "Why? You said you are content with your work here."

"I am, I mean . . . I was until now. I want to go back to the sea. I feel that it's calling me."

Isabella kept quiet momentarily. She then said, "I know how you feel."

It was Avram's turn to raise questioning eyes.

Isabella continued. "I also want to go back to the sea, but I'm a prisoner of my body right now. I can't let you go without me."

"Why is that?" shouted Avram.

"It's not that I don't trust you, Avram. You've shown great skills with sailing and taught me all I know. It's just that I'm responsible for the only ship we have, and as the owner, I must be there too."

Avram threw his hands in the air. "I don't feel useful right now. My thoughts are with my father. I want to find him." His voice rose with a muted sigh.

Avram saw that his words had reopened Isabella's wound and despair at finding Miguel.

"I know exactly how you feel," she said. "I also want to find Miguel, and I'm desperate to begin looking for him."

"But—"

"I know what you're thinking." Isabella continued. "That it's useless searching for a man who might've drowned. That he was killed before they threw him in the ocean."

Avram gasped. "Who told you—Ana?"

"No. Ana didn't say a thing to me. I could read it in your minds, not on your lips."

"So you still believe that he's alive?"

"Yes. Just as you want to believe that your father is still living, I'm also comforted by the thought that Miguel is alive, because I believe it."

Avram looked down, his head hanging low. He said in a mourning voice, "I'll wait until your son is born."

Isabella cracked a smile. "You see, Avram, my conviction that I'll have a son has influenced you too. That's how I believe that Miguel is alive. It's faith."

Avram didn't reply. He wanted desperately to get away from Isabella, not only to find his father but also not to pine for her. Her closeness, her voice, and all that made her a most loving woman stirred his love for her, but she was in love with the memory of a dead man. He could never compete and win her love.

100

Smooth Sailing

Monday, January 21, 1493

THROUGHOUT THE LAST FOUR DAYS much sailing had been done. The *Niña* and the *Pinta*, one respectively after the other, covered a total of 84 leagues or 252 miles. Columbus sailed a quarter east and southeast all along, then a quarter southeast, turning the prow to the north, then northeast. By January 19, he had turned the prow northeast with a strong wind, and then a quarter to the north. That day they spotted masses of tunny fish, turning the sea into a metallic-blue carpet of moving and darting fishery. The tunny fish followed along the caravels, flying sometimes above the waters in a frenzied race with the ships.

"Watch them swim!" The men on board egged them on as if the fish could hear their cheering.

Other signs came along that gave Columbus peace of mind, such as pelicans trying to land on deck, and some ring-tailed birds. Other large frigate birds, with iridescent black feathers, flew above the decks but didn't land. They circled the ships displaying their large wings, then turned around and flew away.

Columbus was sorry to see them disappear from view. They were excellent indicators for weather and pattern changes by flying on the updraft.

On Tuesday January 22, the caravels navigated north and quarter northeast with a good wind blowing east and northeast. That day and night they navigated twenty-six leagues. At noon, Columbus ordered to fall back to the *Pinta* to confer on the leeward with Pinzón.

"Is the water still seeping through in the hold?" Columbus shouted across to Pinzón.

"We're down to pumping five buckets per hour!" Pinzón shouted back.

"I blame the poor job done in Palos!" Columbus grumbled, and saw Pinzón throwing his hands up the in air. The insult was directed at him for not supervising the dockworkers before they'd left. Even the hasty repairs on Española Island weren't sufficient to stop the flow into the hold.

"How's the *Niña* faring?" Pinzón's voice replied across the ships.

Columbus didn't reply to his question. He hollered, "I can send you a couple more sailors to help with the bilge!"

"No thank you, Admiral."

"If we lose you, stay on a north-northeast course!"

"All right, Admiral!"

The *Pinta* took off suddenly, instead of waiting for the admiral and the *Niña* to overtake her. Columbus felt the affront, but he already knew Pinzón's insubordination and ill will toward him. He mainly feared that Pinzón would reach Spain first and take all the credit for himself. Vicente, who had seen his brother take off with the *Pinta*, stood by at the railing in silence.

Columbus knew that Ruiz was aware of the rivalry between him and Pinzón. He turned to Ruiz at the tiller and said in a grumbling voice, "We must keep up with the *Pinta*."

"Si, Admiral. I will catch up to the *Pinta*. The *Niña* is lighter and faster."

"Good work, Ruiz!" Columbus said, and left for his cabin.

On the way, he ran into João. *He's probably still stalking me.*

"Admiral, I'd like to talk to you."

"There's nothing to talk about. Return to your job!"

"But, Admiral, I have new information for you."

Columbus came close to João's face and looked into his eyes. "Are you going to blackmail me again?" he yelled into his face.

The men washing the deck around them stopped their work and raised their heads.

The attention on him was enough to make him back off from João. He calmed down and said, "Follow me to my cabin."

After Columbus closed the door to the cabin he turned to João. "You have till the next ampolleta's call, and it's due soon."

Columbus could see João's face reddening under the rushed ultimatum, and he briefly closed his eyes, then opened them up.

"Admiral, you have a grown daughter back in Spain!"

Columbus knew this was a new ploy for João to obtain another favor. He folded his arms across his chest and nodded his head. "What is it this time—you want gold for your threat?"

"No, Admiral. It's the truth! When you left Sarita, she was already pregnant with your daughter. She didn't know that you wouldn't come back to her."

Columbus stood dumbfounded for a moment. "I can't believe it! Are you saying that I have a daughter born from my union with your sister?"

"Yes, Admiral. She's at least eighteen years old now."

Columbus stood dumbstruck. He had fathered a daughter without his knowledge? It couldn't be true! "You're trying to hold me slave to your machinations."

"Admiral, I have no reason to do that. I have now strong reasons for returning home."

"You mean a reason to rush home and denounce me as a Converso! Isn't that it?" His voice rose volumes.

João's mouth fell open. He stood in front of him speechless, with his green and piercing eyes bulging out. When João found his voice, he repeated, "You! You, Admiral. A Converso?"

Columbus stood aghast and dismayed at his blunder, but it was too late. The slipped revelation sealed his fate. He had just exposed a deep secret buried inside him from as long as he could remember. His adoptive father had revealed this secret to him, just before he had sailed on a merchant carrack many years ago. It was now his turn to be in shock. It seemed his soul had just presented to him an abject secret he had tried to bury for years. He shuffled back a step or two, and feeling his legs weak, he went to sit down on a chair.

Columbus's voice came out choked and gravelly. "It's something I had forgotten many years ago. Only Sarita knew of it."

João eyes were fixed on the past, and he uttered with a dreamy voice, "She never told me."

Columbus shook himself out of his trance and said, "Now that you know, are you going to denounce me?"

"Admiral, how can I do that to you, to the father of my niece?"

"What do you intend to do with this information?"

"It's a secret I'll carry to my grave. I swear to God!" João's voice sounded true.

Columbus had to trust his words and rely on his oath of secrecy.

"Can you tell me about this daughter of—"

A bell rang for the ampolleta signaling the half-hour turn of the sandglass, when a cry was heard. "Admiral! Admiral come quickly!"

Columbus ran out on deck with João in tow. On the horizon by the prow, they saw a moving mass of grasses floating on the surface with ringtails flying high above them that were looking for crabs nestled in the floating grass. But the sight that greeted him with fear was the *Pinta* reappearing and lagging in front of them. His fears returned that if the *Pinta* broke up or sank, they'd be finished! With only one ship loaded to capacity, the chances increased for capsizing in bad weather. He ordered for the *Niña* to catch up and sail leeward alongside.

"What's the problem?" Columbus called out to Pinzón.

"We found a crack on the mainmast!"

"How long is the crack?"

"About two hands."

"That's easy. I'll send my woodworker to you!" Columbus yelled out.

The next hours were taken up with transporting Antonio de Cuellar, his carpenter, as he crossed with fear over to the *Pinta* to repair the damage done to the mast, then back to the *Niña*.

"Report?" Columbus asked Antonio.

"I stuffed cloth and glue in the crack, then I mixed more glue with linseed oil and painted the mast with it."

"Thank you, Antonio." Columbus sent him back to his work.

"I'll be in my cabin," he told Juan de la Cosa.

João, who worked on the main deck, gave him a long glance.

Back in his cabin, Columbus sat down with wobbly legs. The shock he had experienced earlier resurfaced. João was holding him captive by his own past, and he now had a daughter somewhere in Spain. But where was she and who cared for her? Those were troubling questions that racked his brain without providing an answer. João would have to fill him in on the details. For now, he hoped his secret would be safe.

101

First Buds

WARM WEATHER BEGAN TO FLOW over the vineyards, and the citrus trees began to bloom. A light and delicate scent from fragrant white flowers on orange trees filled the air and wafted to the back garden, where Isabella now rested most of the day. She felt her weight slowing her down considerably, and Ana forbade her to lift or do any work. When restlessness took hold of her she got up, leaving this heavenly world for the house, then entered the kitchen to watch Ana kneading the daily dough. On the table, a plucked chicken and chopped onions for the daily soup waited to be immersed in the boiling water.

"Let me help you, Ana." Isabella approached the table.

"No!" Ana said, looking down at her work. "If you want to help me, go and supervise Raquela and Juanita with the linens."

"I'd rather stay here and speak to you."

Ana raised questioning eyes. "What about?"

Isabella sat down in front of her and let her eyes follow Ana's sturdy hands at her task. "You know that my deliverance is soon."

Ana said, smiling while still working, "We're all looking to this blessed event."

"So am I. Once my son is born, I intend to go back to sea."

Ana stopped pounding the dough. "You have a child to nurse, remember?"

"I'm well aware of that. I'll leave right after that."

Ana raised her voice. "That's nonsense. You must feed your baby for a year."

"I know that. I'll find a wet nurse for him."

"I don't think it's wise, but why do you want to go back to sea? Avram can take care of it. He's already confided in me that he longs to go back to the *Liberação*."

"I know. He approached me with that request, but I told him to wait till I'm ready."

"But, Isabella, your child is more important."

"He is. So is his father."

Ana stopped from sprinkling flour on the wet dough and looked at her strangely.

"I know. I know what you must think," Isabella said. "You think I'm crazy for thinking that Miguel is still alive, but I know better."

Ana wiped her hands on the apron around her waist, came around the worktable to Isabella, then sat down and hugged her. "My poor child. You're still missing and pining for him. You'll see, with time, the pain will lessen."

"You don't understand—" Isabella's voice broke with a sigh. "That's why I want to go back to sea and retrace his steps where he was captured."

"All I know is what Avram told us. He was captured like Avram, but he was beaten on the head and—" It was Ana's turn to stop abruptly.

Isabella said in one breath, "You can finish what you're going to say—that he was thrown overboard and drowned."

Ana lowered her eyes with distress.

"Ana, I can talk about it because I know that Miguel is alive somewhere. I know—no, I *feel* he's alive and not able to come back to me."

Ana said, *"Mi povrecita, mi povrecita."* She repeated it over and over. "My poor child, you're still suffering deeply."

Isabella held the tears back. She said in a strong voice, "Don't you see I must find out?"

Ana got up, pushed her sleeves back, and went back to her work as if nothing had happened. She then said to Isabella in a determined voice, "I will take care of your child like my own."

102

Signs of Home

Friday, February 1, 1493

FOR THE LAST WEEK, COLUMBUS made great progress sailing northeast and east-northeast with slight adjustments, when strong winds came from south and southwest. He jotted down his measurement and found they had now sailed 161 leagues with the aid of the ampolletas turned every half hour. The crew had caught many tunny fish and a large shark. This was a great addition to their diet. Their reserves in fresh meat had dwindled, and all that the men had been eating before the catch was bread and ajes swallowed with wine.

Throughout each day, he aligned and tacked the *Niña*'s sails on port side and ran it by the lee, or with the moving downwind leg. The strong winds helped push both vessels forward. At other times, they sailed *a la relinga*, or with a boltrope sewn to the bottom of the sails' skirts to stop them from rending and splitting. All night that Friday they sailed sixteen and a half leagues, and Columbus began to notice the weather becoming colder—another sign they were getting closer to European waters.

The next few days the sea was calm, and he thanked the Lord for it, and then the North Star appeared in the skies higher than before—another sign they were closing in on Cape San Vicente in Sagres, Portugal. Upon sighting the cliffs rising vertically from the Atlantic, he'd know he was finally home. They saw more and more petrels diving into the waters for fish and little floating sticks. That was a sign they were nearing land.

On the night of February 6, Martin Pinzón sent word from the *Pinta* that the island of Madeira lay windward to the east. For Columbus, they were near home and near Porto Santo, where he had lived and had married his first wife, Filipa Moniz Perestrelo. It was due to his noble wife that he had become a noble, adding legitimacy to his request to explore the Indies. Without a title, the Spanish court would have been closed to him. For that he was most grateful to his deceased wife.

Columbus shook himself out of his reverie and looked down at his journal. According to his calculations, they had sailed 526 leagues from the island of Hierro in the Canarias by the time they saw the first floating grass on the voyage west. He put his quill pen into the ink bottle and got up to stretch his limbs. His sore joints were stiff in the morning and bothered him every day. His eyes as well were dry and itchy. He also felt a constant urge to urinate.

On the morning of February 7, Pedro Alonso, his pilot on the *Niña*, confirmed that they were passing between Tercera Island that lay in the north and Santa Maria Island to the south. All signs now pointed to sighting land any day now.

Columbus went on deck to clear his mind and lungs from the wax smell coming from his candle in the cabin. The night was sweet with a smooth breeze and a moonlit sky. A few birds circled above the masts but didn't land on deck.

All was calm, with his men snoring and lying all over the deck, except for a few sleeping in ceiling hammocks gifted by the Indians that hung under the deck in the hold. His mind was now at peace, knowing that his achievement was about to change the world's notions of the dark seas. The Indies had been reached by going west, and he was its discoverer, along with new lands for the crown.

Just then recalling what João revealed pierced his peace of mind and congratulatory thoughts. If he had a grown daughter, his duty was to find her and present himself as her father. But then his true identity might be discovered. No one should learn of his Converso past, least of all the crown, and especially not Martin Alonso Pinzón. His enemies would use it to discredit him and undo all his past accomplishments. That he couldn't allow.

103

𝕿he Court in 𝕷isbon

COURTIERS AND NOBLES AWAITED KING John II of Portugal to make his grand entrance. All present waited in their plumed hats and finest robes, and red cloaks covering their swords showed their outlines jutting at the hips. The ladies of the court wore Hennin hats with braids, and richly colored velvets and woolen gowns with their kirtle and voluminous slashed sleeves.

The announcer pounded his metal stick three times on the parquet floor. "João II *o Príncipe Perfeito!*"

A seasoned monarch of thirty-eight years of age, the tall and portly King John walked vigorously to his throne, where he sat down with great energy. "What is the order of the day?" he asked.

"Sire, we have several requests by the emissaries of Castile."

King John said, "What are their demands?"

"They request an audience with Your Majesty."

"Let them in."

Two envoys from Queen Isabella came forward into the assembly hall and bowed to the king. He waved his hand at them to commence speaking.

"Your Majesty. We're here at the behest of your cousin, Queen Isabella I of Castile, and King Ferdinand II of Aragon and their eldest daughter, Isabella of Aragon."

"Go on," King John encouraged them.

"It's with great sadness that we're still grieving over the death of your young son Afonso, prince of Portugal, and for his widow, young Princess Isabella."

The king lowered his head in grief for the death of his son a little more than a year ago.

"Yes, I still mourn him too." He let out a sigh. "But what is the reason for your visit?"

"Sire. The young princess is still grief-stricken and wants to enter a convent." Before King John could stop the envoy from speaking, he added, "That is why Queen Isabella is sending us with the request to find her another husband."

"And who is the queen looking at for a husband for her daughter?"

"Your widowed uncle, Sire, and your successor: Manuel I of Portugal."

King John turned to his advisors standing by the throne. They all nodded in agreement. One of them whispered a few words into King John's ears, at which he, too, nodded.

"You will hear from Manuel as soon as we put the request to him."

"Thank you, Sire. We have another request."

King John raised an eyebrow. "Go on."

"Queen Isabella of Castile is a pious queen and faithful to the Roman Catholic religion."

"Yes," King John said.

"Upon the marriage of your uncle and the young princess, Portugal must be unified under the Catholic religion."

This time, the king's raised both eyebrows. "What could she mean?"

"All subjects in your realm must be or become Catholic, Sire."

King John's face took on a bewildering look. "I'm the king of all my subjects. I don't make divisions among all Portuguese. Furthermore, I have extended a gracious invitation to all Jews to come and live in my realm. They are industrious and abide by the law. That is nonnegotiable." His voice rose on a higher note.

The Spanish envoy lowered his head with a sigh of failure.

"Go and tell your queen my message, but I will confer with my uncle on a prospective marriage." He waved them on.

As soon as the envoys left the assembly hall, a medley of voices rose in crescendo.

"Who is the queen to give us orders?" said one courtier.

"Castile is still meddling in our affairs of state," another courtier said.

The king raised his hand. "We'll wait until we hear from the Castilian court."

104

Spring

THE DAYS WERE NOW BECOMING clear and free of rain. The vineyards were also sprouting new leaves, and the gardens were beginning to emerge from the wind and cold of the season. Isabella watched Ana preparing her jams as usual, filling the clay pots with the still-warm and translucent marmalades. The sugary aroma of citrus fruit, mingled with the soup cooking in the cauldron, filled the kitchen.

"Your jams have brought us many dinheiros since we've started selling them," Isabella said.

"Amen to that," Ana replied. "Wait until we sell the wine from last season."

"Isn't that what you've been selling?"

"No. What we sold came from the previous years. We always have a few years in reserve in the cellar."

"How did you manage it?"

"I had nothing to do with it. As you know, I came to my cousin's house with Queen Isabella's edict to exile all Jews from Spain."

"I know," Isabella replied. "I was part of that exodus with the Beneluz family. I came to love them as my own—" Her voice broke, and she stared down, then took a deep breath. "Somehow," she continued, "everything I loved has been taken away from me."

"My poor child." Ana stopped doling out the marmalade and said, "You've suffered enough."

Isabella took a cloth from her long dress pocket and wiped her itchy nose. Her eyes, though, were dry. She was learning to face her disappointments by fighting back. She wasn't going to remain home and accept her fate. The only avenue opened to her was the sea. As a young girl, when her dada Hannah accompanied her into the city of Seville, she begged to be taken to port to see the carracks and ships docked there.

"I need to leave on a voyage. I have to!" Isabella said.

Ana raised her eyes with surprise. "I didn't know you liked the sea. Why this ardent desire?"

"You know my reasons."

Ana lowered her head in despair. She then raised her head and said, "Yes. I promised you I'd take care of your child. Have you found a wet nurse?"

"I intend to search for one at the next market day."

"All right, but time is growing short. You have two or three weeks left," Ana reminded her.

"Yes, I know." Isabella smiled. "His weight tells me every day he's ready to join us."

Both Ana and Isabella broke out in laughter.

Then Isabella stopped and looked at Raquela nursing her son in a kitchen alcove, and she slapped her forehead.

"*¿Qué estúpido soy*! I can have Raquela nurse my baby after he's born!"

Ana smiled and looked pleased. You should talk to her soon."

"I will."

105

Storm at Sea

Tuesday, February 12, 1493

THAT NIGHT BOTH SHIPS NAVIGATED eighteen leagues going northeast. As they crossed another league, the temperature dropped drastically as a cold curtain fell upon them. The sea became high and tempestuous. To allay his fears, Columbus quickly took refuge in the belief that his caravel was sturdily build and well equipped. The men were still pumping and emptying the bilge waters in the bottom of the hold, but they were seasoned mariners and used to hard work. Those two sailors were switched at different watches, coordinated with the watch switches at the tiller.

On the following morning on Wednesday the thirteenth, great winds rolled over the sea throughout the day mixing and stirring up the waves coming from north-northeast. By nighttime, he gave the order to sail with bare masts and spars that took an hour to clew up, except for the lower topsails and bonnets. All they had sailed that night was thirteen leagues. The morning of the fourteenth saw a frightening sea with high waves splashing against each other, with the ship taking the brunt of the fury.

By the night of the fourteenth, the howling wind magnified and sent the waves across each other in terrible and thunderous sounds of crashing heard on the *Niña*. The ballast in the hold had been lightened by the dwindled provisions eaten since they had left Española Island, which made the ship about to topple at any moment by rolling and swaying dangerously. The men on the ships were thrown with force to and fro against each other with seawater splashing from above and below. The *Niña*, meanwhile, was obstructed from going forward, and they lost much time.

"Secure the tacks and the *papahigo!*" The papahigo was tacked on to the foot of the lowest sails, and to keep it from tearing to shreds was raised back on the mainsail, foresail, and mizzen sail, to keep the vessel afloat and moving forward.

The men ran to the masts to follow the admiral's orders, and João lent his able and knowledgeable hands to help raise the bottom sails clewed down. Meanwhile, several men pulled on the rigging lying in piles on the decks and secured them around the base of naked masts. The sea was terrible, coming back at them over and over with waves of seawater drenching the ship and all on it.

Several times, João came in contact with Columbus on deck helping the men.

"See to the pilot at the tiller!" Columbus yelled to João over the frightful roar of the sea.

"Aye, aye, Admiral!" The sound of his voice was lost over the waves. Columbus saw him advancing toward the tiller against the wind on the main deck, each time ducking from the monstrous waves crashing on him. At the tiller, Vicente, and Ruiz applied force on the lever about to break in two by the force of wind and waves. João added his hands to the others', and all three kept the tiller from flying off its rudder's post.

Columbus, drenched to his bones, turned and squinted to look for the *Pinta* but couldn't see it in front or behind him. He ordered all lanterns lit throughout the night to project a beacon to the *Pinta.*

Columbus thought the end was near. The ship would break, and they were going to perish, and no one would know of their discovery and feat of landing on the Indian continent. His older son, Diego Colón, would become an orphan, and Fernando Colón, his youngest, would only have his mother

Beatriz de Arana to care for him. He then thought of his third child, a daughter called Isabella. She would never know him, and be no better than an orphan.

Columbus called to the men. "¡*Escucha, hombres*! The sailors turned at the sound of their admiral to hear his words against the wind.

"If the Lord . . . if the Lord gives . . . salvation . . ." Columbus spit out the waters splashed into his mouth, then continued. "We will make a pilgrimage . . . Santa Maria de Guadalupe!"

To which the men replied with strong belief, "To pilgrimage!"

A sailor's voice rang out then was drowned by the noise of the wind. "The *Pinta*! The light from the *Pinta*!"

Columbus looked in the direction of the light, and he could see it bobbing up and down with the *Pinta*. The sight warmed his heart in the midst of despair.

"The Lord has answered our prayers!"

"Hurrah! Hurrah!" the sailors shouted before the voices were drowned by a new high wave.

Columbus murmured words of faith. "I will offer a four-kilo wax candle to the Virgin."

With great difficulty, he held on to the ropes leading to his cabin and succeeded in reaching the quarterdeck. He pushed on the heavy wood door, and it flew from his hands and banged back against the doorpost from the strength of the wind. A splash of seawater penetrated and washed over the cabin as he staggered in. He went to grab the letter he'd been preparing for the monarchs relating his discovery, then rolled it up and melted candle wax all over it, wrapped it in a waxed cloth, and slipped it into his deep pocket. He then took a pouch lying on his table and made his way back out into the storm and with the help of the ropes tied on deck to find the cook.

"Give me many peas!" he hollered into Diego's ears.

"What?" Diego hollered back.

"Peas! Peas!"

"All right, Admiral!" Diego tore himself away and limped down into the hold, then reappeared with a wrapped cloth. "Here, Admiral!"

Columbus took one of the peas and slashed it, then dropped it in with the others into the pouch. "Take this pouch to the men and let them draw one for pilgrimage at the first island we land!"

Diego fought his way from man to man as each one drew a pea from the pouch. When Diego came back, Columbus put his hand inside the pouch and drew the last pea. It was marked with the slash!

Columbus fell to his knees and prayed. "It's a miracle! I should be the one called upon for pilgrimage!"

Columbus called another lot to be drawn for a pilgrimage to Santa Maria de Loreto in Ancona, and it fell to Pedro Villa of Santona.

"I will pay your pilgrimage expenses!" Columbus hollered to the sailor, who was down on his knees and praying.

"Let's all make a vow at the first land we reach to go in our long shirts to pray in their church!" Columbus told the men, and they agreed by crossing their foreheads and praying to the Virgin.

"Bring me an empty barrel, a hammer, and nails!" Columbus ordered Diego, who went down into the hold for the second time and came back up hauling a small wooden barrel.

Columbus took the waxed and wrapped document out of his deep pocket in the gown that was dripping and clinging to his body. He dropped it into the barrel and nailed the top down.

The men watching him crossed themselves again, believing that Columbus was performing a religious rite to protect them.

"Throw it in the ocean!" Columbus yelled.

For a moment, Diego and João standing near him stood frozen.

"What are you waiting for?" Columbus blasted.

The two men lifted the barrel and threw it overboard. The barrel bobbed up and down for a short time, then a large wave took it down, never to be seen again. *Now the record of my discoveries will be found someday to affirm my claim to a passage to the west.*

Just then a cry was heard. "Admiral! We lost the *Pinta* again!"

Columbus ran to the railing and tried to pierce the mist and the waves still drenching them on deck, but no sign of the *Pinta* appeared. Now his men were frightened and moaning, "We're lost, Admiral. We're lost!"

"Have faith, men!" Columbus ordered them.

"Diego, Juan, and some of you men." Columbus pointed at random to the sailors in front of him. "Fill the empty barrels with seawater for ballast in the hold!"

The men scrambled to bring up the empty barrels. They then threw them in the ocean with hemp ropes and hauled them back up, covered the lids, then rolled them to the opening in the hold and lowered them down. The work took many hours, while the sea still soared with high waves, but now the *Niña* pitched and rolled less.

Columbus felt somewhat at fault that he had ignored the all-important ballast that steadied the ship. He had planned to execute it on the Island of Women, but then changed his mind, pressured to get the voyage underway. Now he was reassured, and he could see it in his men's eyes as one or two smiled now and then. His fear of never returning had got the best of him, as he had rushed to cross the Atlantic back home. His fear also made him lose faith in the divine hand that saw to his protection. After all, hadn't God favored him and helped him discover the new lands? He must now believe and trust the power of the Lord. He now knew that he would return home in safety.

The sea was still soaring and angry, and the *Niña* tossed on the waves throughout the night without direction. Columbus then ordered to remove the lower sails rather than lose them to the wind.

On the following morning the clouds in the west tore open, revealing a small opening in the sky, and the sun's rays penetrated the sea, spreading its shining light on the water as in a cathedral during service for its congregants. Then the subsiding wind grew again, but without force.

"Place the bonnet on the mainsail!" Columbus ordered.

They sailed east-northeast that night for thirteen leagues, and no one slept, keeping a vigil in case the vengeful sea rose again.

By sunrise, Columbus, who hadn't slept, went down with great pain on his knees and began his Lauds prayers by seven, when cries came to his ears.

"Land!" The numerous voices came from all the men on deck.

He staggered out of his cabin and came on deck. There, by the prow, in the direction of east-northeast, a line grew on the horizon—a familiar coast—and the men yelled out many names.

One sailor screamed, "It's Madeira Island!"

"No. It's the Rock of Sintra! I recognize it!" another confirmed.

"Yes! It's the same one near Lisbon!"

The wind suddenly changed and blew high, coming from the west.

"We are near the Azores!" Columbus yelled at his men from the quarterdeck.

Throughout the night the ship beat against the wind, and by the morning of February 16, the obscure weather had hidden the island, and the coast disappeared. And yet, by the stern, Columbus saw another island behind them. It couldn't have been more than seven or eight leagues from their ship, but he couldn't take the chance of coming any closer without running into shoals.

For another night, Columbus didn't rest and suffered from joint pain and lack of sleep. By morning on the seventeenth, he sailed around the island and couldn't recognize it. At sunrise, he approached the island and dropped the anchor. Before him were red clay soils and rocky mountains in the background.

"Lower the boat down!" Columbus sent five of his men to land on the island.

Columbus didn't trust the Portuguese king, as he had known him before to break his promise to subsidize the voyage. By that token, if the men were taken or arrested, he would be safe to sail away without his men, but safeguarding the treasures he had brought back to Spain.

When the men came back, they were excited and all talking at the same time.

"One at a time!" Columbus thundered.

"Admiral. We're on the island of Santa Maria on the Azores," one of his men declared with glee.

"We were told to dock here in Baía dos Anjos to celebrate tomorrow the feast of Santa Maria Madalena," another said.

"We will spend the rest of today on board," Columbus replied. "Tomorrow we'll visit the inhabitants."

He then went to his cabin and sat down to write to the sovereigns in Castile. Before climbing into his bunk bed, he said a prayer of thanks to the Lord.

❧〜❧

João stood alone on the *Niña*'s deck, regretting having endangered his niece's life. Where was she now? Téresa had promised to care for Isabella and dispatch her to her relatives in Cordoba if found out in the Alhambra. And where was Téresa? Back in Seville, or had she too left with the decree? If Téresa's family, the Beneluzes, had left Cordoba, then Isabella must have left with them. That meant Isabella wasn't in Spain any longer. Or she may have returned to Seville to her parents, and all his plans and promise to Sarita, his sister, may have been in vain.

He reeled under the thought for having utterly failed. No matter—the minute he reached Spanish soil he'd search for Isabella, and face the wrath of her adoptive parents, Don Arturo and Estrella Obrigon.

106

Lisbon

Tuesday, February 18, 1493

T DAWN, COLUMBUS, WHO HAD slept soundly through the night, jumped from his bed and went in his nightshirt to check on the sea. It was calm and peaceful. He dressed without Salcedo's help and ate a hurried breakfast, then went to find Sancho Ruiz.

"I'm going with the men ashore."

Ruiz raised his head from the tiller, but kept the pressure on the rudder with his knotted strong hands. "But, Admiral, are you certain it's safe?"

"What do you mean?"

"We don't know the inhabitants on this island or what they're capable of doing."

"There's peace now between Castile and Portugal. What can they do to us that hasn't happened by the sea?" Columbus said.

Ruiz shook his head with a perplexed look on his face. "Didn't King John deny you funds for this voyage?"

"Yes, but he relented with the Treaty of Alcáçovas in the division of the Atlantic Ocean. Spain stays on one side of the Atlantic and Portugal on the other. We found the Indies on the side of Spain."

Ruiz wiped beads of sweat from his forehead and said, "How do you know they won't arrest us all and throw us in a dungeon? Who's going to know, then, that you found the Indies?"

Ruiz's sound argument stopped him short. "You're right, Ruiz. I trust your judgment. I'll remain on ship and send a few men ashore."

Ruiz let out a sigh of relief, and Columbus left him to give orders for his men to head for land.

By sunset the men hadn't returned, and Columbus suspected treachery, but when three men called to them from shore, he signaled for them to board the ship.

The three men came on board bearing bread and cooked chickens. "We bring tidings from our governor Juan de Castaneda for Carnival Day. Our captain knows you, Admiral," one man said to Columbus.

Columbus didn't search his memory. He was worried why the sailors hadn't come back. "Where are my men?" Columbus said.

"They remain on land. We enjoyed their stories of your voyage. They'll return tomorrow with fresh food for all your sailors."

"Admiral, we heard of many ships that broke apart with many having perished and drowned. We're amazed you made it alive through the storm," another delegate said.

Columbus was plunged again into the raging storm of the previous night. "The Virgin protected us, and tomorrow we'll make pilgrimage to give our thanks."

"We'll deliver your request to Juan de Castaneda." With those last words Columbus saw them go back in the *Niña*'s only boat.

By morning, he rejoiced to see his men return, loaded with provisions as promised.

Columbus turned to his men on the *Niña*. "I'm sending ten men to say Mass at the local church, and I'll make pilgrimage when you return."

Columbus exchanged glances with De la Cosa. The men going ashore would serve as bait for the Portuguese. The next hours would prove whether the Portuguese were good at their word.

The men descended in their long nightshirts to say Mass, and Columbus bid them good luck.

Then the wait began. The hours of the morning passed, then late afternoon ushered in without the men returning.

De la Cosa said, "Admiral, I fear foul play. Our men should've returned by now."

Columbus, who wanted to believe that the men might just be tardy, or involved in imbibing and celebratory feasts in their honor, decided to wait till morning.

"We don't have a boat to go ashore, Admiral. I suggest we sail around the island," De la Cosa advised him.

Columbus gave the order to raise anchor, and the caravel avoiding large rocks, began circling the island and made its way to the other side to a promontory hiding the church building.

One look at mounted and armed men by the church convinced him of danger. The armed men boarded the *Niña*'s boat and approached the caravel.

"Your Excellency, Admiral. We wish you no harm, and Captain de Castaneda requests your presence on land."

Columbus said, "But where are my people? I can't leave the ship until my men return." He then thought of an idea. "Why don't you come on board? I will vouch for your safety."

"I cannot enter your caravel, Admiral, as I'm not ordered to do so by my captain."

They were now at an impasse. Columbus was losing precious time.

"When in the land of Castile, our visitors are received with security and trust. Your monarch, King John, would surely be annoyed at how you're treating us. I have letters of recommendation from the sovereigns in Castile, and I'm their viceroy for the Indies, which I've just discovered for the monarchs."

This list of credentials may have convinced the armed man standing in the boat. "With due respect, Admiral, may I see those letters?"

"You must come on board then." Columbus reiterated the same invitation.

"Perhaps you can show them to me from your perch?"

Columbus saw that he wouldn't succeed in capturing the armed man as a hostage. He left the railing and main deck for his cabin. Returning shortly, he unfurled the parchments and exposed the monarch's seal for all to see in the bobbing boat below them.

The captain's voice became antagonistic and menacing. "We don't recognize the Spanish king and queen's jurisdiction in Portugal, and we're not afraid of you!"

Columbus used great restraint to withhold blasting at him. "You can't stop us from sailing. We have enough men to go back, and you'll be punished for holding my men!"

A silence followed in which the men in the boat consulted each other by nodding their heads. The speaker bowed to Columbus. "I'll report to my captain. Meanwhile, don't leave your ship."

Columbus felt blood rising to his face. "I give you my word we won't leave this ship. Don't forget that we can depopulate your whole island! And we have the means with Lombards to blast you!"

Columbus watched the men in the boat sail back to shore, and all present on the *Niña* erupted in laughter, relieved that their admiral had won the argument.

"Ha-ha-ha! We showed them!" Sancho blasted.

"Yes, those bastards wanted to fool us!" De la Cosa added.

Several men slapped each other with excitement and roared with laughter.

Columbus tried to restore silence. "All right, men. Let's be patient and courteous when they return."

"The weather is turning bad, Admiral."

"We're too exposed in the open. Let us find a better harbor on this island."

"What about our captive men, Admiral?"

"We'll wait till tomorrow." Columbus put an end to the anxious questions by his men.

107

Alpujarras

IN THIS CORNER OF THE Alpujarras Mountains, south of his beloved and now lost kingdom of Granada, Boabdil found relief from the struggle baiting him all these past years. He was no longer a king, but his subjects still considered him their caliph. They attended to him each morning in the court they had managed to form in the small villa, and courtiers presented requests daily from the inhabitants. His trusted vizier, Moussa El Zayari, informed him each morning of news concerning the Moors' last retreat in this lush and fertile valley.

"We have had many visits now from the infidels' clergy wanting to request an audience with Your Excellency," Moussa said.

"They took my kingdom and my lands, and now they want my peace!" *Why must I be tormented?* Boabdil lowered his head under the demand.

"That's why we have to grant their request, Sire. So they can leave us in peace."

"But do you know what they're seeking?"

"No, Sire. They pretend, though, that it's for our own good."

Boabdil shook his head. "I don't trust these men who pretend to carry their God's words."

"I agree, Sire. But if we find out, then we can decide what to do," Moussa insisted.

"All right, then let them in."

The word went out of the small hall, and two priests cloaked in black with heads covered by beanies and rosaries attached to their robes came silently into the room. They stood in front of Boabdil without bowing to him, but with hands clasped in prayer.

Boabdil scrutinized them for a short time, then said, "You're standing in my principality and kingdom, and as such you must bow to me."

The two clergymen turned and glanced at each other, then turning back around made a slight bow of the head.

"Your Excellency, we're here to bring tidings to you and your family."

Boabdil remained silent.

The other priest said, "King Ferdinand wants to inquire on your health in your restful retreat."

For a moment Boabdil had to restrain himself from shouting at the inopportune visitors. He was in this exile because of their infidel king and his perfidious scheme to conquer his land. He had ceded his realm to Spain, abiding by the one-sided treaty that had forced the Moorish crown off his head. He suddenly felt his blood boiling.

"What does your king want this time?"

Both priests protested in unison. "We're only carrying out our king's wishes, that's all."

Boabdil replied between his teeth, "My health is good, and my retreat was peaceful until you two came into it."

"We're here also on another mission."

Boabdil raised an eyebrow.

The priest continued. "We have received a request from several of your populace that they want to convert."

"You had no right to contact my people!" Boabdil's voice rose volumes. "If some of my people are discontented, they can always turn to me!"

"But Your Excellency, it was a direct request. We came with good intention to fulfill their request."

"You will wait for my answer until I speak with those concerned. Off you go now." He waved them away.

The two priests nodded their heads, turned around, and left the hall.

"The insufferable goad to my face about conversion!"

Moussa, who stood close to Boabdil's chair, nodded to him. "That's not a new request, Sire. They've been traveling in the valley trying to convert anyone in their path."

"Why wasn't I told of this?"

"We didn't want to disturb your peace, Sire."

"Has my mother or the Sultana Morayma been told of this?" he said to Moussa.

"No, Sire. Your mother has left all decisions to you, and the sultana is very frail and still not in good health."

Boabdil rubbed his forehead back and forth. "Take this down."

Moussa rushed to get his script table and waited for Boabdil's dictation.

To the Marinid Sultan of Morocco, Allah grant you a long life.

If it is in my power to undo the past grievances you may have had with our line, I will do so with great obedience to you and to Allah. Your line has been illustrious and successful to all your people in your lands. I have only myself to blame for wrongdoing and for not listening to my ancestors in fighting the enemy. My ancestors should have listened to your ancestors in their wisdom.

The king of Spain, Ferdinand II, gave us the assurance in writing and lands in which to live in perpetuity and peace for all the years of our reign. We, the descendents of Banu al-Ahmar, cannot live in a land of the infidel and without our God.

We have received many goodwill letters for us to join you in your land, and we thank Allah and your most magnificent offer. My people are ready to cross the stormy seas and the dangers to come to your land, and be forgiven as brothers.

Your most ardent and faithful supporter. Inshallah!

Signed Abu `Abdallah Muhammad XII, King of Granada

"Get this letter to the king of Morocco with the utmost haste!" Boabdil urged.

Moussa nodded and left the hall in a hurry.

108

Visitors on Board

Friday, February 22, 1493

COLUMBUS WAITED FOR SEVERAL DAYS to hear from the island's authorities and from his captive men. The sea was turning stormy, the night was coming, and he ordered his men to check the ballast in the hold. The bad Atlantic weather off the coast of Portugal had taken him by surprise. He remembered that in comparison to the Indies' winter where he had only encountered good weather. He also recalled reading great philosophers' predictions that when earthly paradise would be discovered at the end of the Orient, it would always have smooth and gentle weather. Columbus had found the most temperate islands in the Indies; it followed that paradise had now an earthly place.

"Admiral! Admiral!" Ruiz's voice called him out of his cabin.

He rushed out to find three men poised on rocks facing them and shouting across the water. Subsequently, a boat appeared around a crop of rocks bearing sailors, priests, and a notary.

"We ask for protection for our men!" one of the three men shouted at Columbus.

"What of my men?" Columbus shouted back.

"As soon as we take down your words, we will send them to you."

Columbus waved his arm for them to board the ship. "You're welcome to remain on board for the night," he told his visitors. He then proceeded to feed them and to make them comfortable for the duration of their visit.

Immediately after the meal, the bell rang. Columbus, his crew, and the visitors prayed at Compline, and an air of peace descended on the caravel.

Columbus faced them. "What is it you need now?"

"With your permission, Admiral, we would like to see those documents giving you orders for this voyage."

Columbus hesitated at first. A few days ago he had been threatened with an obdurate delegation of ignorant townspeople, his men were taken captive, and now they wanted to see proof. Apparently, they had relented in capturing and tying him in chains. Now they wanted to prove that they were right, when they had been wrong all along. *But two can play this game*, he concluded.

"Why don't you follow me to my cabin."

When they entered the small cabin, Columbus lit several lanterns that immediately shed light on his table holding all sorts of documents.

His voice came out in a measured tone. "What would you like to know?"

"We want to see your orders from the Spanish monarchs."

Columbus searched among the piles of documents piled up on the table and pulled out a rolled parchment that he unfurled.

"You are honorable servants of King John II, and you can see the great seal of Queen Isabella and King Ferdinand giving me full power to undertake this voyage."

The king's officials examined the document and conferred by glances to one another.

One of the priests spoke to Columbus. "We see with the great guidance of the Lord that you had the monarchs' benefaction to accomplish this voyage. We'll report all this to our king."

Columbus nodded and bid them good night, then down they went onto hammocks in the hold.

By morning, the visitors disembarked with salutations and assurances of safety on their part that his men would be restored to him shortly.

By noon that day, his shaggy and unwashed men came on board, happy to find their mates and the admiral.

"Admiral, they captured us because they thought they could capture you in chains."

"I was aware of that threat," Columbus said. "That's why I had decided to join the second party on land, but waited to see to your safety. You have shown great courage, men!"

"We will now lift anchor and head for Spain."

A good portion of the past days had been lost waiting for the men's release, and the sea now was becoming agitated with white-crested waves rolling toward shore. The ship moved forward with Sancho Ruiz at the tiller, and the *Niña* surged into high seas. Just then, Columbus thought of the *Pinta* and Martin Alonso Pinzón. *Where could the ship and its crew be now?*

109

The Pinta Lands in Galicia

Friday, March 1, 1493

FOR MARTIN ALONSO PINZÓN, LIFE was a game, and winning belonged to the bold. As far back as he could remember, he had worked on the docks with his father and his grandfather, building ships with his two brothers; by following in the family's marine business, and that had made him become rich in Palos. At a young age, he made his way on a ship by starting out as a gromet or cabin boy. Many days were spent talking and dreaming with his brothers about the day he would sail westward, where the sun set over the horizon. His brothers laughed at him, but nevertheless they came to believe in his lifelong dreams. Now this dream had become a reality with the voyage west to the Indies.

He still relished the steps he had taken in guiding the *Pinta* on a northern course for Spain and on beating the *Niña* and Admiral Columbus. The *Pinta* was now ahead, and he'd be the first to reach Spain and declare having found land. He couldn't begin to imagine the splendors and riches heaped upon him. But first he had to cool a small fever that had plagued him for the last few days.

He wiped his warm forehead with his coat.

"Captain Pinzón, the sea is becoming a jealous wife. She roars at us!" The voice of his brother, Francisco, came to his ears. He looked over at the tiller and saw Francisco applying all his force to the handle.

"Hold on!" Pinzón ran to the tiller post and helped Francisco take control of the rudder.

"You're right—we're running into a stormy sea," Pinzón said. "Man the sails!" He gave the order to his men to also secure all rigging on board.

He then made his way to the cabin near the tiller and tried to fix his position. The needle pointed northwest for Baiona in Galicia! They were home at last. Now if they could approach land as soon as it was revealed, he'd be the first to contact the court in Barcelona. The fact remained that the *Niña* may have been lost at sea, since it hadn't reappeared on his horizon.

Meanwhile, the sea took a turn for the worse with waves crossing each other at great heights and breaking on the ship. With great force and difficulty, his men battled the waves rocking the ship, drenching them on board.

"Make sure to secure the men!" Pinzón yelled from his station on the deck to the men holding on to the masts and anything they could hang on to.

Another great wave washed upon them, splashing its salty waters on the men, and some of the loose rigging slid and disappeared from deck onto the sea.

"¡*Dios Bendichos, ayudarmos! ¡Dios mío! ¡Nos ayudan!*" The men were terrified.

It was still daylight, and the gromet yelled at the top of his lungs, "I see it! I see it!"

Pinzón looked at the horizon and could barely make out a line at five leagues ahead of the ship.

"Land ahoy!" the man yelled from his perch on the mainmast.

The ship was now directing its course in an eastern line, toward the land ahead. Within two frightful hours where Pinzón thought he was done for, the land surged in front of them. He recognized the fortress tower on the rocky cliff of Monte Real, and the sandy beaches being pounded by the winter surf.

"We'll go into the harbor by Rio Lerez!"

The battered *Pinta* with torn sails and missing rigging entered the river bisecting the small town, and the anchor was dropped into the muddy and murky waters. The boat was lowered and ten men descended into it, including Pinzón and his brother Francisco Pinzón.

"We must make a holy pilgrimage to Santiago de Compostela!" Pinzón shouted at Francisco over the roar of stirring waters.

"Take us to the—" Pinzón's voice died down.

"What is it, Brother? Martin?"

Pinzón felt faint and turned to his brother. "Don't fret. I'm just cold in these wet clothes. We could all use a warm fire."

"We're almost there," Francisco shouted.

The boat docked at a wooden pier, and all the men disembarking were surprised to see the townspeople there to greet them.

"¡*Bienvenidos, buenos amigos*!" The townspeople hailed.

"Where do you come from?" said one villager

"You braved the sea with courage!" another said.

Pinzón tried to quell the questions flying at them from many mouths.

"*Amigos!* We come from a great voyage across the dark sea! We're here to prove we found new lands for Spain!"

"¡*Viva*! ¡*Viva*! ¡*Viva*!"

Just then Pinzón collapsed. "Francisco, my brother, take me to an inn and prepare a letter to the monarchs. We must do any repairs before we sail for Palos," he said before blacking out.

110

The Court in Barcelona

THE WINTERS FOR QUEEN ISABELLA were now spent at the court in Barcelona with her five children: Isabella, princess of Asturias and Aragon, the eldest and widowed; her son, Juan, the heir, prince of Asturias; her second daughter, Joanna of Castile; Maria of Aragon, her third daughter; and Catalina of Aragon, her youngest—all still too young to give her grandchildren.

She sighed with regret. "All my children have been betrothed to other royals to become queens and kings, but will I see any children born of them?"

Her councilor, Don Coronel, standing next to her by her writing table, said, "Patience, Your Majesty. They will marry in time, and they'll bring you many, many grandchildren."

Queen Isabella sighed again. "My husband, the king, is now away in Sicily, and I find myself alone. Please, Don Coronel, give me some good news. What of the state of the economy?"

"Your Majesty, as much as I want to give good tidings, I'm afraid we're still suffering after the Granada wars, and . . ."

"Why are you hesitating, my good man?" Isabella said with a smile. "Whatever it is, I can bear it."

"Majesty, commerce is still floundering. Merchants can't deliver goods as before. There are fewer purchasers in goods, and revenue has suffered, with scarce taxes to be levied."

Queen Isabella stepped out from her downcast mood and with her eyes questioned Don Coronel's statement. "How can we have less revenue? Last year's taxes were sufficient to feed the armies and sustain many of the clergy in the region. Please explain yourself." Her face was flushed with surprise and indignation.

Don Coronel hesitated at first. He then explained in a calm voice, "The revenues last year were based on the population at hand. We have grown less in households and number of family heads."

Queen Isabella always tried hard to contain her impatience when she was at a loss to understand a complex problem, but usually with her fine mind she delved into the problem head-on to find a solution.

"Don Coronel, you're my tax-farmer-in-chief, can you please simplify your words?"

"Simply put, dear queen, we have grown smaller because we have two hundred thousand less citizens in the country."

"I know what you're getting at. It doesn't explain how a group of people of another faith had any bearing on our economy."

For an old man of eighty years of age, Don Coronel tried to collect his dwindling strength. He took a few steps forward toward the queen and missed his step. With concern, Queen Isabella extended her hands to protect him from falling. He steadied himself as another courtier rushed to his aid.

"Thank you kindly, my good man." Don Coronel bowed to the courtier. "Please, my queen, do not concern yourself with an eighty-year-old man. I feel steady now with your benefaction."

A ruckus of voices and sounds from beyond the council hall made all present turn around toward the noise and listen intently. The gilded doors to the hall opened up, and a courier entered with a rushed and steady gait. He removed his hat and approached Queen Isabella's dais and bowed before her.

"What is it, Courier?"

"My queen . . ." He tried to catch his excited breath. "I bring the most astounding news! One of the captains of the *Pinta* ship that left last August has reached Castile and requested an audience with Your Majesty. Here is the request by Captain Martin Alonso Pinzón." He handed her the letter.

Queen Isabella's heart fluttered. She put her hand across her chest and tried to contain her excitement. The ships were back! All was well with the blessings of the Lord! She made the sign of the cross, and everyone in the hall followed suit. She then handed the letter to her advisor, Don Coronel.

While Don Coronel read the letter, she turned to the courier and spoke with a shaky voice. "Are all the ships back?"

"Not all of them, my queen. Only Captain Pinzón and his brother Francisco Martin Pinzón came back on the *Pinta* to Galicia. They're well and waiting for a reply from Your Majesty to come to Barcelona. The other ship, the *Niña*, was last seen along the Portuguese coast with the admiral in charge."

Queen Isabella tried hard now to contain her joy at the news. "You'll send Captain Pinzón a reply that I'll wait for the admiral to arrive and tell me in person all about his voyage."

The courier bowed to the queen and left the hall to convey the orders.

Queen Isabella turned to Don Coronel with a triumphant smile. "The Savior has seen to the success of the voyage. He will also see to Spain's inheritance in the Catholic faith and her well-being. Send word to the king in Sicily to join me at the court in Barcelona for the good news."

111

Portugal Welcomes Columbus

Monday, March 11, 1493

THROUGHOUT A GOOD PART OF a week, the *Niña* wavered back and forth in a soaring sea, and Columbus thought they were done for. He sailed in an eastward course and netted a mere total of forty-five leagues. And yet he found the caravel to be at an average of one hundred leagues' distance between Cape St. Vincent, and the island of Madeira in the Azores. He then thought that the *Pinta* must've gone through the same resistance and being forced back by the winds. Hopefully the *Pinta* hadn't arrived in Spain yet. He dreaded Martin Alonso Pinzón arriving at the Spanish court, then smearing his good name. Perhaps the *Pinta* had been lost at sea. *The sin of it!* How could he wish such a dreaded end on so many men? He made the sign of the cross to atone for his sinful thought.

The bell rang for the hour of Compline, and Columbus dropped on his knees along with the men on the ship. By now the ship was being tossed on large waves that lifted and dropped it dizzyingly from great heights. Columbus held on to the mainmast and hurried his prayers.

"Drop all sails! Leave the Papahigo on the lower bonnet!" he ordered his men.

The waves washed overboard with the men teetering on being washed away at sea. Ropes were tied around each sailor's waist and tethered by this lifeline to a mast or hook. Several plants were washed to sea, but the bulk of them were solidly tied and reinforced with coiled ropes around the masts. Through howling winds a crash was heard when the mizzenmast broke and plunged into the sea with rigging still attached to starboard.

"Quickly, cut the ropes, cut the ropes!" Columbus yelled at his men.

Five men reached the starboard deck and began to cut with hatchets the solid coiled ropes. Within ten minutes, which felt as an eternity, the last rope gave way and the mast disappeared below the waters. Afterward, the hours went by slowly for the men gripped by fear that the mainmast and foremast might follow the same fate. Columbus was drenched from head to toe, with his face dripping with saltwater, and no one slept through the night with the winds still howling in their ears. By four in the morning, the sea somewhat abated, but they were all exhausted and wished for sleep.

"Keep your eyes open for an island!" Columbus yelled at the men.

As dawn appeared on the horizon, it revealed a still-unforgiving sea with waves coming from two directions and battering ship and men.

"The island! Admiral! It's Cabo da Roca!" Pedro de Terreros, his cabin boy, called out from the quarterdeck.

Trying to steady himself on the rocking deck, Columbus took great pains reading his compass that gave him the distance for Portugal's shores. This was the rock of Sintra's location with one hundred kilometers of rocky cliff promontories. They were also thirty kilometers from the court in Lisbon, which created an awkward moment for him. Though Spain and Portugal weren't at war any longer, they were still enemies in commerce and exploration. The gold mines in Guinea were jealously guarded by the Portuguese crown from the Spanish monarchs looking for gold for their coffers. Now he, Cristóbal Colón, was bringing a future wealth to the Spanish crown.

His spirit and mood became elevated, and he gave the order to approach Portugal's coast.

"We will enter through the river of Lisbon. We can no longer remain in high seas!"

The order given, the men raised the sails on both the mainmast and the foremast and without the mizzenmast sailed haltingly into the Tagus Estuary. Above their heads a flock of pink Flamingos flew over the two standing masts, and light-gray Booted Eagles circled high above the ship.

Juan de la Cosa came to him while bouncing and sliding on the slippery deck and said, "Admiral, are you sure it's wise? The Portuguese monarchs will accuse you of returning from Guinea."

"I'm forced to do so. They can see with their own eyes the different plants and foods from the Indies and the people we carry."

"Aye, aye, Admiral. It's your decision."

Avoiding the rocky cliffs, the *Niña* advanced slowly on breaking waves on the Tagus River and sailed toward the town of Cascais.

As the caravel neared the town, they saw hundreds of people hailing them. Fishermen and their boats stopped fishing to see the battered *Niña* advance toward port.

"Bom dia! Bem-vindo! Bem-vindo!" The inhabitants stood on the shore waving their hands with, surprisingly, smiling faces.

The *Niña* docked into port, and Columbus turned to Juan de la Cosa. "I'll voyage to Lisbon with one of the Indians. Meanwhile, make sure anyone coming on board is an official. All in the hold must be protected at all costs, including the gold locked in my cabin."

"Aye, Admiral. I'll guard it with my life."

"Mucho gracias. I trust you will defend it from robbers."

Under a strong wind coming from the sea, Columbus disembarked with his pilot, Sancho Ruiz, and the Indian under the scrutiny of officials waiting for him.

"Bem-vindo, Admiral. We've heard of your exploits and finding new islands in the Indies."

Those words made Columbus wince. Had Martin Pinzón reached land before him?

Columbus bowed to the official. "I'm here to pay a call on King John."

"Follow us then," the official said.

Columbus, Ruiz, and the Indian followed by three officials, entered a covered carriage, and the driver whipped his horses and took the road to Lisbon. They passed several, small villages on the way and finally arrived by late evening at Sacanben, a small village not far from Valparaiso, a mere nine leagues, or fifty kilometers where the king awaited him. After a hasty meal at the nearest inn, Columbus crashed into bed and slept through the night.

The following morning, the carriage left for Valparaiso with Columbus looking forward to meeting King John. Now, he noted with some inward satisfaction, he would be vindicated for having been rejected years earlier.

Upon arrival, he was immediately escorted through the entrance to the castle and into the main square furnished with cannons that were aimed at the sea. Entering a vaulted-ceilinged room, he met King John and his court seated at a dining table.

"Por favor, entrar em!" The king's voice welcomed him and indicated he wanted Columbus sitting next to him.

Columbus and Ruiz bowed deeply to King John and went to sit down at the head of the table by the king.

The king waited for Columbus to be served, then told him, "You must tell us all about your voyage, Cristóvão Colombo."

Columbus bowed to the king, acknowledging his name in Portuguese. "I'm honored, Sire."

King John said, "Admiral, we look upon you as a son of Portugal and are very happy for your success. You also married Filipa Moniz y Perestrelo, a native Portuguese, and a noblewoman, and we're proud of you."

Columbus bowed his head again, pleased with the praise lavished upon him by King John. But he couldn't resist making it known to the king that his refusal to subsidize the voyage to the Indies had lost him a glorious opportunity.

"With respects, Sire. I'm very sorry that this victory didn't go to Portugal. Perhaps, the next time a deserving Genoese comes to you, I hope that you won't refuse his offer to discover new lands for Portugal."

Columbus's offense didn't perturb King John. He kept silent for a moment while Columbus waited respectfully. King John then said, "You must understand that because of the capitulation between the Spanish sovereigns and me, and the Treaty of Alcáçovas promulgated by the papal bull and signed on September 4, 1479, that conquest belongs to Portugal."

Columbus was stunned by the king's statement. He replied, "Sire, I know nothing of the capitulation between your country and that of the Catholic monarchs. All I do know is I was commanded by the king and queen of Spain to stay away from the mines in Guinea and sail west of the Portuguese coast. Furthermore, the monarchs made sure of it by a proclamation in all towns and ports in Spain."

Ruiz threw him an appreciative glance.

The king stayed silent to Columbus's prudent explanation. To save face he said graciously, "I'm sure we won't need any arbitration in this matter. We are now at peace with the kingdom of Andalusia and wish to remain so."

Columbus nodded his head with respect to the king.

"Many ships in Flanders were lost this winter. You're a lucky man that heaven protected you," the king said.

Columbus kissed the silver crucifix medal hanging from his neck. "I'm most grateful that the Lord's benediction shone on us. We could've been drowned in several storms."

"So, tell us. How did you find this passage to the Indies and the mainland?"

"Sire. I believe that we found the Indies, but the mainland was so large we had only begun to explore it."

"But you must have had some coordinates to find those islands. What were the coordinates?" King John's voice was insistent, sounding like an order.

Columbus froze. If he gave away those coordinates, the Portuguese would commission ships immediately to sail to his newly discovered islands. Then the Spanish monarchs would have to fight for their rightly won new territory.

"With great respect to you, Sire, I don't carry these coordinates in my head. I keep then on board in a locked chest." Columbus felt reassured by the cold metal key tied to his chest.

Ruiz nodded to Columbus then looked down at his plate.

King John's face reflected deep disappointment as his lips pressed tight and he lowered his head down. His two hands, with their fingertips touching, showed bulging knuckles.

"Sire, I did bring you some samples of what we found on the islands." Columbus made a sign to one of the attendants, who left the room and came back shortly with an Indian attired in colorful feathers, a loin cloth tied around his hips, and holding a spear.

Everyone in the room recoiled at the threatening spear.

"This Indian is very gentle, Sire, and he'll become an obedient Christian for Her Majesty, Queen Isabella."

King John looked for a long time at the Indian and nodded silently.

The rest of the assembly examined the Indian and ventured to touch his feathers and spear. Each one nodded his head and in turn murmured their amazement.

"My dear Cristóvão Colombo, I would be most delighted to have one of my courtiers accompany you to the Spanish court. It will be more convenient to travel by land."

Columbus reflected for a moment on the king's offer. "Sire. I'm most honored by your offer. I will confer with the captain of the *Niña* and send word to you."

Here again King John had a sad look upon his face. "I will assign the prior of Clato, who will see to your comfort and good wishes."

Columbus bowed. "I'm deeply honored, Sire."

"We'll wait for your reply, Admiral, concerning travel by land."

Columbus bowed again and felt a great urge to take leave from this court.

After leaving the court of King John II, Columbus and his two companions traveled back with speed to the *Niña*. Upon arrival, he went to look for Juan de la Cosa.

"Make haste! We're leaving tonight. Raise the sails!"

To Juan's raised eyebrows, he said, "I'll explain when we're underway."

Hours later, the *Niña* gently sailed away south with all crew on deck watching the coast of Portugal recede from view.

Columbus then let out a sigh of relief. *I could've easily been murdered in my bed by my foes.*

112

King John Appeals to the Vatican

OHN II SAT ON HIS THRONE aghast. He seethed inside with anger, regret, and a need for vengeance to be redeemed in the eyes of his people. He had failed miserably by rejecting Columbus and was shamed in front of his ministers, but then, he had been counseled unwisely. The Spanish court would announce their victory to the world, when it could have been his. He still had the Vatican, though, who had vouched for Portugal in the Treaty of Alcáçovas signed between Portugal and Spain in 1479.

His minister lamented, "Sire, what are we going to do about Spain?"

King John stepped out of his troubling thoughts and replied, "We have the treaty. This peace signed between us and Spain specifically outlines that Portugal has the right of navigating and trading in the Atlantic Ocean south of the Canarias Islands. Read me that map again!"

His minister unfolded a map that marked the conquered territories, and he read, "Lands to be discovered, found, and all the islands already discovered or found from the Canarias Islands beyond toward Guinea."

"That's it! Right there signed and agreed by all parties!"

"Sire, let's not forget the Romanus Pontifex papal bull signed and written January 8, 1455 by Pope Nicholas V to King Afonso V of Portugal. It confirms our right for the crown of Portugal dominion over all lands discovered or conquered during discovery."

"Yes," the king affirmed. "All we do now is petition Rome for our right to claim the New World of the Indies for our crown." King John rubbed his hands with glee. *He had them now in the palm of his hand*!

113

Sailing Home

Thursday, March 14, 1493

BY EVENING, THE *NIÑA* HEADED for the Saltés Bar's high tide and with a moderate wind and a relatively calm sea. The sails were blowing fully on the two remaining masts, and the men were busy washing all decks while the rigging was checked again for weak or worn connections. Columbus now felt a great sense of peace descending upon him. The ship and crew had met violent seas, storms, and threats on the islands and from the Portuguese crown, and they had survived all dangers.

He now looked forward to touching the coast of Andalusia. Once there, he'd send word to court that he'd arrived safe and sound, but without the *Santa Maria*. Since the flagship had been torn apart, beam by beam, to build a new fort in the Indies, the Blessed Virgin had seen to their safety and survival and he hoped would continue to do so with her blessings upon him. Life and fate had served him well and in perpetuity for his descendants.

He uncovered the ink jar and grabbed the quill to begin several letters. The first one was addressed to Luis de Santángel, the *Ministro de Finanzas* who oversaw all finances for the king and queen. Santángel had been his most ardent believer in the voyage that Columbus undertook and his faithful benefactor.

> *B"H*
>
> *Don Luis de Santángel, Escribano de Ración, comptroller of the king's household expenditures: It is with great pleasure I'm announcing a great victory, which the Lord hath given me in this voyage. It took me thirty-three days to pass over to the Indies with the fleet of the most illustrious king and queen, where I found many islands beyond belief and peopled with inhabitants. I have taken possession for Their Highnesses with proclamation and the royal standard displayed, and I was not gainsaid . . .*

When he finished writing, he dated it the fourteenth of March of the year 1493, and signed the letter with his sigla.

$$.S.$$
$$.S. \quad A. \quad .S.$$
$$\mathsf{X} \quad M \quad \mathsf{y}$$
$$: \mathsf{X}_{po} \; \mathsf{FERENS}. /$$

Underneath his sigla he affixed the Hebrew letter *Fe Sophit* on the left bottom of the page as a monogram.

He sealed the letter and began a similar one to the monarchs in Spain. He briefly stated to Queen Isabella and King Ferdinand that all the islands conquered in their names, and the ones still to be discovered, would be managed by a governing body of men sent by Spain.

In the letter, he suggested that two thousand settlers should go there, and that two or three towns be founded to house them. In each settlement a mayor and a clerk would govern. Likewise, a church should be built with priests or friars to administer sacraments and undertake the conversion of the Indians.

He also suggested that the mayors and friars report periodically regarding all the gold mined, melted, and weighed. All vessels returning from the Indies should come and unload at the port of Cadiz with faithful transactions made.

He finished his letter by adding: *May Your Highnesses keep me in your minds, while I, on my part, shall ever pray to God our Lord to preserve the lives of Your Highnesses and enlarge your dominion.* He signed it, this time without the Hebrew letter and acronym.

114

La Rábida Monastery

Friday, March 15, 1493

IN PALOS A GREAT COMMOTION was heard with people milling about curiously to see the *Pinta* sailing into port. The word circulated that the ship or its master was ailing. Some of its sailors went about their chores and prepared to unload the ship's cargo, while others clewed the remaining sails.

By noon, a procession descended from the *Pinta* carrying a stretcher on which Martin Alonso Pinzón, owner and captain of the *Pinta*, lay still with a pallid face. Quickly, sailors, dockworkers, and bystanders came forward with curiosity.

"Is it Pinzón? One of our town's sons?"

"Where are you transporting him? To his family home?"

His brother Francisco and his son, Arias Pérez Pinzón, angrily pushed the assailing bystanders aside. "Make room! Don't you see he's weak?"

At that moment, Pinzón opened his eyes. "Where are we?" he said with a weak voice.

"Hush, Father. We're taking you home."

"No. Not home! Catalina Alonso, my father's widow . . ." He coughed then continued. ". . . will see that my half brother and half sister will finish me. Take me to La Rábida."

Arias Pinzón grimaced, then shook his head sadly. He eyed the stretcher bearers and directed them to a wooden wagon, on which they placed Pinzón.

Pinzón opened his eyes again and saw the *Niña* down at the docks swaying gently on the waters and without her mizzenmast.

A deep moan escaped from his mouth. "Ahhh . . ."

"What is it, Father?" Arias said.

"Is that the *Niña* I see in the harbor or is it an evil apparition?"

Francisco remained silent, afraid to upset his elder brother.

Arias said with a sad voice, "No, Father. It's not a vision. It arrived early this morning."

Without another sound Pinzón closed his eyes.

⌇⌇⌇

Sunset was descending fast on the Franciscan Monastery of La Rábida, which at one time had been a Moorish fortress between the Tinto and Odiel Rivers. Through the dusk, Fray Marchena hurried across the columned cloister to the last cell at the end of the friary. He carried with him two wax candles, holy water, the pyx or wood-box receptacle containing the Blessed Eucharist, and a small communion cloth. He opened the wooden door and entered a dark miniscule cell. At the threshold he said, *"Pax huic domui,"* and replied to himself, *"Et omnibus habitantibus in ea."* He entered the room, and then put on his stole.

Under the flickering lantern light, a form lying on the bed was still. A physician, aided by Friar Fray Perez and a young choirboy, attended to the patient by wiping the man's sweat with a wet cloth. The physician listened to his chest with his ear, then wiped his finger on the patient's forehead and tasted the perspiration.

"It tastes acidic and sticky." The physician turned to Fray Marchena and shook his head. "Not much longer now," he whispered in Marchena's ear.

Marchena turned to the man lying still and spoke to him gently. "Alonso? Alonso? It's time for Viaticum." He then placed the communion cloth under his chin.

Martin Alonso Pinzón opened inquiring eyes and with a feeble voice intoned, *"Credo in Deum . . ."* Pinzón's voice faded. Fray Marchena shook him again with a paternal expression on his face, encouraging Pinzón to continue. *". . . Patrem omnipotentem; Creatorem . . . coeli et terrae."* Alonso finished his sentence with his eyes closed.

Marchena then said, "This is the Lamb of God who takes away the sins of the world. Happy are those who are called to his supper."

Pinzón's lips moved. "Lord, I am not worthy . . . say the word and I shall be healed."

Marchena said, "The body of Christ."

Marchena waited for Pinzón to reply, but he fell silent. Marchena looked into his eyes and could see Pinzón's lips moving without a sound. He genuflected and bent close to his mouth to hear his last words.

"May the Lord forgive me for my deeds." Those were Pinzón's last words asking for forgiveness, and for everyone to hear in the room. Marchena rose slightly to see Pinzón's glassy eyes staring vacantly into space.

"May the Lord Jesus protect you and lead you to eternal life." Marchena closed Pinzón's eyes. He covered Martin Alonso Pinzón's lifeless body and turned to the physician standing near him.

"Thank you, Master Diogo."

Diogo said, "I'm sorry we couldn't do anything for him. The seas and the voyage are what killed him." With a bow, Master Diogo left the small cell.

Marchena shook his head with sadness. "I'm sorry, too, I couldn't get a full confession. May his soul be blessed in the hereafter." He turned to the fray and said, "You and José will take care of the body now?"

"We will, Fray Marchena. Won't we, José?"

The young apprentice's eyes were fixed on the corpse lying now at rest, and he nodded without turning his head.

Out of a dark corner in the room, a cry pierced the silence in the cell. A young man approached and collapsed on the dead body. Near him, Francisco Pinzón sobbed quietly.

"¿Padre? ¿Padre? ¿Me oyes?"

Fray Marchena came to him and tried to console him.

"Arias Pérez, he's with his maker and in a better place now."

To which the young man sobbed harder. "My father was spurned by the monarchs and lost all his deserved honors for the voyage. I will fight to my last breath against those who'll dishonor my father!" Arias Pérez screamed in agony.

115

Birth of a Child

OR THE LAST TWO WEEKS now, Isabella felt restless and jittery. She couldn't sit or stay in one place for any length of time. At meals when the three of them—Ana, Avram, and she—sat around the table, she would stand up suddenly, go to the kitchen, then come back empty-handed. She saw Ana observing her behavior without comment. Avram had become taciturn, not speaking for long periods of time, and was moody throughout the day. Isabella knew why, but she made no mention of it.

Finally, after Isabella left the table for the third time, Ana said, "If you need anything, Isabella, just ask me."

Isabella stopped mid-motion.

"*Muchas gracias*, Ana, but I don't need anything."

"Then why are you getting up all the time? Are you feeling all right?"

"I said I'm fine!" Isabella's voice was sharp.

Ana was taken aback. She lowered her eyes to her plate and kept silent.

Avram said in a measured voice, "If Ana's asking, it's because she cares."

Isabella looked at him surprised. "I thought you were absent from the table," she said, and folded her arms against her chest.

Avram was about to reply, when Ana put an end to the barbed conversation. "All right! That's enough!" She turned to Avram and said, "Isabella has good reason to be impatient or irritated."

Avram didn't reply. He went back to his silence and continued eating.

Isabella looked at him sideways, then smiling slightly she said, "I'm sorry, Avram, I didn't mean to be harsh."

Avram looked up from his plate and nodded his head. He then quickly said, "We're ready to hire the workers from last season again. I'm meeting them after breakfast."

"That's good news, Avram. We need to prepare for the next shipment. In two months we'll sail—" Isabella felt a sharp pain in her abdomen that made her crumple in half, and she let out a sharp scream.

"What's wrong?" Ana got up and ran to her seat.

Her breath held up for a moment, Isabella couldn't answer. She then felt a second excruciating pain that made her lose her breath again.

"This must be the time!" Ana screamed. "Raquela, Raquela!" she called from the dining room.

At the calls, Raquela, working on the second floor, came in running. "*Por la vida del Dio*! What's happening?"

"It's time for the child. Go boil some water and bring me clean linens, soap, scissors, and twine," Ana said.

Raquela left them to carry out Ana's requests, and Avram came to Isabella's chair, helped her stand up, walked her to a divan near a window, then helped her lie down as she moaned in renewed pain.

Ana turned to Avram before she left the dining room. "I'm going to help Raquela. See after Isabella."

Avram nodded silently.

On her temporary bed, Isabella tried to breathe periodically between the pain coming back to stab her.

"Avram . . . Avram?" she asked in a weak voice.

"What is it, Isabella?"

"If I don't survive . . . I want you to take care of my son . . ." Another sharp pain came down on her.

Abram quickly said, "You'll live to see your son. I saw my mother with the same pain when she had both my younger brothers. It will pass," he reassured her.

"I don't know . . ." Another wave of burning sensation invaded her body and radiated through her back.

"Here I am!" said Ana as she reentered the dining area, carrying a heavy cauldron of hot water. Avram ran to help her. Raquela followed with the linen sheets and a birthing chair. "Thank God I had this water boiling already. Go and get another cauldron ready, and tell Juanita to look after little Aron," she told Avram and closed the doors after him.

"Now, my child," Ana said, "I have here a birthing stool for you."

Isabella lifted herself slowly on her elbow. She took one look at the horseshoe stool with a hole on the seat and blurted aloud, "No! I won't use this old way. I want to lie down instead."

Ana shrugged her shoulders and acquiesced to Isabella's wishes. She then prepared Isabella for the birth of her son. Both women undressed and washed Isabella thoroughly, then covered her with clean sheets.

Ana pulled out all of Isabella's hairpins and loosened her long hair. She then spread herbs around her on the divan and rubbed an ointment on her belly that smelled of sweet almonds.

The hours went by as the pain grew in intensity and beads of sweat covered her forehead, Isabella grew weaker. "Take care of my son!" she screamed.

"We will. *You* will." Ana patted her head.

A new wave of burning and searing pain came back to take her breath away again. She overheard Ana say to Raquela, "I can't understand why she's going through this terrible pain."

"Perhaps the child isn't in the right position," Raquela replied. She looked at Ana and said, "I went through the same—"

Before Ana had a chance to reply, Isabella wiggled and screamed from the pain stabbing her in the back. "I'm burninnnnng!" She felt her own sweat drenching her in wet sheets.

Ana prepared Isabella's legs to receive the child. "Listen, Isabella. I want you to push with all your strength. You hear me?"

Isabella nodded between the contractions and pushed with all her might.

"Push, push again!"

Again she pushed, and could feel the pain descending her body down to her legs. Then another wave traveled from her back to her legs, back and forth.

Ana said suddenly, "I see something. Push, Isabella, push!"

Isabella gathered all her dwindling strength and pushed the mass inside her.

"I see it now! I see the feet! Again push! The baby is coming with feet first!"

Isabella felt her last moments on earth had arrived as she pushed for the last time, when she heard a small scream filling the air. With that scream came great relief as if the vise holding her body prisoner had been lifted.

"It's a boy! A boy! You were right, Isabella!"

Isabella, weak from the last effort, rose slowly on her elbow to see Ana holding a rosy and fleshy form in her arms. Ana brought the child to her and placed him on her chest. The small body wriggled with his little hands, and gentle struggling sounds came through his well-formed mouth. She caressed the tuft of reddish hair on his small head and looked into his blue eyes staring at her.

"You look just like your father," she whispered to him. "But where did you get this red hair!" Isabella laughed with relief and amazement at her small son.

Both Ana and Raquela joined her in a good laugh. Just then a knock was heard at the door.

Ana quickly covered Isabella with a sheet and went to find Avram standing pale at the threshold with a water cauldron at his feet. She touched the water with her hand. "This water is lukewarm," she said. "Come in and see mother and son," she said to him.

Isabella saw Avram approach the divan and smiled at him. "My son just joined us." She looked at her son and felt an immense joy filling her.

"What will you call him?" Avram asked.

Isabella looked at her infant son. "He will be named after a great man and savior." She then made herself a promise. *You have liberated me to find your father. And I promise you that someday you'll live as free as the wind and the sun!*

116

A Triumphal Return

OLORFUL BANNERS OF PURPLE, RED, yellow, and carmine flew above the crowds lining the streets of Barcelona. The whole population was given a day off to celebrate a hero's return. The brass trumpets, tambourines, and the lute music playing at the head of a procession became drowned by human voices and shouts aimed at the mariner's triumphant return. The city had never seen such rich display of excessive joy and cheer among its citizenry. Many pigs and cows had been slaughtered for the crowds to feast on throughout the night's festivities; wine would flow as promised by the queen and the king for all of their subjects. The court wanted to show all their sons and daughters that Spain was now rich with land beyond their wildest dreams.

At the head of the procession going down the cobblestone street was Columbus on horseback, at present a favorite son to Queen Isabella, who helped make it happen by her wisdom to foresee this victory. Behind the long train of city officials were the captive Indians in their colorful feathers, walking half-naked with a loincloth wrapped around their hips and holding their reed spears. Several porters carried a chest filled with Indian artifacts and the gold brought back from the Indies. The Indians also carried the unknown plants they burned and smoked, the root plants called ajes, and the various palm fruits wrapped in a hammock.

Columbus saluted and nodded to all the excited people that came out to see him or were lucky enough to touch his robe.

"You are most revered, Don Cristóbal Colón," Luis de Santángel said while riding next to him. His eyes looked benevolent, and he had a satisfied smile on his lips.

"I'm most honored, Don de Santángel. It was your foresight and belief in me that made this voyage possible."

"I was fortunate to be finance minister to King Ferdinand II and *escribano de racion*. As chancellor and counselor to the royal house of Aragon, I was in a position to raise the funds."

Columbus quickly interjected, "But those funds were raised from your own coffers and a few other generous men. Every maravedí of those seventeen thousand ducats you invested will be paid back to you. I swear, I'll see to it, with the gold we find in the New World!"

"My dear Colón," Santángel said, "I appreciate your gratitude. I did it because I hold the queen in great estimation. Don't forget that it was mainly due to her belief in you and your skills that this voyage became a success."

Columbus turned sad for a moment. "I do deplore and elevate one of my sailing mates for his absence." He was careful not to mention the word *death*, lest he'd be called callous and insensitive to a colleague's death.

"If you're referring to Martin Alonso Pinzón's death, it was most unfortunate. He was an able seaman and rallied all of Palos's residents to support your voyage."

Columbus kept quiet and made sure not to release all the conflicting emotions he had against Pinzón and the grief that Pinzón had personally caused him. Now wasn't the time to dwell on bad feelings. It was his time to rejoice.

"We have arrived," Santángel announced.

Columbus looked out to see a vermillion carpet lining the steps to the palace and thousands of Barcelona's citizens standing on both sides cheering him. He dismounted and smiled at everyone. This was his time to feel blessed and reap the rewards of all the years he had struggled and begged. With a light step, he entered the palace's portico.

I have now earned the title of "Admiral of the Ocean Seas and Viceroy of the Indies," with rewards to follow . . .

⚜

On the docks in Palos, João Treves looked beyond the port to the city of Palos de la Frontera, where his search for Isabella would begin by purchasing a mule. From there he planned to travel northeast to Seville, where his search would end. If his niece had traveled with Téresa's family to the port in Seville, chances are she would've gone to see her adoptive parents. He hoped the long trail would end there. He would then reveal to Isabella her father's true identity. Next in his mission was to bring forth the quest for a new land for all Jews to live in peace.

flower from Castile Trilogy: Book Two
The New World
Cast of Characters

Spanish Court

Queen Isabella I of Spain in Castile and León

King Ferdinand, King of Spain, Aragon, and Sicily

Isabella — Princess of Asturias and Aragon, the eldest and widowed

John — Prince of Asturias, and heir to Castile and Aragon

Joanna — Princess of Asturias and Castile, second daughter

Maria — Princess of Asturias, third daughter,

Catalina — Princess of Aragon, fourth daughter

Tomás de Torquemada — grand inquisitor

Don Fernando Núñez Coronel of Castile — financial advisor to Ferdinand and Isabella and a converted Jew

Luis De Santángel — Columbus's friend and Converso

Fray Juan Pérez — friar of Convent Santa Maria de La Rábida

Fray Antonio de Marchena — friar of Convent Santa Maria de La Rábida

Bartolomeu Perestrello — II Porto Santo's governor and third captain of Porto Santo

Dona Beatriz de Bobadilla — Queen Isabella's retinue

Dona Leonor de Bobadilla — Beatriz's sister

Alfonso Fernandez de Lugo — governor of La Palma Island in the Canarias

Carmela — palace servant, friend of Maria Donarojo

Portugal and Portuguese Court

John II — King of Portugal

Dom Joam do Allgarve — king's councilor

Alvoro Gonçallvez — merchant mariner from Belmonte

Bartolomeu Perestrello II — governor and third captain of Porto Santo. Columbus's brother-in-law

Filipa Perestrelo e Moniz — Columbus's deceased wife, sister to Bartolomeu Perestrello

Arias Pérez Pinzón — Pinzon's son in Portugal

The Vatican

Pope Alexander VI, Rodrigo Lanzol Borja

Cardinal Raffaele Riario —Chamberlain (Camerlengo)

Cardinal Oliviero Carafa — Pope's advisor. Office dean, and suburbicarian bishop..

Cardinal Ascanio Sforza — Pope's advisor. Suburbicarian bishop.

Spanish Nobles

Isabella Obrigon — seventeen years old

Dona Estrella Obrigon — Isabella's deceased and adoptive mother

Don Arturo Obrigon — Isabella's adoptive father

Dada Hannah — Isabella's nanny

Carmelita — Obrigon's maid

The Exile Ship, Morocco and Portugal

Téresa Costa — Miguel's mother, deceased

Isabella Costa (Obrigon) — wife of Miguel Costa

Miguel Costa — Isabella's husband, deceased

José Costa — Miguel's brother

Ana Sarauel — Don Abravanel's cousin

Don Isaac Abravanel — aka Dom Fernandez de Carvalho

Isaac Beneluz — Jew from Cordoba

Rivka Beneluz — Isaac's wife

Avram, León, Guerson and Mica — children of Isaac and Rivka Beneluz

Benvenide Matigoro — purchaser of slave Jews in Tangier

Pedro — Avram's apprentice

Raquela — Jewish refugee

Sarina — Raquela's daughter

Aron – Raquela's little son

Sarita Treves — sister of João Treves, deceased

Juanita — gypsy girl aboard ship

Juan — old man at the inn

Estrellita — old woman in a cottage

Dom Manoel do Allgarve — Councilor from King John of Portugal

Abdul-Azim — Moroccan slave trader

The *Liberação* Ship

Miguel Costa — captain

Avram Beneluz — first in command

Lourenço da Sintra — second in command

Joham Alvaro — pilot

Hanrrique — cook

Fernando — sailor

The *Nina*, *Pinta*, and *Santa Maria* Ships and Crew *

The *Santa Maria* Crew

Christopher Columbus — admiral and captain-general

(Cristofõm Colon and Cristóvão Colón — Portuguese and Spanish
   names for Columbus)

Juan de La Cosa of Santona — captain, master and owner of the
   vessel

Sancho Ruiz — pilot

Maestre Alonso — physician of Moguer

Maestre Juan Diego — cook and boatswain (contramaestre)

Rodrigo Sanchez — comptroller from Murcia

Diego de Arana — master-at-arms, cousin to Beatriz Enríquez de
   Arana and mother to Columbus's second son, Fernando

Terreros — steward (maestresala)

Rodrigo de Jerez of Ayamonte

Ruiz Garcia of Santona

Rodrigo de Escobar

Francisco de Huelva of Huelva

Ruiz Fernandez of Huelva

Pedro de Bilbao of Larrabezua

Pedro de Villa of Santona

Diego de Salcedo — servant of Columbus

Pedro de Acevedo — cabin boy

Luis de Torres — Converted Jew of Murcia, interpreter

João Treves of Seville — Converso sailor and Columbus adversary

Hernán Çavallos of Seville — João's co-sailor

Alfonso Sabatin of Seville — João's co-sailor

Gomes of Seville — João's co-sailor

Pedro de Gutierrez — royal steward

Rodrigo de Escobedo — royal secretary

Alonso Chocero

Alonso Clavijo

Andres de Yruenes

Antonio de Cuellar — carpenter

Bartolome Biues

Bartolome de Torres

Bartholomé Garcia of Palos — boatswain

Chachu — boatswain

Cristobal Caro — goldsmith

Diego Bermudez

Diego Perez — painter

Domingo de Lequeitio

Domingo Vizcaino — cooper

Gonzalo Franco

Jacomel Rico

Juan, servant

Juan de Jerez

Juan de la Placa

Juan Martines de Acoque

Juan de Medina

Juan de Moguer

Juan Ruiz de la Pena

Juan Sanchez — physician

Lope — joiner
Maestre Juan
Marin de Urtubia
Pedro de Terreros — cabin boy
Pero Nino — pilot
Pedro Yzquierdo
Pedro de Lepe
Rodrigo Gallego — servant

The *Pinta* Crew

Martin Alonso Pinzón of Palos — captain
Francisco Martin Pinzón of Palos — master. Brother to Martin
    Alonso Pinzón
Cristobal Garcia Xalmiento — pilot
Juan de Jerez of Palos — mariner
Juan Perez Vizcaino of Palos — caulker
Juan Rodrigo de Triana — also known as Juan Rodriguez Bermejo
Juan de Sevilla
Garcia Hernandez of Palos — steward (despensero)
Garcia Alonso of Palos
Gomez Rascon of Palos — owner of the vessel
Cristobal Quintero of Palos — owner of the vessel
Juan Quintero of Palos
Diego Bermudez of Palos
Juan Bermudez of Palos
Francisco Garcia Gallego of Moguer
Pedro de Arcos of Palos
Alvaro Perez
Anton Calabres
Bernal – servant
Fernando Mendes
Francisco Mendes
Gil Perez
Juan Quadrado
Juan Reynal

Juan Verde de Triana
Juan Vecano
Maestre Diego Perez — surgeon
Pedro Tegero
Sancho de Rama

The *Niña* Crew

Vicente Yanez Pinzón of Palos — captain. Brother to Martin Alonso
    and Francisco Martin Pinzón
Juan Nino of Moguermaster
Pero Alonso Nino of Moguer — pilot
Bartolome Roldan of Palos — pilot
Francisco Nino of Moguer
Gutierrez Perez of Palos
Alonso Gutierrez Querido of Palos
Alonso de Morales — carpenter
Andres de Huelva
Diego Lorenzo
Fernando de Triana
Garcia Alonso
Juan Arias — cabin boy
Juan Arraes
Juan Romero
Maestre Alonso — physician
Miguel de Soria — servant
Pedro de Soria
Pero Arraes
Pero Sanches
Rodrigo Monge

* Source: Immigrant Ships Transcribers Guild™©®
Copyright © 1998–2013
http://www.immigrantships.net/v4/1400v4/santamaria_pinta_nina1492

Appendix A

Letter from Columbus to Luis de Santángel

on Luis de Santángel, Escribano de Ración, Comptroller of the king's household expenditures: It is with great pleasure I'm announcing a great victory, which the Lord hath given me in this voyage. It took me thirty-three days to pass over to the Indies with the fleet of the most illustrious king and queen, where I found many islands beyond belief and peopled with inhabitants. I have taken possession for their highnesses with proclamation and the royal standard displayed, and I was not gainsaid.

I named the first island San Salvador in commemoration of His High Majesty, who marvelously hath given all this; the Indians call it Guanahani. The second I named Santa Maria de Conception, the third Fernandina, the fourth Isabella, and the fifth La Isla Juana. Española is a marvel with rich soils for planting and sowing and breeding cattle of all sorts, and where we can build many towns and villages. I followed La Isla Juana, and the coast was so large I thought it might be a mainland, the province of Cathay. On the coasts of these islands were hamlets, where the people could not speak with me because they all fled.

The lands are high with many rivers, most fertile fields that are a marvel. I brought many samples of plants and foods, some similar to Castile, but better-tasting to the palate with the spices they use. There are beautiful trees and palm trees of six or eight species with green and marvelous foliage with fruit.

The people on these islands have no iron or steel, nor any weapons other than the stems or reeds, on the ends of which they fix little sharpened stakes. All the Indians are fair and go as naked as their mothers bring them forth and of fair stature and wondrously timid. They are also gentle people and can become obedient Christians.

I was not able to speak to them in their language, but some of the Indians we took from one island served as translators as we learned a few words of their language. I gave them gifts and cloth at every island we landed. I forbade and made sure my men didn't take anything not fairly bargained. Any gold they had in small quantity to the weight of two and a half castellanos, or one-sixth of a gram of gold, was exchanged for scraps of metal, broken glass, or broken barrel hoops. They welcomed us and called us "the people from heaven"!

I took possession of a large town, which I named the city of Navidad. I have made fortifications there, and a fort (which by this time will have been completed), and left enough men there with arms and artillery, one boat, and provisions for more than a year.

Since our Redeemer has given to our most illustrious king and queen this victory, Christendom should rejoice therein and give solemn thanks to the Holy Trinity for the great exaltation they shall have by the conversion of so many people to our holy faith, and for the benefit that will bring hither profit not only to Spain but to all Christians.

This briefly, in accordance with the facts, dated on the caravel, off the Canaria Islands. Dated the 14 of March of the year 1493.

At your command, the admiral.

* Modified letter from *The Northmen, Columbus and Cabot, 985-1503: The Voyages of the Northmen, Volume 1.*

Appendix B

The *Santa Maria*, the *Pinta*, and the *Niña*
Lying in the North River, New York

The caravels, which crossed from Spain
to be present at the World's Fair at Chicago 1912

Appendix C

The *Santa Maria*, the *Pinta*, and the *Niña*

"Die Schiffe des Columbus," historisierde Darstellung aus dem späten 19. Jahrhundert, 1892

"The ships of Columbus," historical portrayal of the late nineteenth century, 1892

Courtesy of Wikipedia